PARADOX

The Templar Thriller Series

BOOK IV

By

PJ Humphreys

PARADOX

THE TEMPLAR THRILLER SERIES

Book IV in the series
ISBN 978-1-9163167-4-4

Compiled by: Jackie Harding: 16.04.2023 / 30.07.2023

ALSO BY PJ HUMPHREYS

THE 'TEMPLAR THRILLER' SERIES:

BOOK I: ARK
ISBN:978-1-5272203-8-6

BOOK II: PROPHECY
ISBN:978-1-9163167-2-0

BOOK III: PERDITION
ISBN:978-1-9163167-3-7

BOOK IV: PARADOX
978-1-9163167-4-4

STAY IN TOUCH:

Website:	https://thetemplarthrillers.com
Instagram:	PJ Humphreys Books
Instagram:	pj_humphreys_books_
Facebook:	The Templar Thriller Series
Email:	info@thetemplarthrillers.com
YouTube:	PJ Humphreys

Where can I get PJ Humphreys' books from?

Amazon: PJ Humphreys Books

Also available to order at selected Bookshops

Please follow our Facebook page for more information and to keep up-to-date with upcoming events

ACKNOWLEDGEMENTS

Joanne, for her unwavering support and steadying hand through the entire journey of 'Paradox' and the 'Templar Thriller' series of books. For her ability to unblock the blockage when I am stuck and staring at empty pages — screen.

Jackie and Kevin Harding, for their invaluable diligence in making sure I made as few mistakes as possible, and for their creative input on the cover design and book promotions.

ABOUT THE AUTHOR

PJ Humphreys is the author behind the Templar Thriller Series of books. He has consistently denied any direct involvement with the Templars or the Illuminati, but undoubtedly there is a close association somewhere.

His novels are described as exciting, passionate and informed. Like his characters in the book, PJ has spent his life travelling the world and now splits his time between several continents in order to continue his research and writing, and, as he puts it, his search for answers and meaning.

While PJ's skill in writing was honed at an early age, it was interrupted by a career in the British military and then, international education. But he re-engaged with writing and began creating the now popular and much-loved Templar Thriller Series of books.

PJ currently lives in Spain and Kent with his wife Joanne, his two adored dogs and Sam the cat.

Paradox

A seemingly contradictory, unbelievable, or absurd statement
that can be explained or shown to be true.

To Noel Gallagher:
Hope this changes your mind. Yes, No, Definitely Maybe?

Chapter 1

Priya

Date: Present day
Place: End of the world
Time: Dawn

A dull, flickering light from a candle seeped weakly out of a small, barred window. The candle was cheaply made, the wick poor, and the light it gave off was jaded, almost lifeless. Its luminosity was almost non-existent – more a hue than light; more nothing than something. The window was slightly cracked open – ever so slightly.

Outside a vast snow-covered wilderness stretched out for hundreds of miles of nothing but flat snow and ice-covered terrain. The Polar days were well into their darkness – when the sun wouldn't breach the horizon for two months, the days would remain in total darkness.

It was cold and eerily quiet outside. Then the faintest sound of ice crystals breaking – muffled. A white Snowshoe hare was zigzagging across the snow, its movement almost imperceptible to the human ear. Skittish in movement for fear of prey. Stopping, listening. It was foraging for twigs and bugs – anything.

It was about twenty yards away from the building, a single-storey, concrete complex from the 1960s. The hare had passed it many times; it had never seen any life, any movement or heard any noise. It had only seen light from the window twice before.

It was a low emitting light from the small, barred window close to the ground. There was no reason for the hare to be afraid. He

1

foraged, digging into the snow seeking the scent of scarce food. Then it sensed something, a feeling; it was a bad feeling. Instinct kicked in. The hare immediately froze. Its head was still. Its eyes searched for the thing that had triggered the feeling of danger. Its heart pounded. He had detected a movement in his peripheral line of vision. The hare waited. Motionless.

Then he saw it. In the gloom of the small, barred window. The candlelight was weak, as always but then, just then, the weak light caught something. The hare strained to see. Then he saw it again, he saw them. Eyes. The dull light caught the small, peering eyes and lit them up momentarily. They were human eyes. Dark and sunken. Sad. They were a child's eyes.

"What is the Paradox, Mr Hare?" The whispered question came from the child, the question seeped out of the small, barred window. "What is the Paradox?" It whispered again.

Then, moments later there was another voice. A male. Older.

"Priya. Close the window now, you know we cannot have the window open. Close it and pull the black window cloth back down." Each window had a thick black cloth covering it, like blackout curtains, no light could seep out, seep out into the blackness and the wilderness.

"I was talking to the hare; he was back again."

"That's lovely Priya but close the window now."

The window closed quietly but for a faint sigh and then, the eyes, the dark, sunken, sad eyes of the child were gone along with the dull light and only the silence and darkness of the sunless winter day remained.

Inside, the man kissed his nine-year-old daughter, then stroked her head lovingly. "Priya, promise Papa you will not open the window again."

He tucked her into bed. She slept in the bottom bunk, he in the top: bunk beds with three dirty blankets each - the only furniture in their six foot by six-foot cell.

"I asked Mr Hare, Papa. I asked him what the men keep asking you. I asked him, what is the Paradox?"

"Shhh, my sweet."

"I have heard them, Papa. I have heard them all the time,

asking and asking you, and then they hit you."

"Sleep now, my sweet child." The man extinguished the candle. His bruised and puffy face no longer visible.

The child slept.

The man wept silently.

*

The hare turned, leapt and sped away into the blackness.

Chapter 2

The Bearded Warrior

Date: 1313 – Over 700 years ago
Place: A rural farm seven days hard walk to Paris, France

Young Thomas Dumas lived on his parent's farm. It was a poor, low yielding small holding in the harsh, rustic countryside of northern-central France. An ill-built stone farmhouse, with rotting roof timbers, a thatched roof that was more repair than roof and the only water source was from a small stream a quarter of a mile away. The farm was near nothing in particular. It was a hard five-mile walk away from the closest village, Lubea, but there was nothing there. The farm had no particular redeeming features. No one could ever remember why the first owner had built the farmhouse where he did or even why he built it in the first place. It had changed ownership several times but none of the owners had ever worked the land themselves, they always leased it to tenant farmers. The farm had come into the possession of its current owner, a mean-spirited landowner from Paris, as payment for a bet he had won in a card game. The landowner leased it to Thomas's father for fifty per cent of the farm's yield, this left little for the Dumas family. The farm had few visitors and its occupants, Thomas, his five siblings, his mother and his father, rarely left the farm.

Thomas and his siblings did not go to school; however, they could read and write, and carry out elementary maths thanks to their mother who had had an education. In fact, their mother had had a good education because she had come from a middle-class family in

Paris. Unfortunately, her family would always say when lamenting her fate, that she had met and had fallen in love with, and then married – much to their disapproval and the cause of them disowning her – a poor farmer who had had no education and worked a poor yielding farm. Now she too was poor, worked long hours on the farm for little reward with her husband and had poor children. However, Thomas's mother was determined her children would have some kind of education and had stoically taught them to read and write each day after their farm chores were done. Even if she couldn't always feed them, she ensured that they could count the chicken eggs, tell the days of the week, the months of the year and count down the days to the religious festivals and even their birthdays. She was poor but she was with the man she deeply loved, had six beautiful children and felt richer than most people she knew, and that included her entire family. The only family member who did not ridicule her for falling in love with a poor farmer was an uncle. He had sent money for the children once a year and thus made sure that they would eat a good Christmas meal and have at least one small present each. His name was Benoit Duvall, he had lived in Paris and had worked as a lawyer. News had reached Thomas's mother a few years back that her uncle, Benoit Duvall, had left his highly successful law practice, given away all his goods and was now a senior friar in a small friary in Paris. She didn't know why and there was no family member she could ask – but even if there had been, they couldn't have told her why either.

The land they worked on was poor, and with the landowner's rent of fifty per cent of the yield, and debilitating government taxes, that seemed to increase every year, it meant that Thomas's mother and father, like so many other rural farmers, struggled to make a living. It was difficult for them, as patriotic as they were, not to feel aggrieved as they struggled and the upper classes and royalty went about their days in silk attended to by servants and maids. Rumours that the king had frittered away the country's wealth and France was now steeped in debt had reached even the Dumas's farm. It was said that whilst much of the sovereign debt was owed to many foreign states, most of the debt was owed to the extremely popular Order of the Knights Templar.

Thomas Dumas's father had called his youngest son *Petite Pomme* – Little Apple because of Thomas's rich, red, rosy cheeks. Mr Dumas's *Petite Pomme* did not play much with his other siblings and would often be seen sitting alone. Thomas had a serious nature about him; dutiful and fastidious in his chores, a good scholar and determined when faced with difficulty. He was also a deeply religious child, like his father, both pious and reverent.

As a young boy, Thomas Dumas had seen imaginary things. His parents, raising five other children, were used to the fanciful and meandering nature of young minds, but they had begun to believe that his mind might just be more fanciful than the others! Thomas had told them that he heard voices; he had seen things, that he had visions. By the time he was twelve, his visions and the voices had become more frequent. His parents began to fear for their young son's life. In the parochial, rural village enclaves, if it had become known that he was having visions and hearing voices, his young life would have seen its end in the flames of an execution pyre. He would have been burnt at the stake for witchcraft and sorcery. The infamous French Inquisitions, purging French communities of witchcraft and an ever-growing list of heinous black arts, gripped France with fear and a menacing self-righteousness. Families reported other families with fevered paranoia and authorities openly encouraged neighbours to spy on neighbours. The propagating and proliferating mistrust that stifled the normal life of mainly rural communities, engulfed them in a spiral of suspicion and distrust. Everything that went wrong: the weather, illness, misfortune, bad luck, hair loss, bad teeth, aches, pains, loss, a bad harvest, and death, were all blamed on the black arts and the only way to stop it was to seek out those that practised it. Clearly, the black arts were responsible for all the woes of ordinary French folk.

By the time Thomas had reached his sixteenth birthday, he announced that an angel had arrived in his visions. His parents were distraught. They had managed to keep his secret for years, but they knew, even if they continued to be ultra-careful, sooner or later stories of the farmer's boy who said he spoke to an angel, would eventually get out and then the king's Inquisitors would arrive! Despite their constant pleading, Thomas would not stop talking about his visions. The family even stopped going to church, but this in itself caused rumour, speculation and gossip.

Thomas's father tried to deter his son many times. "We all have dreams, Thomas. They will go as you grow older and be replaced with other dreams, dreams of the land, harvest, weather ... but you must stop talking like this."

"But Papa, I cannot, I have no power to stop him from visiting me; he needs my help."

"Who is this angel, my son?'

"I do not know his name Papa, but he said he is a Seraphim."

"He is one of the seven, the seven Seraphims?" His father was taken aback. "One of the archangels that serve as the throne guardians of God, this is your angel?"

"I don't know Papa; I just know that he said he was a Seraphim but I do not know what that means."

"How many wings does your angel have?" his father asked, testing him.

"Three sets, he has six wings, Papa."

Thomas's father knew that his son could not know that the biblical Seraphims have three pairs of wings. He said out loud. "Isaiah 6, verse 2. *Above him were Seraphim, each with six wings: With two wings they covered their faces, with two they covered their feet, and with two they were flying.* What else can you tell me, my son?"

"The angel told me I must find the *Barbatus Bellator* before the fire takes him and the way back for the one is lost."

Thomas nor his father understood the meaning of the words *Barbatus Bellator*, the language was not French.

Thomas's parents were at a loss of how to protect their son anymore, they decided her uncle was perhaps their only hope; he was Thomas's only hope. The uncle had always been kind to them, so it was decided that his mother would travel to Paris and seek out her uncle at the small friary on the island of Île de la Cité, on the river Seine near Notre Dame, in Paris. One of her eldest sons would make the journey with her and help protect her from any would-be robbers and vagabonds as it would be a dangerous journey for her to undertake and one she had only undertaken a few times.

*

One month later his mother and the elder brother returned to the farm. The journey had taken its toll, but they arrived back safely. His mother was tired but took the time to greet each of her children and tell them of the sights they had seen and the people they had met. Later, once all the children had had their curiosities satisfied and were safely tucked up in bed, she devoured two plates of broth and then told her husband something that both pleased him and dumbfounded him.

"It seems," she began, "well, there is no other way to say this, it seems our son, your *Petite Pomme,* is a genius." Her husband looked quizzically at his wife as she warmed herself by the open fire in the kitchen and drank in gulps the fresh water one of the children had fetched for her earlier. "He speaks Latin," she announced.

Her husband raised his eyebrows in utter amazement and reached for the flagon of homemade ale. "Latin!"

"The name that Thomas keeps repeating, *Barbatus Bellator,* the person the angel says he must help, it's Latin; *Barbatus Bellator* means bearded warrior."

"But—"

"I know, husband, no one here speaks Latin. He has never met anyone who speaks Latin, but my uncle does, both from his former life as a lawyer and now from his monastic life, and he assures me it is Latin."

"Does he know who or what the *Barbatus Bellator* is?"

"He does not. But he agrees with us, we must get Thomas away from the farm. We must get our boy out of here as quickly as possible."

"But where is he supposed to go?"

"I begged my uncle to take him into the friary."

"And what did your uncle say?" her husband asked impatiently, now even more worried for his son's life than ever before.

"He said yes but insists that he leave tomorrow." She knew this would be hard for her husband to hear.

"Tomorrow!" The look of consternation spread over his weather-beaten face.

"My uncle said he will always be in danger here. Their monastic way of life and self-reflection will help purge our son of his fanciful stories and they will keep him safe. But we cannot risk leaving him here a moment longer. My uncle has told me that France has become a dangerous place and the king's Inquisitors are scouring the countryside looking for any scrap of information about possible witchcraft, sorcery or possession."

"My poor *Petite Pomme,*" her husband sighed ruefully, as he drank more ale. "But must he really leave tomorrow, why?"

"Because he will become our poor 'deceased' *Petite Pomme* if he does not!"

*

So, at sixteen years of age, Thomas, and this time his father began their long journey to the friary on the island of Île de la Cité, on the river Seine, Paris, where Thomas was to be taken into the Brotherhood and where he was to spend the rest of his life in servitude to God.

Thomas was sad to say goodbye to his siblings and especially sad to say goodbye to his mother. He didn't know when he would see them all again, but he hoped it would not be too long. He didn't want to leave them, and they all cried when the time came for him and his father to leave. They kissed and hugged and his siblings promised to write to him. He promised to write back, to tell them all his news on his new adventure. However, whilst he was sad, the thought of doing the work of God excited him. His nature of being dutiful and fastidious in his chores, determined when faced with difficulty, and his deeply religious, pious and reverent way would hold him in good stead as he trained to be ordained.

Along the dusty cart-worn tracks they walked and Thomas marvelled at the ever-changing environs. Along the way his father told him that as a friar he would take vows of chastity, obedience and poverty. He told him that after his training he would be required to go out into different communities and spread the word of God. As a friar he would not serve one community as monks do, but that he would serve God amongst the laity communities. He was excited to know that after his training, he would travel the countryside as a mendicant, relying on alms to feed and clothe himself. The thought of helping others and spreading God's word gave him the fortitude to take on the arduous seven-day trip to the city of Paris.

*

Date: 1314, one year later
Place: France, a small friary

Thomas was now seventeen but not yet a fully trained friar. He was still a student preparing for ordination. He had been at the friary for just over a year. He'd promised his father when they said their goodbyes that he would say nothing of his visions to the other friars and would try to become a good servant of God; and this is what he did.

Thomas Dumas applied himself to his new calling. He blended in and he enjoyed his new life. As for his visions, he had not had a vision for twelve months, not since the day he entered the friary. He had tried though. Secretly at night he would lie awake silently speaking to the angel, but the angel never came, only silence greeted him back.

In the March of 1314, all of that changed, Thomas Dumas's visions returned once more.

*

Before becoming a friar, Benoit Duvall, Thomas's great uncle, had been a lawyer, a much sought-after lawyer amongst those with rich and prosperous lives and one of some repute. But then the revelation came. He had taken on a case of a rich land baron. A cruel and unpopular man who was accused of flogging to death one of his farm workers, who worked on one of his many tied farms. Monsieur Benoit Duvall skilfully convinced the court that his client simply could not have committed the crime and so could not be guilty of it. His mastery of French criminal law, riddled with Inquisitorial judges and punitive Ecclesiastical courts, meant most commoners were deprived of their basic rights. Duvall's client was found not guilty. Less than two months later he killed another farm worker, a woman, then he killed her four children because they had witnessed what he had done to their mother. Monsieur Duvall was racked with guilt. He gave away all his worldly goods and severed all contact with past colleagues, friends and most of his family. He became Friar Benoit. He kept only a few contacts from those days. One of those was his niece. She had married for love, despite the family's protestations, and now worked a poor farm with her six children and her husband. There was also a handful of Templars whom he had represented in investment and property cases. He had trusted and liked them, and this was reciprocated. Although he had not spoken to any of the Templars since entering the friary, he had kept up to date with what was happening with them.

Within the friary there had been a lot of talk about the plight of the much-famed *Templiers* – Templars. The heroic deeds of the warrior monks were the stuff of legend in cities, towns and rural villages of France and in most European countries; every young red-blooded male wanted to become a knight and leave for exotic places and righteous crusades.

It was 1314, seven years after the fateful Templar arrests on Friday the 13th, but rumours were still raging about the fate of many of those still incarcerated.

Thomas was naturally intrigued about the famed warrior monks. He, like the rest of France, wanted to know if they were guilty of the heinous crimes that they were being accused of, tried for and for some, executed for – everyone in France wanted to know. He turned to his great uncle Benoit for information.

His great uncle had been sitting in the herb garden, near the old fig tree, with his friend and companion, Friar Pablo. Friar Pablo was a man of very few words; a diagonal, deep, nasty-looking scar across his face hinted at a previous life less tranquil and contemplative than the one he now led. Some of the other friars called him *le Chevalier* – the Knight, but they would never dare to in front of him. It seemed to Thomas that everyone knew more about Friar Pablo than he did himself. Whilst the friary, like many other friaries, was not just occupied by French men, Friar Pablo was the only Spaniard there. It was rumoured that Friar Pablo, like many soldiers from the wars and the crusades, had found God on the battlefields and had swapped his sword for a Bible.

As a lawyer, Friar Benoit had been a thoughtful man, a man not prone to gossip or rash conclusions. He never wanted to enter into the gossip of the day, but he wanted to help the young Thomas understand. The three of them sat huddled together so they would not be overheard.

"It is said by many," Friar Benoit began, "that the Templars are guilty of all charges, but others say they are not guilty of any."

The old fig tree gave shade from the sun in the summer and protection against the chilly eddies of light breezes that swirled around the friary in the winter. He spoke in a hushed whisper, his friend, Friar Pablo, said nothing – but he watched, his eyes serious and intense, very intense. Friar Benoit knew that the subject matter was contentious at the very least, but it was always dangerous. To gossip about such things would be to gossip about the king and the head of their church, the Pope. He knew his views would be treated as treasonous gossip and probably the cause of his own death: a guillotine blade to the back of his neck.

Friar Benoit looked towards his friend; his friend looked around and then he nodded, it was clear to speak. Subconsciously, Friar Benoit rubbed the back of his neck as he began. "We must go back seven years, to 1307 to seek our answers, young Thomas." He adjusted the rope belt around the waist of his coarse, woollen, brown robe. His hood was up, it was cold. "Our king, King **Philippe** IV and our Pope, Pope Clement V, conspired together, some say to dismantle the Order of the Knights Templar. The warrior monks who had fought for our country with their lives and protected Christian pilgrims during the Crusades were now doomed. They were warrior monks but also, they were the architects of one of the first banking systems; they were once applauded, admired and revered by kings and queens worldwide. However, it was also said that behind closed doors the warrior monks held secrets, secrets so profound that if they got into the wrong hands, they would reshape destiny and tip the balance of power between good and evil on Earth." Thomas noticed Friar Pablo nodding in agreement.

"When strange things started to happen to our skyline, through their many building projects, it only served to fuel the growing speculation. Some speculated that they used Hermetic and Hiramic knowledge; Hiramic knowledge passed down from Hiram Abif, Solomon's master mason. The Templars had taught a whole army of French craftsmen and created guilds, quantified by degrees of knowledge, just the same as Hiram Abif had done centuries before when building Solomon's Temple, where the Ark of the Covenant was kept. No one had thought it was possible to build so high and to span so wide.

"Last year, you may remember, the trials began of some of the remaining Templars still incarcerated, on the 19th of October. On the 25th and 26th, Jacques de Molay, the Templars' Grand Master, and some of the others were brought before their accusers. Many Templars had faced them already and some had confessed to the heinous crimes they were being accused of."

"It was the king's men who tortured the Templars." Friar Pablo said. This was the most words Thomas had ever heard him say at any one time. "They got their confessions," Friar Pablo added.

Friar Benoit nodded in agreement and continued, "They sent the transcripts of the confessions to the king; the king sent them to the Pope. He needed the Pope's blessing to eradicate the Templars because they had always previously had the church's protection. Plus, in 1139, Pope Innocent II ordered by Papal decree *Omne Datum Optimum* – International Independence to be granted upon the Templars. This meant that the Templars no longer answered, paid taxes, tithes or dues to any royal house in any land. The king needed the Pope.

"The Pope wanted to appease the king but he was worried how his actions would be received in the Catholic countries around the world," he went on.

"Because in many of those countries the Templars were revered?" Thomas asked.

"Exactly, the Pope holds enormous power, not only in France but also in many other countries where Catholicism is practised."

"Then he is as powerful as the king," Thomas stated in a hushed whisper.

"Far more powerful in those Catholic practising countries. I think the Pope was worried that the warrior monks had confessed a little too quickly and perhaps, to a little too much and that others would see that too. I think he must have worried that the royal interrogation had been inhumane torture to force the Templars to confess to anything. Not wanting to be seen as unjust, the Pope sent two of his cardinals with orders to speak to the Templars and find out how the confessions had been gained and, if necessary, to take the Templars into papal custody. However, the king would not allow the cardinals to see the Templars, nor would he release them into papal custody."

"Stalemate," Thomas announced.

"Indeed, Thomas. So, the Pope sent word to all European heads of state to hold Templars in their countries and seize their lands for the church. He was showing the king his power. Remember, Thomas, the king wants the Templar wealth, that's why he wants them, needs them, dishonoured and disbanded."

"Preferably dead," Friar Pablo said. "His largest debt is owed to them! This is not about religion, this is about politics, power and money."

"We know that the Pope yet again sent his two cardinals to Paris," Friar Benoit continued, "but this time the king, I guess fearing ex-communication from the church and in doing so isolation from other state leaders, allowed access to the Templars. The king had been excommunicated by a previous Pope, Pope Boniface the Eighth, who was Pope from 1294 to 1303. Back then, the king had prevented religious clerics in France to travel to the Holy See in Rome.

"As Templars, these Knights denied that their confessions were given freely and truthfully and showed the cardinals proof of their festering wounds and hideous burns and deep scars, gained from the terrible torture that forced their false confessions. The Pope then suspended the Inquisition."

"So, stalemate number two."

"Indeed Thomas. So, the king then went to see the Pope and reminded him of the Third Lateran Council of 1179 that said: *heretics and all who defend and receive them shall be excommunicated.* The Pope himself was now in a vulnerable position and feared for his life; he feared he would become known as the Heretic Pope! Eventually, though, the king agreed to release seventy-two selected Templars to be interrogated by the Pope's own people in Poitiers. They were interrogated for five days. And now here we are, seven years later and the Templars are still in prison."

"Will the king win?" Thomas asked. "Will the king see them all dead and take all their possessions?"

The ex-lawyer thought about it for a moment or two. "I believe the king just might get their wealth, but I have always thought that there is something else about those Templars. I don't know what it is but ..." his voice trailed off as he got lost in his thoughts. Then he said, "Brother Pablo, what do you think?"

The Spaniard stood up. He took one last look around and then said, "I fought with those Templars, so I know." Then he slowly walked away and left them.

Thomas leant towards Friar Benoit, and whispered, "he stares."

"He does stare, I agree there."

"But I mean a lot."

"I know."

"He looks right at you, into you. Why does he stare so much?"

"Because he is trying to learn from you. From you, me, from the others."

"What is he learning from us?" Thomas asked, confused.

"He is trying to find how to forgive. He is trying to find his salvation."

"He scares me."

"He should."

"He should! Who is he?"

"His name is Don Pablo Santiago de Aragón and he was a commander knight in the Christian military army of Aragón, Spain. He fought the Moors there for most of his adult life and won many battles. He was a revered soldier and his name is well known throughout Aragón. But when he finally returned home after two years away at war, he found his entire family dead. He was told that a small Moor scouting party had discovered their village on the terraced mountainside where it had stood quietly and peacefully for over a hundred years. Only one man had managed to escape the invaders, all the rest of the men were butchered: they had their throats cut. His wife, his children and all the other women and children of the village were locked inside the village's wooden meeting hall, then they set it alight. Everyone inside burnt to death. This had happened just one month before Friar Pablo returned home. He was due to leave the battlegrounds six weeks earlier but had stayed on those extra six weeks because they had needed soldiers to drive back a large force that was attacking a major city north of where he lived."

Thomas was shocked. "Oh my God. He ... he could have been there; perhaps he could have saved them but he decided to stay."

"And he thinks about that fact every excruciating second of every day. It eats away at him. He returned to the battlefield two days later but this time he was a bitter, angry man and intent on only one thing, to exact revenge. For three years he fought but this time he fought within the ranks. It was said he had gone rogue; some say even a little insane, others that he went totally insane. He became a cold, heartless, merciless bloody killer and killed just for the killing of it. He had lost himself. Then, one day he turned up here, at the friary. He was half his body weight, dirty and bloody, his clothes in tatters. He wore a haunted look that terrified me. It was like he had had his morality squeezed from his very soul. I was the one who met him at the gate. I nursed him back to health. Physically he regained all his strength but mentally, well, that's been a bigger challenge for us to climb. And so, Friar Pablo hides away here, here in this small friary, blaming himself for the hundreds of lives he has taken and for the death of his beloved wife and three small children. After a year he took his clothes and his sword from the storeroom where they had been kept and he walked into the forest and threw them away; he threw away his old life and his sins."

Thomas thought for a moment. "You know he wears beads."

"I know," Friar Benoit said.

"Why?"

"Santeria."

"Santeria?"

"It is Spanish, it means the cult of the saints, or way of the saints."

"But ... but he is a Catholic?"

"He is a Catholic, Thomas. Santeria is a strange cult that mixes Catholicism with the teaching that every person has a destiny from God and you fulfil that destiny with the aid of energy and the help of the Orishas. For people like Friar Pablo, the Orishas are the saints."

"And the animal skulls that he keeps in his room?"

"Part of their sacrifice to the Orishas."

"I'm never going to sleep with my door open again!"

Friar Benoit laughed, "says the boy who has visits from an angel in his visions." He laughed again as he walked away, this time more heartily as the irony amused him.

*

News travelled slowly in rural France, relying on travelling merchants, wandering minstrel players and the king's tax collectors to relay it – inevitably it became more slanted the further it travelled. So, news of the demise of the Templars had only reached Thomas and his family in dribs and drabs. However, now he was a stone's throw away from where the top five Templars, which included the Order's Grand Master, were being held. The small friary was just a few miles from where they were incarcerated. Now there was daily news of their interrogations and the authority's proclamations regarding the Templars' guilt. There had been talk all week that something was about to happen. The friars watched and listened with intense interest. They, like the rest of France and large parts of Europe, Asia Minor and the Middle East, waited to see what would happen to the renowned warrior monks. And just like that, it came. It was announced that five of the Templars, which included their Grand Master, were about to be charged. That was the week Thomas's visions began again.

By the end of the week, the most important Templars were finally sentenced. The judge read the verdict: they were to be held in prison for the rest of their natural lives. But that was not the end of it. At the court hearing, two of the Knights, the Grand Master Jacques de Molay and Geoffrey de Charney, the second in command, shouted publicly that all the confessions had been extracted by torture and force. There was uproar in the court. The king, after hearing of Jacques de Molay and Geoffrey de Charney's outburst, commanded that that night they were both to be executed. They were taken from their cells on the small island of Île de la Cité, on the river Seine, close to where the small friary lay and where the dominating *Notre Dame de Paris* – Our Lady of Paris cathedral stood.

On that tragic cold night, the 18th of March 1314, the king's armed guards and the Templars' jailers, wrapped in thick cloaks and holding burning torches to light their way, marched their two shackled, beaten and tortured prisoners right past the friary on their way to the Templars' final destination. The friars could see the light of the torches in the distance, long before they saw the execution group and their prisoners pass by. The friary's main gates were already locked and secure for the night, when a few of the younger friars, and one student in training, slipped quietly out of one of the side gates and followed the execution party to see what was to become of the Templars: Thomas Dumas was one of them.

It was a clear cold night. The friars quickly caught up with the group of two bedraggled prisoners, four bad-tempered jailers and twelve king's guards. The guards paid no mind to the friars, they just wanted to be rid of their prisoners and be back in their beds with their wives, girlfriends or their Parisian whores. Thomas got closer, almost by the side of the prisoners: they looked in a bad way. Their clothing was tattered – it was literally rotting away. Once, they had been recognised by their white surcoat and distinctive red cross, signifying purity, symbolising their abandonment of darkness for light, evil for good, now they looked like street beggars.

At one point Jacques de Molay, the Templars' Grand Master, weak and exhausted by the years of incarceration and terrible torture, stumbled and nearly fell. Thomas was closest, he reached out to steady the old Templar from falling. The guards ignored him, if the friar wanted to waste his effort on a man soon to die that was his lookout, besides, it gave them an excuse to stop and take some wine and warm themselves from the cold Parisian night air.

As Thomas reached out to de Molay's arm to steady him, de Molay sank to one knee, he was weak and exhausted. Thomas knelt beside him. He held onto de Molay, holding him steady.

Do you know who I am?" Thomas whispered, afraid but leaning even closer to de Molay.

"I do, Friar," de Molay said, his voice was hoarse and his lips swollen, dried and cracked; he struggled to form his words. Thomas took his small pewter flask from within his robe and gave de Molay some water. Then handed his flask on to another friar so he could give water to the other Templar. The guards still took no heed of the friars. "I am not a friar," he told de Molay.

"You are the farmer's boy, the one I have been seeing in my visions?" de Molay asked him.

"I think so," Thomas replied. "And you are the one I have seen in mine. You are *Barbatus Bellator* – the bearded warrior," Thomas whispered. "And ..." he paused.

De Molay grabbed Thomas's arm and pulled him a little closer. His hands bent and claw-like through the countless broken bones that without treatment, had healed badly and hideously misshapen. Most of his fingernails were missing. He smelt of putrid prison decay, sweat and blood. Yet Thomas caught a glimmer in the old man's eyes, it was resolute and intense, a defiant glower that told him that the Templar was not yet done with this world. The jailers and the guards were still huddled, sharing a buck skin of wine, telling their brothel stories and trying to warm themselves whilst they rested.

"Finish what you were going to say, I know my fate."

"You are the one the angel told me I must find before the fire takes you and the way back is lost."

"I've been waiting for you." de Molay told him. He pulled Thomas closer still.

Jacques de Molay's face was aged, ashen with a deep haunted look. He had once been a great warrior, brave and strong. He had stoically led the Knights Templar from April 1292, until 1312, when the Order was officially disbanded by Pope Clement V. He was the 23rd Templar Grand Master and all thought he would be the last Grand Master. Jacques de Molay shot a glance towards the guards and his jailers to check they were still deep in their brothel stories and drinking their wine.

"When the first of our Order went to the Holy Land, only nine Knights went; Hugues de Payens was the Grand Master then. They went to find that which many thought had been long lost, but not our Order, we never thought it lost, just hidden. Many have speculated what our Order found deep underground in that holy place, the place they call the Temple of Solomon."

Thomas did not speak; inside his stomach churned. He tried to remain calm, but the seventeen-year-old was scared. He began to pull back. De Molay caught his arm again with his broken hands.

"Stay your fears young friar, for God, is on your side and it is God's work that is to be done." de Molay looked at the other Templar. They held a gaze that seemed to last an age to Thomas, but it was just seconds. The other Templar nodded in agreement to de Molay and then he smiled.

Jacques de Molay turned back to face Thomas. "We have the Ark of the Covenant." He didn't wait for Thomas to absorb this startling revelation, there was too much to tell and too little time to do it in. "We protect it. We have kept it safe as our 'Charge' for hundreds of years. But now it is gone from this wretched place. Seven years ago, when the arrests started, the king, Philippe, sent his guards to the port of La Rochelle, where some of our brothers had made their escape with the Ark, but the king's men were too late they had escaped across the water to England. The king then tried to persuade his son-in-law, Edward II of England, who is married to Philippe's daughter, Isabella, to hunt down the Templars. However, the Templars had actually landed in a remote part of Scotland, at the Mull of Kintyre.

"Now you must find the one who has the key. Get it and hide it. The Ark has always been separated from its key."

"A key to open the Ark?" Thomas mumbled.

"No, my young friar, not to open it. It is not that kind of key. This key does not open the Ark, it opens what the Ark really is: the *weapon*, and the *way*. It is written in the prophecies that the Cathars brought with them. But only the last Seer knows how the key works. He knows the answer to the Paradox. We must protect the key until the Seer comes."

"Who is the last Seer?" Thomas asked.

"We do not know. We have been waiting for the Seer for the past two hundred years. You must protect the key, you cannot let it get into the wrong hands. They are looking for it. They want to know what the Paradox is."

"Who?"

"Followers of the Man of Lawlessness."

A guard coughed and they both shot a look towards them. They were still occupied with their stories and drink.

"You must go from this place, this night," de Molay continued. "You must travel to Spain and to the Cañón del Río Lobos, near Soria. There you will find a hermitage called San Bartolomé, once there you must seek out a hermit called Caleb, an Essene from the Essenes of the time of Christ. Although, the hermit you seek will not be found in the hermitage as he has not been there for seventy years. No, you will find him high above the hermitage in the mountains to the east, he will not be found easily though. He has spent nearly all of his life not being found."

"How will I know such a man?"

"You will know him when you see him. He is one hundred and three years old and around his neck hangs a small wooden cross with a rose within a crown of thorns carved upon it. Now, go from this place young friar; go and do the work of the *Pauperes Commilitones Christi Templique Salomonici,* the work of the Knights Templar. Go do the work of God."

De Molay looked at the other Templar. "We are the last who know the identity of the guardian of the Ark key and where he is to be found, and soon we will be gone. Take only one or two others with you; trust no one else. You know such men, men you can trust?"

Thomas knew immediately who he would ask to go with

him, his mentor and his great uncle, Benoit Duvall. "I do." He replied.

"Good, then go to him. If my resolve holds, then they will not get what they want but should it not, then you are in mortal danger and so is the key. I have not asked for your name, so I cannot tell them, but it will not take them long to work out where you have come from. Go back to your friary and gather whatever you need, but you must leave tonight. Travel only on the back roads; do not use your real names and travel in disguise. The Ark key must reach the last of the Seers. I cannot tell you how long it will take as we have already carried this secret for nearly two hundred years."

Again, the jailers and guards began to stir. They had now finished their whoring stories and their wine and besides, there was an execution party waiting for them. The wood had already been stacked around the two stakes that would hold the old Templars. The stakes had been fixed into the ground before the wood pyre was piled around them so as not to fall. The rope that would bind the Templars had been thoroughly soaked so it would take longer to burn through. The heat of the flames would melt their skin, but the Templars would be upright, for all to see, as the king had wanted.

I have one question, Thomas said as he started to rise and help de Molay to his feet.

"Then ask your question."

"What was his name?"

"Whose name, my son?" de Molay asked.

"The angel; our angel?"

"Ah. His name is Michael, the Archangel Michael. He is the leader of the Seraphim, the fiery ones. He is one of seven, the seven archangels that serve as the throne guardians of God, he is our angel."

"I will not let you down," Thomas said as they now stood face to face, de Molay finally back on his feet.

De Molay smiled at Thomas, "then now I can die in peace."

*

The friars and one trainee friar got back to the friary just before 10 o'clock. Thankfully the full moon illuminated their way. No one spoke. At the friary gate, they eased the wrought iron ringed handle to open the gate. It creaked. As soon as they entered, they saw him, Friar Benoit, Benoit Duvall. He did not look pleased. He scolded them, then told them to get off to bed before anyone found out they had left the friary without permission. They scurried away quickly but Thomas stayed behind. Benoit Duvall locked the gate. As he turned around, he was surprised to see Thomas still standing there: but not as surprised as he was twenty minutes later when Thomas had finished telling him about his meeting with Jacques de Molay that night.

*

They hurried down the corridor, Thomas and Benoit. Their bare feet – sandals in hand – grew cold on the grey, flagstone floor. Silently they headed for the friars' sleeping quarters, the burnished orange light of the full moon illuminating their way.

Benoit Duvall had not had to think twice about Thomas's request that he go with him to Spain. And when Thomas said they should take one other, in unison they had turned to each other and said, "le Chevalier."

They turned the handle and pushed lightly against Friar Pablo's door, then quietly crept inside. There was just enough light in there for them to see an empty, unmade bed. The door closed on them. Friar Pablo was there, standing behind the door with a knife in his hand.

"You shouldn't creep about at night Brothers, you are no good at creeping, too noisy," he said, lowering his knife.

"How did you know we—"

"Saw them leave. Saw them come back. Heard what he told you, Benoit."

They looked down at his left hand, it held a small bag.

"I have three donkeys ready at the west gate."

"We can't steal the friary's donkeys," Thomas protested.

Benoit smiled. "Well, I guess, legally they actually belong to God, and we are going to do God's work so, He might forgive us."

By the light of a full moon beaming orange out of a clear sky, and on three stolen donkeys, a small band of two friars and one trainee, left the small friary on the island of Île de la Cité, on the river Seine near Notre Dame, in Paris and headed south for Spain.

Chapter 3

A Rooftop Getaway

Date: The 17th – 700 years later and the day of the rooftop escape
Place: A Catholic school, Barcelona City, Spain
Time: Afternoon

His breathing was heavy and laboured. He struggled to stay upright. His frantic escape was precarious at best. The sun was beating down relentlessly, one slip and he would fall to his death.

He checked that he still had the pointy thing tucked into his belt. He did. He let out a sigh of relief, if he'd lost it then it would have all been for nothing.

He was trying to make good decisions as he ran but he was running for his life and found it hard to remove the fear from his decision-making. Good decisions would mean he stood a chance of making it; bad decisions and he wouldn't.

They had all studied the street map for days before the meeting, but he was now disoriented and lost, it had all gone south very quickly. All hell had broken loose; the noise had been deafening. Bullets started to fly, there were loud bangs and lots of smoke. He didn't know who fired the first shot or why, but as soon as its explosive sound reverberated around the empty school gym, everyone took evasive action. He knew the safest option was to disperse: no central target, not a cluster of bodies making an easy target, just lots of individual ones spread out.

She'd told him to get out. He'd ran towards a window, his egress partially covered by stacked chairs. He'd reached the window and flicked the latch, there was no lock. Now he was in an unfamiliar place; he didn't know where he was or where he'd been; he was alone.

He'd taken several wrong turns. He knew it was easy to do in a firefight but still, he was annoyed at himself. He'd memorised the street map but lost his way. He was lost, alone, unarmed, out of breath and the target of some very pissed off villains, plus, he'd stabbed himself in the leg with the pointy thing whilst making his escape.

He left the narrow street he had just run down and quickly tucked into a building through its narrow archway entrance. The three-storey apartment block was one of many along the *calle del Torro* – street of the bull. He ran up three flights of stairs towards the roof – there was nowhere else to go other than up. What he was going to do when he got up there, he hadn't figured out yet, he was too focused on getting away from his assailants. He had the artefact, the pointy thing, he needed to keep it from falling back into their hands.

Behind him, the salvo of gunfire had stopped. He knew the Templars inside the derelict building were regrouping. He also knew the Templars outside would already be searching for him. They would find him; she would find him; he just needed to stay alive long enough for her to do so.

He burst through the door at the top of the final flight of stairs. The half wood half wired-glass door sprung open and crashed against the wall as he pushed hard against the panic bar. It led him out onto a rooftop terrace. He stole quick glances trying to find the best escape route. Each apartment block along the road was joined to the next. There were sixteen three-storey apartment blocks, with red-tiled roofs and all had a small rooftop terrace in the centre. There were six apartment blocks to his left and ten to his right. He stopped and hesitated: *go left or go right*? he thought. He wanted to use his coms to call the others but knew it would be too dangerous, if one of the others had been caught, then the criminals would have their coms and would be listening. Besides, he had no idea where he was anyway, so he couldn't tell them, plus, his bodycam had snapped during his escape. However, as Bertram had told him, the credit card he was carrying was made of polymagnetite multilayer skins, compressed together with nano circuitry embedded within the centre skin layers. It had a built-in nano chip tracker, which meant he could be found almost anywhere because it transmitted by bouncing its signal off any nearby satellite. It had a battery life of around three months; however, it constantly recharged through either body warmth or solar. Bertram was precise like that! Jonathan had no idea what all that meant, he just knew he was being tracked by the team back in the control room in Scotland and they would relay his position to the Templars on the ground.

Either left or right meant running across the precarious looking red-tiled rooftops to get to the next rooftop terrace and a possible way out.

He heard shouting from downstairs. He knew they must have seen him enter the building. His hand reached for the pointy thing again, he wanted to reassure himself he still had it. The voices were getting louder – their language was not English; he couldn't make it out. A barking dog started on one of the terraces to his left. It sounded like a deep bark, which only meant one thing, a big dog. He was left with only one option, leap over the small rooftop terrace wall to his right and try to run across the tiled roofs and exit via another apartment block.

As soon as his feet hit the red tiles, he knew he was in trouble. He could hear them cracking underfoot. Every frantic step he took, set off another ear-piercing crack. The red clay roof tiles, relentlessly baked over many years by the Spanish sun, were not meant to be walked on, let alone run on. They were brittle and fragile.

He heard his name being called over the coms, the secure nano coms earpieces were crisp and clear. He heard the password, *Longinus* – Aldrich Manwin Tucker, the professor at Cambridge University and the infamous witch hunter, had aptly given their mission that name. Now he knew that their coms were secure and safe to use.

"Where is everyone?" Jonathan called. Now he was more out of breath and leaking sweat. His earpiece was struggling to stay in his ear as he ran erratically high above the ground and across the roof of the three-storey apartment block in a dodgy part of Barcelona. The splitting and cracking, causing him to second guess his footing, only served to hinder his getaway. Hot, slippery, dusty, undulating, like the shape of small, corrugated sheeting, and exceptionally brittle from years in the baking sun, his lofty escape was proving potentially terminal.

"Almost there, Honey." Dominique's voice rose from his earpiece like sweet velvet. "I can see you now." Her voice was calm and reassuring, despite the situation he was in.

"Remind me, Dear ... why am I doing this?" Jonathan gasped as he tried to control his breathing, balance, footing, courage, head, limbs, bones ... life! And the pointy thing!

"Because you're a ... steady Husband, watch your footing you almost ..."

A roof tile under Jonathan's left foot cracked and broke into several small pieces. It started to slide off the roof, his left leg with it. He saw an ageing configuration of aerials and grabbed at them. He was lucky, they were still secured and anchored to a whitewashed chimney stack.

"Good reflexes, Husband; I got you through the binos, you're doing great. Watch out for those telephone wires."

"I see them."

"And the seagulls?" Two seagulls took fright and flight as he approached them, he nearly fell backwards as they surprised him.

"Nope, didn't see them."

"Watch your six, incoming," she called to him.

Jonathan Rose, the ex-priest from Washing DC, turned around quickly. Two men were hot on his trail. They were carrying knives – big knives! Now they too had cleared the small rooftop terrace wall and were following his path across the tiles. He couldn't help noticing that they looked far more adept at rooftop sprinting than he did.

"Damn it," he cursed. He ran on.

A bullet barely missed him, it hit one of the terrace area's small utility buildings where the apartments' gas bottles were kept. It ricocheted off the rendered wall and spun off in the direction of the heavens.

"Damn it," Dominique cursed. "Sniper at your nine. Rifle.

High velocity and scope. Look for some cover."

"Cover! Cover! I'm on a rooftop. No cover!" Jonathan shouted back, "the two on my back are gaining. And they have knives, big knives!"

"You have a gun."

"I dropped it."

"You dropped it?"

"I was running, and the pointy thing stuck in my leg and I couldn't see anyone and—"

"Jonathan, watch out!" His wife yelled, as she watched the sniper on the adjacent roof ease the butt of the rifle back into his shoulder and aim the barrel along the crosshairs of the sights once more.

A new voice came over the coms.

"I'm thirty seconds away; on my mark in thirty, twenty-nine, twenty-eight ..." Luther Jones, the ex-SAS veteran and newly appointed to the Order's Higher Council, announced over their earpieces. "Wolf is with me," he continued, "and we have your new extraction route covered. Just make sure you get here Jonathan, Dominique will guide you in."

The second bullet narrowly missed his head. This time the rogue round hit a small gas bottle next to a rusting barbecue on the rooftop terrace of an adjacent building. The explosion woke up the siesta-sleeping residents and most of the slumbering dogs within a three-mile radius. It was 2 p.m. and nearly 40 degrees in Barcelona.

People started to hang their heads out of their apartment windows to see what had happened.

"*Que diablos* – what the hell," rang out in general unison.

"*Tenga cuidado alli arriba* – be careful up there," followed by some of the concerned residents.

"*Bájate de nuestro puto techo* – get off our fucking roof," was offered by a number of others. All of them gawped in amazement at the high-octane rooftop chase.

"... Fifteen, fourteen ..." Luther's voice was clear.

Jonathan saw the black ball-like object pop up above the top of the roof, and then it disappeared. At first, he thought it was a large black balloon, but something was out of place, this balloon had a nose and a pair of glasses, and hair "What? What was that?" he asked.

"What?" Dominique asked. "What was what?"

"That was my question. Where did that head come from?"

"What head?" Dominique asked, confused.

"The head. It had a black crash helmet on top of it with hair sticking out and a pair of flying goggles, like first world war pilot goggles. And ..."

From out of the corner of his eye he saw it again, bobbing up and down, appearing and then disappearing above the rooftop. It was like a buoy in a rough sea, chaotically rising and falling.

"Jonathan, focus, what are you talking about?" Dominique asked him.

Again, the head appeared. This time it turned to Jonathan and waved.

"It waved at me!" Jonathan said incredulously. "The head just waved at me!"

Dominique saw the sniper on the adjacent roof adjust his scope. She knew he would not miss again; he had zeroed in his sights with the first two shots. He placed the rifle butt into his shoulder and panned along to just in front of Jonathan, he stopped where Jonathan would be when he took his next step.

She saw it and knew what it meant. "JONATHAN," Dominique shouted over the coms as Jonathan went to move forward. "The shooter he's ... don't mov ... he's waiting for you to take another step."

Jonathan had already begun to move; he stopped suddenly – his left leg stopped mid-flow.

"I got this, Mrs Dominique." Bertram's voice came over the coms. "Mr Rose Jonathan, if you could just leave your left leg where it is for a moment."

Jonathan stood on one leg, the other hanging there waiting to finish its step. He was in freeze frame, three storeys up on brittle, sun-baked, red clay roof tiles that cracked every time he tried to shift his weight to steady his balance.

Bertram's head appeared above the rooftop again. He was wearing a black helmet, with strands of unkempt hair protruding out and was looking out through World War I flying goggles.

The shooter momentarily lowered his rifle, not sure what he was seeing.

"Ber ..." Jonathan was stunned. "Bertram, what are you doing up in the air," he yelled breathlessly into his coms.

"If you want to catch a tiger you need to tether a goat nearby, Mr Rose Jonathan. Just stay where you are."

"Goat!" Jonathan snapped. He was still gasping for air. "Goat ... damn it, Bertram, how are you flying?"

The shooter put the rifle to his shoulder again: the target was now motionless; it was a better shot for him. He had lain flat and in an uncomfortable position when he took his first two shots; he didn't want to be seen but now he had nothing to lose and everything to gain. He raised himself from his prone shooting position. He stood upright. He widened his stance and leaned forward slightly on his lead leg, his left leg. His index finger closed in on the trigger. He felt the steel of the trigger and slowly started to squeeze.

The whirling sound distracted him. The view through his telescopic sight had changed from a clear and full view of the target, now something was blocking his line of fire and whatever it was, it was coming straight for him. He squinted to try to make it out.

The helicopter was coming towards him but by the size of it, he decided, it was still a mile or so away, even its sound sounded distant. He knelt down, one knee on the floor so he could see his target with a clear line of sight again. The sniper wiped away the sweat from his forehead with the sleeve of his thin, gaudy cheap shirt. He eased the butt of his rifle into his shoulder once again, his left elbow resting on his lead leg, his left hand underneath the stock of the rifle. He leaned into the shot once more and breathed out gently.

Bertram's stealth sky-eye was a two-foot-long helicopter drone. The drone had nearly sixty rounds of ammunition on board where a payload would normally be. They were low calibre rounds, but enough calibre to fell a shooter – many times over.

The two men chasing Jonathan had also stopped. They saw their shooter and waited for him to put a bullet into the man they had been chasing. Once he pulled the trigger, they would go and retrieve the object he had stolen from them twenty minutes ago.

The sniper looked at the helicopter again, but this time not through the sights. Something about it niggled him, he lowered his rifle. At that moment he figured it out: it wasn't miles away. It was a drone helicopter, and it was just ten feet away. He uttered a slew of swear words, annoyed that he had allowed himself to be caught out.

Enhance your calm, Bertram thought to himself. He saw the face of the shooter via the onboard camera of the helicopter, relayed through his smart pad monitor that was hung around his neck. "Don't fire Bertram," he said to himself out loud. He increased the fuel to the burners of his jetpack, and he rose another five feet. "Wait for it," he said out loud again. "Wait for it, Bertram, you'll be right there in a minute, and breath, and breath. If you put the cart before the horse, the horse won't see the road—"

"Bertram!" Jonathan screamed at him, able to hear everything Bertram was saying over the coms. "Stop talking and—"

"Ah, Mr Rose Jonathan, you're such a cool dude in a loose mood." Bertram started to hover forwards. "*Ubi positus est, ut omnis* - where one stands, so stand us all."

"BERTRAM!"

"Yes, Mr Rose Jonathan. This is Cerebral, to infinity and beyo—"

"BERTRAM!" Wolf shouted. Wolf was sitting next to Luther in the truck almost directly below Jonathan's position. "NOW, DO IT NOW."

"Yes, Mr Indian Wolf," Bertram responded. And with that, a hail of bullets struck the shooter's body. The rifle fell from his hands and crashed to the floor, followed by his bullet-ridden body. Now Bertram turned to the two men who had been pursuing Jonathan across the Barcelona rooftop. He turned the throttle of the jet pack and the two thrusters roared again. He leaned forward and eased the thruster handles forward but then one of the thrusters spluttered, then it died, Bertram shot off!

"Where's he going?" Jonathan called over the coms.

"Well," Dominique's voice came back, "by the look of it, France!"

"Fran—"

"Okay, Jonathan, I need you to now take ten paces forward and then I want you to fall," she announced in a matter-of-fact way.

"Fall? What do you mean, fall?" Jonathan shouted to his wife through their coms. "Do I look like a guy that likes to fall off roofs?"

"Ten paces forward then just let go and slide down the roof. Relax, Luther and Wolf are there." She knew her husband would want to discuss it. He would try and talk himself out of it. She wouldn't give him the opportunity, if he didn't move, his two pursuers would be on him in less than twenty seconds.

"And so, in three, two, one," she called.

Jonathan let out a scream, "Aarrgghh!" He ran ten paces and then ...

He was no longer upright. Horizontal, feet first, he was sliding down the undulating roof of the three-storey building, snapping and cracking the red roof tiles as he went. He felt like a child on a snow slope helplessly falling, unable to stabilise his position.

His left foot struck the rickety metal guttering first, then his right, then the guttering broke away from its rusting brackets and hurtled towards the ground, followed by red tile debris and a screaming ex-priest from Washington DC.

He didn't know what '*splat*' looked or felt like, but he envisaged he was about to find out. His landing, however, was much different from what he had imagined it would be.

Luther had followed Dominique's instructions and was perfectly positioned with the canvas covered 3-ton truck directly under Jonathan. Jonathan landed on the roof of the truck they had stolen when Scotland had given them Jonathan's position and told them he was on a roof, a high roof! Luther's foot poised over the accelerator pedal, ready to press it hard to the floor, waiting for the instruction.

"Hold, hold Luther." Dominique's instructions were clear in his earpiece as she focused on the two pursuing thugs through her binoculars. "Wait for it. Wait for it."

The two thugs watched Jonathan slide off the roof but they didn't hear a splat, they heard a much softer landing sound. They looked over and saw the truck. One of the pursuers shouted for them to jump. The other one didn't want to jump but knew that if there was no soft landing, it would still be a less painful death than if he didn't jump and his boss got hold of him. They both followed Jonathan down the roof. Just as their feet started to appear over the eaves of the roof, Dominique gave the instruction to Luther.

"Go, go, go."

Luther forced the accelerator pedal down towards the floor as hard as he could and the truck moved forward thirty feet.

Jonathan sat up and looked back to where the truck had been – now he knew what *splat* looked like! He let out a heavy sigh. He didn't like taking lives but was reconciled by the fact that the two dead thugs would never take another life themselves. Luther reversed the truck back and he and John Wolf searched the two dead men. Then they painted a small red cross on each of the dead men's foreheads with their own blood – the Templars always painted their dead enemies this way, so that the Devil would know whom to take!

Two shots rang passed his ears. A third thug was now on the roof and firing shots at him, he was like a sitting duck stranded on top of the truck.

Bertram's voice came over the coms. "France indeed, just a slight miss calculation. Back now."

Dominique watched as Bertram hurtled through the air towards the new pursuer, then he crashed into him like a man who had been shot out of a cannon. The man fell. He was lying sprawled on the floor of the rooftop terrace; he was out cold. Bertram was lying next to him, his jet pack helped break his impact. He unhooked it from his torso, set a small explosive charge on it, placed it next to the unconscious thug and then headed for the door that led down the stairs and out onto the street where Dominique was now waiting in a getaway car.

The signal went over the coms from Luther, "*Omnis Templars tatum* - All Templars safe." The Knights in the control room back in Scotland breathed a sigh of relief, their plan to protect the ancient, priceless artefact, the Longinus spear, despite they themselves taking it out into the open to try to capture the criminals, had worked: just!

*

Back in Scotland, there was jubilation in the control room The main communications control room in the castle, the heart of their operations called exactly that: 'the control room', or CR for short. All around them were computers and other technological wonders. A 256-way symmetric multiprocessing mainframe running Unix, Linux operating systems, Quad TFT Plasma display terminals. Hard drives with petabytes of storage, satellite uplinks, combined CPU speeds cloaking into terahertz stealth technology and the people in there knew every relay, every plug, hard drive and connection, every wire, every router and screen. They kept the Templars' eyes and ears working day and night, monitoring thousands of sites, networks and communications: and they kept their Order secret. The people who worked in the CR were especially jubilant because their boss, Courtney Rose, had worked her magic and secured the vital evidence they needed to put the cardinal away for a long time and to entrap the criminals. But their celebrations were to be cut short. The next day, the 18th, would turn out to be a dark day.

Chapter 4

Charlie B

Date: The 8th – nine days before the rooftop escape
Place: The suburbs of Rome, Italy
Time: 7 a.m.

The radio was on, it was an English radio channel. A George Michael medley boomed out. His wife was dancing in the kitchen, and their daughter, Uma, was sitting at the table laughing. The Nef family were trilingual: Italian, Spanish and English and they wanted their daughter to be the same. At her local Italian school, she only spoke Italian. She had Spanish classes twice a week for thirty minutes and in the house, the whole family only spoke English, watched English TV and listened to English radio channels.

Uma's father stood watching his wife and daughter, his wife dancing and his daughter giggling at her mother. He was smiling and tapping his foot to George Michael's 'Freedom' song. Uma's father was tall and distinguished looking. He kept himself fit and took care of his appearance. He was a nice man and people liked him. He sported a well-trimmed beard and moustache; he was slightly thinning on the top. He always wore a broad cheery grin whenever he was around his wife and daughter, his name was Dámaso Nef. Nef was the chief of police of the *Corpo della Gendarmeria dello Stato della Città del Vaticano* – the Vatican City State Gendarmerie Corps, globally just known as the Vatican police. He was intelligent, liked by his staff and respected by most of the cardinals. His father was Spanish, so Nef had a Spanish surname as his first name.

The doorbell rang; it rang four times before Nef finally heard

34

it above George. He left his wife to finish her dance and went to open the door. Out on the street, he saw a BMW K 1600 GTL on its rest-stand, its engine idling. Its rider, his helmet off and under his arm, stood in Nef's doorway. "Package for Mr Nef," he said in a strong *Romanesco* accent.

Nef quickly checked the street, both ways. It was all quiet; nothing unusual going on, no strange cars parked up or people hanging around. He lived in a quiet suburb of Rome. It was a nice neighbourhood; it had a few local shops and their house was within walking distance of Uma's school – the main reason they had bought the 1970s townhouse. He looked both ways again – an occupational habit! It was clear. The rider thrust a handheld device at Nef and indicated for him to sign on the screen with his finger! Then he handed Nef an envelope. The rider walked back to his bike and put on his black crash helmet. He mounted it, twisted the throttle handle and made his 1649cc engine roar into life. With a quick check behind him, he pulled sharply out and roared down the street. The rider may well have been a little bit more careful had he known he had just delivered a letter to the Vatican's chief of police! Nef noted the bike's registration plate. He sent a text to his office and asked for them to run a check for ownership by any known criminals or stolen. The reply came back within thirty seconds: registered to a company called DNN, a Rome-based dispatch and delivery service. It was clean.

Back inside George had gone and his voice had been replaced by a news reader – his wife had turned the sound down lower for the news.

"Who was it?" Elena, Nef's wife, asked him.

Nef mumbled something back as he opened the envelope. His exclamation after reading the letter was much clearer. "Merda!" The rare times either Elena or Nef swore, it always naturally came out in Italian.

"What?" his wife called as she walked over to where he was.

"It's a letter."

"A letter needs a merda? Who is the letter from?"

"It doesn't say."

"Well, what does it say?" she asked, somewhat impatiently.

"Why the merda?"

He gave his wife the letter to read. It had been written by hand and in blue ink. The handwriting was neat, fluent, purposeful and elegant. It read:

Dear Mr Nef

Mr Eden will receive important information in a week's time, on the 15th at 3 p.m. I fear greed and temptation will again possess him.

The information he will receive is that an artefact that once belonged to Mr Longinus, will be moved from Vatican property in Barcelona to Vatican property in Venezuela. The move will take place on the 17th, nine days from now and two days after Mr Eden finds out it is being moved. He will know it is fact and not rumour because the information will be given to him directly by the Vatican.

If greed and temptation does possess him, he will have just two days to make arrangements to have it taken. Might I suggest you keep a watchful eye on him from around 3 p.m. on the 15th.

Perhaps you might consider calling upon your friends from abroad for help.

Charlie B

Nef and his wife both looked at the letter for a long time.

"Do you know a Charlie B?" she finally asked.

"No. But whoever sent it is either British, learnt their English from a native speaker or went to school with a British curriculum." Nef announced.

"How do you know that Sherlock?" his wife asked him teasingly.

"The words *rumour* and *artefact*. British English comes mostly from old French and German. American English is spelt the way it sounds, they would have written rumor and artifact if they were American or were educated in America, my dear Watson."

"Do you know who Mr Eden is?" she asked.

"Oh yes," he said, his smile was now fast becoming a grin. "Oh yes, I know who he is."

"Well, are you—"

"Got to go," he abruptly said. He kissed her, grabbed his car keys and jacket and left, calling as he closed the front door, "say goodbye to Uma for me, I will see you both tonight. Love you."

His journey into the office was as hectic and at times as dangerous as it always was. Today though, he was excited, keen, eager, although slightly irritated and impatient to get there. The Rome traffic had a cadence all of its own: chaos, but it worked. The three, four, and sometimes five lines of traffic on two and three-lane roads took some navigation but Nef knew that if anyone tried to drive normally it would probably cause an accident.

Nef's route was full of streets with antiquated aqueducts and viaducts, screeching brakes, sounding horns, tired engines and exasperated drivers; Kamikaze pedestrians darting across streets, walkers, joggers, and runners. Historical facades nestled between modern shop fronts and three and five-storey apartment buildings. As he got closer to the centre the labyrinth of streets increased. His vision was bombarded with traffic lights, brake lights, hazard warning lights, some drivers even, occasionally, used their indicators! Weaving motorbikes and scooters with scantily clad girls and macho boys resting their helmets just on top of their heads, headed for the university, shopping malls or cafes on street corners. His green Peugeot growled as he adeptly manoeuvred around one waiting accident to another, abiding by the no right turn, no left turn, no U-turn, no everything!

The thirty-five-minute drive took him fifteen minutes less this morning! His green Peugeot had made it through the Rome rush hour traffic once again: unscathed. En route Nef had made three calls, now he knew how the Mr Longinus artefact was going to be moved and from where to where. He had calls to make!

*

Place: Police headquarters, Vatican City
Time: Later that morning

Nef had a lot to do this morning. He asked his secretary for coffee and told her to hold all his calls. He told her he would deal with his emails later but asked her to flag any urgent ones. She then brought him coffee and a plain biscuit – as always. Nef finished the biscuit and then wiped away the crumbs off his desk. Dámaso Nef disliked untidiness. Despite his desk being awash with papers and files, they were all stacked in neat piles, they always were.

The office, with its two large metal windows and pale cream walls that had been recently painted, never represented anything else to him other than a place full of pending case files and endless paperwork. For weeks he'd cracked the windows open to ease the pungent smell of the paint, but it just wouldn't go away.

He closed the door of his office. Whilst he trusted his staff, he did not trust all of the cardinals. He knew that should any of their acolytes be about, they would certainly report back to whichever cardinal held their loyalty – the Vatican was an ecclesiastical dog-eat-dog place to work.

He knew for his nascent plan to work he would need to convince Cardinal Paradiso to meet him at or just before 3 p.m. on the 15th. He also needed to ensure that the cardinal received the news himself. It was well known that all calls to the cardinal's home were taken firstly by his housekeeper, as he believed he was far too important to answer the telephone himself. So, for Nef's plan to work he also needed to get the housekeeper out of the way on the 15th , normally she would take a message of any call received and at some point later, the cardinal would return the call. Nef could not take that risk; he needed the cardinal to get the information straight away and then to make a call the moment he heard the information he was given! He didn't know who the call would be to, but he was sure that a call would be made. So, he needed to ensure he was in the room when the cardinal got the news, and out of the room when the cardinal made his call. However, for his plan to work he needed to know to whom the call was made and more importantly what their plan would be to steal the item that used to belong to Mr Longinus. To have any chance of achieving all of this, he would need the help of a covert organisation that had assisted him before. They would be his ace in the hole. If they agreed to help him, it would be the sixth time they had freely rendered their help to the Vatican. Nef knew them to be a group of extremely high-principled professionals with FBI, Interpol, and Omega 1 and Omega 1S clearance with MI5 and MI6 security clearance. In the beginning, he had been told that the group normally only got involved in crimes against religion and its people, and that meant against any of the mainstream religions. They were unprejudiced when it came to their help. Whilst there were no formal or structured lines of communication between them, Dámaso Nef and Payne St Clair, the Templars' Grand Master, had always kept the back channels open. He would not use any of his own officers for this assignment. Time was tight, perhaps too tight he thought but he knew from the posted schedules he had received at the start of the month, that the cardinal would be on vacation on the 15th at his home in the country.

He braced himself, he did not like the cardinal, he had cutting sarcasm in abundance but Nef needed to make the call. He lifted the receiver of his black, dated, desk phone. True to form one of the cardinal's acolytes answered. He was cordial enough to the chief of police but Nef was still kept waiting for four minutes. He knew this was deliberate, the cardinal always kept him waiting, as he did with almost everyone. This was his way of showing he was in the top echelon within the hierarchy of the Vatican.

"Nef." His voice was gruff and laced with irritability.

"Cardinal Paradiso, how are you?" The cardinal did not respond – no pleasantries. "I will be brief; I know you're a busy man."

The cardinal made a scornful grunt.

"I have a complaint on my desk that may, but I only say may involve one of your staff. I do not wish to discuss the matter over the phone, and I know you are very busy but I see on the intranet that you have a vacation booked. I wouldn't normally bother you on your holiday, but I thought you might want to be kept informed about this and even render your advice."

Nef knew that the vanity of the cardinal would make sure he did not want any bad rumours about his staff and the request for advice would mean he could control it and then squash it. "I'm afraid I only have the fifteenth because of internal audits but I can come out to you in the country on that afternoon, say 2:30 p.m.?"

Normally, the cardinal would not agree to anyone's times and dates, it was always at his convenience but a possible shadow hanging over his department and his team ensured his hubris went down slightly.

The cardinal grunted again scornfully, "don't be late." Then hung up.

For Nef's second call he would not use a landline. There was no proof, but he knew the likelihood was that someone would be listening in. Someone's eyes and ears were always watching, listening, snooping and spying. The cardinal's priests were loyal to a fault.

He searched for the number on his mobile's speed dial list; it was listed under J Bond, only he would see and get the irony. He pressed the green call button. He waited. He knew the drill. He would first speak to a female he'd never met. He knew the call would be recorded and that it would be traced – they would place him in the Police headquarters of Vatican City. He knew the woman answering his call would be exceptionally pleasant and engaging. She would hold a brief conversation with him but all the time she would be busy confirming his location. He didn't know where she was located or that only a few months before she had been appointed to the Higher Council of the Knights Templar. All Nef knew was that she was British, and even suspected Welsh, because of her slight accent, so assumed that she was somewhere in Great Britain. He could have traced the call himself but suspected they would be using a cloaking device, and he didn't want to waste time. His past experiences of them were that they were far more technologically advanced than his own force and far more tactical and covert than any other organisation he had come into contact with.

He heard the ringtone. The last time he reached out to them he had been given permission in the form of formal confirmation in an email from the prefect that he could contact the outsiders. Cardinal Paradiso was cc'd into that email, along with several others from numerous departments within the curia, the administrative institutions of the Holy See and the body that all affairs of the Catholic Church are dealt with. There were representatives in that email from the secretariats, congregations, pontifical councils, pontifical commissions, tribunals and many more. This time, he didn't seek permission. This time it was his trap to set, and he didn't want to risk anyone leaking it. This time he was on his own – or so he thought.

His thoughts were racing. It rang three times. He didn't know but the call automatically routed to a secret address in Islington, United Kingdom. Nef had never heard of Islington. The computer in the electronically protected shell (EPS) in Islington, checked the number's authenticity. The Controller focused on the computer screen with scrutiny. As 'Controller' her job was to ensure that no one from outside the organisation was hacking into the system. She checked the meter on the cloaking software. It was normal. The software would then direct the call to a private number in Scotland. The conversation would take place via the computer. The computer would cloak and scramble the conversation. If the EPS room's security was breached, the scrambler would protect the identity of the Templars and the contents of their part of the telephone conversation if they were talking to an outside person.

Nef was excited, he had just got his first lead for the case file that read *Sancti Furem*– Holy Thief, that morning. He had always suspected the cardinal, now he would set out to prove it. It was the 8th, in seven days' time, on the 15th, he needed to be sitting in Cardinal Paradiso's home in the Italian countryside. Two days later, on the 17th, he hoped he would have enough evidence to arrest and charge the cardinal that he despised so much. Thanks to an unknown letter from someone called 'Charlie B', he knew that an artefact that had once belonged to Mr Longinus would be moved from Barcelona, where the artefact had been kept for the past three years. On his way into the office, he had made a series of calls and now knew that the artefact was being moved to Venezuela on the 17th as part of the Vatican's rotation policy of valuable artefacts.

When Nef had last spoken with Luther, the second of the newly appointed Worthies on the Higher Council of the Knights Templar, Luther had told him that St Clair had sent him a message from Spain, where he was leading an operation to capture Salah El-Din. He asked Luther to pass on the message to Nef, he said that they would help the policeman find his *Sancti Furem,* his Holy Thief. Now it was time for Nef to speak to Payne St Clair.

Place: Glennfinch castle, Scotland

The Templar castle, fully restored and renovated, had never been breached. It was surrounded by thirty old, tied cottages. The cottages were run, operated and manned as fully equipped garrison posts. Heavily armed, fitted with infrared cameras, sound sensors, perimeter sensors, night scopes, and a range of small arms. The garrison posts were the Templars' final ring of steel protecting the castle and their holy 'Charge', which lay hidden. It was protected and secure below the castle, as it had once been below Solomon's Temple in Jerusalem. Two Templars lived and worked in each of the cottages. Every three months there was a rotation of each of the garrisons. Jonathan and Dominique Rose did not rotate, they lived in one of the cottages, which was called *Gleann Ceó* - Glen Mist. Ever since the episode with Salah El-Din's men on the beach, they had moved onto the castle estate where Jonathan, the Seer, could be protected by the might of the Order.

Their operational centres around the world, the Satellite Stations, like the cottages, were all connected to the Castle's control room. Their on-the-ground eyes and ears, small bands of men and women, hidden in plain sight, running electronic surveillance and data capture operations. When there was a mission in their area, they would act as the command and relief station. They enjoyed the digital wizardry that the ex-FBI desk operative, Courtney Rose, brought to the Order and that of an Oxford graduate who had a first in Computer Science, specialising in Nanotechnology, Artificial Intelligence, Blockchain, Advanced Electronics and Gaming. His name was Bertram De'Ath. He was a genius – albeit eccentric. He was born Bertram Hubert De'Ath, in Calcutta, India, in 1987. Bertram had a distinctive look: white teeth, deep black skin, curly unkempt hair and acne. He looked twelve but he was twenty-five years old. His father had been a

Templar and so had his grandfather. After his friend the Russian, Nickolin Klymachak, died during a firefight in Romania when the extraction team went in to save André Sabath from the Abaddon leader, Zivko Gowst, Bertram changed his name to Bertram Hubert Klymachak De'Ath.

*

St Clair had taken the call from Nef straight away. Nef explained the Charlie B letter and his plan to trap the *Sancti Furem,* the Holy Thief. St Clair told him he would call him back in thirty minutes. Exactly thirty minutes later, Nef's mobile phone rang, it was the controller in Islington, she then connected the call through to the castle in Scotland.

The castle had several meeting rooms, accommodating three to five people, others ten to fifteen. All were furnished with comfortable and efficient conference furniture made up of long teak or walnut tables and black high-back comfortable swivel chairs with castors. Some had plain white walls, others oak panelling on the walls – nothing too fussy and all done with functionality at its core.

The three Templars were gathered in room 3. A plasma screen was on – waiting for another to join them. The screen, like the rest of their coms, was protected by the new firewalls and scrambling technology that Courtney, Bertram and their team had installed. The castle windows were stained glass, casting a thousand vibrant colours into the castle but they had a high-density reflective coating to block any electronic spy software. On the roof, three heavy-duty jamming masts cast an invisible arc around the castle.

Whilst the Nine Worthies, the Higher Council of the Knights Templar, always held their meetings by candlelight, as tradition was important to the Templars, at all other meetings they used electric lighting. No one sat at the head of the table; chairs were not placed at the head of any conference table in the castle; they were always placed along the sides. The only time someone sat at the head of a table was in the great hall when the Higher Council met, then the Templar Grand Master, Payne St Clair, would sit at the head of the table. The other times were when they were gathered in the banqueting hall for formal ceremonies, introducing new Knights knighted, promotions or retirements.

The meeting room's phone buzzed. St Clair hit the receive button; he knew who it was. "*Ciao amico mio come stai* – hello my friend, how are you?" St Clair asked him.

"*Tutto bene* – everything is fine," Nef said.

"Dámaso, I have the Priest, Jonathan and Luther with me and Aldrich will be joining us by conference call, all of whom you have already met on the *Gwrach Marwolaeth* Hag sanction." Luther and Jonathan both said hello to Nef. "Dámaso, will you read out the letter you read out to me so that the Priest and Luther can hear it?"

Nef relayed what happened that morning with the letter. Then he read it out loud to them.

"Dear Mr Nef

Mr Eden will receive important information in a week's time, on the 15th at 3 p.m. I fear greed and temptation will again possess him.

The information he will receive is that an artefact that once belonged to Mr Longinus, will be moved from Vatican property in Barcelona to Vatican property in Venezuela. The move will take place on the 17th, nine days from now and two days after Mr Eden finds out it is being moved. He will know it is fact and not rumour because the information will be given to him directly by the Vatican.

If greed and temptation does possess him, he will have just two days to make arrangements to have it taken. Might I suggest you keep a watchful eye on him from around 3 p.m. on the 15th.

Perhaps you might consider calling upon your friends from abroad for help.

Charlie B"

"So, now we know for sure who the *Sancti Furem* – the Holy Thief, is. It is your friend, Cardinal Paradiso, Paradiso is Eden in English: the Mr Eden! Whoever wrote the letter, knows he's the thief within the Vatican."

"Ah, Aldrich, did you hear?" St Clair called.

"I did," Aldrich replied.

"Dámaso, I asked Aldrich to join us because of the Mr Longinus ref. He is on a conference line from another part of the world."

"Nef, my old fruit," Aldrich barked excitedly, nearly deafening everybody on the call.

Nef was taken aback. "Old fruit? What does it mean, old fruit? Like rotten apples or bad grapes old fruit?"

"He means it as a—" St Clair started to explain.

Aldrich roared with laughter at Nef. "No, no, no old fruit. It means we are friends. Besides, old fruit, I took a sword from right under the noses of the Vatican and you didn't grass me up."

"Grass?"

Aldrich let out another great, hearty laugh. "You Italians, you do make me laugh. Now, less of this chatter old fruit." Then he started. "On the twenty seventh of November 1095, the Pope, Pope Urban the second, chaired the Council of Clermont's clerical delegates in an open field. He told them about the dire situation across Europe and in the Holy Land. He asked the people to take up arms and launch the very first crusade to liberate Christians and holy places. The words of the fourth century Bishop of Augustine of Hippo rang in his ears: '... with a worthy and honourable purpose and with peace as the aim, violence could be justified'. Those that joined and took their solemn oaths, then sewed red crosses on their left shoulders of their surcoats showing their commitment and their entitlement to the new privileges the Pope promised them. The phrase 'taking the cross' was born and the word crusade came about from the Latin *crux* - cross.

"The Pope's crusade was not ready to go. However, there was another crusade that had started at the same time called the Peoples' Crusade. There was a man called Peter the Hermit. He was a zealous monk who went around passionately preaching that the common folk needed to take arms against the anti-Christians. He amassed an army of over fifteen thousand, men, women and children from Germany and France. Peter's followers set off for the Holy Land ahead of the Pope's organised army. However, some of the tailenders started their own little war and slaughtered nearly ten thousand Jews along the way, calling them Christ's murderers.

"The emperor Alexius was so horrified, he made sure the Peoples' Crusade had quick passage across the Bosphorus and into Asia Minor. But, waiting there for them was the powerful Seljuk Turks. Starving and depleted the Peoples' Crusade came to a bloody stop!"

Finally, St Clair was able to get a word in. "We asked Aldrich to join us because, as you can see Nef, he has expert knowledge of the First Crusade."

"But I ... I'm confused."

"He's getting there," St Clair said. He turned to Aldrich. "Can we skip some of the boring bits?"

"Bugger me, Brigadier. Boring bits! Boring bits, why, this is one of the—"

"Aldrich!" there was some pleading in St Clair's voice.

"Fine. So, the Peoples' Crusade was dead in the water. The second, first crusade, or the real first crusade, was on its way to the Holy Land via several countries, and not all of them friendly. They too reached Emperor Alexius's domain and again he was horrified by what he saw. Other than the knights, who made up just one-third of the crusaders, the rest were made up of mostly rabble and ruffians. They set up camp outside his city walls during the winter of 1096 and 1097. Then they started looting around Constantinople.

"So, now we near the zenith of our story, as I like to say, on this subject, we are getting to the pointy thing! Eventually, the crusaders made it to Nicaea, that's Iznik today, in northern Turkey. But, like the ill-fated Peoples' Crusade, the Seljuk Turks were again there, standing in their way. In fact, the Seljuk Turks had already captured the city of Nicaea in 1071.

"But the Christian army laid siege and five weeks later the city had been taken. They now had the wind-in-their-sails. Several battles later, that wind took them to the city of Antioch, now called Antakya in southern Turkey. It was famous because it had never fallen to a siege, only by treachery.

"The crusaders arrived at Antioch on October the 20th, 1097. Unable to enter the city walls they surrounded it and stopped any supplies from getting in. By the start of 1098, the Christian army's own supplies were falling perilously low, they were starting to starve to death. Through bravery and skill, they eventually managed to break through the city walls and get into the city. Only problem they had now was that once they were inside, they had become cut off from leaving because an army of seventy-five thousand Seljuk Turks arrived from what is now Iraq and blocked their route out again."

"And there was no one around to save the crusaders?" asked Jonathan.

"Splendid question, Corpse. The Byzantine army was on their way to help the crusaders but reports got through to them that said the crusaders had all starved to death. So, they just turned around and went back to Constantinople."

"Leaving the crusaders trapped inside the city?"

"Indeed, Corpse."

"So, what did they do?"

"Well, enter stage left our man and the pointy thing."

"Enter stage left? And the pointy thing?" Nef asked. "*Non capisco* – I don't understand."

"He means now comes the artefact you are interested in. Aldrich is a professor at one of Britain's finest universities, he lectures in medieval studies, in the Department of Supernatural, Occultism and History of Satanic Medieval Renaissance." St Clair said.

"Can we get back to the pointy thing?" Jonathan urged.

"Yes, Corpse, my dear fellow, of course. Ready? The pointy thing I am referring to is the lance of Longinus. The note from someone calling themself Charlie B, called it an artefact that was once owned by Mr Longinus."

"Ah," said Jonathan, now realising the reference, "of course. Longinus was the name of the Roman soldier who pierced Jesus' side whilst he was dying on the cross. In the New Testament, it says that his body was pierced by the Lance of Longinus to make sure he was dead. As it says in the Gospel of John 19:34, *but one of the soldiers with a spear pierced his side, and forthwith came there out blood and water.*"

"Precisely Corpse. And in Mark 15:39, when the soldier

proclaimed, *Truly, this man was the Son of God,* but which *one* are we talking about? Was it Constantine's mother, Empress Helena, that found it. She decided she would take it upon herself to locate all religious sites in Jerusalem, and so, she went, along with an army of servants to find them. Christ's tomb was found beneath Jupiter's temple, the site of the crucifixion a short distance away. Helena herself discovered wood from the True Cross, nails and even the Longinus lance. She even reported that she had found the spot where Jesus ascended to heaven. What is most miraculous is that she did all of this three hundred years after the events took place! And two hundred and fifty years after the Romans had destroyed the city!

"So, it's all a bit messy and there are numerous spearheads that carry one of the names given to the lance that pierced Jesus' side: the spear of destiny, the lance or spear of the Roman Longinus, the Holy Lance, they are all the same thing and yet, they are not. There is the *one* and then, there are the ones that have been wrongly thought of as the *one*. Many have claimed to have owned the true *one*, Herod the Great, Constantine the Great, Charlemagne and Alaric the Visigoth, the man that sacked Rome and started the fall of the Roman, Empire.

"You can actually find a proclaimed Longinus spear in a number of different countries, in their museums. The one in the Kunsthistorisches Museum, in Vienna, Austria, is bound by silver. It is said to hold a nail from the True Cross and has a gold sheathing with the inscription: *lancea et clavus Domini* - the spear and nail of our Lord." Aldrich continued.

"But the real Longinus relic is in Rome, in one of the four pillars over the altar in the Basilica of St Peter." Nef said.

"Well, it would seem the Vatican has been rather sneaky about the whereabouts of the spearhead because now we know it has been in Spain of late." Aldrich let out a laugh.

St Clair could have told them that that was wrong, the Vatican didn't have it and the real spearhead wasn't in Spain either. He wanted to help Nef catch the Holy Thief and the best way he thought he could do that was to let people believe they were dealing with the real spearhead, for now, anyway. However, Jonathan noticed St Clair's look and it caused him to wonder what St Clair might be withholding.

"But I must finish my story." Aldrich took a deep breath. "So, the crusaders on the first crusade were all but done," Aldrich continued, getting them back to the Crusades. "Trapped and dying with no hope. Their fate seemed to be ending like the Peoples' crusade. But on the 10th of June 1098, a man called Peter Bartholomew, a peasant accompanying the crusaders, requested a meeting with the Pope's Bishop, Adhemar, who had been appointed as the Pope's representative and spiritual leader on the crusade.

"Peter Bartholomew told Adhemar that he had had recurring visions that the spear that had pierced the side of Christ was buried beneath the altar in St Peter's Cathedral in Antioch, their prison. He told them Christ and St Andrew had come to him.

"Then, the very next day, a monk called Stephen of Valance, said that he had been visited by Christ and the Virgin Mary and they had promised to help the crusaders. The next day a meteor was seen falling into the army that had them trapped and slowly dying. Bishop Adhemar told them to start digging for the spear.

"After much digging, Peter jumped into the pit and unearthed the relic. Not everyone was convinced; even the bishop was highly sceptical; but whatever it was, news of the find spread and the crusaders chanted that God was on their side. It rallied them. It filled them with renewed energy and purpose. When Peter told them he'd had another vision, they all listened. He said that St Andrew had come to him and told him that they should fast and then they would be victorious – by now there was nothing to eat anyway!

"Then on the 28th of June, the crusaders mounted their horses, the head of the lance was carried at the front of the charge by Raymond D'Aguilers. Although the Turks were larger in number, more rested and more fed the crusaders won the day."

"So, Mr Eden will steal the artefact," Nef announced.

"He will indeed," St Clair told him.

"I need to stop him. I need to put him in jail, somehow."

St Clair looked at his Knights, then he looked to Luther.

Luther smiled, *"ubi positus est, ut omnis* - where one stands, so stand us all".

49

"Dámaso, we are with you," St Clair said.

"Bugger me, Brigadier, we're off again, hooray," roared Aldrich, with his very indefectible, untrammelled and complex personality of mayhem, enthusiasm, and ruckus eccentricity. "Let's call it the Longinus Missions."

*

By the time Nef had finished the call with St Clair and the others, it was already mid-day and his day's work was still to be started. He was way behind; emails and phone messages were stacking up that needed his attention and he knew it was going to be a long day. He asked his secretary for more coffee, strong coffee, then he called his wife, Elena. He told her he would be late and that she should not hold dinner for him, he would get some food on the way home. His wife was used to this type of call and took it all in her stride.

"Then I will see you when I see you. Don't work too hard, Darling," she told him.

"Thank you, I will see you later, old fruit," Nef said; then hung up.

Elena was left holding the phone in the hallway and staring into the receiver trying to work out if he had said what she thought he had just said. *Old grape?* She thought. *Did he just call me an old grape? No, he wouldn't, would he?*

Chapter 5

Sancti Furem – Holy Thief

Date: The 15th – the day of the call
Place: Anzio, Italy

Both Nef and the Templars knew there was a long list of buyers waiting to buy the un-gettable, those historical artefacts and relics they were not meant to have. But nearly all were hidden away, secured like a fortress. The Vatican library held over a million books and was one of the world's oldest libraries. It was where scholars worked – with limited access, so as to limit any one person's ability to steal the priceless. It held a collection of ancient books, parchments, scrolls, essays and treaties, kept safe in secure underground rooms, including the Vatican Secret Archive, the central repository containing official papal paperwork from the Holy See over the centuries. More was hidden away in even more secret vaults, deep underground, with engineered atmospheres, impenetrable walls, ceilings and floors, sealed doors, combination locks, alarms, cameras and sensors, all guarded day and night by well-trained armed guards. The vaults contained some of the Church's most secret assets: religious, historical, intellectual, most related to art, science, mathematics and philosophy. But every time anything was moved from its safe place, it would offer an opportunity for the unscrupulous. It offered an opportunity for the *Sancti Furem.*

Nef was pleased he'd taken the decision not to go into the office. He'd decide to work from home until it was time for him to leave and drive for his meeting with Cardinal Paradiso. He hadn't been able to do much work that morning though; he was too excited, on edge, trepidatious: he was worried. He knew this could be his chance, probably his only chance to catch the cardinal. If he tried and subsequently failed, the cardinal would be alerted and he would go to ground. He would stop his activities and blend back into the amorphous, ecclesiastical multitude that is the Vatican – hidden in plain sight! And there wouldn't be a thing Nef could do about it. He knew it could take years for the cardinal to commit another crime – if he ever did.

He'd spent eight days trying to piece together evidence that would allow him to indict and then convict the cardinal but he knew what he had, was pointless. The evidence was scant at best, it was wholly circumstantial and ninety-nine per cent hearsay. His case file report was only one and a half pages long. The *Sancti Furem* – Holy Thief, was smart, elusive and so far, had left no trail. However, all of Nef's instincts had pointed him to Cardinal Paradiso. The letter from someone calling himself, or herself Charlie B had confirmed his suspicions but he was not comfortable that he now also had a mystery informer – more hearsay. Nef's best guess was that it was another cardinal or another senior member of the clergy who would not reveal themself for fear of retribution – the cardinal was a powerful man. So, all his hopes now rested on an organisation he knew practically nothing about. All he knew was that Pi was a code name the British Secret Service, MI6, had given them and that they had Omega 1 and Omega 1S clearance by all branches of the British Secret Services. All they had to do now was help him catch one of the most powerful men in the Catholic Church, red-handed, and with irrefutable evidence that the cardinal's expensive lawyers, whom he would undoubtedly engage, could not discredit. The cardinal had wormed his way out of a number of controversies over the years, so, there was no reason to believe he wouldn't do that again unless there was cast-iron proof. Nef knew that Charlie B had been right when he or she wrote that once the cardinal knew the decision had been made to move the artefact, it would prove too much of a temptation for him. Nef didn't know how Paradiso would plan to have it stolen, but he hoped he would soon find out.

Nef accelerated; the villa he was heading for was the country residence of Cardinal Paradiso – he didn't want to be late. He'd taken the SS148 when leaving Rome, then onto the SR207. Now his green Peugeot sped along more rural country roads as he headed towards the villa on the outskirts of Anzio. The scenery went from the autostrada, with nothing but vast stretches of flat countryside on either side of it, to rural roads. The tree-lined, winding roads wove their way through a patchwork of green hills and downs scantily peppered each side with mostly whitewashed, light brown and beige houses and villas, with humpbacked red tiles, shuttered windows – mostly green – wood stained and light blue wooden frames and doorways. Worn flagstones and sun-kissed courtyards. Slow-moving shadows stretched ever longer as the day wore on. Punctuating the vista, old villages with arches and arcs; belltowers ringing out; vines and olive trees, citrus and cherry trees. Old maids dressed in black, sitting on wicker chairs in the shade of their doorways, crocheting and watching the villagers stroll unhurriedly through their day.

The villa he was heading for was the country residence of Cardinal Paradiso. The plan needed to ensure that he would be in the room with Cardinal Paradiso, when the call came in at 3 p.m. and allow him to be out of the room directly after that so that the cardinal would make his call to whomever it was that he had used to steal the venerated artefacts over the years – from which he had become very rich. For Nef's plan to work, they would need to know whom the cardinal called and more importantly, how they planned to steal the item that once belonged to Longinus.

Their plan was that members of Pi would take the place of the Vatican curators, who normally would deliver artefacts to the appointed Vatican couriers. They suspected that the criminals would make their move at this handover point because it was the weakest link in artefacts transportation. However, they didn't know where the exchange would take place other than:

Mr Eden will receive important information in a week's time, on the 15th at 3 p.m. I fear greed and temptation will again possess him.

The information he will receive is that an artefact that once belonged to Mr Longinus, will be moved from Vatican property in Barcelona to Vatican property in Venezuela. The move will take place on the 17th... two days after Mr Eden finds out it is being moved.

The mysterious Charlie B had not given any information about where the handover would take place. Charlie B worried them. The fact that they didn't know who he or she was, how he or she knew about the arrangements but not the location, nothing quite added up but it was all they had. Nef had tried to find out who the note had come from by having it analysed. He believed it was another cardinal, or a trusted priest working for a cardinal because that kind of information was highly sensitive, for obvious reasons the circle of 'need to know' is extremely small. Nef had two of his most trusted officers working with forensics. All they had come back with was that they thought that the author had not used their normal writing hand. They thought it had been written by a person using their less dominant hand. Whilst it was a well-written letter, and the person was obviously capable of writing with both hands, he or she was right-handed and had written the letter with their left hand. They knew this because there were obvious weaknesses in the structure and form of certain letters, mainly the e's, p's and u's. They suggested it was not written by the writer's dominant writing hand and because of the way some of the longer letters slopped, it suggested the writer was right-handed. He was told by forensics that as only ten per cent of the population are left-handed, the writer was in all probability part of the remaining ninety per cent and in Italy alone, that was some fifty-four million people. That was it, that's all they had. St Clair, Luther and Nef, decided they could not wait to find out who Charlie B was, they needed to move ahead with their plan, or they would have to alert the Vatican that the Longinus spear was at risk. However, if they did that then they might not get the opportunity to trap and catch the *Sancti Furem*.

Nef's satnav announced that he needed to take the next right turn onto the ring road. He checked the satnav screen; he was fifteen minutes away. Notwithstanding any last-minute hiccups, he would make it in time and even be a courteous five minutes early. He nudged the indicator down and took the slip road onto the Anzio ring road. His eye caught the small, brown padded envelope, marked 'fragile' and stamped with a Rome mail stamp, that lay on the passenger seat: his heart started pounding. He reached across and fumbled inside for its contents. He placed the tiny earpiece receiver in his pocket. *Another part of the plan that could go disastrously wrong*, he thought as he was running through possible scenarios in his head.

*

Place: A small grassy outcrop of wildflowers, eight hundred yards from the Paradiso villa

The mission leader, Luther Jones, watched Nef's green Peugeot pull off the road and take the long shingle drive up to the cardinal's villa. He relayed events as they unfolded to the team in-situ there and the Templars, back in the control room in Scotland, could see it live through the Templars' bodycams.

Luther, an ex-SAS operative, had been a Templar 'active' Knight for many years and one of the Order's most experienced fighters. He'd saved the lives of many Knights, including the life of St Clair's niece and Zakariah's daughter, Dominique. He was now a member of the Higher Council of the Order of the Knights Templar, but he was still an 'active' Knight and as far as he was concerned, he would remain so for as long as he could.

Just a few feet away from Luther lay John Wolf, known as the Indian. He was a true-blooded Shawnee Indian from Kentucky and one of the Templars' most combat-experienced Knights. He lay still with his favourite weapon of choice, a fourteen-inch bone-handled knife holstered in its sheath by his side. He was also packing a six-round Beretta M9 semi-automatic handgun, and a specially modified .357 Magnum handgun which St Clair had given him some years ago. Wolf was tall and lean, with solid broad shoulders, and shoulder-length jet-black hair parted in the centre. He lay still and vigilant. Wolf was a hunter; his skills were legendary.

The Templars were heavily armed not so much because of this mission, but because of the recent emergence of *Le Fantome Blanc* – the White Ghost, Zivko Cesar Gowst. The Templars were on red alert. He was their greatest threat and that meant the greatest threat to their 'Charge', which lay hidden deep underground, beneath the castle in Scotland.

Both Knights lay hugging the outline of a small grassy outcrop of wildflowers in the vast Italian countryside, some eight hundred yards away from the target villa. They had been there since the day before; arriving around lunchtime on foot, having left their rental car a few miles back, tucked away into a small coppice where it could not be seen from the road that circumvented the sage, maritime pines and junipers. Their current position was close enough for their binoculars but only just because at eight hundred yards out, they were at the maximum range to have clarity in their line of sight. Their position was recce and eyes in stage one of the mission. They were the first lookout and RV (rendezvous point) should anything go wrong in the early stages.

Parallel to their position, and some one thousand yards from the villa, two more Templars lay hidden in the undergrowth. The Lionheart held a semi-automatic weapon. However, he wore the same style coat as all the other Knights because it hid their weapons well, especially their favoured weapon, the Katana sword of the Samurai, which they concealed in a back-body webbing that held a lightweight titanium *saya* – scabbard, with only an inch peeking out of the top of their long, black coats.

Ten yards to his right, Marie-Claude lay in a prone position, her MK13 bolt-action sniper rifle, which used larger calibre rounds that were needed because of the distance they were from the possible target, was trained on the villa, safety off.

*

Place: The home of Cardinal Paradiso, the Anzio countryside, Italy
Time: 2:25 p.m. – five minutes early

Nef eased himself out of the car. He knew he was being watched. Some outbuildings off to the right had activity. Two men watched him. He saw they were armed. Whilst he was expecting it, it still shook him. He fingered the tiny earpiece in his pocket: it gave him comfort. He knew the people from Pi would be watching. They were close by. He had been told where to head to if it all went wrong. Other than that, he didn't know where they were or how many of them were out there, but right at that moment, he was mighty thankful they were.

His footsteps crunched on the gravel drive. The two heavily armed men drew closer, they tracked his every step. He figured they'd been told not to accost him, not to search him – although it would have been futile because he was unarmed, a decision he, Luther and St Clair had taken early in the planning. He would not be searched because the cardinal would not want to give the chief of police any reason to look at his affairs any closer than what was required by Vatican policy and protocols.

Nef pulled the handle of a hanging wrought iron linked chain and somewhere off inside the villa, a bell rang. He waited. And he waited. *Farcical*, he thought. *They knew I was coming and at what time, and they would have seen my approach for some time along the long driveway.* He knew the cardinal was making a point. Nef was making his own point – he only rang once; now he just waited. It was a battle of wills. He was left standing for nearly six minutes.

A young priest answered the door. He looked tired and harassed; Nef had noted that all Paradiso's staff tended to look tired and harassed. The young priest introduced himself as Father John from Nairobi and beckoned Nef into the house. Inside a melodic Mozart concerto idled around the villa's corridors but Nef didn't recognise it, not that he would anyway, not his thing. He wiped his feet. He was standing in a large hall, plainly decorated but with vaulted ceilings – it was impressive. The place was thick with the smell of Lily of the Valley and stale cigarette smoke. The same dense musk and nicotine smell as the cardinal's office and his Vatican quarters – Nef hated it, it made him feel sick, always did. There was a reception room off to the right and Nef headed towards it. The young priest, Father John lightly coughed; it was a nervous cough. "His Eminence has asked if you would wait for him here." He pointed to an uncomfortable-looking chair in the hall.

Of course, Nef thought to himself. *Of course, I have to sit out in the hallway like a naughty schoolboy waiting outside the headmaster's office.* Nef was agitated but he didn't show it. "*Graze*, Father," he said courteously and sat down.

The young priest smiled and then left, hurriedly.

This time he was made to wait a full ten minutes before he heard the barking voice of the cardinal issuing out orders to his bullied, frightened and browbeaten assistants and aides. The household staff appeared to be in a constant state of alert. The cardinal entered the hallway with the same sense of importance he always entered anywhere. The craggy-faced man with silver hair and a stern look about him smoked like a trooper. Nef stood. The cardinal didn't bother to greet the chief of the Vatican police. He grunted and pointed to the reception room. Then he gave an imperious wave of the hand and the two priests who had been following at his heels, left. To Nef, they looked like people who knew they had made a mistake. The mistake being by going to work for their Machiavellian master. *That look is the price of blind servitude or ambitious progression*, thought Nef.

The cardinal brusquely imperious, arrogant and domineering, lit another cigarette and walked with pace into the reception room tutting as he went.

Well, the first part of our plan went to plan, Nef thought, breathing a silent sigh of relief as he followed the cardinal into the room. *I'm here and I have his attention; hopefully, he will be off guard. Now for poor Father Alfonso.* He checked his watch; it was 2:46 p.m. fourteen minutes to go.

When Cardinal Paradiso was not in the Vatican and being chauffer driven about, he drove his one-million-pound Porsche 911, 2.7 RS, 1973. It was a sign that he had money, but having money was not a crime, not for the rest of the population and neither for cardinals. However, like the rest of the population, it all depended on how you obtained your money. Thus far, however, Nef had failed to prove that the cardinal became wealthy through ill-gotten means. Secretly, Cardinal Cristoforo John Paradiso, regularly communicated with a criminal called Mackintosh, mainly about dodgy Bell and Ross watches, and shares in Tottenham Hotspur and Milan football clubs. His poor housekeeper in Anzio, Mara Di Venanzio, had suffered his bellicose nature for years. He drank heavily, watched his favourite film, 'Where Eagles Dare,' endlessly and had a cellar full of long overdue, unreturned videos from Blockbuster, dating back to 1995. Originally, his links to the criminal fraternity had been through an ex-lover, who was also an ex-priest and had spent a long time in prison. The arrangements he had with a man called Michael, nee Father Michael, meant that the cardinal's bank balance grew to nearly five million Euros – in his private bank account for supplying secret information. Paradiso had supplied information about Solomon's ring – which nearly ended his Pope's life, information about the whereabouts of Saint John's skull and he had told Michael about the whereabouts of the last *Gwrach Marwolaeth* Hag, the last witch of death. The Vatican had secret files on such people, and he had access to such files. He was paid well.

The cardinal's job gave him direct access to the Pope. This gave him power. As Nef had told the people at Pi, he holds an important job in the Vatican's secretariat of state, a department of the curia, the administration of the Holy See. Through this his Holiness the Pope directs the Roman Catholic Church. The cardinal has many friends, mostly within the Congregation for the Doctrine of the Faith – *Congregtio pro Doctrina Fidei*. It's the oldest of the nine congregations seated in the palace of the Holy Office here in Rome. The main sponsor for his appointment to cardinal is the congressional leader, the prefect of the *Congregtio pro Doctrina Fidei*. He was well protected.

The cardinal also had access to funds and to the president of the Pontifical Commissions. The Pope is the ex-officio sovereign of Vatican City but he in turn delegates executive authority to the president, who is the ex-officio president of the governate and head of the government of the Vatican.

The Vatican moves certain artefacts, venerated religious pieces, from time to time to different places and different countries. They do this for security reasons but also to make sure they are available to be seen by its flock in as many countries as possible. They would often keep certain items in the last place someone would expect to find them because they are often safer there than somewhere where everyone would expect to find them, especially the criminals. Nef had told them that Paradiso was also on several select committees including the committee that was advised when an artefact was going to be moved: when, how and to where. The people at Pi now hoped they would also get this information.

The cardinal was smoking yet another cigarette. He huffed and growled out his words. Each word left his mouth engulfed in a haze of grey and blue cigarette smoke. He poured himself a drink from a cut glass decanter. He didn't pour Nef one, nor did he offer. He then pointed to a verdant green velvet-covered chair next to a pile of books – the room was full of books. Nef sat down.

"I don't have long," he barked curtly. The cardinal didn't sit, as if to emphasise the point that he didn't have long and that he was a very busy and important man. His irascible, capricious nature, always on full show.

Nef took out a brown envelope from the inside pocket of his jacket. He did it slowly because he wanted the whole charade to look more official than it really was. He took his time to open the envelope, then slowly took out two pieces of A4 paper that he'd actually typed the night before. He'd typed out his concocted story just in case the cardinal asked to look at the file but he knew he wouldn't. He knew the cardinal would ask for a copy to be sent to his executive assistant, a man Nef knew he had been sleeping with for years. The cardinal wouldn't look at it because he would not give Nef the satisfaction of seeing him concerned. If the allegations were bad enough and might possibly hurt his own position, the offender would be re-assigned within hours – he had no care for any of his staff, no matter how loyal they were.

Nef drew out his concocted story for as long as he could. The cardinal was completely disinterested. For ten minutes, Nef did his best to hold the cardinal's attention, but it didn't work. At 2:56 p.m., the cardinal had had enough. He started to make for the door and Nef's plan was unfolding rapidly. Then the phone rang. Nef's heart missed a beat. If it was the Vatican, they were early. They were not known for being early. He crossed his fingers and hoped.

The cardinal lifted the receiver. "Si." He listened for what seemed to Nef to be an age. Then Nef heard him say the word Longinus and he knew it was indeed the Vatican. Now he had to get out of there. With the cardinal still on the phone, Nef stood up, pointed to his watch and indicated that he had to go. The cardinal shrugged his shoulders and returned to his call, completely indifferent to the policeman. To support the ruse, Nef left the file on the table.

Nef was now outside in the courtyard and quickly placed the tiny earpiece into his ear.

"Is he on the call?" Luther's voice was in his earpiece. Nef brushed his fingers through his hair. This was their pre-arranged signal that the cardinal was on the call with the Vatican.

Luther nodded to Wolf and Wolf pressed his coms and spoke to the rest of the Templar team. "*Ubi positus est, ut omnis* – Where one stands, so stand us all. We are go, I repeat, we are go."

Then Luther spoke to Nef again. "Go to your car and wait for my call."

Nef brushed his hair once again to signal he understood and walked over to his car. There he stood, pretending to be answering a call on his mobile phone. The two minders had eyes on him again and they moved a little closer. He felt their menace. To Nef, it was the longest pretend call - in history. If their plan worked, he would be going back inside the villa and arresting the cardinal but for now, he had to stand by the car and keep the two menacing minders occupied with eyes on him.

*

Place: Mobile phone mast station, five miles from the Paradiso villa

Courtney Rose prised the door open with a small, black crowbar. It gave easily. Inside there was a mass of relays, terminals, and wires in vertical stacks; a low hum filled the stuffy room. Outside the mobile phone masts received and then transmitted the mobile phone signals that the terminals collected and redirected to the intended recipients. The Templars guessed that the cardinal would not use a landline to call his criminal friends about the opportunity they could not pass up. He would use a mobile phone and, in all likelihood, it would be a burner phone – once used, then disposed of; untraceable: almost! The Templars had no idea where that phone would be or its

61

number. So, the only way was to home-in on any mobile phone signal coming from the Paradiso villa. If they were right, it would be very soon after the cardinal received information about the Spear of Destiny being moved under the Vatican's rotation policy. It was Courtney's job to spot the call, electronically infiltrate the coms and then, record it, and all without the caller or the receiver being any the wiser.

The ex-FBI agent was smart, mega smart. She had upgraded and installed an advanced, robust and protected electronic superhighway of servers across the Templar network, which made tracing and tracking digital crime easier. She had a Double honours degree in criminology as well as a Doctorate in computer sciences. She liked science, maths and puzzles. Her mind was logical, clinical and rational. She had been a desk-based FBI agent that worked on one of the most powerful computers in the world. A Middle East Theatre Strategist, a desk job that required a very powerful computer, linked to the FBI's cloaked mainframe, 'Colossus 1'. She had an intellect only found in the top three percentile of the world's population.

Courtney saw the relay light up. She triangulated to a single location, it was coming from the Paradiso villa. She clipped a small black digital box into the relay system. Her handheld tablet was connected to one of the black box's input ports. She pressed record. As soon as the conversation was over, she encrypted the file and sent it back to the castle in Scotland.

Bertram removed the encryption and then played the recording to St Clair, who listened to it, twice. Then St Clair made a secure call to Cardinal Gino Del Luca. The cardinal was expecting the call. He listened to the man with the slight Scottish accent. Then he heard the recording.

Nef had made the cardinal aware of the plan after his call with St Clair. He and St Clair agreed that they would need a powerful cardinal inside the Vatican to help them; to stop Paradiso from slipping their net. Paradiso was an extremely powerful man. He was a bad man with dark secrets, but he also knew the dark secrets of a number of powerful cardinals. So, Nef and the Templars knew they would need a direct route to the Pope himself. Del Luca was a natural choice. Del Luca in turn informed the Pope what had been going on and what their plans were. He promised the Pope that he could contain it and it would not get out to the press; the Catholic Church didn't need another public relations disaster on its hands.

After St Clair played the tape for the second time, Del Luca gave him the green light. Del Luca's parting words were, "may God be with Nef and your team."

"We pray for his guidance, your Eminence. I will let you know when it is over," St Clair replied.

"Thank you, my son. When this is over, we have another matter to discuss, you and I."

"I suspected that to be the case after your conversation with Jonathan in Rome but I have been waiting for you to get in touch."

"I will my son, I will. I have a number of meetings and speaking engagements in the UK, I leave in three days' time and will be away for about six days but I will call you as soon as I am back, there is no rush." The cardinal had already decided that the man he was talking to was either the Templars' Grand Master or he was one of the Worthies. He was in no rush to tell St Clair or Jonathan what he needed to tell them, after all, it had already been seven hundred years!

St Clair gave the cardinal a telephone number to use. "They will find me day or night. I am looking forward to speaking again." Then St Clair hung up.

Two minutes later, Del Luca made a call to the Vatican security team on detail at Paradiso's villa. Less than five minutes later, they had left.

At the same time, St Clair told the Templars watching the villa that Del Luca was doing his part, they should go and go fast. Luther, Wolf, Marie-Claude and Cameron Jack all rose from their positions. Keeping low they ran towards the villa.

With a few hundred yards to go, Luther told Nef the news.

*

Nef was getting really uncomfortable pretending to be on the phone. He had been standing there for nearly ten minutes, pacing up and down, mouthing non-existent words of a non-existent conversation. Then finally, his wait was over. His earpiece crackled.

"We got it Dámaso." Luther was breathing hard. "Paradiso made the call just like you thought he would, we have it on tape, and we have their plan. We have Paradiso."

Nef's heart rate increased as adrenalin started to pump around his body.

"We just played it to Cardinal Gino Del Luca. He gave us the green light and has already called the Vatican security detail guys who are on rotation with Paradiso. He knows them well; they are sometimes rotated to him. He told me that he knew they hated Paradiso and wouldn't need any convincing to leave when he told them what was about to happen. Go, Dámaso, you have your green light. He's all yours. Go get your man. We are one minute away."

Nef inhaled deeply. He had been waiting so long to be able to arrest the cardinal, whom he so despised. The cardinal he always knew, deep down, was the *Sancti Furem* – Holy Thief. He closed his eyes and savoured the moment. *Sixty, fifty-nine ... three, two, one.*

The Vatican chief of police reached for his badge from his inside pocket. He held it tight. He turned around in the direction of the minders. They could still stop the arrest, but he had no reason to worry. He saw one minder falling to the ground, being disarmed on his way down by a woman dressed in a long black coat and a sniper's rifle slung crossways over her shoulders, Marie-Claude struck hard. The second minder seemed to react and was raising his handgun, which he then proceeded to quickly drop when a man drew a Katana sword and sliced the air in an arc towards the minder's neck. The razor-sharp blade now pressed against the minder's neck. Nef had never seen the skill of the Lionheart, neither had the minder.

Nef now turned towards the villa. A figure came in from the left. He recognised him, it was the man whose voice he had been listening to through the earpiece. It was Luther Jones, the man who had helped them kill the last *Gwrach Marwolaeth* Hag. Nef no longer needed his earpiece. Luther's bodycam was on. The Templars back in Scotland were watching everything that was happening. They were part of the mission, more eyes and more ears; they were feeding information to the team on the ground. They recorded all the bodycam footage, they always did.

"You ready?" Luther asked Nef.; he was still breathing hard.

"Si," Nef said, then he took an envelope from his jacket pocket and handed it to Luther. "This formally deputises you and all your team. You are now official deputies of the Vatican police, for one day." Then Nef turned towards the door and rang the doorbell. Instantly he heard footsteps coming from inside. He smiled to himself, *expecting me, make me wait, not expecting me, answer the door straightaway*, he thought.

The door opened and the same young priest stood there, opened mouthed. "Chi ... I'm, er ... I'm sorry but the ..." He struggled with his words. He so desperately did not want to let Nef back into the villa; he knew he would incur the wrath of the cardinal if he did so. "I'm afraid you ca—"

Nef showed him his badge. "I'm afraid I can, Father."

"No, no you can't bec..."

The Indian John Wolf approached. "The back is clear," Wolf told Luther. He then grabbed the priest standing in the doorway blocking Nef's entrance back into the villa. Wolf lifted him up until the priest's feet were dangling six inches off the ground. "I don't think you mean can't, I think you mean can, right?"

"R ... right," said the priest, with a trembling voice.

It wasn't a gamble arresting the cardinal because they had already decided that he would not want any more contact with the criminals until the job was done. So, they would not be expecting a call from him. He had played his part; it was now up to them. The next contact he would want from them would be to be informed that the Longinus artefact was in their hands, a buyer had been found and had already transferred the money he was to receive into his Swiss bank account. And when they listened to the call he'd had with the criminals, that is exactly what he had told them, no contact unless it was about his money. Of course, what the cardinal didn't know was that the Templars had been tracing and then hacking into his private account. Nef had spent months trying to find proof of the cardinal's offshore, off-grid account. With limited resources, he had failed. Without real proof of any wrongdoing, he would not ask permission to investigate the cardinal. The cardinal had many friends and if Nef spoke out, the cardinal would have known within minutes. The Templars had no such restraints. Morgan Clay and the Barbados forensic accountancy team, led by John Edison, had been on it ever since the Templars' meeting with Nef, in Rome, when they killed the Hag. When that mission team left Rome directly after the mission, Luther had shaken hands with Nef and said, "St Clair sent me a message earlier from Spain. He told me that we are going to help you find your *Sancti Furem,* your Holy Thief, although, I think we all suspect who it is. I want you to know that we will be back in touch in the New Year." And from that day the Templars had redirected some of their resources to track and locate any offshore bank accounts belonging to Cardinal Paradiso, under his own name or any pseudo names. Just days ago, they got the evidence.

With the trembling priest leading the way, Nef, Luther and Wolf entered the villa of Cardinal Paradiso. The priest took them straight to where the cardinal was, his private study. He was sitting behind a large, regency-style desk full of papers. The room was heavy with cigarette smoke and the stifling musk Nef hated so much; it was also heavy with anxiety and fear – it oozed from the priests who were working in there. To one side a priest sat typing on a computer, another was hovering over four large filing cabinets. Both priests had facial bruises. They had been bullied and abused mentally and physically by the cardinal. The sight of three intruders sent them into sheer panic, fearful of what the cardinal would do.

The cardinal stood up from behind his desk, his face like thunder, his colour reddening with every second that went past. The priest that had led Nef and the two Knights into the study took the opportunity to escape and he ran, less fearful of the intruders than the growing wrath of the cardinal. "You had better have a good reason to be in my house, Nef!" The cardinal roared at him, whilst eying the two strangers.

Nef had many reasons, the cardinal was impious, wicked, immoral, and ungodly but right then, there was only one he needed. "Cardinal Paradiso, I arrest you for conspiring to steal a venerated object owned by the Vatican. Conspiracy to steal is a criminal act."

The cardinal erupted and hurled abuse at Nef. He reached for his mobile phone and began punching in numbers.

"They're not there," Nef said. "They are outside and in custody."

The cardinal looked out of the widow. His two minders were lying on the ground, bound and gagged. He started screaming for his security detail.

"Gone," Nef said. He then turned to Luther and nodded. Luther played the tape of the cardinal in conversation with the criminals earlier.

"It will never stick," he rasped mid-way through the recording. "Prove it was me, you idiot. Anyone's voice can be mimicked, copied, or digitally changed. You have no witnesses."

There was a silence, only for a brief second or two, but then a timid voice spoke up. They all turned. One of the priests, the one that had been sitting at the computer, stood up and turned to the cardinal. "I ... I will be their witness." He then turned to Nef. "I was in the room when he called someone about the plans to move the Longinus spear. He gave them his private bank account details, but I cannot remember them."

Luther stepped forward. "It's okay, Father, we have them." He then called out the name of the cardinal's secret account, the account number and the sort code. "We have his bank account and every transaction for the last five years."

"Cardinal Paradiso, I am further arresting you in relation to a series of thefts of Vatican property over a period of fifteen years. In addition, for tax evasion and conspiring to defraud the *Ministero dell'Economia e delle Finanze*. And finally for the subjugation of members of your appointed staff: assault, battery, and aggravated assault."

Both priests broke down and sobbed uncontrollably.

*

Date: The 17th – the day of Jonathan's rooftop escape
Place: A Catholic school, Barcelona City, Spain

After the arrest of Cardinal Paradiso, the Lionheart, Marie-Claude and Courtney Rose all left for the UK. The remaining two, Luther and the Indian, John Wolf, flew to Barcelona and were met by Dominique, Jonathan and Bertram. It was another intervention by Cardinal Del Luca that made what happened next, possible. He had pulled off a small miracle and managed to get several Vatican administration departments and several other decision-making cardinals, to agree to the swap – having his Holiness's support clinched it. The Templars were handed the spear just two hours before the real curators were meant to hand it over to the real couriers.

*

They were on the ground floor of a school. It was the weekend and the meeting between the curators and the couriers had been planned to take place in the gymnasium of a small, two-storey Catholic school in the *Sarria-Sant Gervasi* district of Barcelona. The diocese told the local caretaker to leave the school unlocked on Friday night. They told him it was needed for a diocese meeting over the weekend. He did not question it; they had done it before.

Jonathan and Dominique stood together, masquerading as the curators. Jonathan held the Longinus spear in his hand – tightly. They waited inside the gymnasium, which doubled up as a dining room for the children's school dinners. Bertram was outside, hidden, keeping watch. He would signal on their coms when the criminals arrived. The Indian and Luther hid inside the gymnasium. The Indian was behind a small staging platform, used for school plays and assemblies; Luther was tucked away in a small recess that held balls, long low benches, green rubber mats, rope and a medicine ball. All the Templars were facing the door. There was only one way in. They had no idea when the criminals would arrive. They didn't have to wait long; Bertram gave the signal over their coms, they had just arrived – they were twenty minutes early.

At first, the criminals seemed flustered that the two curators were already there. They had arrived early so they could recce the school, but there was no reason for them to be suspicious, so they followed their original plan. Outside they left two people, they would stop the real couriers from entering the building. They also had a sniper placed on one of the rooftops close by – as it would turn out, it was the one opposite to the rooftop Jonathan would choose to make his escape route.

Four criminals entered the gymnasium. They were armed but as yet, they had not drawn their weapons – they did not want to spook the curators. The criminals believed, the information their boss, a Moroccan called Matue, who was with them, had received from someone within the Vatican, that they could pass for the couriers and take the artefact. It would make them enough money to live the good life for quite a while.

"Hasta," Matue smiled and took one step forward. It was the password to be used between the curators and the couriers.

"You're early," Dominique replied politely. She knew the Indian and Luther would be watching, sizing up where everyone was and trying to secure all the lines of fire. She just had to keep the conversation going until Luther gave the green light.

"We have a long way to go," Matue offered cordially. "Do you have it?" he asked.

Jonathan raised the spear a little. "We have it," he said. He was nervous and would normally reach into his trouser pocket seeking out any coins that he could rattle – his 'tell'. But ever since the battle with Salah El-Din in Cumbria, Dominique had taken to removing all the change from his pockets before a mission.

"Then we should get on with it," Matue suggested. All the time the other three criminals were making their way around the gymnasium, circling – eyes everywhere.

Over their coms, they heard Bertram. "There were three out here. I can only see two now. They are waiting twenty yards down the road; it looks like they are waiting for the real couriers. I don't know where the third person has gone."

Luther came on the coms. "Okay, it's time. Remember, we want as many alive as we can." He paused, and then said, "close your ears, here it comes." And with that, there was a loud explosion.

The flashbang, used by the military to create confusion, shock and awe, exploded. The flashbang lived up to its name. The plan was to rush the criminals and, in the confusion, restrain them, question them and try to collect as much additional evidence that might be useful to Nef. Either way, they wanted to get the criminals off the streets and behind bars for as long as possible. But then all hell broke loose. Whilst the other criminals all had small handguns, one of the criminals had brought a GK 53EA3 5.56mm carbine machine gun with a 3-round burst trigger; it had a roller-locked bolt system and had unmatched controllability in its calibre range: and he was using it to great effect. Now it all seemed to move in slow motion as Luther and Wolf returned fire.

Dominique pushed Jonathan forward and shouted for him to run. "Go and take the spear. Keep it safe." She then turned around and faced the criminals.

Now she stood motionless. If the criminals thought that the woman curator wouldn't be a problem, they were very much mistaken. The small petite woman, with short mousy brown hair, standing motionless, did not look threatening, that was until she threw open her long, black leather coat and retrieved a Heckler Koch .40 and a pump-action 12-gauge shotgun, designed for smaller shooters. The 12-gauge had a seven-shot magazine and a specially modified handgrip stock. As the sides of her coat opened, it also revealed a shoulder rig, where she carried a backup gun with a 13-round magazine. They could not know that the woman in the mirrored Ray Bans, was a 7th Dan in Karate and a highly skilled shooter. Like all the other Templars, she also carried their favoured weapon, the Katana sword of the Samurai, which they all concealed in a back-body webbing that held their lightweight titanium *saya* – scabbard on their backs, with just about an inch peeking out of the top of their long, black coats.

Dominique didn't take off her Ray Bans, she rarely did, but behind them her eyes were darting everywhere. It took her seconds to assess the situation. She returned fire. Five quick bursts then she saw one of the criminals was down, he was dead. The Indian had sprung from his hiding position and launched himself at the criminal. Wolf, his fourteen-inch bone-handled knife in his hand, caught the shoulder blade of one of the criminals; he let his handgun fall as he reached for the wound. Wolf was now on him and a powerful blow to the man's head knocked him clean out.

Dominique spun around to see where her husband was. The Seer was twenty yards away, he had the spear tucked into his belt. He'd stopped.

"Jonathan, run. Take the Longinus and run."

"But—" he started to shout above the din.

"No buts. Run, I'll find you; we'll find you."

The bullets started again as the remaining two criminals were now fighting for their lives.

The ex-priest from Washington DC looked for an exit. A window offered the fastest way out, it didn't look like it had a lock. Part of the way was obscured by stacked dining chairs. He started to make his move.

Dominique saw the direction he was heading. *Thank God,* she thought, *he has cover, good work Darling.*

Jonathan made it to the window and flicked the latch, he was right, there was no lock. He started to ease himself out, but his bodycam got caught and it snapped off. He turned around to see where his wife was. He saw her.

"Just keep going Jonathan," she called. "It's fine, but stay away from the rooftops, don't go up there."

"Okay."

"They're brittle and it's a death trap up there; it will be a bad idea as an escape route."

"I won't, I pro—"

A spray of bullets barely missed her, she dived forward, did a forward roll and as she came up, she fired a short burst. A second criminal lay dead. She turned once more, Jonathan had gone.

The leader, Matue, dropped his gun and raised his hands. Luther was on him in seconds, and put him to the floor. Luther zip-tied his feet and hands, and then checked him for weapons. The Indian zip-tied the other criminal, checked him for weapons and then placed a field dressing on the injured man's shoulder.

The firefight didn't last all that long, but the Seer and the Longinus spear had disappeared into the Barcelona streets. He was alone and didn't know that the two criminals that had been positioned outside, were now right on his heels and even more worrying, the sniper lay in wait.

Dominique hit her coms, "Jonathan, Jonathan, where are you?"

Bertram's voice came back, "he headed for the rooftops, two in pursuit. I think he's out of range for our coms, but I can guide you."

*

Date: The 18th – the following day

The email arrived at the regional headquarters of the *Policía Nacional* – National Police. Controlled by the Directorate General of Police and Civil Guard and ultimately the State Department of Security in the Ministry of the Interior. Two policemen, just finishing their nightshift, were closing their computers down when their email 'inbox' flashed. They looked at each other. Then towards the clock on the wall, there were seven minutes to go before their shift ended. The older of the two started to clear his desk and pressed 'shutdown' on his computer, his screen started flashing and the homepage icons began to disappear; he was looking forward to breakfasting with his wife before she left for work. The other, had no one to rush home to, he would eat breakfast alone, as always. He opened the email. It was a short email with an untitled M-JPEG file attached. The email read:

Please call Dámaso Nef, at the Corpo della Gendarmeria dello Stato della Città del Vaticano - Corps of the Gendarmerie of Vatican City state: the Vatican police.

There was a phone number. It then had an address:

This is the address of a school in the Sarria-Sant Gervasi district of the city. It is just twenty miles from your headquarters. The school is open. Inside, in the gymnasium, you will find four men, two are dead. Two are alive; one is a Moroccan called Matue, he is the leader. They have their hands and feet restrained by zip-ties and have been there since yesterday. They each have a small rucksack on their backs, a bottle of water in each rucksack and a sucking tube from the water to their mouths – it's taped to their cheek, so accessible for them. One is wounded but you should find them in fair health but not in fair spirits.

Yesterday, they attempted to steal a priceless object belonging to the Vatican. The file attached is live bodycam footage of the robbery. As you will see, our faces have been blurred out, do not try to reinstate the images, you will not succeed. The thieves were not successful in their attempt and the object is already on its way to its intended new home, transported by Vatican couriers.
  Nef will know what to do.

There was no name. They checked the email address but it wasn't traceable, it no longer existed. The older of the two policemen called his wife and told her not to bother to make him breakfast, he might be a while. The other policeman then called the *Grupo Especial de Operaciones* (GEO) - Group of Special Operations, the police tactical unit of Spain's National Police Corps. He was put through to the officer in charge. He forwarded him the email and the file. Five minutes later the officer called them back.

"I know Nef," the officer in charge said. He had remembered him because it was unusual for an Italian to have a Spanish surname as a first name. "He's the chief of police at the Vatican. Good guy. Good golfer." He chuckled.

The call to Nef happened less than twenty minutes after the two policemen first received the email. Nef had been expecting the call. He could not be directly involved in the trap set for the criminals trying to steal the spear, nor could he be there at their capture because it was outside of his jurisdiction and any involvement would have seriously jeopardised any case at trial. So, the Templars hatched a plan that would secure Nef's involvement through the invitation of the Spanish police. They sent the evidence to the Spanish police and then left it to them to formally invite Nef to become involved. The Spanish authorities would class the crime as larceny, with a classification of grand theft, punishable by a sentence of between five to twenty years.

*

73

About the time the Spanish police were calling Nef, the Templar mission team were at a provincial airport in northern Spain. They had tickets to a provincial airport in France, where they would split up, half catching a flight to London City Airport and the other half would hire a car and drive back via Calais and then the Euro Tunnel.

They were sitting around chatting; they were pleased with how the mission had gone. They were extremely pleased that Cardinal Paradiso would soon face trial, although his case would have to be put before his Holiness the Pope first. The Templar mission team were relaxed for the first time in days and even joked about Bertram's flying skills – or lack of flying skills over the rooftops. However, an autopsy in Rome a few days later would only serve to destroy their relaxed mood.

Chapter 6

Morto Vivente

Date: The 18th – the first day of Cardinal Del Luca's UK trip
Place: London, England

The cardinal's UK trip had been in his diary for over a year, it was to last six days.

His schedule included a number of meetings with church leaders; a number of meetings with diocese elders; and there were a few with politicians – the part of any trip he disliked the most. He also had four lectures to give, the part of his trips he loved the most. So, cancelling the trip was out of the question. But Del Luca didn't want to go. It had only been three days since Nef had arrested Cardinal Paradiso. Del Luca wanted to stay in the Vatican and help Nef, and assist his Holiness the Pope, in handling the Paradiso matter and the serious issue of a senior clergyman about to be found guilty of abhorrent crimes. It would engulf the Catholic Church. The aftermath would be horrendous and the inevitable PR nightmare would follow. His Holiness would need all the support of his cardinals. However, Del Luca knew all too well that decisions made within the Vatican hierarchy had a pace all of their own – grindingly slow. So, he'd resigned himself to the fact that he would probably be back from his trip long before anything happened. Besides, he took comfort in the fact that Paradiso was now safely locked away in one of the Vatican police holding cells and under the very watchful eye and jurisdiction of Dámaso Nef.

However, there was a far greater reason why Del Luca did

not want to go to the UK. He had every intention of calling St Clair when he got back from his trip, as he'd promised on their last call together but, he didn't want to wait that long. He really wanted to cancel his trip and make the call. Patience, cautiousness and discretion had always been their watchwords, and now he needed to heed those words. He could not rush it. He needed the resolve to wait – but he so desperately wanted to know if his suspicion about Jonathan was correct. Was the ex-priest one of the famed lions, those Knights of temperance they had looked for, for so long, the legendary warrior monks, the Templars? And, if Jonathan was, was he the *one*? So, calling and meeting the man with the slight Scottish accent had been on his mind ever since his call with him a few days ago and even before that, in fact, ever since his first meeting with Jonathan Rose. However, he was resigned to the fact that he must go to the UK – but he couldn't wait for it to be over.

He was worried he might lose contact with the man with the slight Scottish accent; he needn't. Had he known the man, he would also have known that the man's Knights would not be too far away. In fact, ever since Del Luca had had that conversation with Jonathan in the Church, at the slaying of the Hag, the Templars had had a tail on him – their best.

Morgan Clay was average looking, average height, with average features and average ways. Nothing ever changed about Morgan Clay – leastways, not outwardly. The kind of man you could see every day for a year and not be able to describe him when asked. He had learnt his craft from his previous employers, the British Secret Service. He had spent thirty years defending the Crown, then he joined the Knights Templars. He was ideal for the job and the best ghost man the Order of the Knights Templar had ever had. He had been sent by St Clair to watch over the cardinal because of the conversation the cardinal had had with Jonathan. The Templars needed to know who the cardinal really was, what he knew and how he knew it!

*

The cardinal and his two companions arrived in the UK early morning. Grey skies sucked the colour out of the day. It was cold

76

and it was wet but as a frequent visitor, he'd packed for it; he was dressed for it, and he was ready for it.

After a frustrating car journey into the city of London, through early morning, slow-moving traffic – 'as bad as traffic in Rome', he'd commented to his UK Government's security service female driver and the male bodyguard sitting beside her. He'd not seen her face, just the male's, who had met them inside the airport, presented his credentials and then took them to their waiting car.

Despite the motorway's best efforts to the contrary, he finally made it to his central hotel – an old Victorian building that had once been a workhouse that housed the poor but was now a top London hotel. The absurdity was not lost on him. After checking-in at reception, the cardinal had gone to his room, unpacked, freshened up a little, checked his emails and responded to a few of the more urgent ones. He'd sent an email to Nef as soon as he'd landed. Now there was an answer in his inbox from Nef confirming there was nothing new to report. His Holiness was still praying about what to do with the Holy Thief, who was still incarcerated and still complaining bitterly. The cardinal closed his laptop down, got his lecture prompt notes in order and then left the hotel. The male bodyguard opened the car door for him and he got in. The two priests who had accompanied him, Father Declan, his personal aide and Father Ronan, who would assist him during his lectures, were also booked into the same hotel, they had also freshened up in their rooms and were now in the car with him. They were then driven to the first speaking engagement.

Many thought the cardinal foolhardy when they found out he was undergoing an overseas trip and not taking his own protection detail with him, just his personal aide, Father Declan and the priest Father Ronan. Many of the other cardinals knew he was never comfortable having bodyguards but Del Luca, *l'esorcista del Papa* – the exorcist of the Pope, the revered Devil slayer, regularly received death threats. Most came in the form of telephone calls to the Vatican switchboard. Some were emails and some were scribbled and disturbing letters mailed to him. He saw very few of them as his office and the security services dealt with them. However, he was aware of them and aware of the number he received. Some could be traced to people who had serious issues with the Vatican, Catholics, or just religion in general. Most of them were from people who clearly suffered from paranoia, neurosis and psychosis and for a few, insanity. He told everyone he did not want to take a protection detail on this trip because it would just become a media spectacle. If he had his detail with him, he would, he argued, be inviting headlines like 'entourage', 'bodyguards', and 'Hollywood style visit' in the UK tabloids and then he would be hounded for the rest of his trip as the papers' hacks pursued a non-existent story to sensationalise their front pages. 'Why spoil a good story for the truth?', he was once told by a rather disagreeable reporter. The Vatican asked the British if their Secret Services might help secure the cardinal's welfare whilst in their country. MI5 stepped in.

Many thought that the head of *Corpo della Gendarmeria dello Stato della Città del Vaticano* - Corps of the Gendarmerie of Vatican City state, should have shown more concern but he didn't. Nef was one of a handful of people who knew the real reason the cardinal didn't travel with his protection team on that trip!

It had been an interesting few months for the cardinal in the lead-up to his trip. He'd trapped the *Gwrach Marwolaeth* Hag. Then, he had helped a small group of talented people destroy the witch who was evil and extremely dangerous – the witch had killed countless times. He'd watched Nef skilfully gather enough evidence to lure and then ensnare the Holy Thief; he even knew who Charlie B was, the author of the letter that was sent to Nef about the Longinus spear being moved. And on top of that and far more importantly, he may have found the 'someone' whom they had been searching for, for nine hundred years. Then, just a few weeks before his trip, at a wedding where the cardinal was a guest of the father of the bride, who was a high-ranking government official, the real reason he did not take his protection detail to the UK happened.

At some stage during the long, lavish wedding reception, which was taking place within the sprawling grounds of the father's very large country residence, a luxurious Renaissance villa, there was a bomb scare. At first it was received in disbelief and no action taken, then, shortly everything changed. The mood went from celebrations, eating and drinking, dancing and socialising, to blind panic, a raw survival. The presence of the bomb was announced loudly over a microphone from a central stage. The bride's younger sister had convinced her father and her sister that they should hire a new up-and-coming grunge band called Spider, fronted by the lead singer, 'Street Boy' – whom she was secretly dating. Her father and sister had never heard of grunge and so, to appease the younger girl and to stop the tantrum that had erupted over the fact she felt she was not part of the wedding or the plans, they hired them. It was a mistake the father and sister would regret, that regret setting in soon after the first line of the band's first song, 'my baby did it to me big in the back of a yellow taxi!' The rest of the song didn't get much better. Fortunately, most people were too occupied drinking, socialising and eating to listen to the noise emanating from the central stage, with its oversized speakers and deep reverberating base.

Three songs in and mid-verse the band's manager, who looked pale and out of breath, shouted something to Street Boy. Street Boy pointed to his ears and indicated he did not hear what was said. The manager repeated his words, gesticulated with his arms in a windmill motion and then he ran. This time he heard it. Street Boy stopped singing and so the band stopped playing. "A bomb!" Street Boy screamed down his microphone at the realisation of their certain death before they'd even got the chance to cut a record. Off to the right, he saw the emergence of a small group of people starting to run in the same direction his manager had gone. Then he heard the screaming, the same as his manager had done. All of them were heading with great haste for the car park, and more were joining them with every step.

"Fuck this," he screamed down the microphone now totally panicked. "Fuck this, there's a bomb. We're all dead. Get the fuck out!" He screamed again.

And, with that he leapt over the drums and the drummer, sending them sprawling all over the stage and he headed for the car park, along with the human stampede. His announcement of death had blasted out of six multiway, six feet stack, Bose speakers. No one was left uninformed as to what was about to happen to them.

The security personnel, who had been hired by the father of

the bride, did their best to try to keep everyone calm, as they tried to move people as quickly as they could. They struggled to keep the guests in order. They gave it ten seconds and then, they ran too, most heading for their cars and the rest heading for the large ornate electric gates and the road beyond.

Three priests quickly gathered around the cardinal. A fourth, his personal aide, Father Declan, stood to one side and made a visual sweeping check to decide on the safest route out for them. It was difficult to see a safe route.

"The villa," Father Michael called. He was an older priest, with dark hair and deep olive skin. He was tall and muscular. He pointed towards the villa; no one was heading towards it, they were all going in the opposite direction. "We will have protection from the blast if we can get inside; the walls are thick. Quickly." He started towards the house.

The others followed, unsure of a better strategy at that moment. It was chaos outside.

Father Declan was conflicted. His instincts were screaming at him, telling him it was the wrong decision. He wanted to get away from the grounds of the house as quickly as possible. However, he had no way of knowing how long they had before the bomb went off. He did not want the cardinal out in the open when it did. He didn't want anybody out in the open when it did but he could only focus on the cardinal right now.

Father Declan wasn't the only one having doubts about the decision they had just made. The cardinal had doubts, too.

There was lots of screaming and blind panic gripping the fleeing guests as they pushed and shoved others out of the way to escape the bomb. The bride was hurt during the chaotic exodus. She fell and several people ran over her heading for the twisting shale drive and the two electric main gates that meant their survival.

The eating area, sixty trestle tables covered in white starched linen tablecloths, covered with silver, stainless steel trays, bowls, tureens, containers, chafing dishes and an array of Italian and international foods, both hot and cold, starters, main courses, desserts, the bread of all descriptions and shapes, had been upended in the peoples' blind panic to get away and was now strewn across the churned grass in a grand, culinary mess.

The car park and the drive were now log jammed with cars because the gates were not working. They would not open – someone had disabled their sensors an hour before the alarm had gone out about the bomb and no one had the metal handle that would turn the small electric motor to manually open the gates.

People on foot were also now backed up and a number of fights broke out. Even if the emergency services were on their way, they would never get through the fleeing barricade.

As the cardinal's protection team approached the sixteen-bedroom villa, they did not look up, their focus was straight ahead on the grand, double ornate carved wooden doors beyond which, they believed, offered protection from the impending blast. If they had looked up at that moment, they would have seen figures making their way across the crest of the villa roof. They had climbed onto the roof from the east side, the side only used by tradespeople. It was hidden from view. The climb to the flat roof was short, but it led to the main roof another forty foot higher up. Grappling hooks secured their ascent onto the main roof. Keeping low and hugging the crest tiles, the two figures, dressed in black, carrying their grappling hooks on long ropes and small-stocked submachine guns strapped across their shoulders, moved quickly. Only Father Michael looked up and saw them: but he didn't say anything.

The priest-protection team burst through the front door and into the large and decorative reception room. The whole house was empty. Everyone had fled and like the rest, they were now heading for the car park or the gates, both of which were in the same direction. They frantically looked for a safe place for the cardinal.

"Top floor," Father Michael called. "The higher up we go, the further away from the blast arc we will be." The others didn't argue, they just followed, adrenalin keeping them fuelled on high alert, although at least two of the priests were also gripped with terror.

It had now been ten minutes since the alarm had gone out and the announcement by Street Boy. They had been in the house for just two of them. The cardinal asked if the presence of a bomb had been confirmed. Had they themselves confirmed it; had anyone? It had not and they had not, they informed him. He then asked them who had given the initial warning, before the singer announced it. "Father Michael told us," one of the bodyguard priests said. "Father Michael raised the initial alarm." Now the cardinal knew what was really happening.

Outside on the expansive, red-tiled clay roof, grappling hooks had been secured around two pillars of the parapet wall of a secluded roof terrace. The two figures, clad in black, were now rappelling down the front of the luxurious Renaissance villa. The whole wedding reception was totally oblivious to their presence and their murderous intent. Skilfully, the two figures made their way down.

. They seemed to know exactly where they were going. Above a large bay window, they paused. Suspended above the ground, they knew that one slip and they would fall to their death – they would not survive a fall from this height. They waited.

Inside the priests were in the large master bedroom, huddled down against what they thought was the furthest wall from where the wedding reception had been taking place. Four of them waited: two of them knew what was going to happen next, the cardinal and the cardinal's assassin.

"Pray for us, your Eminence," one of the priests said to Del Luca. "Ask God to help us in this hour." His voice was shaking.

The cardinal smiled as he finally stood up. "Oh, I don't think we need to bother our Lord today, my son. I don't think we have need of His bomb disposal skills." He chuckled a little.

They looked confused.

"There is no bomb," he explained. "If there had been, we would have been told of its detonation time by now, because they would be using it as leverage to extort a large sum of money from Mr Giordano, our gracious host. If the bomb was not for money, then it would have gone off by now; they would not have waited whilst six hundred guests were already halfway down the drive." He paused and then turned to Father Michael. "Isn't that right, Father Michael?"

As the cardinal spoke the older priest pressed the button of a small electronic device hidden inside the pocket of his cassock. There was a deafening sound of breaking glass and for a second, they thought the bomb had actually gone off. Then, two assailants crashed through the large bay window. They were at the far end of the large master bedroom. Glass shattered everywhere. The assailants raised their submachine guns. All hell broke loose. Bullets started flying everywhere. Everyone took cover, but Father Declan, his handgun now in hand, spun around on the imposter, Father Michael, as he was trying to move away from the priests who were drawing fire. Father Declan hit him hard on the side of the head. He hit the floor, dazed. He groaned as blood seeped from the wound.

The large room was full of furniture, it saved the priests, shielding them from the salvo of bullets.

"Get the cardinal out of here," Father Declan called to the other two priests, but they were crouched low and already running for the door.

Father Declan fixed his focus on the assailants. He fired off six rounds from his handgun – he was skilled. The 9mm bullets drove the assailants diving for cover themselves. He saw Michael's gun lying on the ground next to him and grabbed it. Now with both guns firing and moving at the same time, he zigzagged as quickly as he could and took cover behind a large, ostentatious ebony drinks cabinet. One of his bullets had hit an assailant and he was already lying on the ground dead. He reloaded his own gun and tried to slow his breathing, waiting for another assailant to make the next move. Father Declan had nowhere to go and the only way out was back the way he came and he didn't fancy his chances a second time. It went eerily quiet. He waited. He was not scared. He was a priest who had been through seminary, but he was also a soldier. He had been trained by the Italian elite special forces, the 9th Assault Parachute Regiment, the *Col Moschin Incursore* – Col Moschin Raiders when he had first joined the Cabal, just three years after meeting Cardinal Del Luca. He had become the cardinal's aide, – his bodyguard, his protector.

No one outside heard the gunfire coming from the house. No one outside knew what was going on inside the house. Outside the noise was already deafening, shrieks and screaming, hollering, the hooting of over a hundred car horns and the roaring sound of car engines frantically trying to inch forward in the long line of traffic. Besides, they were too busy saving themselves from the ticking bomb. Some sent text messages to loved ones, and some prayed. A small band of men at the front hammered on the electric gates with anything they could find in their car boots. It was a vain attempt to get the gates open.

It would take twenty seconds to breach the building and then kill the cardinal. That was their plan. It was their best chance to get the cardinal. He was always too well-guarded in the Vatican; it was impossible to get to him there. The wedding, they had decided, was the perfect place. What they needed was a diversion. Something that would distract a large crowd, something that would have every pair of eyes looking in the opposite direction to where the assassination would take place. It had been planned as a three-man hit team. One on the inside and two would enter the house once the cardinal had been lured there. Michael had spent years undercover, deep within the Roman Catholic Church. He loathed every second of it; he despised every Christian, regardless of the church they worshipped in.

Lying there, still dazed but now aware of his situation, only the death of the cardinal was on his mind. They had planned for the fact that bullets might not get him. A curved blade drawn laterally across the cardinal's neck would render any attempt to save his life useless. It would take around thirty seconds for the blood loss and lack of oxygen to kill him. Michael, still a little dazed but driven by his devotion to evil, eased his hand down the side of his leg and retrieved a small but razor-sharp flick knife that was tucked into his sock. The imposter ripped the white dog collar from around his neck and spat at it. He called the cardinal's name. He needed the cardinal facing him – it would make his strike more accurate. All he had to do was to extend his arm and then, make a quick but deep sideways movement with the knife. Less than five inches and it would be enough to kill the man of God.

The cardinal turned towards Michael, the assassin, as he tried to strike out like a viper's bite. But Del Luca hadn't forgotten any of the lessons he had learnt during the war; lessons that had saved his life and allowed him to save countless others. Raising his right arm he blocked the viper's striking arm with his wrist. Then with a turn of his wrist he caught the assassin's wrist of the hand holding the knife. One hard twist and the knife, still in the assassin's hand, was now facing the assassin. His wrist locked. The cardinal took a powerful step forward. His body weight fully behind his forward motion. The assassin screamed as the knife, still in his hand, sunk deep into his own heart.

The remaining assailant looked for a way out. He raised himself slightly. He looked around and then saw Father Declan. The priest had his feet apart, leaning ever so slightly forward, handgun raised. He fired one round. It hit the last assailant in the middle of the forehead.

Cardinal Del Luca made a call to Nef. Nef was there within twenty minutes. Whilst his policemen started to clear up the chaos outside, he entered the large country residence of the well-known government official. Inside the luxurious Renaissance villa, he found Cardinal Del Luca, Father Declan and three dead bodies. The crime scene was outside of his jurisdiction, but the cardinal had asked for his help, Nef was only too pleased to help the man who had helped him get the Holy Thief and had trapped the Hag so that they could kill her.

By the time the local police arrived, the bodies were gone. There was shattered glass and there were bullet holes, and there was also blood (although all the bullet cases had been collected and taken away by Nef and his men).

A day later, the owner of the house received a confidential communication sent to him at his office at the *Senato della Repubblica* – Senate of the Republic, it read:

During the bomb scare, three armed men tried to steal works of art, jewellery and cash from your home. It is believed they created the bomb scare as a decoy. Because a member of the senior clergy was also there, the cardinal, I was alerted to the bomb scare. Fortunately, we were quick on the scene. When we went into the house, we came across the thieves. A shootout took place. The three thieves were shot dead.

I hope you understand the sensitivity around this and so, I suggest that we do not release this information to the press.

Dámaso Nef.

Corpo della Gendarmeria dello Stato della Città del Vaticano

*

The cardinal did not take a protection team on his trip to the UK because the last time he did one of them had tried to kill him. He knew why there was an attempt on his life. It was not the first time *they* had tried to kill him; perhaps next time *they* might succeed; he concluded he was safer with strangers; he was safer with British security services protecting him. His office made a call to MI5 to ask if they would assign a detail to him whilst there. He was assigned a two-person close protection unit to guard him. One male and his driver, a female operative.

*

The cardinal's afternoon speaking engagement was at the 'City of London and Boroughs University of Law'. The subject of his lecture was how, within Christian countries, civil law still had layers of Mosaic law within it, emanating from the period of the 'giving of the law' on Mount Sinai, until Jesus' death. His audience was young, eager and enquiring, and largely students. It was a full house in the lecture theatre. Many had booked a seat at each of his four planned lectures – he was a much-liked speaker and because of who he was and what he did, a much sought-after speaker. Of those who couldn't attend all four of his lectures most had made sure that they had booked a seat for his second lecture, which was due to take place the following morning. The subject matter was the most contentious of all the lectures and not to be missed: 'God versus science'.

Cardinal Del Luca didn't need his notes. There were slides put up on a large screen, by Father Ronan but these were references for his audience, not prompt notes for the cardinal. He was well prepared; his lecture, as always, was fluid and thoughtful. His delivery style was charming and engaging. The lecture was advertised to last one hour, with a further twenty minutes for questions. However, less than fifty minutes into it, that changed very quickly. A side exit door at the back of the lecture theatre opened and Del Luca's personal aide, Father Declan, entered the auditorium. He had stepped out for a few minutes to take a call. Father Declan made his way down a side aisle and round to the side of the stage. Del Luca saw him out of the corner of his eye, but he didn't skip a beat. However, when his aide started to mount the stage, Del Luca knew it was not good news. He leaned forward into the microphone and said to the audience, "forgive me, but Father Declan here knows only the Pope and God himself can interrupt my lecture, both have far more power than I, so I'd better see what it is." He laughed and the audience laughed with him. The cardinal took a few steps to the right – away from the microphone. His aide got up close and the cardinal listened. Some in the audience fidgeted. Others checked their notes, but most watched the cardinal, intrigued to know what the Pope or God wanted. Then it all went very quiet. Those in the first few rows could see the cardinal was visibly alarmed by whatever he had just been told. Del Luca moved back to the microphone again. "Forgive me, Father Ronan here will now continue with the lecture. You're in for a treat, he's far better than me." He pointed to Father Ronan, who had been sitting at a table to one side of the lectern, displaying the slides through his laptop and onto the large stage screen. The cardinal promptly left the stage with his assistant.

The male member of his protection detail hurriedly followed them. Once off the stage he led the way, making sure their route was clear. He didn't know what was wrong but, like most of the audience, he too had seen the visible alarm on the cardinal's face. As he walked, he sent a message on his mobile phone, the message read: *the Italian* – the codename they were using for their ward – *is leaving. Not happy. Something's up*. The message was sent to two people, a man in Scotland who looked a little like Sean Connery with a slight Scottish accent, and the cardinal's driver, the other member of the protection team, the Templar, Dominique Rose.

The car engine was already running when they got outside, Father Declan did not notice this, but the cardinal did. His instincts fired warning messages inside his head. He saw the litter bin at the bottom of the steps, to the right of the waiting car. He walked over to it and pretended to put something in. Now he turned and was able to approach the car from the front – he wanted to get a good look at the driver. Her head was down but then she lifted it as he approached. The cardinal looked at her through the windscreen, it was longer than he should have, longer than he wanted to. He'd let himself down, he knew better. A look would last a second or two, but a look of recognition would last longer. His lasted longer. *Did she notice it?* he thought. *Did she recognise me? No, surely not, she was too young.*

The cardinal got into the back of the car, and Father Declan followed him. The man St Clair called the Lionheart, Cameron Jack, who was their other protector, sat in the front with the driver, Dominique.

A senior member of the UK Government Communications Headquarters, GCHQ, Proctor Hutchinson, had also advised on the Communications Electronic Security Group, CESG. He was also known and respected within MI5. Proctor Hutchinson had also been a member of the Order of the Knights Templar since the age of twenty-nine. And, for a number of years, one of the Nine Worthies, but of course, his employers were not aware of this fact. When the Vatican sent a request to MI5 for support with the protection of the cardinal during his visit, a number of people across the security services were consulted. Hutchinson saw it. He waited for a couple of hours before suggesting the use of the organisation known to the UK's Secret Intelligence Service as Pi. From time to time, like secret intelligence services all over the world, the UK's SIS used private, outside agencies that had Omega 1 clearance, to carry out certain classified assignments. The thing that made Pi substantially unique was that it truly was an unknown source. However, it was known to have advanced intel and a communications network that spread worldwide. Both MI5 and MI6 approved using Pi. The telephone call was placed in the usual way, via the normal covert lines; the call was then re-routed to an unknown address in Islington.

As they pulled away from the 'City of London and Boroughs University of Law', Father Declan told the cardinal that their things had already been gathered from their hotel rooms, packed and their cases were waiting for them in the foyer. He said they could collect their luggage on the way to Heathrow Airport. He told the cardinal they were booked on the first available flight back to Rome; they had just over two hours to get to the airport and check in.

Del Luca asked the driver to raise the glass partition that would separate the front of the car from the back. The driver obliged and the partition slowly ascended. She did not look into the rear mirror once. *She suspects*, he thought.

They were in free-flowing traffic, the weather was good and they were making good time. Father Declan was busy typing a message on his mobile phone to Father Ronan, informing him that the cardinal had been called away and to leave London when he could and return to Rome. He told Father Ronan that they would cancel all other engagements. Father Declan did not elaborate – he would have struggled to know what to say without it sounding absurd: Father Ronan was not one of them!

"I need my phone please, Father Declan," the cardinal asked. Father Declan handed the cardinal his mobile phone. The cardinal searched the contacts folder on his phone, looking for the letter C, and then the name *crucesignati* – crusader came up. He rang the number, the number St Clair had given him on their call during the Paradiso arrest.

*

The controller called St Clair on his mobile phone. She told him that she'd carried out the checks and confirmed it was Cardinal Gino Del Luca; she put the cardinal through. The conversation was short. Billy Jack, the Templars' Sergeant at Arms, was in the room. He only heard St Clair's side of the conversation and he didn't know with whom the Grand Master was talking to.

"I didn't think we would be speaking so s—"

Billy Jack assumed the caller had just interrupted St Clair and told him he had called for a different reason, or something had changed.

"When? Are you alright?" St Clair asked, now with a concerned voice. "Do you know who ordered the assassination attempt?"

Billy Jack did not hear the answer.

"Are you sure about the post-mortem? Are you one hundred per cent positive?"

Again, Billy Jack did not hear the answer.

"I see?"

Billy Jack saw the effect the answer from the person on the other end of the phone, had on St Clair. St Clair was clearly rattled. The caller asked St Clair a question.

"No, I have not known post-mortem results like this," St Clair told the caller. "But I have read about it."

The caller spoke.

"Yes, I have a copy of the book, *Morto Vivente*."

The caller spoke again.

"I know copies are rare, but I did not know only three were left. I assume you have one, I have one ... that leaves just one more. Do you know who has it?"

Again, Billy Jack did not hear the answer, nor did he know what *Morto Vivente* meant, but he saw the look on St Clair's face.

"Okay." St Clair continued. "I will call you later tonight, there are some friends I need to talk to. I will call around midnight, US east coast time." Templars often gave times in a different time zone to where they were, a simple ploy but it would often confuse the other party into thinking they were somewhere they weren't. "I suggest you stay in the UK, Cardinal. Stick to your agenda, let's not raise the alarm or suspicion." St Clair then ended the call. He kept his mobile phone in his hand and typed an SMS to Jonathan, it read:

Priest.

Can you get here straight away, we have a big problem.

Watch your back. Bring the dogs with you and lock down your home, you may be here for a while.

St Clair rang the Controller back. Tiffany Clarke, in Islington, was expecting the call, she was expecting a flurry of calls.

"Tiff, call them, call all the Higher Council together, we're going to need them. Get them here as quickly as possible, tonight, or early morning at the latest. If they can't make it or they are abroad, arrange to have them join by conference call. Tiff, can you make it here yourself, I'll need you?" Tiffany Clarke had recently been appointed to the Higher Council, she confirmed she could. "Good. Make the calls then catch your train." Then St Clair turned to Billy Jack, "we have to get ready, Billy; it's beginning."

Billy Jack didn't know what was beginning, but he knew from St Clair's tone and a sudden air of urgency that whatever it was, it wasn't good.

*

When Cardinal Gino Del Luca had finished his call with St Clair, he tapped the glass lightly and the screen came down. He apologised to the driver and asked to be taken back to the hotel. He also said that they were resuming the schedule as planned.

Father Declan, like Billy Jack in Scotland, had only heard one-half of the conversation. "We are not leaving for Rome, your Eminence?" he whispered.

"No, Declan, I think we are staying, we have evil to fight ..." he thought for a moment or two, "and perhaps with new friends." Now he leant in close to Father Declan. "Call the Watchers, Declan. Tell them I believe our journey might finally be coming to an end."

*

Later that night

They were sitting in the reception area of the cardinal's hotel. Their wards were safely tucked away for the night in their rooms. The two Templars planned to hang around for a few hours, one of them would get some sleep in a room they had booked at the hotel, then they would relieve the other after three hours.

He knew something was niggling her, she'd been quiet all day, ever since they had picked up the cardinal and his aide from their lecture. Cameron Jack knew that behind those mirrored Ray Bans – which, when she was on a job, she was rarely without, even

91

in the evenings – something was going on. He knew her as a Templar, a 7th Dan in Karate, a skilled shooter who favoured a Heckler Koch .40 and a pump-action 12-gauge shotgun, designed for smaller shooters. Inside her shoulder rig, she also carried a backup gun with a 13-round magazine. She was small and petite with short mousy brown hair. She was a skilled Backgammon player. Her mother had been Italian, a maths professor and a Templar. Her mother had also been a Seer. But he had got to know her more of late because he was a frequent visitor to their cottage. His friendship with Jonathan had flourished and he was often invited to dinner, toasted ravioli and Dolcetto red wine. The three of them would either sit and talk late into the night or watch old black and white movies together. He knew her well now, so he knew the 'Guardian of the Seer', was rattled about something. She was pacing the floor; she seemed distant.

"Do you want to tell me what's going on?" Cameron Jack finally asked her.

"I don't know ... it's probably nothing. But ..."

"But?"

"But ... maybe. I'm not sure but I think he made me."

"Who made you?"

"The cardinal."

"There was nothing that would have raised his suspicion. We played it straight, two secret service operatives on a job. We played it cool, no drama."

"I know, that's what makes it so strange. I've gone over and over it in my head, we did nothing out of the ordinary."

"Then, if he made you, and we did nothing to alert him, he must know you?"

"No. I don't know him; I've never seen him before."

"You sure? No disrespect to the cardinal but a bunch of old guys wearing red and white frocks and a small red skull cap all tend to look the same."

"Zucchetto."

"Excuse me?"

The skull cap is a Zucchetto ... but you are right, they do tend to look the same. Even so, I think I would have recognised him if I'd seen him before, I have a pretty good memory."

"Tell me why you think he made you."

"He held his gaze too long. Just before he got in the car, he looked at me and he held his stare a little too long. It wasn't a casual stare, it was..., well, it was recognition."

"If you are right and you have never seen him, it means he knows you but you don't know him." Cameron Jack thought for a moment. "Shall we call Scotland?"

"No. Let's wait for a while and see how it plays out, it's probably nothing." Despite her words, she could not get the blurry picture out of her head of a priest holding a blanket, standing in front of her but she had no recollection of it or even if it was a memory at all. "Listen, I'll take the first watch," she said, "you go get some sleep. I'll let you know if anything happens."

Cameron Jack went to bed but didn't get much sleep.

Chapter 7

A Dead Man Walking

Place: Glennfinch castle. The remote castle in Scotland
Time: 3 a.m. the following morning

Glennfinch Castle had electricity and had done so for many years, however, the great hall always smelt of burning wax. The Higher Council of the Knights Templar held their meetings by candlelight – tradition important in Templar life. The atmosphere conjured by their light and shadows was always intoxicating and somehow, it was right for their meetings and the serious subjects they discussed.

Reverence and veneration were everywhere at Glennfinch. There were places inside the castle that were consecrated ground, embodiments of spiritual grace. There were sanctuaries that were as sacred as the innermost subterranean passageways and catacombs of the Temple Mount itself, the Holy of Holies in Jerusalem.

Tapestries depicting medieval adventure and stoic heroism decorated the tall stone walls of the great hall. History radiated from every direction. Carved into the large stone hearth where a fire raged, were the words, *Nil nisi clavis deest, Templum Hierosolyma, clavis ad thesaurum, theca ubi res pretiosa deponitur* – Nothing is wanted but the key, the Temple of Jerusalem, the key to the treasure, a place where a precious thing is concealed. The same Latin inscription that once adorned a precious jewel held by the Royal Arch of Freemasonry many centuries ago.

The Worthies were pious people, dedicated to the holy vows of righteousness; warrior monks who worked in the shadows, dedicated to the sacred science of the Qumran – the original Nazarene Church. At the head of the great hall hung the Baussant, the black and white chequered war banner of the Knights Templar.

The Nine Worthies of the Higher Council represented the Order of the Knights Templar, the most secret Order of ancient and modern times; it had remained hidden from the eyes of the world for centuries. They seldom met; they had too many secrets to protect. They seldom came together face-to-face because the risk was too high. The death of André Sabath, thirteen Knights in Abu Dhabi, five in Romania and the death of Nickolin Klymachak, the Russian, just last year, had the ultra-secret group on high alert, on code red. No one was taking any chances: the problem was, they were expected to take chances!

*

It was late. They started the meeting late. It took the whole night of the 18th and early into the morning of the 19th to arrange for them all to attend the meeting. Because of the differing time zones, some were asleep, others were about their daily routines: in meetings, jogging, picking up the mail; one was on a commercial flight above the Red Sea. However, by 3 a.m. they had gathered, the Higher Council of the Knights Templar, the Nine Worthies, some in person, others that could not make it, attended via video conferencing.

Inside the great hall, in person or on wall-mounted screens, they waited for him, Knights who worked in the shadows to keep their 'Charge' safe, the Ark of the Covenant, and to protect those that needed their help.

St Clair had promised to call the cardinal by midnight, US east coast time. It was now 3 a.m. UK time. At 5 a.m. it would be midnight on the east coast. They had two hours to meet, discuss and decide. There was much to discuss. Much at stake. Much to decide. They all knew there would be sanctions to consider – the process they used to decide and vote on the taking of lives. They would not rush those decisions, they never did. He knew that but he knew time was not on their side.

Inside the great hall they had already donned their white surcoats with the distinctive red cross, during their initial welcoming ceremony of intoning chants and secret gestures. Now, those present sat around the long mahogany table which dominated the great hall of Glennfinch Castle, the others looked down from their wall-mounted screens, but they all waited for their Grand Master to arrive.

As was his way, St. Clair had paused in the flagstone hallway, outside the door that led into the great hall. He checked his dress in the tall 17th century French mirror hanging on the stone wall. And as always, he checked and adjusted his white surcoat, centralising the distinctive red cross. He took a deep breath.

He needed to hold two meetings in two hours. The first meeting would be held in the great hall, only the Worthies would attend this meeting because the content was highly secret, it contained restricted information; it was Higher Council only. The second meeting would be held in one of the larger meeting rooms in another part of the castle where Jonathan and Aldrich would join the Worthies.

St Clair turned the black iron ring handle, the door groaned and creaked and he entered the great hall.

Once inside he took his seat at the head of the table. Four Worthies were seated at the table, four others had dialled in via their secure video conferencing network, St Clair made the ninth: the Nine Worthies.

After the ceremony of welcome was complete, they each took the Eucharist, the embodiment of Christ. Then St. Clair eased himself out of the high-backed, black Jacobean chair to address them. He stood tall and proud; he personified reverence and dignity. "My Brothers, my Sister, Knights, by God's grace we are called again. May our Lord watch over this Council and give us the wisdom we will need." He sat back down and lowered his head in respect. They all sat in silence. Their prayers were silent. The vows they had taken, and for some taken many years ago, were explicit and absolute. They left no room for compromise, no second thought. Once pledged, they were forever followed. They had all made many sacrifices over the years, but their lives were not theirs; they had already given them to the holy Order of the Knights Templar.

After a while, again St Clair eased himself out of the high-backed Jacobean chair to address them. "Knights of our Order, there are four items before this Council, I must warn you that one of them, item three, will shock and alarm you. However, we should be shocked and alarmed because of the devastating, destructive impact it will have on us, on our Order, on the world if we are unable to defeat it."

Serious faces looked on at their Grand Master. None of them knew what was coming. Bodies tightened; faces now grave, stern and sombre. No one looked at one another, they all looked at their Grand Master.

"First though, Item one. This one is all but resolved. It is the Paradiso affair. Zakariah has kept you all up to date with our mission with Nef. I think our work there is all but done, it's now down to his Holiness the Pope to decide what to do with Paradiso. In the meantime, Nef has him firmly locked away. They have enough evidence to lock him up and throw away the key for good. My thanks, our Order's thanks and congratulations to the Templar team that helped Nef trap and arrest this criminal. It was a good job, well executed and, our anonymity remains intact."

The others nodded in agreement.

"However, that said," St Clair now continued, "there is one thing that I have to clarify to this Council. To you. One thing that I must tell you because only a few of you know, those who have served on this Council for a long time."

Some knew what was coming but the others didn't; they waited.

"The spear of Longinus that Paradiso tried to steal, well, it was not the real spear of Longinus."

"You swapped the real one for the meeting with the thieves in Barcelona?" a Worthy asked from a wall-mounted screen.

"No, it was the spearhead the Vatican had, the one they thought was the real one." It was clear St Clair knew something the Vatican didn't.

"Then, does the real one still exist?" one of the Council asked.

"It does," St Clair confirmed.

"And do you know who has it?" he asked.

"I do."

Luther asked the question. "Who?"

"Me. I have it," St Clair said. He paused, then added, "it is the reason I became a Templar."

Now, most wanted to ask questions. There was a wave of voices.

"Knights." St Clair held up his hand. "I will tell you when we have more time; there are far more pressing matters before us right now, as you will soon see. Just know it is safe and less than five hundred yards from this great hall, from where the five of us sit right now."

The other Worthies went quiet again.

"We must get through our agenda because for our last item we will be moving to one of the meeting rooms to talk about what Del Luca said to the Priest in Rome and what the cross he gave him might mean. For that, we will be joined by two others. But right now, let's get to item two, Gowst."

He turned to the wall-mounted screen that held the image of John Edison, the Worthy in Barbados who ran their forensic accounting team that was based there. "John?"

John Edison's voice was clear, despite the four thousand miles that separated him from the meeting in the great hall. "Despite our best efforts, there has been no progress in our search for Zivko Cesar Gowst, *Le Fantome Blanc* – The White Ghost. The trail has gone cold and all our efforts have resulted in dead ends so far. We have exhausted all our forensic financial investigations and whatever we have found out about his shell companies, bank accounts and money flow, is useless now because he's closed them all down, everything. We have our Knights at our satellite stations looking for anything that will help us find out where Gowst is. Our eyes and ears on the ground are looking for anything that will help us." Each station was run by a small band of men and women, Knights running electronic surveillance and data capture operations.

"We will stay vigilant because one thing I think we all believe is he will come out of the woodwork soon. Men like that cannot stay hidden forever, and when he does, we will be waiting for him."

The other Council members all nodded in agreement. Then slowly it went silent again. They turned back to their Grand Master: they had come to item three. He didn't disappoint.

"The reason I called this emergency Council meeting was because of a call I received some hours ago. The call was from Cardinal Del Luca. You will remember we needed his help with the arrest of Paradiso, so I called him. He told me on that call that he would call me when he returned back to Rome after his lecture tour here in the UK. That call was on the 15th, just three days ago. He's still here in the UK but earlier today he called me out of the blue. What he told me has meant that I have needed to call you altogether because it changes everything. I explained to him there were people I needed to consult with, so we agreed I would call him later. We now need to decide what we are going to do. I am going to suggest that we meet, in London, later today. I have already asked the Lionheart and Dominique to find us a safe location to meet him. Thanks to Proctor and MI5, they are with the cardinal right now acting as his close protection unit."

"And the subject of his call, Grand Master? What has you so rattled?" a Worthy asked. They all knew their Grand Master did not get spooked easily, but it was clear that he was seriously concerned, they wanted to share his burden; they wanted to know what had got him so concerned.

"*Morto Vivente.*" St Clair said with trepidation in his voice.

The portentous words left his lips and an ominous feeling descended on the meeting.

Some knew what it meant, but not all.

"First he told me that there had been an assassination attempt on his life a couple of weeks ago, it was not the first."

The Worthies spoke amongst themselves again in hushed whispers. Their words carried like distant echoes in the great hall.

"One of his own protection detail, an imposter priest, who had hidden inside the Catholic clergy for nine years." St Clair continued.

"A sleeper," Proctor Hutchinson said.

"A very deep sleeper. This was a long-term plan," Luther said. "Can you imagine the patience and resolve needed to go undercover for all those years?" he shook his head.

"He had two accomplices," St Clair went on. "Obviously, they failed and they are all dead. The cardinal arranged for an autopsy to be carried out on the bodies. Today, he was given the autopsy results. The two assailants died from gunshot wounds. This, and their time of death matched their demise. The sleeper had a stab wound directly into his heart. It punctured the heart completely. Yet the coroner's report said that he had died from electrocution, and scars on his wrists, ankles and scalp were commensurate with the electric chair. The coroner recorded the time of death, twenty years ago."

They all waited. Those that had already guessed what was coming, because they had read *Morto Vivente,* started to move uneasily in their seats. Their pious eyes looked around at the other Knights.

"*Morto Vivente* means living dead. The book is the only account we know of, where a person died and then was found months later on a different continent, alive. The case remains unsolved to this day."

"Is this even possible?" One of the Worthies asked from a wall-mounted screen.

"The Ark saved the Priest," St Clair told him. "He was dead. Shot. Bled out."

"But that's the Ark."

"Enoch and Elijah went to heaven without dying. Water got turned into wine; a blind man sees; a dead man rises ... We don't know everything that is out there. We don't know what's possible and what's not possible; maybe everything is possible.

"But it gets worse, Knights. There are only three copies of the book left. We have one, the cardinal has one and when I asked him if he knew who had the third copy of the book, he said yes, he told me it was the same person who had ordered his assassination a few weeks ago. The same person who had tried to have him killed two months earlier. When I asked who this person was, he said he would not speak his name but I was to look toward the second

Epistle, to the Thessalonians 2:3."

Now the Worthies realised the full gravity of the situation – all but Luther Jones.

St Clair told them they would need to vote on far-reaching sanctions this time; they may need to take a number of lives.

"Our pursuit of Gowst has already cost us dearly. We have already lost so many Knights, but I want to propose a blanket sanction against any and all associates of Gowst and any and all that threaten our Order, our 'Charge' or any civilians. These are strange days we are moving into; dark foes await us."

The sanction he was proposing was a sanction to cover all. Normally, only named people would be targets for a sanction. However, St Clair was acutely aware they had not seen the last of Gowst and felt he was somehow connected with what the cardinal had told him. He knew he would have to ask more Knights to risk their lives as part of the sanction team. He told them that the sanction team would have to include all 'active' Knights because they just didn't know who would strike first and from where. He fell silent and waited for their decision.

There was no heavy, protracted debate like normal, this time approval of the sanction team was instant, and they showed it in their usual manner: each on the Council made the sign of the cross across their white surcoats and in unison, they whispered, "by God's grace and by His word, that which was cast in stone, we humbly seek your forgiveness. Amen."

It was now time for them to vote on the sanction itself. Despite agreeing on the sanction team, the sanction itself was always left until last. The Order was steeped in tradition and ceremony. St. Clair made his case one more time, and then each of the eight Worthies would remain seated, to signify their approval, or they would get up and leave their chairs, signifying their disapproval. Every sanction had to be unanimous.

Nobody left their seats, approval was given.

*

The Council meeting lasted just under two hours. St Clair had little time to spare. The Worthies quickly changed out of their formal dress and started to make their way to the next meeting room. Quietly they walked along the flagstone corridors of the castle. Those who had dialled in via video conferencing were already transferred onto wall-mounted screens in the new meeting room.

Outside, the first blushed pink fingers of daylight were reaching upwards and their light piercing through the stained-glass windows of the castle, cast an array of striking colours.

Luther was thoughtful as he left the great hall. He had so many questions but he didn't want to keep asking questions in the Council meeting. He was a Worthy now and he would be expected to figure it out; but more so, he expected that of himself. He let the others walk on. He slowed down. He found a quiet spot. He would catch up in a short while. He took out his mobile phone and selected her number. He sent her a message, it read 'you free?'. A message came back in a few seconds, 'here, what's up?' he called her number.

"How's it going?" he asked her.

"Quiet," Dominique said. "I think the cardinal's awake but he's still in his room."

"And the Lionheart?"

"Bored but sleeping now. I took first watch." She was waiting in the reception area of the cardinal's hotel. St Clair had told her that he and the cardinal had spoken and that he intended to speak to the cardinal again. Depending on that call, the cardinal might still be delivering the second lecture, but then there would be a meeting with him, in London later, and at the venue St Clair had asked them to find.

"What's up?" she asked Luther.

"I like to think I am a pious man," he started, "but I am a soldier and ... well ... I don't always understand a biblical reference."

"Jonathan's not there, is he?"

"No, he's in one of the meeting rooms waiting for us. Why?"

"Because you all go to him if there's a Bible question. You only come to me if he's not about," she laughed. "Don't tell him I told you, but he's had to start reading it again because he's so worried that one day he won't know an answer to a question."

"I would have ... well—"

"What do you want to ask me, Luther? Just spit it out."

"Second Epistle to the Thessalonians 2:3, what is it?" he blurted out. He could not see Dominique's expression, but he felt the change, it was grave and serious. The joking had gone.

There was no one else in the reception area – no early check-outs, or early check-ins. The night porter was in the back making coffee. Despite the fact she was alone, she cupped her hand over her mouth and the phone and spoke quietly. "2 Thessalonians 2:3 tells of the coming of the Man of Lawlessness; he is called the 'Man of Sin', in other versions, the 'Man of Perdition or the Son of Destruction."

It dawned on Luther. "I'm guessing the Son of Destruction is ..."

"You're guessing right, Luther. He is the Antichri—"

"I got it," Luther said interrupting her. "I got it, you don't need to say it." He turned and started to walk slowly towards the next meeting room.

She didn't ask him why he wanted to know – though she wanted to, she so desperately wanted to know. She knew that she would be told when and if she needed to be told. Information was not freely shared. She belonged to the most secret Order in the world, so secret it did not exist. Information was always on a need-to-know basis: lives depended on it; their 'Charge' depended on it. She was about to hang up but she couldn't, she had to ask.

"Luther." Her voice seemed even more serious now and was tinged with emotion. The one St Clair called the Girl, was not known for outward displays of emotions. When Jonathan had first met the small petite woman with short mousy brown hair, he'd liked her a lot, despite her caustic manner towards him. She was pretty, intelligent and had a presence he really liked. He had a sense that there was a softer side to her nature that she rarely showed. In some ways, she reminded him of his sister Courtney. She seemed to have the same drive, same focus and ambition. Her skin was tanned, like Courtney's, although slightly darker. She always smelt nice, something he had noticed that first day. Now the hardened Knight, the Girl, could not help her emotions slipping out for a second or two.

"Luther, if this is going to ..." she began hesitantly, "if this is going to involve my husband, if Jonathan needs to be in the centre of it, please let me be the one to tell him. He is not like the rest of us. We have seen a lot of things Luther, but ... but he has not. He was a priest; he spent his days as a priest-school teacher. You know how he'll get if he hears what I think is coming our way, is coming his way!"

*

St Clair was running out of time. It was late. They were all tired. He had to call the cardinal and yet there was still so much to get to.

The Worthies had moved into one of the larger meeting rooms. Jonathan was waiting for them. He'd been asked to join them because of his conversation with Del Luca after the death of the Hag. They had all received his report, of course, but they needed to hear it directly from him. St Clair told them they had to understand the cardinal's conversation with the Priest when he and the others left Rome for the airport.

"Anybody who knows anything about us already knows too much. Anyone who knows what the cardinal seems to know is a danger to us, a big danger," Tiffany Clarke said.

St Clair turned to Jonathan. "The Priest furnished us all with his report, which gave us the details of his conversation with Del Luca in Rome. I now want us to hear directly from the Priest, our Seer. I want to judge the tone of the interaction, his body language and anything else that will tell us more about the cardinal's intent." He indicated to Jonathan to stand.

Jonathan stood to his feet. He reached for the coins in his pocket and started to jangle them – it was his 'tell'; his giveaway that he was nervous. St Clair put up a copy of the report on a large wall monitor and he shared his screen with those Worthies that had dialled in by video conference call. The report was the one he had written after Del Luca's conversations with him, St Clair had emailed it to each of the Worthies at the time.

REPORT: Meeting with Cardinal Del Luca
Just before the slaying of the witch, the Gwrach Marwolaeth Hag, Cardinal Gino Del Luca had arranged to meet me first before the others had arrived.

I didn't know why.

The Cardinal told me he knew who 'we' were, and it certainly seemed that he did! This is what he said, '... you think we didn't know?' He told me to remember that before I spoke [answered], I was to remember my words would go from my lips to God's ears in a millisecond.

Stalling, I asked him what it was he thought he knew, and he replied, 'the Templars were not wiped out'. He also said that the original nine Knights, who were sent to the Holy Land to protect the Christian pilgrims, went for another reason, not what history books teach, but a more secret one.

He told me that the Knights' quest was to search for and then rescue the lost Ark of the Covenant. '... when the Ark was found, we think', and here he did say 'we', 'that the Templars, like the inner sanctum of the Holy of Holies, formed their own inner sanctum, an inner circle, a cabal, a council. And its reason for being was to protect the Ark at all cost'.

He then spoke about the year 1307, here are the bullet points:

1. *'... we think in 1307, the Cabal, sworn to protect their 'Charge', escaped from France via the port of La Rochelle and disappeared from the eyes of the world*

2. *He said, 'actually, Father, we don't think this, we know this'.*

I asked him how he knew that I used to be a priest. He told me, 'in the same way that I knew your name; the same way I knew what Luther was; the same way that I know what you all protect'.

He told me that I was not the only one with a secret, not the only one with senza volto cabal, Dominique told me it means 'a faceless cabal'.

When the cardinal walked me to the car that he'd organised to take me, Luther and Aldrich to the airport, he said the following, 'we will talk soon, you and I. There is much for us to discuss'. Then he gave me the small wooden cross. All we know for now is that it is very old and has a faint engraving of a crown of thorns and in the middle of the crown of thorns, a small rose.

Jonathan told the Worthies that he had not confirmed anything to Del Luca. "The last thing he said to me as I got into the car taking us to the airport was, 'we will talk soon, you and I because there is much for us to discuss'. Then he gave me the small wooden cross and said, 'to keep you safe, my son'. I thanked him and we left."

"I agree with Tiff, it is clear the cardinal knows a lot about us. Too much." Proctor Hutchinson started, his voice and image coming from one of the wall-mounted screens – he was in London because he was not able to get to Scotland in time. "He said he knew who we were; about La Rochelle, he said you didn't think we didn't know? He said we don't think this, we know this; he is part of a Cabal. This is all very, very worrying." The others nodded in agreement.

"What do you think, Jonathan?" Tiffany asked. "You're the one who has spent the most amount of time with him. How much do you think he really knows?"

"He told me he had read the Interrogation Roll, kept in the French National Archives. He said the sixteen-mile-long scroll, handwritten on dozens of individual sheets of parchment and then all finely stitched together by hand, was an account of the Templars' interrogations. But he knew more. More about King Philip IV of France, Philip the Fair. I know, it's all information that is out there but, he told me that the Templars were not wiped out. He said the original nine Knights who, it was said, were sent to the Holy Land to protect the Christian pilgrims, actually went for another reason, 'not the quest our history books teach', he said, 'but a more secret one. Their quest was to search for and then rescue the lost Ark of the Covenant. It wasn't taken by the Babylonians, and neither was it in Axum, in Ethiopia; it was still in Jerusalem'. He told me the Templars who found it formed an inner circle, a cabal, a council. And, its reason,' he said, 'was to protect the Ark'."

"Obviously, we need to find out what else he knows," Tiffany said. "I get the impression he didn't tell Jonathan everything he knows and I suspect he knows quite a lot," she added.

"Almost like he'd heard all of this from one of us, from one of our own, a Templar!" John Edison's image again sharp and clear on the wall-mounted screen, despite the four thousand miles between them. "Perhaps we have a leak?" he added. It's what they were all thinking now.

"Then I will ask him," St Clair said. "But we really need to find out what the cross with the crown of thorns and the rose means, and if he knows you are the Seer, Priest. I have Aldrich waiting on the other line, let me call him in, I want him to join in with this conversation." Aldrich was extremely knowledgeable on the history of religions, mainstream and many of the more obscure ones. He was also an expert on the occult, especially medieval occultism. St Clair hit the red flashing light of line 3 on the multi-buttoned black desk phone, it turned green. He thanked Aldrich for staying up so late and for waiting on the line for them. Aldrich was not on video conferencing, he was on a landline and so could not see the others, but he could hear them as St Clair had him on loudspeaker. No names would be used now during the discussion: Aldrich was not a Templar.

St Clair told Aldrich they needed to try and find out what the cross meant, the cross Del Luca had given to Jonathan before the Templar team had left Rome.

"I think I have an idea what it might mean, well, but I don't want to cloud the discussion right now. Let's listen to everyone's opinions first. Let's see where a bit of blue-sky thinking might get us on this one."

A discussion broke out about its most likely meaning. As a Council, most were knowledgeable in religious history and doctrine – in the law and the lore of all of the major religions because of the glaring repetitive crossover and replication and very close similarities of many of their main stories and central tenets! One Worthy thought the cross was not significant, a token, a gesture. There are many crosses, he argued. Crosses of all shapes and sizes, this probably was just another. Two others joined him in that thought and made a good case for it and for a while, that view seemed to dominate the discussion. However, slowly the thought that the cross was perhaps more than a token or a gesture, took hold and that soon developed into the likelihood that it was very significant. One of the Worthies quoted Genesis 3:18, and then Mathew 27:29 and John

19:2-5. Someone suggested Mark 15:17. They talked about their possible interpretations, the hidden meanings, opaque metaphors and verse allegories within the verse texts in relation to the cross, the crown and the rose. It became clear to them that you could pretty much interpret and adapt any of those verses to fit the cross.

"Perhaps there is merit in looking at the real crown of thorns held in Notre Dame Cathedral." someone asked from a wall-mounted screen.

"Too obvious," Proctor said. "So is the fact that the red rose symbolises the shedding of Christ's blood. But then again, Isaiah 35:1 tells us that *the desert shall bloom like the rose* and some believe that the mystical rose is the poetic title of Mary. Not helpful because she had a litany of other titles and names."

St Clair looked at his watch. They were running out of time. He needed to call the cardinal.

Aldrich's voice drew their gaze to the multi-buttoned black desk phone with the green light on line 3.

"I would look at only two places for the possible meaning of the cross with the rose and crown of thorns."

Everyone went silent, they were waiting to hear the eccentric, Cambridge professor's suggestion. His voice, as stern as ever, roared with bravado, confidence and high jinks over the phone's speaker. It was sharp, it was haughty, like an ex-public-schoolboy who had become a parody of himself in adulthood, complete with a mix of an ageing colonel and an eccentric landed gent.

He took his time, but finally. "The first is the Rosicross of course, the Rosicrucian Fellowship, the Fraternitas Rosae Cross or more commonly known as, Rosicrucianism. There was a lot of fuss about them back in the 17th century because they wove Gnosticism, Hermeticism and mysticism from the Jews and a large helping of Christianity and occultism thrown in. Some say Sir Francis Bacon was the Lord Chancellor of the Rosicrucian order, but I don't think anyone knows for sure. Anyway, if that's its origin then you will need a lot of luck to determine its meaning because Rosicrucianism is notoriously vague on interpretation and elucidation. Not a fan myself. I say, if you can't articulate, shut up!" He paused as if his statement warranted a dramatic pause, as if the others needed to catch up. They waited. Then they waited some more. He took time to build the suspense of his second suggestion; it was a bit too long for some.

"And the second," Jonathan asked, somewhat impatiently.

"Ah, Corpse old boy, I'd recognise that colonial accent anywhere."

St Clair smiled – Aldrich always cheered him up with his eccentricity.

"Well, now that you asked. I would say that the meaning of the cross is none of the above. I saw it in the car when we were going to the airport and I had an opportunity to look at it closely because you kindly let me study it for a while. It is obviously old, very, very old. I would suggest far, far older than Rosicrucianism. I would suggest its age is the key to its meaning. However, I don't think you, or I will ever know it's true meaning. Only Cardinal Del Luca knows that and he will tell you dear Corpse, just as soon as he is ready.

"The problem we have, is that there is no starting point to it, no reference point to link it to, so you will never guess its significance or its true meaning. You need a least one anchor point to get you going. I suggest you all wait for the cardinal to tell you what it means, that's my counsel."

What he said made perfect sense to everyone. St Clair thanked Aldrich for his time; he promised to let him know what it actually meant, as soon they knew, then wished Aldrich good morning. Aldrich left the meeting and the green light on line 3 went out.

St Clair waited for a second or two, and then he spoke again. "The Priest and I discussed this some weeks back and I think this is linked to the sixth prophecy: *The flower of the martyrs and the plaited crown shall join to battle 'El S'hhan te Abyann' for the way back.* The red rose is sometimes the sign of the martyrs because red signifies the blood they have shed. And a plaited crown?" St Clair turned to Jonathan.

"Matthew 27:29," Jonathan started. *"And when they plaited a crown of thorns, they put it upon his head ... And they bowed the knee before him and mocked him, saying Hail, King of the Jews."*

"Then the red rose means the martyrs" Proctor Hutchinson announced. "The flower of the martyrs, the rose. And of course, the crown of thorns is Jesus Christ."

"Perhaps," St Clair replied. "Perhaps."

"Whoever they are, they will join to battle *El S'hhan te Abyann*, who or what is *El S'hhan te Abyann*?" Luther Jones asked, Dominique's words of his earlier phone call still ringing in his ears.

Everyone waited.

"We do not know," St Clair told them. "That phrase has never been translated because no one has ever been able to trace or determine what language it is. The closest we have come to its origin is when a particularly gifted professor of ancient languages in Israel, suggested it was most likely an archaic form of an Aramaic dialect.

"As for which or what battle, well, the Priest and I believe it is linked to *the way back* referenced in the prophecy." He let this sink in for a moment or two.

"And *Morto Vivente,* living dead," Luther said, "and the second Epistle to the Thessalonians 2:3, all this leads you to the same conclusion about the way back and the battle?"

Jonathan heard Luther but didn't understand it, then he wished he'd not heard it. He had not been in the meeting when St Clair had explained. This was the first time he had heard the expression living dead. For a moment he thought it was a reference to him: he'd died, and now he was living: living dead. Then he heard 'second Epistle to the Thessalonians' and he knew it was not him!

Their Grand Master rose from his seat. He looked around at his Knights; at the people sitting in the room and those on the wall-mounted screens. "It does, Luther. Search your hearts Knights. We all know who is meant to come back: *the way back*. And we all know who will try and stop that from happening, *the battle*, and what Thessalonians 2:3 refers to."

Everyone got it at the very same time. Everyone went deathly silent.

*

Place: Glennfinch castle, Scotland
Time: 5:30 a.m. on the 19th

He'd started the first meeting, his meeting with the Higher Council at 3 a.m. It was now 5:30 a.m. he'd been awake for almost two days. To maintain his ruse, he would refer to the time as 12:30 a.m. east coast time.

St Clair hoped he might come to know Cardinal Del Luca better and perhaps, at some point trust him, he would like that. The Templars trusted few, mistrusted most, disbelieved many, and were weary and suspicious of the remainder: it had kept most of their Knights safe over many centuries and had kept the Ark from falling into the wrong hands, the hands of criminals, and the hands of those who had embraced evil and would use it for criminal or malevolent reasons.

"Did I wake you?" St Clair asked him.

"No, I've been waiting for your call."

"I'm sorry I'm late and that it is so early for you."

"And so late for you."

"Indeed."

"Did you speak to your friends?" the cardinal asked.

"I did. My friends agree with me, we will help you."

St Clair suggested they meet in London after the second of Del Luca's lectures which would take place that morning. He told Del Luca he had found a safe place for them to meet, a café near London Bridge train station. The cardinal agreed but said he wanted Jonathan to be there. St Clair understood and agreed. He also said he would arrange for Aldrich Manwin Tucker, the Cambridge professor, to be there because they might need him. St Clair heard the cardinal chuckle at this.

"I was hoping you were going to say that Aldrich would be there, my son."

St Clair then gave him the time and place for their meeting later that afternoon in London.

"Will you be there?" the cardinal asked.

St Clair smiled to himself, *nice try* he thought. "I couldn't get there in time."

"Ah, of course," the cardinal replied, "you are in a different continent. Maybe next time then. But, as you and I are not meeting, do you think you can share with me who you and your friends are?"

"Oh, I think you already know, Cardinal." St Clair said. He thought he heard a slight, muffled chuckle from the cardinal. "Can I ask, did you learn so much about us from one of our own?"

The pause was only three seconds, but it seemed a lot longer to St Clair. Then the cardinal answered. "Yes. From one who knew all your truths, my son."

St Clair knew that if he asked the cardinal who the person was, he wouldn't tell him. But he had to try. "Might I know his name?"

"You know his name!"

"Mmm. Well, as you have me at a disadvantage, perhaps you might tell me who you and your friends are?"

"Ah, we are very few these days, my son," the cardinal said ruefully. "But you see we have only ever been here for you, for your Order. And when our work is done, we will be no more."

Chapter 8

Head for the Mountains

Date: 1314 – over 700 years ago
Place: A small friary on the island of Île de la Cité
Time: Night-time

Fortunately, the burnished lunar light was now veiled by gathering clouds sweeping westward. *le Chevalier* – Friar Pablo – had wrapped the donkeys' hooves with cloth, so they would not make their clip-clopping sounds as they left the friary – the noise of twelve hooves would carry in the night's still air and barking dogs and light sleeping friars would raise the alarm. If anyone was awake, they would have seen the outlines of three stolen (borrowed) donkeys, two friars and a young trainee friar, leaving the small friary. They were travelling light, with small packs containing meagre rations on their backs, a bedroll each on the donkeys; they would have also seen that they were heading south and in a hurry.

After about ten miles, Friar Pablo disappeared into the woods that ran along their right flank and seemed to stretch out for miles. He told the other two to carry on, he would catch them up. They didn't see him again for about two miles. At first, they thought it was a small tree along the dusty dirt road but as they got closer, they made out a shape, a human shape and then as they got closer still, they saw it was Friar Pablo. They waved but he did not wave back, Thomas found him aloof at the best of times, now he was travelling with him, he just found him odd. What happened next did nothing to dispel his view of him.

As they got closer to where Friar Pablo was standing, he waved them off the road. "Go round me," he called.

They did as he asked and led the three donkeys off the road and as they did so Thomas saw a line of fresh blood. It was running right across the road. At each end of the line of blood was the skull of a rabbit. Each skewered on a stick that was driven into the ground. Both skulls had been stripped of their fur and flesh and, draped over each skull was a set of beads. Without saying a word, they re-joined the road ten yards further on and continued their journey. Thomas looked back at the line of blood, the rabbit skulls and the beads.

"The black beads are for Protection; the purple beads link the blood line to the third eye." Whoever crosses it will have bad luck. It will buy us some time." Friar Pablo took the reins of his donkey and strode off.

"Santeria," Friar Benoit reminded Thomas. "Remember, I told you, it's Spanish and means the cult of the saints. And the skulls are part of a sacrifice to the Orishas. To the saints because they believe every person has a destiny from God, and you fulfil that destiny with the aid of energy and the help of the Orishas."

They walked through the night. None of them had slept since the night before and tiredness was fast becoming their enemy. It was cold and it was hard going. Whilst they were working donkeys, they had not endured having to walk long distances. They were used to going to the crop field and back again, less than a mile, several times a day and then their work would be done. They too, were fatigued. Now they were all beginning to feel the pain of distance.

The three travellers pressed on and disappeared into the night.

*

Place: The Headquarters of the king's commander of Paris

The retinue of soldiers and jailers who had taken the two Templars from their jail to the place of their execution finally returned to the king's commander's headquarters. They stood there, four bad-tempered jailers and twelve king's guards. The commander lived lavishly; they did not. He kept them waiting in the courtyard while he finished his supper. It was late, very late. It was cold; they were cold. There were large, flaming torches steadfast in the wrought iron wall holders, casting streaks of light across the courtyard, accompanied by flickering shadows as the king's commander of the Paris district approached them.

"Attention pour le commandant," the execution detail sergeant barked as he snapped to attention. His motley crew, who earlier had burnt alive two of the most important men in the now banished, hunted and hounded, Order of the Knights Templar, did the same.

The king's commander was a serious man, short, stocky, cruel. The soldiers' sergeant stepped forward as their commander approached. He saluted; the commander did not, he merely grunted and told the sergeant to get on with it, it was late. The sergeant's face was haggard, his eyes red with the smoke from the raging execution pyre. He did not want to give the report; he wanted it to be someone else's responsibility, but it wasn't. The commander's fury would be aimed at him and him alone. He decided to get it over and done with as quickly as possible. He reported. Brevity, he decided was the best policy. It took less than thirty seconds. The news would not be what the commander wanted to hear because he knew his king would not want to hear it and the king's wrath inevitably would be dealt out to the messenger, him!

"What do you mean, they did not confess?" he roared, incredulous at the news. "You burnt them. How could they not tell you everything you wanted to know? Burning people always do!" The commander rasped; he was now all but two feet from the sergeant's face. "Did they speak any words?"

The sergeant did not want the commander to ask that question, not that one. He stumbled over his words trying to soften them, but there was no getting away from them, the Templars had spoken to them and now he had to tell his commander what they said. He took in a deep breath – wishing he was lying next to one of his favourite whores, warm and drunk, and began, "He, de Molay, cursed our beloved king and our beloved Pope. He said that both would be summoned before God for a tribunal of heaven, and both would be punished before this year was out."

The others looked at the commander waiting for him to react. He did. He erupted. "You fucking whore's son, why didn't you rip his tongue out. He would dare to speak of our king and our Pope in that manner. His tongue, his tongue, why didn't you have his tongue?"

"Because it was burning, Commander."

The commander raged for another five minutes before finally speaking again. Wine was brought to him. He gulped it down. He hissed his words and wine leaked from his mouth. "So, no one heard them say anything?" he looked at the men assembled in front of him.

The sergeant stood upright. He did not move or speak. He hoped that this was the last question and then they would be dismissed. Then he heard a voice from his ranks and his heart sank.

"Maybe, Sir, the friars, might have."

The sergeant then knew that he would not be lying with a warm whore on this night.

"Friars?" The commander's attention was now utterly focused on one of the soldiers.

The soldier was nervous and now wished he'd kept his mouth shut. It was a spur-of-the-moment thing that he hoped he would live long enough not to regret, in fact he just hoped he would live. "We had stopped for a rest, Sir, when he, de Molay, stumbled and some friars tended to him. Just a little water they gave them, we made sure of that. One of those friars spoke with de Molay for about five minutes."

"While you rested?" the commander asked, almost hissing out his words. Now just one foot away from the sergeant's face. The sergeant went to speak. "Not you," the commander barked. He turned to the man in the ranks, "you."

"Sir, yes sir. We were just following orders."

Right then the sergeant knew he was doomed, perhaps he would be castigated again, maybe even lose his rank, but he didn't see the commander's sabre retrieved from his scabbard. The commander drove his sword straight into the sergeant's stomach. He knew where to drive it. It came out of the sergeant's back. Blood started to seep from the sergeant's mouth. He tried to speak. He coughed and the commander moved away. The sergeant felt a searing cold pain in his abdomen but he was choking to death because his lungs were filling with blood. He gave one last attempt to get air, his face hideously distorted.

"You, do you remember where this was."

"Yes Sir."

The commander took another mouthful of his wine. And do you know where their friary was?"

"Yes Sir. We passed it on the way to execute the prisoners."

"And would you recognise the one who spoke with de Molay?"

"Yes Sir."

"What is your name?"

"Tautou, Sir, Remy Tautou," he stammered out.

"And do you have a rank, Tautou?"

"No Sir."

"Well ...," the commander thought about it for a second or two. "Well, come here and present yourself to me, Sergeant Tautou. And when you have done that, you are going to take me and forty of my soldiers to this friary to meet this friar who seemed to have an interest in one of our prisoners, the Templar leader."

Place: The small friary on the island of Île de la Cité

The friary where Thomas was in training, like all the other friaries in France, was run by the prior, his name was Leroux, Brother Leroux. The friars shared the running and governance of the friary but the community was guided by the prior, Brother Leroux. He was the superior, elected by the friars every three years. He was helped and assisted by a small council.

Leroux was a duplicitous, overweight, wheezing, lazy man whom Thomas struggled to like. Rumour had it that he had been the son of a butcher, in a district of Paris. His father, the butcher would only allow his family, his wife and his son, meat he could not sell in the shop: scraps of fatty, streaky meat, lard fat he rendered from the pig carcasses and tripe – stomach lining from the pigs and sheep he slaughtered in the back of the shop. The boy, fed on fat and fatty food, grew fat. He showed no signs of slowing up when he entered adolescence – in fact, it increased. He was a lazy adolescent and showed no enthusiasm to assist his father in the shop. It was said that when the boy reached seventeen, and still showed no signs of wanting to support his father in the shop, his father packed a small hessian bag for him and marched him off to a friary where he would not find his way back to his home. At the gates of the friary, he told his son, 'if you won't serve my customers, then you can serve God'. That was the last the boy saw of his father, who later died and left none of his money to the boy. The boy became a man. A bitter man who thought the world owed him a living. But he did eventually discover he had a skill: persuasion. He honed it and used it to secure the best jobs – those that didn't require exertion. In his ensuing years, he became an important voice in the friary, serving on a number of councils.

Leroux had spent all of his time the year before Thomas arrived, currying favour from those brothers he thought had, or seemed to have, influence with the other brothers, to ensure his election. It worked. When Thomas arrived, he was the prior and spent much of his days lording it over the other brothers and doing as little as possible. No one believed he would be re-elected.

The sound of the approaching horses left no one in doubt that trouble was on its way. If the sound eluded them, the dust cloud did not – it was seen for miles. Preparations were quickly made as soon as they saw the two banners the riders carried: the banner of the king and the banner of the king's commander of Paris. Leroux busied himself making sure everyone else was busying themselves. Food was being prepared, and the gold and the silver were being hidden.

The wheezing prior had never met the king's commander of Paris, but he'd heard stories of his brutality. He was beginning to wish someone else was prior. He even contemplated appointing someone else in his stead and leaving for urgent Godly business. Too late, the visitors had already entered the friary and the commander set about his business with ruthless expediency. The prior was first on his list, but the commander quickly realised that this man was more of a politician than a leader. He gaslighted, trying to manipulate the question and answer to his own benefit, as he did in life: what was best for him. On the surface, he seemed willing and cooperative, but he merely created confusion, twisting and contorting his answers for his own means. This lasted less than five minutes. The commander did not suffer fools, liars or narcissists, the latter, the commander concluded minutes into his questioning, the prior fitted into. The prior displayed an inflated sense of worth and importance and a need for attention. The commander ordered his men to gather every friar that was in the friary and take them to the chapel. He then took hold of Leroux and almost dragged him through the cold, damp passages to the chapel.

The friars were on their knees – it was not their choice; the soldiers had their swords drawn and left the men of God in no doubt that, for now at least, God seemed to be elsewhere.

The commander stood at the front, in front of the altar. "Some hours ago, friars left this place and went to see two prisoners on their way to their execution. I want their names." Silence. "I want their names." Again silence. The commander withdrew his sword from his ornate scabbard and hit Leroux on the side of the head with the hilt of the sword. He let out a cry and his bulbous frame fell to the floor. The commander nodded to his men and each of them stood behind a kneeling friar. "I want their names," he protested again.

"I went," a younger friar said meekly.

"Stand up."

The young friar stood to his feet. He was trembling.

"I want the other names."

He told the commander the names.

"Stand," the commander barked. And one by one the friars who had gone out of the friary that night stood to their feet. "Is this it?"

"No, sir," one of them said, "Brother Thomas is missing."

The commander ordered a search of the friary for Thomas. He made the standing friars go with some of his men in search of Thomas. Ten minutes later they were back and the newly appointed sergeant, Remy Tautou, told him that Thomas was missing and so were two others, he gave the commander their names.

"Are they away at your request?" he asked Leroux.

Still on the floor, Leroux whimpered back, "no."

"Where would they have gone?" then he got his answer.

"Spain," one of the standing friars spoke up. I heard the Templar tell Brother Thomas he had to leave for Spain this night."

"Why? The commander asked.

"I do not know, I did not hear, I just heard that."

"Sergeant Tautou, take what men you need and search all the roads heading south. Do not come back until you have them. Every one of them. Tell the villages if they harbour them, they will be thrown in jail. If they give them up, they will receive coin from the king. His majesty wants to interrogate them himself. Tell them they are traitors to the crown; they had conspired with criminals and interfered with an execution and the rule of law. Leave one of your men in each village you come across, in case they turn up there."

Date: One week later
Place: On the road through France heading for Spain

It was the end of their first week on the road. They were worn and bedraggled. The weather had not been kind to them; it had hampered and slowed their progress and beaten their spirits down. Their donkeys too were suffering. They were getting thinner by the day and they knew if they couldn't find feed for them in the next day or so, the scarcity of grazing grass would not sustain them much longer.

Their plan had been to administer the word of God as they went, it was, after all, what they were: mendicants. Priests preached to one flock, one community; mendicant preachers, friars, travelled to many communities to preach and treat the sick. The three travellers would rely on the goodwill of the communities they came upon to help feed and shelter them. But the rural communities had seen a poor summer. Crops had not grown, stunted by a mild summer. The poor were poorer. Some offered but the three travellers found it difficult to accept their generosity when they looked into the sunken eyes of their children. They decided they needed to select a route that would take them through larger villages and towns, for there they might find more prosperity.

Friar Pablo had made the journey once before, but from Spain to Paris. He told them that it had taken him a month of hard travelling to make the journey. He guessed however, it would take them longer for two reasons, firstly, they must follow a winding route that would take them through places more likely to be able to help feed them. And the second reason, he did not shy away from it. "Brother Benoit, my friend, you are not the fittest of men to have as a travelling companion. You would not have been selected from a line-up. You have lost that lawyer's look but you have not lost that lawyer's body: portly!" He told them he thought it might take them six weeks to make the journey. There were two routes that would take them to their destination, they needed to take the west pass over the mountains, it was further away but it was passable, even in the winter, the other one was not.

The small village was made up of muddy dirt tracks, free-roaming chickens and corralled goats, along with a little over thirty wooden dwellings and a small, shabby hostelry. It was late when they got there. They had little money. They planned to buy food and maybe ale, then find a place to camp for the night a little south of the village. That was their plan.

Inside the hostelry, it was dark and dank. The lanterns held poorly made candles from beef tallow – the tallow burnt and smelt bad. The place hung heavy with the smell of stale ale. On the far wall, a fire raged in a blackened stone hearth. They made for a table close to the fire; they were glad of the warmth; it was a chilly night. They were regarded with caution, not the usual greeting for men of God. The talking all but stopped and they felt decidedly uncomfortable. Friar Pablo was once a knight. His fighter's senses had never left him. They were there, always, just below the surface. He watched everybody.

The hostelier gave them a board of cheese and bread and a jar of warm ale to share between them. He then left. In the far corner, a small group of men had gathered. Ragged clothes, weathered faces and calloused hands – they were farmers. The hostelier went over to join them. Friar Pablo watched them intensely.

After about twenty minutes the hostelier returned. He was nervous. He told them it might be better if, when they were done, they moved on and did not linger in the village. Friar Benoit asked if they had offended him in some way. The man looked aghast.

"No, no, no Father, far from it," the hostelier said apologetically. "You are men of God, I am a Godly man, despite what I do for a living," he added. "But you are in trouble." He then told them that the king's men had been through there just a few days past looking for three friars travelling together, they matched the descriptions they had been given. He told them that the king's men offered coin for information about them, and more coin for their capture.

"We are poor people, Fathers. Temptation is always a greater chore for those who are poor and have children to feed. Do not judge us badly. We were told you were on your way to Spain; you were traitors to the crown; we were told you had conspired with criminals and interfered with an execution and the rule of law. They threatened us with punishment and jail if we were to see you and not inform them. They left one of their own. He sleeps across the way, there in the small barn. He spends his day drinking and is now passed out in the hay. My son ran over there to check as soon as you came in, he said he was snoring like a wild boar.

"They will have told all the villages around here. Told them what they told us, if we see you, we were to apprehend you and then fetch the soldier. We were told to use any necessary force required but, not to kill you."

Friar Pablo started to stand; his eyes fixed on the small group of men still gathered, watching the hostelier talking to them.

"Father," the hostelier said, "there is no need to worry, you are among friends here. Please, sit down and rest and allow me to finish my story."

Friar Pablo sat down.

"They told us that the king himself wanted to question you. They said you faced the rack, and then a slow painful death."

"Then we must go, my son," Friar Benoit said. "We are putting you all in peril." He reached for his money to pay for the food and drink.

"No, no," the hostelier protested, "you are my guests, no payment is required."

They insisted; they paid. As they left the village – at pace! – Thomas asked, "why haven't we seen any soldiers?"

"Because we've been lucky; we've stuck mainly to the tracks and not the roads. Our luck won't hold though."

An hour or so later, they felt they were clear enough of the village. They found a secluded spot in a small glade and tethered the donkeys with long enough rope for them to be able to graze and forage on the sparse forest floor.

They were all quiet. Thomas started to prepare a fire but Friar Pablo told him not to, it was too dangerous, the light would be seen for miles.

Benoit and Thomas retrieved their bedrolls from the backs of the donkeys but Friar Pablo walked off into the forest.

"Should we go after him?" Thomas asked.

"No. he is best left on his own. Besides, I know of no other man who would be safer in a forest, in the middle of the night, with the king's men on his trail. Remember what I told you about him? He was a commander knight in the Christian military army of Aragón, Spain. He fought the Moors for most of his adult life."

There was a crack of wood from behind them. "And for that, I am eternally grateful." The tall figure of Friar Pablo came out of the trees. He removed his friar's robes and hid them in the thicket. Then he took the bedroll off his donkey.

"What are you doing?" Friar Benoit asked him.

"I cannot be a friar anymore."

"What do you mean? Put your robes back on, my brother."

"I cannot."

"Do not give up on God like this."

"I can no longer be a man of God."

"Why?"

Don Pablo turned on him. "Because I cannot protect you as a man of God. I cannot do the things I must do to keep you both safe."

It went quiet. Benoit hung his head. Thomas didn't know what to say.

"Benoit, my brother, you have been a true friend to me, a brother to me. You saved me. Without you, I would have surely been lost forever. But you and the boy will not make it to Spain; you will not even make it out of France." He turned to Thomas. "Do you believe in this quest; do you believe what de Molay told you?"

"I have not seen the Ark, I have never seen an Essene or a hermit, I have never seen Spain but yes, I believe in this journey, in this quest; I believe in de Molay."

"Why?" Don Pablo asked him pointedly.

Thomas didn't need to think about it. "Because I have faith. We don't always need to see it if we have faith in it."

Don Pablo nodded. *"For we walk by faith, not by sight,* 2 Corinthians 5:7. Then, let's get on with it, my brothers; let each of us do our part."

"But—" Benoit began to protest.

"Shhh, my brother." He had retrieved his old battle clothes from the bedroll and dressed – they were the clothes of a knight. The leather tunic had seen years of war, it was old and worn. Up on the right chest and barely perceptible, a crest.

Also hidden in the bedroll were his sword and scabbard.

"You didn't throw it away?" Benoit asked him when he saw them; he was surprised. "I thought you went to the forest that day to throw them away."

The warrior stood in front of them. "Well, I guess I can never leave the soldier behind; he is in my soul," Don Pablo said, sliding the sword into the scabbard. He turned to Thomas. "Besides, you said we are doing God's work, so perhaps God will forgive me."

"Blessed be the Lord, my rock, who trains my hands for war, fingers for battle," Thomas said.

"Psalm 144:1. But just in case," Don Pablo took out his Bible from his pack, he kissed it, and then gave it to Thomas. "Perhaps, if we make it, and all this is done and I don't need my sword anymore, and the killing is done, you can give this back to me." He smiled.

Thomas had never seen him smile; he took the Bible. "I will give it back to you one day." He paused and suddenly looked puzzled. "But what will I call you now, I mean if Friar Pablo is no more?"

"By my name, Don Pablo Santiago de Aragon, or you can just call me Don Pablo or Pablo, but I would like it if you called me friend."

From that point on, Don Pablo made sure they continued to use the less travelled roads; where possible, they travelled through woods and forests, keeping to the game trails so their tracks mingled with the wildlife. He hunted for food where he could, mainly small game and they sought out what was left of the winter berries. The new route slowed their journey; it meant less food, but it gave them a slim chance of fulfilling the quest the Templar Grand Master, Jacques de Molay, had given Thomas. They knew that news of them would already be on the tongues of wandering minstrels and players, of local tax collectors, traders and, ironically, other friars.

*

Date: Four days later

When Thomas first saw the mountains that they had to cross, he was awe-struck and mesmerised, but that very quickly turned to dread and foreboding as they got closer, the mountains and their task grew larger. Thomas had never seen mountains so high, so long and so inaccessible. He asked their name.

"Pyrenees," both older men said in unison.

Thomas was about to ask another question when a wagon containing a large family came along the dusty road towards them. The man tipped his hat as he pulled on the reins and beckoned his team of two horses to come to a stop. "Fathers," he said looking at Friar Benoit and Thomas.

"You've been on the road a while my friend," Friar Benoit said. The lathered horses and the dusty condition of his family were evidence of the many miles they had travelled.

"Two days but just a few hours left to go," he said. "Seen some of the king's guards about twenty miles back down the road." He looked back at the way he'd come, the way the three travellers were now going.

"Trouble?" Friar Benoit asked.

"They were looking for three friars heading south for Spain. Say they are wanted men. Traitors. There's a reward," he added.

Don Pablo moved closer to the horses. He held the lead horse's halter. The man saw him. He got edgy.

"My guess is they are going to all the villages along the way to the west pass. They said the traitors are heading for the west pass. They do right if you ask me. No one uses the east pass in the winter and with spring late in coming it's going to still be hard going; locals call it *L'étroit de l'enfer* – Hell's Narrow. It is the shortest way over the mountains, I'll give you that but it is treacherous. Not many use it, even in the summer, there are robbers and brigands up there and they'll cut your throat for your saddlebags or half a bag of flour. But the pass is always blocked by snow in the winter. Those that try, well, they don't come back, ever. I hear tell the current count is over fifty."

They thanked the man.

The man flicked his wrists and the leather reins slapped the backs of the horses and the family moved off. The three travellers started to walk in the direction the cart had just been, in the direction of the west pass. Less than ten minutes later, the wagon was out of sight. The travellers changed tack, skirted a tree line and then headed to the base of the mountains and towards the east pass Their decision to go through the closest pass, and not the west pass, was a daring one but it was that or face the king's guards. They knew, sooner or later, they would come across a village that was not as friendly as the last one; either that or they would stumble across the soldiers, no matter how many remote tracks they stuck to. If the traveller told the soldiers in the village they had just passed though, they had maybe five hours, less if the soldiers had scouts or outriders. Either way, they would be on them by nightfall.

*

The east pass lay ahead. It was a hard two-day climb up to the mouth of the pass, then it would be another five days through the pass if they could get through at all and make it out alive. They stood looking up at the climb. They were on level ground; another half a mile and the accent started. There was a large spruce forest that had a winding river running around it. They decided to rest up for a few hours and start the ascent to the pass at first light. They would not risk the ascent in the dark. They tried to sleep.

Friar Benoit Duvall saw them first: the king's guard had outriders! He saw the flames in the river; he counted seven. They flickered orange in the current of the river. Stretching across the undulating water; their reflections were stretched and distorted.

The others woke. The outriders had dogs – Irish wolfhounds. They had picked up their scent on the wind.

"Take Thomas," Friar Benoit called to Don Pablo. "Take him and make for the mountain. I will distract them and join you when they're gone."

"No." It was a stubborn no from Don Pablo.

"You have to get him to Spain. I can't do that, you know I can't, only you can do that. The imperative is to get the boy to the hermit. You know this makes sense. Besides, I'll be one friar on the road, they're looking for three friars. I will tell them I am preaching to villages in the area. After all, it is what us friars do."

Don Pablo knew he was right but every instinct told him it was a bad plan. He wanted to stay with his friend. To protect him, to look after him, to keep him safe, as his friend had done for him.

The flames of their burning torches were getting closer. They were on their side of the river, walking along the river's embankment looking for tracks. The dogs were howling. They were following the path the friars had taken.

"Please go before they get here, otherwise it will be too late. Go and I will go to them, there will be no need for them to come this far, if they do, the dogs will follow your scent."

Don Pablo growled through gritted teeth. He knew his friend was right but he hated it. He grabbed the reins of two of the donkeys and then Thomas's shoulder. "Go." He barked. "Go."

There were no long goodbyes, no hugs or shaking of hands. They all just looked at each other for a moment or two. Then, Don Pablo and Thomas began to run as fast as they could without making a noise – the donkeys resisted every step. They made for the mountains. They had less than an hour before daylight. They would need to be out of sight by the time the sun came up. They needed every second.

*

The king's guards were dispirited. It was cold and wet; they were stiff and their bodies ached – they'd been in the saddle for hours riding throughout the night. They'd been away from their barracks for days. Living around campfires and riding miles every day was not their idea of a good time. They talked every day about finding a village and holing up there for a night or two. Availing themselves of some home-cooked food and ale. Who'd know, they reasoned. But they never did. The punishment for disobeying a direct order and leaving their post would result in desertion charges, along with a handful of others. They knew five years in the stockade was not worth one or two nights with homemade broth and bitter ale. So, they pressed on searching for the traitors. As the days passed, each time they came upon wayfarers, or a village, the telling of the traitors' crimes grew in number until even the soldiers started to accept the list of lawbreaking, misconducts, delinquencies and God, Country and king violations, as true.

"What is it boy?" one of the soldiers called to the baying dogs. "They're on to something, I tell you."

The others agreed. The three dogs, noses close to the ground, twitching with every step they took, could smell the same smell they had smelt on each piece of clothing they had been given for each of the traitors – happily supplied by Leroux! The soldiers, torches aloft, strained their eyes to see into the pitch black night that lay ahead of them.

Then, a snap of wood pierced the blackness ahead. The soldiers halted their horses. The dogs started growling, snarling. They called the dogs back – they came back but only after being scolded with some choice words several times.

"You'd better show yourself in the name of the king," one of the soldiers called with a deep, bellowing, authoritative voice.

"My sons," a reply from the blackness. "Stay your weapons, I am a man of God merely journeying to my next flock."

"A priest?"

"No, my son. A mendicant, a friar." Friar Benoit Duvall told them. He moved out of the blackness and into the light of their torches. "As I said, a friar." He held up his arms so they could see that he was not armed and he was indeed a man of God.

"How many travel with you, Father," a soldier called back at him. All the soldiers eased forward on their saddles to hear his answer.

"It's just me, my son, just me."

"Alone?"

"Alone."

But the soldiers knew there was something wrong because the dogs were going frenzied and they had to leash them.

"Come closer, Father."

Friar Benoit moved a little closer. This merely agitated the dogs even more.

Two of the soldiers had dismounted. "Come to us, Father, let us see each other on this cold night."

"Morning," his companion corrected him.

"What?"

"Morning, it's nearly morning. Look." And he pointed to the amber skyline pushing itself up from the horizon in the east.

"Ah, the Lord's splendour," Friar Benoit said.

"We'll check on ahead," one of the soldiers said to the two dismounted men.

"No. No, my son. Stay here and I shall say mass and we shall pray together on this glorious daybreak." Benoit knew he was sounding desperate because he was desperate. He was a man of words, an ex-lawyer, an ex-trial lawyer. He once talked and argued for a living. He knew how to persuade, manipulate, coerce and compel but it wasn't working and the mounted soldiers began to move off. He sighed to himself. He knew he needed to buy Don Pablo and Thomas more time. Vicariously he had been charged with finding the last of the Essene. The man who held the Ark key. He was not a rash man, but ...

Despite his frame and his vocation, he struck one of the dismounted soldiers hard across his chin; he grabbed the reins out of his hands, lifted his leg as fast as he could, losing a sandal as he thrust his left barefoot, as hard as he could into a stirrup; then he hauled his frame up on to and then over the saddle. He snapped his heels as hard as he could into the horse and it took off at great speed, followed by mounted soldiers, two soldiers running on foot and the three snarling Irish wolfhounds.

Breathing heavily and desperately trying to keep control of his horse, he stole a glance behind him and for a moment he thought not only had they not gained on him, but he might also have extended his narrow lead.

The first arrow struck him in the neck. He felt it. He felt a blow to his neck, a dull thud. Then he felt the pain of it, the excruciating pain. Moments later he was aware of the blood, it ran down his neck and then down onto his chest inside his robe. It was warm and he was frightened. It was dawn but the light was slow to appear. He strained to see; to pick a way through the trees. Ahead he saw the forest edge. If he could make it there, he thought, he might be able to outrun them.

The second arrow hit him in the back and drove straight through into his left lung, it collapsed instantly and he gulped for air. The third struck his waist from behind – this one went straight through. The horse did not stop, it ran manically with the baying dogs at its heels.

Benoit Duvall was unsteady in his saddle. He started to feel faint, then sick, then dizzy, then a wretched feeling of hopelessness came over him. He faltered again, he'd lost all his strength to keep himself upright. His body now listing sideways, hanging over the side of the horse. His eyes had already closed. His breath was barely perceptible. The fleeing horse swerved to avoid the trees. Benoit's body was now leaning over too severely, he struck a tree and was ripped from the saddle, his head exploded into a messy pulp. Benoit Duvall, the only family member to help Thomas's mother when she was in need, the man who took Thomas in, tutored him and cared for him, the man that risked it all to save his two travelling companions, now lay dead.

Chapter 9

L'étroit de l'enfer – Hell's Narrow

Don Pablo and Thomas ran along the riverbank as fast as they could, it was still dark and they couldn't risk lighting a torch, so the route was hazardous. They hoped the sound of the river would mask their escape. Thomas's heart was pounding. He was on the run from the king's guard, soldiers notorious for their brutality.

After ten minutes they turned left, left the river and the riverbank and started their trek across a mile or so of flat land before it melded into the base of the mountains and started to rise.

They worried that if they pushed the donkeys too much, they would start their braying and their 'hee-haws' would easily be heard. Despite this, they ran for as long as they could. There was about one hour left before the sun would be fully up, so there wasn't much time. Thankfully, the base of the mountains, and for a few miles up the mountains were covered with a spruce forest. It wasn't as dense as the one they had just left and as they went higher it began to thin out until only the mountains and rock remained. For now, at least, it gave them much-needed cover. They needed to get as high and as far away from the soldiers as possible because two people trekking up the side of the mountain with two donkeys, in the day light, would not be hard to spot.

They kept looking back. They could see the light from the torches. At first, the torch lights were evenly spaced, almost in a circle and moving in their direction. But now as they looked back, they could see that the torches were bunched together and heading away from where they were. The lights were moving downriver and at pace, they guessed the soldiers were riding. They prayed Benoit Duvall had managed to sell them his story and the soldiers were heading back from where they had come from – and Benoit was making his way up the mountain. They figured he should be with them by nightfall.

Nightfall came and Benoit had not shown. Daybreak the next day came and still there was no sign of him. Neither man spoke about it; they just stayed vigilant and every thirty minutes or so, they stopped for a few minutes, looked back and waited to see if they could see him.

Place: Pyrenees Mountains, France

A four-hundred-foot-deep ravine ran most of the way through the mountains but it was impassable, there was no way through. Large fractures in the floor, leading to bottomless chasms, and fallen rocks, as tall as the tallest trees, blocked most of the way and rock falls from above were a constant threat; two or three times a day the widow-makers would fall. It would have taken them months to get through that way. From where they were, the only way to get to Spain was either the long, treacherous walk over the top of the mountains where they knew they would probably be dead within two days, or to carry on and take the east pass, a narrow ledge some two hundred foot above the ravine floor.

It was a slow, winding climb up, two days of hard trekking to reach the east pass entrance. The hike up the mountains, the weather, the thinning altitude and the fact Benoit was not with them, made every second of every day miserable.

They lingered at the mouth of the pass; they were reluctant to enter. They wanted to wait there, to see if they could see Benoit's portly frame trekking up the mountain towards them. But, by the end of that second day, they both knew that Benoit Duvall was not coming. They hoped he was safe somewhere, but neither really believed that either.

The pass was just a three-foot-wide ledge; it was not wide enough for more than one person at a time; one donkey at a time.

There was a sheer vertical wall, hundreds of feet of rock and granite on their right side and, just three foot away, the edge of the ledge that dropped into a forty-foot-wide ravine, with a two-hundred-foot drop below into a black, jagged abyss. The ledge floor was always covered with shale and fallen rocks, but now it was even more treacherous, it was covered with deep snow drifts. Some of the drifts hung over the ledge, making it difficult to know where the ledge ended and the abyss was waiting!

*

Time: Day four in the Pyrenees Mountains

It was day four in the pass and they were in a bad way. One of the donkeys had slipped over the ledge on the first day and had fallen to a grim death – smashed on the ravine floor. Another had broken its leg on the third day and Don Pablo had to put the beast out of its misery.

Their progress had been slow. They had to carry everything themselves in their packs. The clothing they had taken with them was completely useless against the wintery snow and the cold. They had only been able to light one fire since setting foot in the mountains when they had come across a cave. They could not risk lighting any more fires. They had barely eaten, and rations were light and there was nothing to hunt, no animals lived up there; it was barren and cold; it was an angry place: ungodly, they thought.

Don Pablo had led the way ever since they had left the friary – despite the archaic conditions the friars lived in it seemed so inviting to them now.

By mid-day on day four, a storm had grown and was now raging as it roared through the narrow pass. There wasn't enough room in the pass for all that force and it whipped, bashed, buffeted and crashed into everything in its path. The two travellers leant into the wind and pushed on: wet, cold and exhausted. Don Pablo, taking point, took his life in his hands with every step because he would be the first to fall if he stood on a snow drift that had no ledge underneath it. He had not used the east pass when he had previously travelled from Spain to France, despite the fact it was much later in spring when he made the journey. Its reputation was of death: treacherous rock falls, loose shale, and thieves who preyed on travellers. The heavy snows of the slowly retreating winter added avalanches, freezing temperatures and snow drifts blurring the ledge's edge.

Towards the end of day four, the snow had turned into freezing sleet, it was beating down, it drove into their skin and stung their eyes – it was unrelenting. They were cold and they were wet. Their legs ached; their hands were numb with cold. Lightning lit the ravine in a macabre, bright flashing light. The thunder roared and crashed, reverberating and vibrating through the pass, the deafening sound bounced off its stone and granite walls and seemed to shake the mountains' very foundations. Thomas grew weaker with every miserable passing day and with every miserable step.

Don Pablo was still out in front, testing the snow, prodding it with his staff, making sure there was rock below it and not a void. Thomas, exhausted, was barely able to stand, hunched but leaning forward against the wrath of the storm. He could barely make out his companion ahead of him. He strained against the incessant driving sleet.

*

Day Five

As the pair continued on their treacherous journey, exhausted from battling mother nature, they came out of nowhere. Four of them were on the pass in front of them. Outlaws, dirty and half-starved. They were armed. Thomas was not, only Don Pablo was.

The crossbow bolt hit Thomas's chest. It drove into his chest seven inches deep, only stopping when it hit his shoulder blade – it was inches from his heart. The wound bled quickly and badly. He fell onto the snow – the snow around him reddening quickly. He screamed; the pain took his breath away.

The outlaws saw their opportunity and charged at the only person left standing, Don Pablo. The first, brandishing his sword and screaming obscenities. He fell instantly – he was the first to die on

Don Pablo's sword for many years. The outlaw had held his sword aloft, leaving his entire midriff open and unguarded. Don Pablo's sword sliced his stomach and its contents fell into the snow. He lay dead close to Thomas. Then the second and third; they roared at the top of their voices in a bid to scare Don Pablo and bolster their resolve. Don Pablo stood his ground. His feet apart, his body side on, reducing their possible target area, his sword held diagonally just above his head, ready to slice, slash or thrust.

Just behind them the fourth outlaw, the one with the crossbow, knelt and took aim at Don Pablo. Thomas, still screaming with pain, managed to get to his knees. He saw the crossbow being raised. He saw where it was being aimed. He noticed the body next to him had a dagger tucked into its belt. He grabbed it. Then hurled the dagger towards the man with the crossbow with all his might. The outlaw saw it and moved out of the way quickly. He put the crossbow back into this shoulder. He raised it. He Took in a deep breath. Then letting only half of the cold frosty air out of his mouth and nostrils, he held the rest in his lungs. He squeezed the trigger and let the deadly bolt fly. Thomas saw it, instinctively he held out his hand in defence. It went straight through, smashing bone as it did, it struck his chest. The force knocked him over and he fell sideways onto a snow drift that precariously rested on the edge of the ledge. The snow gave way from under him and he felt himself falling. He scrambled, reached out and clawed at the rock face with his hand. The other hand lay by his side, bloody and broken. He held on with every ounce of his strength.

*

Don Pablo didn't wait for a third bolt to be loaded into the crossbow. He sidestepped the two charging outlaws and leapt forward towards the arbalist, bringing down his sword in front of him in a diagonal motion. The crossbow fell to the ground, the bolt still in the stock rail, ready to be fired. Then the body of the crossbow's owner fell and then the owner's severed head. Don Pablo quickly bent down. He retrieved the crossbow. On one knee he took aim. The third outlaw dived at him. Don Pablo dropped the crossbow, reached for his sword again, turned and brought his sword across the man's thighs. The man screamed, then fell. The sword slid across his neck. With his neck sliced open the man died, face down in a pool of red slush. Don Pablo brought the crossbow back up to his shoulder. He fired and the bolt entered the third outlaw's head. The lifeless body buckled and fell over the ledge and into the black emptiness below.

*

He felt his hand slipping. The pain in his chest was unbearable. Thomas's eyes started to close as he began to lose consciousness.

It seemed quiet now. As he opened his eyes, he was standing on the road to Lubea, near his parents' rural farm. The sun was beating down and he thought it looked like it would be a good summer, a good crop-growing summer; his father would be pleased. They would all have plenty to eat. He saw them in the distance, he could hear them playing, his siblings. He would run to them and they would be so excited to see him, but first, he would seek out his mother and hug her. She would probably be in the kitchen; she was always in the kitchen. His father would be outside with the animals. He would seek out his father too and show him he'd grown into a man since they'd last seen each other at the friary gate.

He slipped back into consciousness and opened his eyes. The pain in his chest had spread to every part of his body – the piercing, insufferable pain. It engulfed him. It stole away the image of his home, of his siblings and the road to Lubea. It stole away the summer. He looked down into the black abyss.

He felt the sun again. He heard the voice. It was deep, effortless and smooth, like sweet molasses. It resonated. It seemed to come from all around him, everywhere.

He was back on the road to Lubea. He looked up and could feel the sun's warmth on his brow. Then the voice again. The sweet molasses tone. It felt familiar. He'd heard the voice before, many times, but where? He started to walk down the road, which stretched out before him: a long winding road that meandered towards his parents' rural farm. Then again, the voice. This time he knew who it belonged to.

A figure was walking towards him, far off. The heat from the road rose and shimmered. He closed his eyes. He was nearing the farm. He could hear his siblings again. His heart filled. When he reopened them, the man was closer, he could see his face. The face he had seen so many times since his childhood.

"It's okay, Thomas." The Archangel Michael said, placing a hand on Thomas's shoulder. "You can rest now; your task is over."

"But ... I have not found the guardian of the Ark key; I have not found Caleb."

"You found the bearded warrior. That was your part in this journey. That was always your destiny, Thomas."

A little behind the angel stood the Knight Templar, Jacques de Molay. He smiled at Thomas. He looked younger. His body was healed and he looked at peace. Tranquil.

"Caleb was never yours to find, it was not your destiny, it is his."

Thomas looked up and saw Don Pablo standing on the ledge of the pass screaming at him to hang on, he was trying to find a way down to him; his broken body clinging to the rockface.

"Finding the Essene is your salvation, Thomas."

Thomas felt his fingertips slipping from their grasp. He was cold again. He was back on the cliff face. Don Pablo was climbing down the wet, rock face to where Thomas was, still screaming at Thomas to hang on.

"You were right," Thomas managed to say, "Santeria, every person has a destiny from God." Thomas then let go.

*

He didn't know how long it had been. He didn't feel the cold anymore, yet it was still snowing, and the storm was still raging. Don Pablo sat still on the ledge, in the snow. His sword was on the floor along with the crossbow where he'd dropped it. He sat, his legs hanging over the ledge and into the abyss. He stared into the empty blackness. He was now alone.

He noticed Thomas's pack lying on the ground; it had fallen from his back when he fell with the first crossbow bolt. It lay on the ground close by, its top slightly open. There was something jutting out. It was black. He looked more closely. It was a Bible. It was his Bible, the Bible he had given to Thomas to hold on to for him. He reached for the pack and the Bible fell out; the pages fell open. He looked down at the open page, it had opened at 2 Corinthians 5:7 *for we walk by faith, not by sight.*

He gathered his things, shook off the snow, took the fur from the outlaws and wrapped it around himself. He tucked his Bible into his tunic. He turned back one more time, took a deep breath, turned around and headed south through the pass and towards Spain.

Above him, he could see the sky through the ravine. The dark potent clouds announced more freezing snow and if it warmed, the snow would melt and bring with it falling rocks.

He was weak. The fight with the outlaws had sapped every ounce of energy he had left and the death of his two friends stole his resolve. He wandered through the pass for days. His progress was debilitatingly slow. In places, parts of the ledge had all but been broken away from huge falling rocks and he had to edge along it sideways on, with his back to the wall – the ledge barely wide enough for the length of his feet. In other parts, he had to scramble over rocks and boulders that blocked his path.

Three days after Thomas's death, Don Pablo came across a semi decayed body. It was sitting on the ledge, its back to the wall: slumped. There was a rope tied around it. The rope had been tied into a loop around its waist, the other end was only about four foot long, the end wasn't frayed, it had been cut, with a knife. A scribbled note lay in its hand, it read:

> *I failed. Francois broke his leg. I tried to carry him but we stumbled and he fell over the ledge. I could not hold him. He begged me but I was slipping. I cut the rope. You will find him at the bottom of the ravine. Please God forgive me.*

The knife that was plunged into his heart was still stuck in his chest, his decaying hand still grasping the knife's handle.

*

He had no idea how long he had been in there now. He'd lost all sense of time and at night the stars were obscured by the clouds. The snow clouds dogged him. Endless snow. His staff had been his saviour. Time and time again he thrust it into the snow to test there was rock beneath it – step after every painful step, but he'd grown so tired. Often he took the step before the staff had struck the solid ground. His concentration now gone, the only thing that kept him going was his promise to Thomas.

The storm was relentless, it was jammed into the narrow ravine, a vortex between the sides with nowhere to go, forcing, pushing and battering everything in its wake.

Don Pablo's vision started to deteriorate. His eyes felt like grit and he rubbed them profusely. His vision became blurry. Now he moved even slower, his staff in his left hand and his right feeling the wall to guide him.

Day after day, night after night, and then, nothing. It was blackness.

Time: Three weeks later
Place: Spain

He slowly woke. He opened his eyes tentatively. He didn't recognise where he was but it seemed familiar. He was laying on a hard bed, in clothes he did not recognise, in a room he did not recognise, but still, it felt so familiar. The room was small, no more than six foot by six foot. It had one small window, which was cracked open. The smell of flowers and spring filled the room. A small, wooden cross hung on one of the plain wattle and daub walls. A wooden ledge and brace door was closed but it looked unlocked. By his bed was a small wooden table – it only held one item, his Bible. He tried to move and was surprised when his body responded. His body felt stiff but not as beaten and broken as he had last remembered it. He wondered where he was. The sense of familiarity lingered. He remembered taking the knife out of the Skeleton, he looked for it, it was gone. He was defenceless.

It had been two months since he and the others had left the small friary on the island of Île de la Cité. Spring was late and it was taking its time launching its floral splendour onto the world again as the winter was very slowly and reluctantly ebbing into retreat.

The door opened and a small rotund man entered the room carrying a wooden bowl with broth in it. He was a monk and Don

Pablo realised why the place felt so familiar, he had lived in a friary and the two places looked, smelt and felt the same, he was in a monastery.

The monk noticed he was awake. He seemed pleased. "Ah. At last." He announced with great excitement. "I see Father Juan has done it again. We are so lucky to have such a skilled apothecarist in our Order. How are you feeling?" He said in Spanish. Then he repeated the whole thing in Castilian, Aragonese and French.

"A little nauseous," then remembering his final days in the pass, he added, "but better than I had been, thank you," Don Pablo said it in French, it was instinctive, it had been so long since he had spoken his mother tongue. Then he said it again in Spanish, Castilian, and Aragonese. His voice was husky, he had not spoken for a while.

"Ha, another linguist, I must tell Father Alejandro we have another linguist."

"What is the tongue of this place?"

"Of course, forgive me, you want to know where you are. The goat herder's son found you; his father, with the help of the villagers, brought you down from the mountains by sledge and brought you here, to the monastery. The boy said he found you just a few miles from the east pass. You are in Spain, my son, close to the small village of Benimordy, in the monastery of Saint Bartholomew. Our tongue is Spanish, Castilian and Aragonese. but as we are so close to France, most of us speak French too. Some of us English and all of us Latin, of course," and he laughed heartily.

"How long have I been here?" Don Pablo asked.

"Mmm, let me see ... about three weeks, now. You woke several times and we were able to feed you but your fever was very high and you have been delirious for most of that time. At first, we thought you were blind, but Father Juan said you had snow blindness. We had to cover your hands in cloth because you kept rubbing them. Luckily the blindness is not permanent and yours went after three days." The monk moved a little closer. He had a warm smile and a caring, honest look that made Don Pablo feel safe for the first time since he'd entered the Pyrenees mountains. "You nearly died crossing the Pyrenees through the east pass. We think you had been wandering for days through the mountains suffering from hyperthermia and frostbite. When you finally made it to the other side and into Spain, your troubles were far from over because you still had to descend the mountains, a difficult challenge even for skilled climbers. You were half starved, your body was emaciated, covered in sores, some festering. Your clothes, dirty and in tatters, hung off you; the fur you wore was also in tatters. You had no weapon, no pack and no provisions."

The monk placed the broth on the small wooden table. "Please try and eat, we need to build your strength up. Oh, and sorry about your clothes, we had to burn them, what was left of them, lice would spread like wildfire in our small community here. You'll find sandals under the bed. The door is not locked, please feel free to get up and move about when you are feeling up to it, the exercise will do you good." He paused and looked at the Bible on the small table. "Who is Thomas?"

"A friend ... but how do you know Thomas?" Don Pablo asked, confused.

"Oh, I don't, but I like what he wrote in the front of your Bible. I should like to meet him one day." And with that, he left.

Don Pablo reached for his Bible; inside it bore the inscription: *I can endure all these things through the power of the one who gives me strength (Philippians 4:13.) Thank you for your strength. Your friend, Thomas Duvall.*

*

Later that day, the abbot asked to see him. Don Pablo was feeling much better, even stronger. Earlier, the talented apothecarist, Father Juan, had called to see him. He checked his wounds, which were almost healed now. He gave him a sweet-tasting potion to drink and told him that in a few more days, he would be back to normal – Don Pablo was already planning to leave.

As soon as he put on the leather sandals, he felt he was back in the friary. He was told the way to where the abbot would be, the common room, which was not too far away. He decided to take the longer route and investigate his surroundings.

Two small corridors later and he'd reached a door to the

outside and to the courtyard. It was a small area where riders could tether their horses or donkeys, it held a deep fresh water well, a small herb garden, a wooden bench and a stone cross made from local stone. The fresh air hit him as soon as he opened the door and walked outside. It rushed at him and he felt faint. He made for the bench and sat down. In front of him, and above the courtyard walls, he could see the awesome sight of the Pyrenees. Miles upon miles of jagged rocks, touching the clouds and dominating the landscape. He took slow deep breaths. He felt claustrophobic. His breathing was now heavy.

"It's because of the pass. You spent so long in there that the feeling you now feel will take a long time to leave you, if it ever does." It was the abbot. He was standing behind Don Pablo.

Don Pablo turned his head briefly. He thought he looked like a kindly man, not at all like the prior in his own friary, yet there was something about him; he felt like a kindred spirit.

"I was just on my way to the common room to meet you, but this will do just fine ... if you're okay with it?"

Don Pablo nodded, now staring back at the mountains.

"Beautiful, aren't they?"

"Deadly."

"Ah, yes, that too. You were lucky."

"Luckier than some." His thoughts drifted off.

"Those mountains have taken many souls."

"Fifty, we were told but we need to add six more." He thought about the four outlaws, the decaying body, and Thomas.

"Oh, my son, there are a lot more than fifty; our count is closer to one hundred and fifty, so I guess we should say one hundred and fifty-six. But praise be to God that it was not one hundred and fifty-seven with you."

Don Pablo did not respond, he was wondering if the number was really one hundred and fifty-seven because the mountains had also claimed Benoit's life, or did the soldiers do that? "How far is it to Zaragoza?" he asked. It was the first largest city he would need to head for. Zaragoza, then Burgos, then Soria and the Cañón del Río Lobos.

"Let me see now." the abbot had to think. "I would guess

three days, maybe four."

"Are the roads safe from here?"

"Well, that depends."

"On what?" Don Pablo asked.

"On what is chasing the person making the journey? But, no more dangerous than any other road, I guess."

Don Pablo did not answer.

There was a pause in their conversation. Both looking out at the mountains – stunningly beautiful but fatal to many that travelled there.

"You were a soldier or a friar?" the abbot asked. He had shifted his position a little and Don Pablo heard a scuffing sound on the ground.

"I was both, but a friar for many years."

"And have you now forsaken God, my son?"

"No Father, I have not. I still do his work, but I no longer do it as a friar."

The abbot thought about it for a second or two. "Do you mind if I ask why not?"

"It matters not."

Again, there was a period of silence. Then, the abbot spoke again.

"There is a legend here in Spain, my son. A legend of a man, a villager who fought for his country against the Moors. He fought so bravely that the king of Spain made him a knight. He gave him a crest by which to be recognised, a noble crest of a two-headed imperial eagle. He was given lands with his title but he didn't take them. The man kept his house in the village and he and his family continued to live there. They say he carries a deep diagonal scar across his face. Some say this man died on the battlefield. Others say he lost his sanity at the massacre of his family and never regained it. A few say he became a holy man, a man of God. What do you say, my son?"

"I would say all three are most likely true."

The abbot smiled. "By the way, I'm sorry we had to burn your clothes but they were in tatters and riddled with lice. I inspected them myself, I wanted to check they were beyond saving.

The crest upon the leather tunic, my monks missed it, but I saw it, the faint inscription of a crest, a two-headed imperial eagle." Now he whispered. "You are amongst friends, Don Pablo Santiago de Aragon. You have nothing to fear here." The abbot walked from behind the bench, limping. His left leg dragging along the floor.

The abbot stood in front of Don Pablo. Don Pablo looked down at the abbot's left leg. It was not there, a metal contraption in its place.

"A Moor blade took it when we were on our way to the shrine of Santiago de Compostela protecting a number of high-ranking pilgrims who had come from Rome."

Don Pablo looked him in the eyes. He saw it. "You were military?"

"I saw it in you, you see it in me, yes. I was a cavalry commander in the Order of Cáceres. You would know them as—"

"*Orden de Santiago* – Order of Santiago."

"My soldiering interrupted my becoming a monk. When I lost my leg just outside Santiago de Compostela, I could finally devote myself to God." The abbot sat down on the bench next to Don Pablo.

The evening was closing in and the long winter had not yet fully receded. It was starting to get cold. The sun would soon be gone and the bell for the evening meal would sound. Don Pablo wanted to trust the man sitting in front of him, but he had been through so much and he still had at least a three or four-day journey. He wondered if he could share the truth with a man he had only just met. Share the most important story he, the abbot, would ever hear.

"We have not met before, Father, but you have given me charity. You saved my life and for that, I owe you some kind of explanation." Don Pablo now turned to face the abbot full on. "I am on a mission. I think it's a mission for the soul of mankind. I don't know what it looks like, I just have faith."

"For we walk by faith, not by sight, my son."

Don Pablo smiled. He thought back to when Thomas's pack was lying on the ground in the pass. His Bible was jutting out. When he had reached for it, it fell out; the pages fell open to 2 Corinthians 5:7 *for we walk by faith, not by sight*.

By 5 p.m. the abbot knew everything that had happened, from Thomas's visions, his meeting with Jacques de Molay, the clandestine departure from the friary, the deaths of his companions, and up to the last thing he remembered, stumbling out of the east pass and trying to make his way down the mountains until he fell and lost consciousness.

The abbot then made plans for Don Pablo to be supplied with a sturdy horse, a full pack of rations, some of Father Juan's potions, a sword and a small bag of coins.

It was still dark when Don Pablo left the monastery the following morning. Only the abbot was there to watch him go – no one else knew about it.

Sitting high on the saddle, Don Pablo looked to the horizon, then he looked behind him at the mountains that nearly took his life. The mountains where Thomas now rested.

"Bad memories?" the abbot asked.

Don Pablo adjusted his stirrups. "They join many more," he answered ruefully.

"You should go before they wake." The abbot turned towards the building behind him. "It will soon be prayer time."

Don Pablo was just about to squeeze his heels into the horse and command him forward when he looked down at the abbot. "Do you know what the Paradox is, Father?"

"I don't my son."

And with that, Don Pablo's heels squeezed just in front of the girth and the horse quickly broke into a canter.

The abbot watched him go; he said a prayer and then, he disappeared inside.

Chapter 10

The Hermit

It played on his mind with every second that slowly went by; with every step the horse took; with every meandering cloud that passed by high above him. Was he too late? He knew that if the Templar de Molay had not been able to hold out against the burning flames that would have engulfed and then melted his flesh, the king's men would already be at the hermitage. And if they were, he feared they would have already found the hermit and he would have failed in his quest. He knew it would be his failure, not the boy, Thomas, or his friend Benoit Duvall, who had given his life so that he and the boy could get away; it would be his.

He had barely made it out of *L'étroit de l'enfer* – Hell's Narrow, alive. It had nearly killed him; it had killed the boy.

He'd spent long painful days in the abbey being treated by the monks – they had brought him back from near death. Their care and their remedies saved him but it took so long for him to heal; for him to regain enough strength to be able to attempt the final part of his journey and his quest: to find the hermit. He knew all the delays meant his chances of finding the hermit and passing on the message from de Molay, grew slimmer and slimmer every day. It played on his mind every second that slowly went by; with every step the horse took; with every meandering cloud that passed high above his head. To him it seemed like an endless journey. The horse he had been given by the kindly abbot was sturdy enough, but it was slow, and it ate a lot. He lost precious time every day trying to find good grazing for the horse to feed. The horse, he regretted nearly every second of the journey, was a typical monk's horse, a slow, steady plodder.

He kicked his heels into the horse; leaned forward and fixed his gaze and his horse southwards towards his journey's end.

*

He kept clear of all the main roads and the frequently used tracks because whilst he was back in his country of birth, where he had once been celebrated, he knew if he was recognised, news of him would soon spread. Spain was full of spies. The French king's agents were everywhere and they paid well for information. Celebrated or not, Don Pablo knew that news of him would feed a family for a month. And it was not just the king's agents he was worried about, peace within the Christian kingdoms of Iberia was fragile. Aragon-Catalonia, Navarre, Portugal and Castile-Leon all had armies, all had mercenaries and all were driven to extend their borders. Currying favour with the French king could secure them new lands and increase their wealth; it could also help them protect what they already had.

The Templars were revered within Spain and mostly protected. When the king of France had asked for all Templars to be rounded up and arrested, unlike France, Spain did not comply. However, the French king had many powerful allies and some Templars were captured and sent to France; others simply disappeared!

*

Don Pablo was tired, dirty, dishevelled, weary and hungry. He was now south of Zaragoza. The rations he had been given by the abbot had long since run out and hunting was scarce. He had no bow and his trapping skills failed him most nights. Throughout the early part of his journey, he had managed to survive on the full pack of rations the abbot had given him, and then bought food whenever he had to, with the small bag of coins the abbot had given him. He did not dare to enter any of the villages to seek food for fear of being recognised. He was getting closer each day and so went hungry.

After many days of travelling in a southerly direction, he finally got to the point where he needed to head southwest and towards Burgos. He was on the home stretch but knew it would be the most dangerous; he would need to be extra careful. He would need all his skills to stay alive – and stay unnoticed.

From Burgos it was still a two-day ride to the Cañón del Río Lobos, but he was close – finally. He decided he would approach his destination through an expansive forest that he knew covered the area to the north of the Cañón del Río Lobos. It offered good cover, a lot of cover, which he so desperately needed as he got closer. It would also offer him food if he trapped well. He would eat during the day, being able to build a small fire to cook his catch on because the fire would not be seen from afar in day light.

He had no idea what awaited him. If the king's men were there already, did they have the hermit? And if they didn't, would he be walking into a trap because they would still be there in the area searching for him. Or perhaps the hermit had already left that place; perhaps he had died. Don Pablo didn't know how long it had been since de Molay had seen the hermit or heard from him. The hermit was one hundred and three years old, he repeatedly told his horse. How could such an age be reached. The horse plodded on.

As he got even closer, he started to feel the same old unease and apprehension he always felt before going into battle. It was like spinning a coin with his life. After the death of his family, he had not cared about his life. He was lost. There was simply nothing for him to live for and the only reason he allowed himself to live, was because it was punishment, his penance, his living hell. He had to live with the grief every day of his life. However, his time in France with his brother-friars and with the patience and understanding of his friend, Benoit Duvall, Don Pablo slowly forgave himself. Now with the quest entrusted upon him by Thomas, and vicariously by the Templar Grand Master, de Molay, he had something to live for. Not only that, he had something that required his old skills but with it came all those old feelings – he was again spinning a coin with his life.

*

The land had become familiar to him; it was more Mediterranean looking, whiter, craggier, full of ravines, outcrops, rocks and boulders, gorges; more barren in parts compared to its greener, more northern regions. The soil was dryer than summer grass; it was gravelly, full of splintered rock. Rain soaked in the winter and sun-baked in the summer. Parched. The mountains were worn by the intense baking sun, the harsh grit-carrying winds; the penetrating and destructive Sirocco winds, born out of the Sahara, hitting north central Spain with blistering winds, sometimes hurricane winds in the summer season. A semi-defaced landscape inflicted by erosion. Lifeless. Yet still there were oases of fertile land. Green plains and sprawling evergreen forests.

His way became slower. Large boulders, as large as houses, strewn everywhere, some balancing precariously, worn by the sun, and the gritty destructive Sirocco winds. As Don Pablo got closer, the sun got hotter, at times it was unyielding, stripping the air of moisture. The land grew more expansive, but still chewed by the elements. Ridges were expansive in places and dark and mysterious Spanish plains spread out for hundreds of miles around him.

*

He was almost there. He calculated maybe five miles to go and he would be entering the Cañón del Río Lobos. Then what? He had asked himself the question nearly every step of the way. He never had an answer for himself. He told the horse he would put his faith in God and pray hard.

He had passed a few outlying farms in the past few days, now he came upon another. It was close enough. "This will do," he told the horse. "End of our journey together." The sun was going down.

The farmer's dwelling was a battered, old, wooden, single storey building with a wooden shingle roof. Whispery smoke curled from out of the stone chimney and drifted into the dusk sky. The only other building was a barn-looking structure.

He got off the horse when he was three hundred yards away, hid the sword the abbot had given him and slowly led the horse towards the farm.

The first to raise the alarm were the chickens, which sent the mongrel dog in to a spin – the dog made sure everyone and everything else knew there was something out there. The farmhouse door creaked as it opened. Lantern light from inside the building came rushing out as the door opened. A man, in his mid-fifties, face and hands worn with toiling the land and growing his black and green olives in the groves surrounding his farm, moved out of the doorway and onto the dirt yard. He held a lantern. He held it up and squinted his eyes. He swore at the dog and it stopped its yapping.

Don Pablo held the horse's rein in his left hand and held up his right hand so the farmer would see he was not holding a weapon. He bid the farmer good evening in the local dialect. "I was wondering if you would trade?" Don Pablo asked the farmer.

"I have little to trade," the farmer replied, "unless you want to take one of my kids off my hands." The farmer chuckled. "They eat a lot and make a lot of noise!"

Don Pablo burst out laughing. "You keep your mouths my friend, perhaps you should not get so cosy with your wife on cold evenings."

"It's not me who gets close."

"Then you are a lucky a man."

"I am that. If it's food and water you need, you are welcome stranger, no trade needed."

"It is and my trade will be this horse." He turned to the horse that had carried him for all the days since he'd left the abbey.

The farmer was stunned. "A horse for some rabbit stew, bread, olives and water, this hardly seems fair."

Don Pablo couldn't tell him that he had come about as far as he could with the horse. He could not take it the rest of the way; it would make too much noise. He figured the only chance he had of getting into the canyon was on foot, quietly! Besides, he knew if there was trouble, they would shoot an arrow into the horse first to stop his escape. The horse had served him well, it was his time to return the deed. "I have no further need of him," he said. He stroked the horse. "I have another horse waiting for me at my next stop. This is a good horse, you will not win any races with it, but he is a worker."

The farmer moved closer. He lifted the lantern a little.

The light caught the side of Don Pablo's face. He turned away. "I will eat out here. I do not wish to trouble you or your family. And once I have eaten, I shall be gone." He didn't want to linger, nor did he want to show his face in the full light of the lanterns inside.

"Are you one of those Cathar's we keep hearing about, or a Protestant, perhaps? I hear both eat like animals."

Don Pablo smiled. "I am neither, I am Catholic."

"Then we shall eat as Catholics, in a Catholic home, with a Catholic family." And with that, the farmer called his eldest son, a boy called Ignacio, to tend to the horse and the farmer and Don Pablo went inside.

The Spanish knight ate well. His stomach had not been that full since leaving the abbey.

The farmer was hospitable, his family a delight and they all talked and laughed so much they lost all track of time. The younger children insisted that the man who had given them a horse should tell them a bedtime story. The older of the farmer's four children, fifteen-year-old Ignacio St. Barrello, tried to dissuade them, to let the tired traveller be but they were having none of it. Don Pablo liked Ignacio straight away. He was respectful to his parents, did his chores willingly and helped the younger children get ready for bed. His parents didn't have to tell him, he just did it. Don Pablo allowed himself to wonder if his own son would have turned out that way, had he lived. Would he have been proud of his son like the farmer clearly was of his. For a short while, Don Pablo forgot about the dangers waiting for him just a few miles away.

The fire in the hearth was warm, the food good and the company better. It was difficult for him to think about leaving, he was so comfortable. He'd risen twice to leave but was convinced to stay just a short while longer by the farmer. However, the night had drawn in and he knew if he didn't leave soon, he would have to wait until the following night. He also feared that if he didn't go, he might never go – he missed his family so.

The farmer accompanied Don Pablo to the edge of his olive groves; he carried a lantern to light the way, although the stars and the moon helped. They had not spoken since leaving the house. Fifteen minutes later they were at the edge of the farmer's groves. They stopped. Don Pablo looked up. It was a clear night. He put the plough and the north star at his back and looked for a feature in front of him.

The farmer noticed. "You're going south?"

"I am."

"I hear there has been activity that way. Soldiers." "Do they say where?"

"No."

This gave Don Pablo hope. If de Molay had confessed, he would have revealed the hermit. As the soldiers were not in any one specific place, he concluded the Templar had remained true.

"Will you be back this way?" the farmer asked.

"I don't know," Don Pablo replied. "Who among us know what fate awaits us, only God knows. If I am back this way, I hope I can visit you again?"

The farmer thought about it for a second or two. Then he spoke. "My home is your home, Don Pablo."

Don Pablo reeled back at the man using his name. He was about to speak, to deny it but the farmer spoke first.

"My uncles fought with you. I heard you speak once, not twenty miles from here when the Moors were pressing further and further north and you were looking for recruits. After that day, I fought for you."

Don Pablo looked closer at the farmer but there was no recognition – he'd led so many men.

"I and my uncles were with you after you lost your family. We stayed by your side and we watched as the loss of your family ate you alive with grief and with hate. When you left, my uncles and I left, many of us did." He looked around him. "My father died whilst I'd been away at the wars, so I took over his olive farm and have been here ever since."

Don Pablo saw the man smile a little but it was a rueful smile, one that gave away a hint of longing for a different life, one not so land tied.

The farmer gave Don Pablo a small hessian sack he had

been carrying. "It's not much, some food, two days' worth, some water in a stitched pelt and a small amount of coin."

"Don Pablo took it. "The food I will take but I cannot take your money."

"Take it," the farmer insisted. "It will give you good reason to come back this way to return it if you do not use it. Besides, you have to come back, I'm never going to match your bedtime stories and the kids will plague me until you return."

*

He had a five mile walk to the Cañón del Río Lobos, he would make it by 2 or 3 a.m. It would be dark enough for him to sneak in, assuming there were no manned outposts. The stars and the moon would light his way a little but he would have to tread carefully. The rocks and boulders were everywhere. The ridges were flat but the foreground was strewn with danger. If he fell, he would be at the mercy of the wild boar, wolves and crows.

The rugged valley was full of dark shadows where enemies could hide and where wolves could lay in wait. At the start of the canyon, he had hidden the sack the farmer had given him, covered it with rocks and marked the spot – he wanted both hands free. He withdrew his sword, bent slightly forward, almost crouching as he walked, his eyes everywhere. His mouth was ajar, making his hearing even more acute. In the distance, although what distance he didn't know because it was difficult to judge in the dark, he saw the lights of five campfires. He assumed all of them were enemies. *Hope for the best, plan and expect the worst,* he kept reciting in his head.

He skirted around the campfires and headed deeper into the valley. He knew most of the soldiers would be asleep, even those on guard – a number were criminal conscripts who had been given a choice, enlist or jail; they owed no allegiance, just their time.

After an hour of carefully navigating the undulating ground, the dark shadow of the hermitage loomed out of the blackness. The white, plastered walls stood solid and robust. The red tiled roof, oblong and round windows all looked odd, in that inhospitable, barren and imposing place.

He was within a hundred yards of the multi-tiered archway entrance that covered the arched door to the hermitage. He knew the hermitage was full of Templar symbology, full of the secret signs and unfathomable meanings. Everyone who lived within a hundred miles of the hermitage knew it was a Templar place. They knew that inside, at the feet of a statue of the Virgin Mary, lay a carved Templar cross: the 'Flower of Life' – a six-thousand-year-old symbol. The large round window, with ten large hearts, ten smaller hearts and a five-pointed star in the centre faced you as you approached the foreboding building. It's mystical pattern associated with Pythagoras and the golden number. Whilst Don Pablo had never been to the hermitage before, he was well aware of what it was and who had built it. However, on this night he could not linger.

He walked to the left of the hermitage searching for a way up to the overhanging, craggy escarpment above and the dense boulder strewn landscape that awaited him there. As he searched, he replayed in his mind what Thomas had told him about his conversation with de Molay. 'There you will find a hermitage called San Bartolomé, but the hermit you seek will not be found in the hermitage. He has not been there for seventy years. No, you will find him high above the hermitage in the mountains to the east. His name is Caleb. He is an Essene, from the Essenes from the time of Christ, and he will not be found easily. He has spent nearly all of his life not being found. You will know him when you see him. He is one hundred and three years old and around his neck hangs a small wooden cross with a crown of thorns carved upon it and a rose carved within the crown. The hermit guards the key. This key does not open the Ark, it opens what the Ark really is: the *weapon*, and the *way*. It is written in the prophecies the Cathars brought with them. But only the last Seer knows how the key works. He knows the answer to the Paradox. We must protect the key until the Seer comes. You must protect the key. You cannot let it get into the wrong hands. They are looking for it, the followers of the Man of Lawlessness. They want to know what the Paradox is.'

*

A pastel skyline had started to emerge from the east – the sun was starting to rise. Scarlet streaks leaked into horse tail shaped clouds; a cool breeze came with it. He was high above the canyon and already on the escarpment. The house sized boulders ensured he had enough cover to move around more freely. He only needed the cover of the night to get into the canyon, now his elevation and the boulders gave him enough cover. He had no idea where to look, just that he had to look. 'You will find him high above the hermitage in the mountains to the east.' He didn't know how far away the chasing torches were, now in the emerging daylight they had become represented by whispery blue smoke but he knew they were not close. He called out – he would risk it; he had no option.

With his throat now parched, he wished he had taken the animal skin water bag out of the small sack the farmer had given him.

He was becoming hoarse, from calling the Essene's name for nearly two hours and had nothing to show for it other than an occasional echo of his own voice. He climbed higher and searched a number of caves but they were all empty and had no sign of life. He didn't know how far east he had to look. It was a hopeless quest but he'd made a promise and it had cost two lives: he wouldn't give up. He found a small stream, although it was more of a trickle, but it was fresh and cool. He drank eagerly.

He'd been searching nearly all day and was beginning to think about finding somewhere to rest up and try again in the morning. The darkness of the night would reveal the light of the torches allowing him to see if he'd strayed too far and was getting too close to the soldiers. He decided to double back towards the caves he had searched earlier. He knew there he would find shelter and sanctuary. Then he saw a large boulder, slightly leaning, it looked like it might offer some cover – the weather seemed unclear if it was going to rain or not and the last thing he wanted, was to be caught out in the open, hungry and wet. He made for it. It looked ideal, but first he wanted to see further than he could. He wanted to check if danger was close by. He climbed a boulder which was over fifteen foot high. At its apex he lay flat so as not to create an outline. Nothing! There was nothing as far as he could see, other than the boulder strewn landscape. He shimmied back down, sat beneath the boulder and decided to rest up there for the night.

*

The Essene had been watching him for a long time. He'd stayed hidden like only someone who had spent decades in amongst the rocks could. With the looming night, he decided it was time to act, besides, hidden less than half a mile away was a patrol of six soldiers. The guardian of the Ark key moved without making a sound. He got within three feet of Don Pablo. With his gnarly old staff he tapped Don Pablo on the shoulder and the Spaniard jumped two foot into the air.

"Shhh," you will alert the soldiers," the hermit's tone of voice scolding him as an adult would scold a child.

"There are no soldier's close by," Don Pablo barked back. "I've checked."

"Checked! Child. Walk that way for some minutes," he lifted his staff and pointed it west, "and you will see them. Likely they will slay you and the world will be rid of your stupidity."

Don Pablo saw the cross de Molay had described to Thomas, it was hanging around the hermit's neck. "Caleb?"

"Dead. Died a long time ago."

"So, you are not Caleb?"

"The Lord has sent an idiot to offend me on this day. What terrible sins I must have done to receive such a punishment."

"De Molay is dead."

This stopped the hermit dead in his tracks. He raised his head and looked directly into Don Pablo's eyes. His face grave. "How do you know?"

"I know you are the guardian of the Ark key and I know I must tell you about de Morlay and I know two good men lost their lives helping me to get de Molay's message to you."

The hermit looked around. He shook his head. "We must go."

"Go where?"

"You have to take the Ark key; it is no longer safe with me."

"But de Molay didn't reveal your name to the soldiers."

The hermit snapped back at him. "We cannot assume that. Always assume the worst when it comes to the Ark key. If it is lost from us, then all is lost: forever. Let's go ..." he paused. "What is your name?"

156

"Don Pablo Santiago de Aragon."

"Ah. I have heard of you Don Pablo Santiago de Aragon. You will make a fine guardian of the Ark key." He nodded to himself in approval.

"Me. Why me?"

"Because I am dying. Now, take my cross." He removed the cross from around his neck and put it on Don Pablo. "This was there at the beginning when the Ark was found by Hugues de Payens, the Templar Grand Master who, along with his other eight Knights, found the Ark hidden deep under the Temple of Solomon. It was he who separated the key from the Ark because he said that no man should hold both, no man should hold such power and they should never get into the wrong hands ..." his voice trailed off.

"Where are we going?" Don Pablo asked as the hermit began to walk away.

"Where," the hermit turned towards him and for the first time since their meeting he smiled at Don Pablo. "Where, why to start the rest of your life, that's where."

Chapter 11

Captives

Date: 700 years later – Present day
Place: End of the world

He was back again, the hare.

It had been a week or so; he looked weaker, skinnier. The thick snow still blanketed the ground, everything including his food and foraging was getting harder.

He stopped and looked at the building, it was not far away. This time he was closer, just ten yards away from the single-storey, concrete complex from the 1960s. He had only seen movement once, that was last time he came by. The window was still there. The dull, flickering light from a candle was also still there, seeping weakly out of the window: jaded, almost lifeless. This time though the window wasn't cracked open, not even ever so slightly.

The hare had been there a while before he felt something. He turned and searched the vast snow-covered wilderness that stretched out for hundreds of miles of nothing but flat snow and ice-covered terrain. The Polar days were still well into their darkness. Then he heard it again: ice crystals breaking. The white Snowshoe hare stayed motionless, he would only run if he had too; if he kept still, he knew he could not be seen, he would meld into the whiteness of the snow. The hare waited. Motionless.

In the gloom of the small, barred window he saw what he saw last time. The hare strained to see. Then he saw it again, he saw the eyes. The dull light caught the small, peering eyes and it lit them up momentarily. They were the human eyes he saw last time. Dark and sunken. Sad. The child's eyes.

Suddenly the snap of a branch. It echoed, reverberated in the extreme quietness of the day. Then the small, barred window opened ever so slightly. The child's voice rang out into the empty darkness of the polar day.

"Run Mister Hare," it warned.

One of the men behind the hare had his finger on the trigger of his rifle.

The hare sprang.

The man shot. He missed. "That fucking child. That was our dinner. Something fresh for once."

"He'll be back. You can get him next time." The other man said, both men spoke in a thick Albanian accent, which almost drowned the English words.

Inside the girl smiled. She was pleased Mister Hare was still alive. She, Priya, had promised her father she would not open the window again but the men were going to kill the hare. Mister Hare.

*

The captives called them 'the dogs', the men who kept them prisoners. The name was given to them by one of the first to arrive there – one of the first to be kidnapped and imprisoned. The dogs, the men who guarded them, beat them, kept them incarcerated. It seemed to the captives that all the guards were Albanians, that much they had figured out. They were thugs, bullies, they lacked compassion; they seemed to thrive on violence – that part took no working out on behalf of the captives. They spoke in their own tongue most of the time but not always. However, when speaking to the captives, they always spoke in English. But the syntax of their English was all wrong; it was disjointed and they ripped and tore at the words like a rabid dog's snarling and snapping. They were gruff, impatient, harsh and humourless.

There were others there, not guards but others. There were four scientists. They too were cruel, harsh people. They did not show respect or acknowledgment for those kidnapped. They had no interest in their suffering, their only interest was in what the captives might know. There were also those others; those in charge. They were not Albanian. They seldom spoke but they were always there, in the shadows, watching. Waiting. They were more dangerous than the guards. More cruel; more brutal. They truly lacked compassion; it seemed its place was taken up by a strange, almost spine-chilling malevolence.

The building was sterile; it had no features. A flat concrete facade. Flat roof, small square barred windows. The entrance door was an iron, doubly insulated door, which lay at the end of a twelve-foot concrete tunnel-porch. It stopped the snow from building up against the door, but drift snow got in the tunnel-porch and every two days it had to be shovelled out. It was the only time any of the captives were allowed outside the building.

It was a one storey, sprawling complex of sterile nondescript rooms and long dimly lit corridors. It was built as a government research laboratory but it had been empty for nearly twenty years and was now leased to a private corporation.

The captives were all kept in cells at night, converted individual sleeping quarters for the original occupiers, now with bars fixed on the small windows and the wooden doors replaced by large grey steel doors. They were not allowed electricity in the cells – or anything else they might use to escape or cause problems with; one small, cheap candle to each cell. Heating pipes ran through all of the cells but their efficiency was mediocre at best. An outer building housed two large generators which delivered power to the building. They had to be constantly maintained but were always breaking down.

Both inside and out the building was stark. Inside it was virtually empty – except for the work taking place in the centre room of the building, the large, sterile, square area that housed the computers which lined the outer walls and the twelve foot by twelve foot, sealed, sterile reinforced glass unit, known as the chamber.

Everything echoed inside the building. Every sound ricocheted off the four-foot thick, bland concrete walls and carried with resounding clarity. The captives knew that a conversation at normal sound at one end of the building, would be clearly heard at the other end. It was eerie. Spooky. It was dangerous. So, the captives only ever spoke in low whispers to each other. The guards spoke in their native tongue and their ravaged English. The guards called the cells' area the *vendi i pëshpëritjeve* – the place of whispers.

The building never changed, it was cold, the air inside was distinctive. It was stuffy, oppressive, almost asphyxiating. It penetrated, leaked and seeped out of every wall, ceiling and corner of the building. It was the overwhelming, stifling smell of Aloe Vera, Llama milk, honey and antiseptic components, like chlorhexidine gluconate, hexachlorophene, boric acid, Lugol's iodine and formaldehyde. The smell was overpowering, ghastly and resembled the smell of a mortuary. It clung to their clothes, inhabited their nostrils and even infiltrated their food and the drinking water.

Inside, the low whirling hum of the complex network of stack mainframe computers never faltered, it hummed twenty-four hours a day. Occasionally, the cast iron heating pipes would groan with age – they were installed in the 1960s. No one could ever find where the problem was, there was four miles of white paint peeling, rusting six-inch heating pipes.

The complex network of stack, mainframe computers had made the same low, whirling humming noise since the day the first captive, the cosmologist, had been taken there. Now there were others, the astrophysicist, who was the eldest and a Nobel prize winner for her work in quantum mechanics and quantum electrodynamics. The theoretical mathematician, the theoretical physicist, the microbiologist, geobiologist, evolutionary biologist, the electromagnetism engineer and Priya's father, the carpenter.

*

None of 'the dogs', their captors, knew about the candle that burnt at one of the windows all day and all night. There was no electricity in the cells. They were only allowed candles, poor candles. At all the windows throughout the complex, were thick black covers. Curtains that allowed no light out. It was prohibited to pull the thick, black curtains open, even for a second or two., It was prohibited to open the windows, despite the fact they were all heavily barred. Punishment for both was harsh.

He'd fashioned a cover for the candle out of aluminium foil. The carpenter used it for shaping the gold mouldings and had taken a great risk by stealing and giving him the aluminium foil. If the carpenter had been caught, he would have been severely beaten again. The cover he fashioned, covered the top, both left and right sides, the front side that faced out the window was not covered. There it glowed dimly, day and night.

The hare had never seen the candle before because it came from the window of the last cell. The one you had to turn the corner of the corridor to get to. All the other cells were in a row except this one. The window of the last cell faced towards a different direction to all the other cell windows. Outside the last cell window, the snow was six feet deep or more in places. There was no cover there and so the snow built up into deep drift-banks.

He'd started to place the candle in the window a week after being there Every day he would put a new candle in the window. The others knew about it, the other captives. They helped him keep the light burning. Every morning one of them would swap one of their candles for his burnt down one. They were only allowed five candles per cell per week. By each taking turn they made sure he was never found out because they all used roughly the same number of candles each week. It was a small act, but it was an act of solidarity against their captors. Every sunless day and every night, the dull, flickering light from the candle seeped weakly out of his small, barred window. The candle, like all the candles they were given, was cheaply made, the wick poor and the light it gave off was jaded, almost lifeless. Its luminosity was almost non-existent but it was something. It gave them all hope; hope that his message had got through and they would come looking for the light, the weak light in the dark, barren wilderness. They all prayed they would be saved.

Chapter 12

The second lecture

Date: The 19th – day two of Del Luca's UK trip
Place: The Thornburg Society, London, England
Time: Morning, the second lecture

It was raining.

Cardinal Del Luca informed the two people from the UK Government protection team, that they would not be needed for the rest of the day, once they had dropped him and Father Declan off for the cardinal's morning lecture, 'God versus science'. He told them the location they needed to go to and which entrance they should use once they got there. Dominique and Cameron Jack, masquerading as British Secret Service agents, already knew where he was going and which entrance to use because they had the cardinal's schedule and had already driven two practice runs along the route to the Thornburg Society. Of course, they told the cardinal that it was not wise for him to travel around London without a protection detail. Although, they already knew where the cardinal would be going directly after his lecture anyway, and other Knights would tail him. St Clair had tasked them with finding the place for the meeting with the cardinal to be held later that day. They had found a small, nondescript café that was out of the way and slightly off the beaten track – away from the hustle and bustle of the centre of London, the metropolis's Square Mile. Still, they kept up the ruse by protesting a little more.

St Clair had called them in the early hours to tell them that the cardinal will most likely want to shake his detail, them. He will not want them to know about his meeting. He told Dominique and Cameron Jack, that the Knights taking over watching Del Luca would be from the Blue team, part of a group of Knights that would be on the ground around the meeting place. He told them to take the rest of the morning off, get some sleep, freshen up and to be at the meeting in the afternoon at the café. He said that their stint as British Intelligence agents was over. Dominique knew exactly where she was going and it was to sleep.

*

The cardinal and Father Declan were on time. Father Declan was the first out of the hotel. He rushed to the waiting car carrying an unopened umbrella and two briefcases, one, which was his and the other the cardinal's. Dominique hit the switch and popped the boot. Father Declan put the cardinal's briefcase in the boot but kept hold of his own and got into the car a little wet. Cameron Jack walked the cardinal to the car holding a black umbrella. The cardinal was dry.

Dominique welcomed the rain, at least it reduced the traffic some and it slightly diluted the frenzy normally experienced in the capital. In the back, the cardinal and Father Declan showed no signs of nerves because of the impending lecture – in front of a sell-out audience; or the impending meeting they would have with the Knights Templars after the lecture.

She eased the car into the flow of traffic and took her time, keeping extra distance from the cars in front because of the wet conditions. Nothing happened on the fifteen-minute drive to the venue, it was uneventful. They arrived warm and they arrived safe.

She pulled the car over by the rear of entrance C, of the society's building, as they had been advised by the organisers because the front would be far too busy with people lining up for the lecture – it was. Just before they got out of the car, the protection team made one more protest and suggested again that they should stay with them. The cardinal thanked them but insisted that he and Father Declan were fine.

Dominique hit the boot switch and it popped open. Cameron Jack was now out of the car and watching the street. Father Declan, carrying his briefcase and an umbrella, asked Cameron Jack if he would hold both for him whilst he retrieved the cardinal's briefcase from the back of the boot. He told Cameron Jack that the briefcase had been a present from his parents when he was ordained and he didn't want to get it wet, it would spoil the leather; it was very, very dear to him, would he mind keeping it under the umbrella. Cameron Jack promised to keep it dry. Father Declan retrieved the cardinal's briefcase, then took the umbrella and his own briefcase back from Cameron Jack.

The cardinal got out of the car, looked up at the sky and, as rain fell on his face he said, "I love London." He chuckled, then he opened the black umbrella Cameron Jack had retrieved from the car for him.

Holding both briefcases and his umbrella, Father Declan reminded the cardinal that Father Ronan was already inside, he had gone on ahead an hour before to check all of the equipment, make the sound checks, and make sure all of the display monitors were working.

The cardinal and Father Declan then thanked their two-person protection team; they assured them once again that they would be just fine and said they would see them in the reception area of the hotel in the morning. Cameron Jack and Dominique got back into the car and as they slowly pulled away and filtered into the mainstream traffic, they saw, as planned, the two Knights from Blue team follow the cardinal and Father Declan into the building.

As they walked up the steps and into the Thornburg Society building, the cardinal turned to Father Declan, who was now only carrying his own briefcase, the cardinal had his one, and said, "did you get it, did you get his fingerprints?"

"Yes," Father Declan said. He showed him the handle of his briefcase. "He held it and I have kept it dry, so we should have full prints."

"Good, my son. I will go inside; you get the prints to our friends. Tell them it's urgent, I will need them by the time my lecture is finished."

Father Declan hailed a black cab.

The rain still poured.

*

Inside it was a full house; the place was packed.

The lecture had been advertised throughout a number of London universities on small, neatly presented A5 glossy pamphlets. They had been circulating for weeks but, of course, it was all over certain social media sites as well, so every seat was taken and there was standing room only. The title of the lecture: 'God versus science', was eagerly awaited. The guest speaker was Cardinal Gino Del Luca, the pamphlet said, he lived and worked in the Vatican, Rome. It listed his role in the Catholic Church as cardinal and *l'esorcista del Papa* – the exorcist of the Pope. It said he was often also referred to as the *Diavolo assassin* – the Devil slayer – for obvious reasons: he slayed demons, the pamphlet said.

The cardinal was already known to most that would be attending. He was known for two reasons, firstly, because he was the Chief Exorcist for the dioceses of Rome, which meant he was the Chief Exorcist of the Vatican. He had carried out hundreds of exorcisms over many years and a lot of attendees were interested in his work – most of his cases were documented, but not all. The other reason he was well known was because as a boy, he had fought in the resistance during the war. What made this particularly astonishing was that Gino Del Luca, orphaned at nine, was just ten years old when he joined the resistance. He was credited with saving more than fifty lives during the war. Back then he was called *Volpe Bambino* – Baby Fox.

The atmosphere in the lecture hall was thick with anticipation. The sound of two hundred feet on the wooden, parquet flooring, hurrying to find their seats added to the atmosphere. A hundred voices resounded around the domed and ornately decorated auditorium in a chorus of expectancy. Students, filling nearly every seat in the tiered, u-shaped rows that gradually rose, were mainly from the sciences, plus students of religious studies; there were undergraduates, postgraduates, professors and an array of other academics; also, a number of people who had come from overseas.

166

In the background, Concierto de Aranjuez II played, the haunting sound of the trumpet solo, which merely added to the eagerly awaited Devil slayer.

Then their wait was over.

The house lights dimmed, then the footlights. It went quiet. Three soft, spotlights came on. Then a central spotlight. It shone on the man standing alone in the centre of the stage. To his right the priest Father Ronan was sitting at a table with a laptop in front of him and a small light. Over the house speakers a male voice filled the room. "Ladies and gentlemen," it announced with some excitement, "we at the Thornburg Society are proud to bring you a man who is renowned, not only for what he does, but also for his views, his honesty, thoughtfulness, openness and humour. His lectures bring with them an authenticity that can only come from experiencing things that the rest of us can only imagine. He always challenges us, brings his insights, ideas, knowledge and wisdom. He might shock you, but he will stir your thinking and get your hearts racing. He is *l'esorcista del Papa* – the exorcist of the Pope. The definition of what he does goes a little like this: to invoke spirits, from Old French *exorciser*, from Latin *exorcizare*. This kind of role can be traced back to accounts of Jesus expelling demons and exhorting his apostles to 'cast out devils'. However, he is much more than that, as you will see. Please give a most Thornburg Society warm welcome to our guest Cardinal Gino Del Luca." There was instant, rapturous applause – it filled the room.

The man with a shock of white hair, neatly groomed, stood in front of his audience. He bowed slightly, then smiled. It was a warm, friendly smile. He looked genuinely pleased to be there. Despite what he did for a living, there was no hint of stress on his face; no outward sign of some of the things he had seen; some of the things he had exorcised from poor afflicted souls. And even more so, there was no sign of the fact that he and his Order had kept a secret that had ensured the safety of mankind for nine-hundred-years.

He moved forward towards the lectern and the microphone. "I am often asked," he began, "if science exists, can God exist? Or if God exists, can science exist."

Already on the edge of their seats, they eagerly awaited the answer, but they would have to wait a little while longer.

"Of course, I am asked a number of other questions as well."

Father Ronan put a list up onto the computer and it appeared on the large monitors.

"Ah, there it is." He read it out loud. "Do aliens exist and did ancient aliens visit us and give us advanced knowledge? Is God an astronaut? Is time travel possible? Do the pyramids hold mystical powers, reflect heaven, was the knowledge on how to build them given by a divine power, or something else, or neither? What happens when I die? Is there a Heaven? Where is Heaven? And, ah yes, the one most asked, do demons really exist if so, what's it like to exorcise one?" He took a breath and let the questions sink in for a second or two. "Please raise your hand if I have at least one of your questions on my list." Around ninety per cent of the audience raised their hands. "Father Ronan, will you please show the final most asked question." It came up on the monitors. *As you have a direct channel to God, can you tell me the six winning lottery numbers for next week, please.*

Everyone laughed. The cardinal laughed. "You don't think there has been a cardinal or two who hasn't asked Him for that answer?" Again laughter.

Some hands went up once the laughter had died down. They were eager.

"I will answer most of those questions on the list," he turned to one of the monitors, the screen filled with the questions. I will suggest possible answers for some of the others and, I will leave time to take as many questions as possible at the end. If I don't get to everyone's question, Father Ronan here," he turned to Father Ronan, "will put an email address up on the screens at the end. Please send me any questions that you have left unanswered. And finally, I cannot answer the lottery question, but if you find the answer to it, please email me that answer to the same address! I can assure you I will bless you at mass."

Again laughter.

"Let's start with some easy ones. Do aliens exist and did ancient aliens visit us and give us advanced knowledge? Don't know. I watched a lot of Star Trek but still unsure." He made the Vulcan sign with his hand. "But shhh, don't tell anyone." The laughter rippled around the tiered seating.

"Is God an astronaut? He doesn't need to be, no point, God is everywhere. Be a waste of an expensive suit!" His audience were loving the informality of the lecture.

"Is time travel possible? Einstein's theory of special relativity says that when you travel at speeds near to the speed of light, time slows down for you relative to the outside world. So, I guess, yes if you can go fast enough... or, there are always shortcuts, blackholes, wormholes. Stephen Hawking believed that wormholes are constantly popping in and out of existence at the quantum scale, far smaller than atoms. By the way, Hawking once held a party for time travellers, he sent out the invitations one year after the party. No one turned up!" Again, the audience enjoyed his delivery and responded with more laughter.

"What happens when I die? Is there a Heaven? Where is Heaven? Phew, now that's a lot, but let's see now. What happens when I die? The people we leave behind will be sad. Is there a Heaven? Yes, of course. Where is Heaven? Does it matter? Let's meet when we are all there, in the Kingdom of Heaven. Let's meet and see if then we can describe it, I suspect not. I suspect we will have no need; it will require no words. No explanation.

"As for the other questions, lets dig right in now and deal with the subject of this lecture. If you would allow me, I am going to start with numbers. When Pythagoras founded his scientific order in Croton, in Southern Italy, he believed in the Orphic mysteries. His message was simple, all things are numbers and the principles of things are the principles of numbers. The essence of the number is the principle of the universe, structured around geometric rules.

"So, all things are numbers. All things are structured mathematically, the trees, us, flowers, rocks, even the space in-between them all. One big mathematical formula. Most of you will be aware of the Golden Ratio, also known as the divine number or the divine proportion. It has been known about for centuries. It is an irrational number because its terms go on forever after the decimal point without repeating. Some say it represents perfect beauty because it is found throughout nature. We see it daily in both man-made things and natural things, geometry, space and time, the human body. Almost everything, if not everything, has dimensional parts that are built upon it, it being one point six, one, eight etcetera; the number which is the building block of nature. Accidental? Science? By design?

"Phi is the basis for the Golden Ratio, phi is also known as the Fibonacci sequence. For example, the Fibonacci sequence means that each number is the sum of the two preceding ones. It directly links into the Golden ratio. Take two successive Fibonacci numbers and their ratio is so very close to the Golden ratio. As the numbers get higher, the ratio becomes closer. The number of petals on a flower will often be a Fibonacci number or sequence; as trees grow, they start to grow according to the Fibonacci sequence. From the tip of our fingers to our wrist, to our elbow; our nose to our mouth etcetera, etcetera. The patterns, the numbers are a Fibonacci ratio driven by the sequence. Numbers, deliberately defined numbers give us building blocks for life. This cannot be explained by the chaos theory, which has often been put forward. Chance perhaps?

"Luca Pacioli, the Italian mathematician, in his book *De Divina Proportione* – The Divine Proportion, wrote about phi, this was centuries ago, in 1509. Friar Luca Bartolomeo de Pacioli collaborated with Leonardo da Vinci. It is said that da Vinci incorporated phi in his drawings used by de Pacioli.

"The question about the pyramids. Do the pyramids hold mystical powers, reflect Heaven, was the knowledge on how to build them given by a divine power, or something else, or neither? You will find phi in the measurements of the great pyramids of Giza, and also, by the way, in the Parthenon built by the Greeks. In fact, in many mystical patterns. Take the height of the great pyramid and multiply it by forty-three thousand two hundred and it equals the polar radius of the earth; measure the entire base perimeter and multiply it by that same number and it is equal to the equatorial circumference of the earth. It is even aligned to true north!

"Ah, I hear some of you say, it's science. So is the big

bang theory but that says there was no time before the big bang, however, we understand that is no longer true. The big bang theory suggests that it is when time began, but they also say that the space inside a black hole is infinite. So, if space and time are relative, we have infinite time. Okay, before I go too deep and get myself lost, let's try and look at this another way. Time is about the past, the now and the future. Space is about what?" He asked the audience.

"Volume, height, width, the depth," someone shouted out.

"A physics student, I bet. So, how about matter?"

"Solids."

"And?"

"Liquids."

"And?"

"Gas."

"So, we know all three need each other, that's the continuum, physics tells us that. All three have to be there for us to exist, right? Space has to be there because if it wasn't, where would all the matter stuff go? Where would you put it all? And, if we have all that stuff, our matter, and we try to find a place for it, space, when would you do that if there was no time? May I offer a solution that does not require a big bang. Okay, let me think ... ah yes, it kind of goes like this: in the beginning, of our time, God created Heaven, our space, then earth, our matter. Phew, and you thought it was going to be more difficult. Creation is easy!"

Many hands went up – eagerness was jumping out from their seats!

Del Luca pressed on. "Okay, back to our friends the numbers. A set, a repeating pattern, that is the mathematical construct for all things. Did God put it there, and if He did, He being our Father, our Lord, the greatest scientist of all time. Actually, before time, because he created time. You see, God is not affected by matter, or by space and He is not affected by time because ... he created it!

"Now, Let me just complicate things a little. What are atoms made of because we are made up of atoms? We know atoms are made up of electrons, protons and neutrons, but what are they made up of. Well, a chap called Max Planck said it wasn't matter. He said they are made up of energy. They have no substance! And this energy holds all the stuff together through vibrations. So, we are not physical, we are an energy … could I use the word spiritual instead of energy? And in quantum mechanics we are pure energy. Planck went on to say that he had to assume that behind this force is the exitance of a conscious and intelligent mind, a divine intelligence. Is this science beginning to explain and confirm our God? But wait, who was this Max Planck? Well, he was a German theoretical physician who won the Nobel Prize in 1918, and founded the quantum theory, this revolutionised modern physics.

"Now, let's see if we can come to a consensus. We all know the word 'natural'. We can say it means ordinary, conventional, mainstream. So, if something is not natural, normal, we can say it is irregular, peculiar, abnormal. A thousand years ago a light bulb shinning from a ceiling would have been unnatural, when in fact electricity was just waiting for Michael Faraday and then Thomas Edison to find it and work out what to do with it. Computers, transport, medicines and healing, aviation, food production, cities, human genetics, space travel, communication. All of them and thousands more, have all been, at some point in their lives, classed as supernatural.

"So, things that have not been seen before and not understood, not experienced before, not thought possible, not thought about at all, then it comes true, is said to be not natural; it must be supernatural. Imagine the first person to rub their hands over something with static and then run their fingers through their child's hair. The child's hair strands stand up, following the hand around. I wonder if that first person, and perhaps the child, sadly were classed as witches because of this. Think of how powerful that static electricity is, more powerful than gravity, which is pretty powerful because it stops us all from falling off this earth.

"Perhaps what we should do, because I suggest this is what history teaches us, we should think that all things are possible, they are and have always been there, waiting to be found, discovered, stumbled on, invented. The light bulb. We just didn't know where to look, and with what, at what, via what, when, how and, for what?

And when they are found, then they are indeed super-natural." He left a pause between the words super and natural to emphasise the point; to emphasise the difference. "The word super means incomparable, sensational, wonderful, magnificent, glorious. At the time it has to be super, think about the original tallow candles for light, now think about the lights in Times Square. Look at using a leech for medicine to using an MRI, or a heart transplant.

"I know people will argue that science and spirituality are incompatible. That they contradict each other. Some argue that one seeks to explain how the world works, the other why the world works. I wonder if I might suggest a thought, a thought that science and spirituality transcend each other. I'm wondering if you might consider that they are in fact one and the same? They are the same, they are the divine truth. As it is written in John 8:32 *ye shall know the truth, and the truth shall make you free.*"

In just under two hours the cardinal had worked his way through the list of questions he was most asked. He answered some in a direct way, others he was more subtle about, left room for suggestion, in those he used 'perhaps' a lot. In all he used well-structured arguments, in a lot he used personal experience. He was fascinating to listen to. Charming. Self-effacing. Calm. Funny. He loved giving lectures to young enquiring minds and it showed.

Towards the end of the 'questions and answers' session, Father Ronan put up the email address the cardinal had promised right at the start. This was Father Ronan's way of letting the cardinal know it was time to wrap up.

"Ah," the cardinal exclaimed when it appeared on the monitors, "it seems that we have run out of time but there is the email address to use if you still have questions. I will answer every email but please bear with me, it might take a few weeks, but I will answer them. So, for now I have one question left to answer, do demons really exist and if so, what is it like to exorcise a demon?"

He knew that there would be those in the audience who were intrigued by the possibility that demons existed, curiosity was a human trait. However, he was also aware that there were those in the audience for whom it would give confirmation, confirmation that if demons existed, then God could exist. It would give them proof that it was possible and Del Luca understood this because it was the age-old issue of faith versus belief. There was much he could have told them. If any of the audience members had read the book *Morto Vivente,* they would have known the truth. It was the only account of a person who had died – from over forty stab wounds – to be walking around a few days later – the only one in the last two thousand years!

Morto Vivente, would have told them about the series of exorcisms that took place in a small, rural, Italian village a long time ago, nearly sixty years ago. The first exorcism was carried out by the local priest, trained but inexperienced. When he failed to remove the demon, he asked his bishop for help. His bishop sent two priests, an experienced exorcist, but he was very, very old and frail – he was in his late eighties – and a younger priest, who was studying to become an exorcist – this would be his first experience outside of Rome. Along with the local priest, the three priests tried again.

The possessed man was a man people called a simpleton, he lived with his brother and his brother's wife and their four children, on the outskirts of the village. Like the rest of the villagers, they were poor farmers trying to eke out a living. Despite Italy being the centre of Catholicism and it being the 20th century, in many of the small, rural villages they still believed in jinns, creatures that lived in the nearby mountains, rivers and forests. These invisible beings would cause trouble and harm; cast spells. Demon possessions were often viewed as spells inflicted upon a person by a witch or a jinn. The villagers ostracised the family. They hunted for the witch and the jinn but found none.

The priests undertook four exorcisms on the man over a three-day period. However, each one became more violent and more intense than the last. The demon was far too strong for a rural priest, an understudy and a frail priest. It was a battle they were losing.

On the fourth attempt, the most violent, they had been trying to exorcise the demon for nearly five hours, when the old priest, faltering and struggling with his breathing, fell ill and died of a heart attack before the ritual could be finished. The other two priests, fearing they would not be able to continue without the experienced priest ceased all further exorcisms and made plans to have the body of the elderly priest transported back to his hometown for burial.

The following morning a journalist from the city arrived. After hearing about a possible possession and exorcism case in a rustic village not but twenty miles from the town he was visiting to cover a corruption story, he decided this new story would make better copy. He telephoned his editor and convinced his editor that he should check it out. The editor sanctioned the visit to the village to check out the story. The journalist arrived by taxi on a hot day. He soon found out that one of the priests was dead and the possessed man, was still possessed. The journalist would document everything; he smelt a book in this story.

He needed the help of the villagers because the priests would not talk to him. He needed background information, details about the possessed man, a man called Vincente. He told the villagers that he had a very small budget but promised, if the story ran, he would be back with payment. He also told them that he would not use any of their real names. That swung it. The mayor of the village agreed on behalf of the village. The journalist began scribbling away and recorded a number of interviews with key villagers. He also convinced Vincente's brother to be interviewed and to let him meet Vincente when the priests had left.

His meeting with Vicente was the most terrifying experience he had ever had. He was in bed, lying naked but for a small sheet covering his groin area, the possessed man was bound by thick rope. His body looked ravaged by illness; his eyes open but dull. He moaned and spoke in a language the journalist could not understand. He appeared to be under a powerful spell. He spoke only once to the journalist, acknowledged him only once, he had said 'kill me, please ki—' Then the demon that possessed him came back again, speaking in a foreign tongue again. The journalist stayed for another thirty minutes but the real Vincente did not reappear after that. The journalist was visibly shaken when he left the farmhouse.

*

With the body of the dead priest on its way back to his hometown, the remaining two priests turned their attentions back to Vincente and the exorcism. The young priest wanted to wait for Rome to send further help but the local priest knew his parishioners well and talk of taking things into their own hands started to circulate. They were afraid for their lives; they were afraid for their children's lives. They worried that people wouldn't buy their produce because they would fear it too was possessed. It was in everyone's interest for the demon to be exorcised or, some were starting to say, the possessed man and the demon with him were killed. The priests were running out of time.

Finally, both priests decided to try one more time. Alone in the house they began the ritual. Reciting the exorcism prayer of Saint Michael, they laboured. *Saint Michael the Archangel, defend us in battle. Be our protection against wickedness and snares of the devil; may God rebuke him, we humbly pray. And do thou, O Prince of the Heavenly Host, by the power ...* Again, and again the two priests worked tirelessly to rid the man of the demon ... *of God, thrust into hell Satan and all evil spirits who wander through the world for the ruin of souls.* The demon proved too much for the priests, too strong, too powerful and they failed. As soon as the man's family came back, the two priests left exhausted. They returned to the church that night to pray. They'd promised to try again the next day.

The local priest, the one who had led the exorcisms since the older priest had passed away, was found that morning drowned. He was floating face down in the stream. There was no sign of foul play. It was not the only death that day. Later that morning, the body of the possessed man was discovered hanging from an olive tree on the south road that led out of the village. He had been hung and had died of strangulation, but his body had also been stabbed over forty times after his death. The body was taken down and buried later that week in a secret place outside of the village by his family. The young priest from the Vatican was present and made sure that Vincente had a proper burial. He left the task of informing the local authorities with the man's next of kin, his brother. The authorities were never informed.

The journalist was aware of the poor man's demise. When he enquired, he was told that the villagers no longer wanted to be interviewed and they wanted all of his notes and his tape recordings. He was left with no choice after a group of angry men surrounded him; he gave them over. He convinced them he would never tell anyone what had happened there.

The following day, the journalist secured a lift out of the village with the young priest. A small group gathered around the car. Again, they made their threats to the journalist, this time it included his family. The priest and the journalist drove away from the village, both men trying to come to terms with what had happened.

They had dusty, country roads ahead of them before hitting the main autostrada. Naturally, they were both eager to put as many miles between themselves and the village as possible. Seven miles outside of the village they came upon a man walking along the road. Taking him for a hitchhiker, the priest slowed down, then stopped to see if the man wanted a lift. The priest honked his horn, wound down his window and called out to the man. The man on the side of the road turned to face them.

The journalist froze, then he swore. "Go. Go, for fuck's sake Father, go."

The man on the side of the road stared at them. The man was Vincente! He started to walk towards them. Clearly visible on the man's neck were the rope burns from the hanging. His stare was fixed. The priest put the car in gear and sped away as fast as his car would allow.

The two men did not speak for an age, miles went by. Finally, the priest turned to the journalist and told him he must never write the story. He said that he needed to find out what it was, what they were dealing with. He did not want to panic the villages and villagers of the region. He told the journalist that the Vatican would deal with this. The journalist agreed not to write the story but would tell his boss it was a wasted journey after all.

The priest and the journalist never saw each other again.

*

However, a year later, the journalist finished writing his book, *Morto Vivente* – living dead. He knew it would be a seller, even perhaps a best seller. He was a good writer and the content was almost unbelievable if it wasn't for the eyewitness that he would name in the book. The eyewitness who could collaborate his story. It had all the ingredients of making him a rich man.

The day before the book was to be published, a mystery buyer purchased the small publishing company from its owners. They promptly closed the publishing company down and destroyed all copies of the book before any sold, they also destroyed the printing plates. They paid the journalist his ten per cent royalty for each book – without it ever going into circulation. The journalist knew he would never see any residuals, he'd sold the intellectual property rights of the book in order to receive a higher royalty. It was no longer his.

However, three books survived. The mystery purchaser who had bought the publishing company had kept one. When they found out that two more were missing, they believed a member of staff at the publishing company had taken them. The journalist, unexpectedly, died within six months.

It took the mystery buyer, a priest called Father Gino Del Luca, five years to track down one of the two missing books. The owner would not sell.

Father Del Luca was one of two men who knew that the story the journalist wrote, was true. The journalist was one eyewitness and Del Luca was the other, he was the young priest in the book.

The whereabouts of the second missing book had finally been revealed to him in the early hours of that morning, by its owner, Payne St Clair.

*

Del Luca looked out at his audience.

"Yes, they exist. And what is it like to exorcise a demon you ask? It is hard because they want to take over the host. They make them say and do things they would never ordinarily do. It is dangerous, both for the host and for the priest that performs the ritual." He thought back to one of the first exorcisms he had ever attended. He remembered the faces of the other two priests with him. One died of a heart attack during a ritual and the other, he was found floating face down in a stream. Del Luca was inexperienced back then, frightened and helpless. How times had changed.

"But I believed in demons long before I experienced one. Why? Belief means to believe in something we know or consider to be true. Faith does not have to be based on proof. Faith can and often is, based on what you feel, inside your soul. What you know deep inside you. As it says in Hebrews 11:1 *Faith is the assurance of things hoped for, the conviction of things not seen,* but like our light bulb, that is until they are seen. And as for faith, I would suggest you look to Mark 9:23 *All things are possible to him who believes.* Maybe he was onto something because perhaps, given time, all things are actually possible. We just don't know where to look, and with what, at what, via what, when, how and for what. But then one day along comes someone with unwavering faith: Michael Faraday, Thomas Edison, Nikola Tesla, Ann Tsukamoto, Alexander Graham Bell, the Wright brothers, Rosalind Franklin, Einstein, Galileo, Stephanie Kwolek, Newton, Alexander Fleming, Marie Curie ..." The cardinal was into his last few minutes.

*

Two men, both armed, one standing on the right side of the room in the aisle by a door displaying an exit sign lit up in green and the other standing on the other side, again standing by a door displaying an exit sign lit up in green, both watched the cardinal. Another man was outside waiting to see which exit the cardinal would leave from, that man sheltered in a doorway from the persistent rain. Their plan was to kill the cardinal at the first opportune moment. So far, there had not been an opportune moment, not without a compromised getaway route. Everywhere he went the cardinal had a protection detail with him. However, earlier that day they observed the protection detail leaving. They didn't know if they would be back. They hoped not. They waited. They couldn't carry out the hit inside the building because the people they worked for owned the Thornburg Society and the building.

The Thornburg Society listed a number of lords as patrons, they also listed a handful of retired politicians, an ex-prime minister, three senators, one Nobel prize winner, two MBEs and even eleven princes, one from India and the rest from various countries in the Middle East, with those from Saudi Arabia making up the majority of the princes. All the listed patrons were all high profile, public figures. Paragons of respectability.

The Society was set up thirty years ago by a small group of benefactors, 'philanthropists of like-minded people', a small brochure, scattered around the building, read that they created the Society as a trust, so any money it made was always put straight back into the Society. It was set up to advance the debate on science and religion – or so it said within the brochure and their website. They had welcomed many well known speakers to their stage and would continue to do so.

The building was purchased for several millions of pounds but the actual purchase price had never been made public. They had spent another five million pounds refurbishing the building and updating all its services, adding a kitchen and a dining room for visitors. It employed thirty-five people. The Society's current chairman was Lord Valkyrie of Perthrenshire. Outwardly a respectable peer who had spent a good deal of his life in service, the Royal Highland regiment. However, he was not one of the paragons! In debt, gambling, and the father of an illegitimate child, born from a high-octane romance with his children's nanny. The nanny was now ensconced in a flat in Kings Cross, with the child, where the lord spent most of his evenings whilst in London. Lord Valkyrie did not know what the real purpose of the Thornburg Society was, its real dealings, he knew though, it was not philanthropy!

As for the other thirty-four employees, they knew nothing of the real people behind the Society. Knew nothing of its real purpose. They would have been shocked and horrified to find out that the people behind the Society, the organisation behind it, had ordered the assassination of Cardinal Del Luca just some weeks back at a society wedding in Italy. Shocked and horrified to find out that they had tried to have him killed a number of times. And they knew nothing of the countless people the organisation behind the Society had tortured, kidnapped and killed over the years.

The three men watched and waited. There were others in London, waiting. The cardinal would not survive the night. And their orders, they came straight from Norway.

*

180

The man that was waiting outside read the text message that he had just received from one of the men on the inside, the leader of the kill team, it read, *he's done and coming out.* The man outside saw the cardinal and his aide come down the steps at exit C. He started to type a text back, *Got him.* He stopped and didn't send the text, he called instead.

"I said no calls. Text only. Y—"

"He's got a tail."

"What?"

"He's got a tail, Two men."

"You sure?"

"Positive. He's walking with the priest, seems like they're heading for the underground. The men tailing them, they're good. Del Luca's not seen them."

"Stay with them, text your position and we'll catch you up. We have his priest tracked anyway but just in case they split, stay with the cardinal." He then rang Norway. It was answered in two rings.

"Dead?" a man in Norway asked.

"No. The cardinal has a tail, two men. Pros."

"Wait."

There was a pause of about twenty seconds, and then a curt command, "follow."

Chapter 13

A meeting 900 years in the making

Date: The 19th – day two of Del Luca's UK trip
Place: A café fifteen-minute walk from London Bridge train station
Time: Afternoon, after the second lecture

It was still raining. It had been all day. It had not abated, not for a second. The storm clouds hung about covering the city on a cold, wet, grey day.

Normally heaving with people, mainly tourists, Borough Market was all but empty, no one was venturing out; city office workers were staying inside their city offices. Tourists were inside their hotels planning what they would see next – when the rain let up. Even the pigeons hunkered down underneath the railway arches, tucked away in the back, in the gloom and waited for respite.

He hadn't gotten much sleep the night before. It was early morning by the time the meetings had finished. He was told by St Clair that he would meet with the cardinal in London. St Clair told him to be careful but to get as much out of the cardinal as possible, the fact Del Luca knew as much as he did about them was not a good position for them to be in – the onus placed on him was the reason he hadn't got much sleep. Jonathan was anxious.

They'd driven down from Scotland early that morning; they'd driven hard to be able to make the meeting in time. They parked the car in a small private car park that the team back in the control room in Scotland had somehow conjured up. It was just under a mile from the meeting place. One Knight stayed with the car.

182

Two Templars walked side by side the short distance down the street to the café with their Seer. It had been found on the web by his wife, Dominique, the day before, as a meeting place for them. They had been told the café would be empty – they needed to keep it that way. They walked to the café, and once outside, they waited.

A few seconds later a voice came over their coms, "clear."

Their entrance into the café was announced by a small bell over the door. Sherry, the waitress, was alone because, as she told them, her colleague, Dawn, had rung in to say it would be a waste of time coming in today because there would be hardly any trade. No tips. No point. The rain was keeping their customers away because London was wet, again!

One of the Templars with Jonathan asked Sherry how many customers she would expect to see on a day like today. She looked out of the window, thought for a moment, then told him if she saw eight customers all afternoon she would be surprised. And when the Templar asked her how much she would expect to take in takings on a day like that, she told him between fifty to eighty pounds if she was lucky. He offered her one hundred pounds for the till and one hundred pounds for herself if they could flip the open sign to closed for about fifty minutes. "Nothing dodgy" he said, "a business transaction, that's all. Real estate." Her boss was away in Tenerife, a winter golfing holiday with his two brothers. She was tempted. Jonathan smiled at her and confirmed it was a perfectly harmless meeting. She heard the American accent from the cute guy, the smaller of the three men. She agreed.

Jonathan sat at a corner table well away from the door. He waited for the others to arrive. He was nervous but he knew she would be there soon; she was on her way.

Low-volume music played in the background, a melody of jazz segments competing with the gurgling, spitting, and hissing sound of a very large, shiny, stainless-steel multi-coffee-making machine behind the counter.

Near the café door, at a small round wooden table, the two Templar Knights now sat, sipping hot drinks Sherry had just made them. Anyone walking past who happened to look in would just see two men, looking like ordinary tourists waiting for the rain to stop so they could go and visit the next city attraction on their list.

Sherry hung around behind the wooden-topped counter, out of the way; she made herself busy cleaning and in between checking her phone messages and her friends' Facebook posts. There was a door behind her that led to a small storeroom. The storeroom held a small amount of stock, although most of the consumables were brought in fresh every day. It was also where the staff left their coats and bags. She went in and out checking the stock and re stocking shelves behind the counter.

The Seer was out in the open and since the beach episode in Scotland, with Salah El-Din in December, Payne St Clair would not take any chances. Even though Salah El-Din was dead, they had enemies even more dangerous and some, who had gone conspicuously quiet, who were far more dangerous: Zivko Cesar Gowst, the one the French called *Le Fantome Blanc*, the White Ghost. St Clair had a group of Knights, the Red team, who would be positioned outside the café, and a group, the Blue team, who would eventually take up position at the back of the café.

The two Knights were strategically positioned near to the front door. The door's quaint bell would rattle to life every time the door opened and closed. The Knights knew who was expected at the meeting with the Seer. Both Knights were 'active' Knights and both were armed. They each carried a Glock 9mm pistol, a bullet in the chamber: safety off. Their swords, the Templars' favoured weapon, the Katana sword of the Samurai, were concealed in their back-body webbing inside the lightweight titanium *saya* – scabbard, hidden by their coats. Through the rain running down the café window, they watched a handful of hurrying pedestrians trying to run from the day's deluge; and London black cabs were fruitlessly seeking out fares on another slow, wet day in London.

Across the street, in an empty office above a Chinese takeaway, the Templar Marie-Claude was in position. Her view was of the café's front door, the entry and egress point. She also had a good view up and down the street. Marie-Claude was a trained sniper and one of the best shots in the Order. Her favoured 7.62

calibre, scoped rifle was tucked into her shoulder and ready. Its barrel resting on a small lightweight tripod. Her concentration was focused, her mind sharp. She had been there two hours before the time the meeting was due to start. She had given Jonathan and the two Knights the all-clear. She watched and waited.

Six other Knights were outside. Four Knights from the Red team were on the street, now hidden. Two just up the street from the café and two were just down the street. The Blue team, the two Knights who were still tailing the cardinal and Father Declan from their speaking engagement at the Thornburg Society, would soon be there and they would position themselves behind the café. A Red team Knight had placed a car there, which the Blue team would sit in. It was next to the canal, just off the towpath, that meandered through the borough.

Soon there would be another two Knights joining the three inside the café, it was a twelve-person operation – St Clair had also invited one eccentric professor.

Back in Scotland, they monitored the operation. Each of the twelve Templars showed on a detailed satellite map imaged on to a large screen in the control room.

They too watched and waited.

Jonathan sipped his green tea – he was trying to keep away from the coffee, he figured his body didn't need any artificial stimulants, it had been stimulated enough for the past few years!

Sitting, he no longer acknowledged the Knights near the door. They were all in position looking like people drinking a hot drink, taking shelter from the rain, not knowing each other. Having the two Knights there made him feel safer. He was looking forward to seeing the people who would soon be there: Aldrich and Cardinal Del Luca, he'd met neither since Rome. He'd been on a call with Aldrich not too many hours before but he had not spoken to the cardinal. The Lionheart would also soon be there and there was a fourth due, someone he had seen just a few hours ago. They had made love and then eaten breakfast together.

Sherry was back at Jonathan's table. She liked the American. Sherry had black hair, a slim, fit-looking body and more than a flirtatious way about her. The other two Knights found it amusing that the Seer was getting a lot of attention. They tried not to look. They tried not to snigger.

The bell above the café door rang out and the person, rain dripping from their umbrella and raincoat, hung their coat on the old, wooden coat stand by the door.

"Do you want me to ask her to leave?" Sherry asked Jonathan. Then she added, "by the way, I get off at 5 p.m. if you are interes—"

"Pleassse," the wet customer who had just come into the café muttered under her breath. She moved to Jonathan's table. "No, actually he's not interested." The wet customer announced.

Sherry looked disappointed.

"In fact, his vow of celibacy forbids any contact with females."

Sherry's disappointed look now changed to a look that suggested she was feeling sorry for him. "What, none at all?" she asked with incredulity.

"Nope. None, Nada," the wet customer replied. "Zilch!"

"Geez. What a bummer for him. So, he's one of those religious types, then?"

"Fire and brimstone to the core. Preacher type. A priest, in fact. He would have you converted before the froth on his coffee had time to settle. Let me just say," the wet customer leaned in a little, "barren!"

"Damn." Sherry empathised.

"You two do know I'm sitting right here, don't you?" Jonathan interjected.

"Just chatting to me sister, Mister," Sherry said. "Keep your pulpit on." She touched the other person's arm in a sister-solidarity kind of way and they both laughed, and then Sherry walked away.

"Celibacy?" Jonathan said.

"It's an option," Dominique replied, sitting down beside her husband with a big grin on her face.

"It's the American accent you know," he said teasing her.

"It might be more than an option if you carry on."

"And we have that really nice room tonight, in that really nice hotel, in that really nice part of the West End, be a shame not to u—"

"Okay, Yank, you can stop now, you had me at 'really nice hotel room'."

There was a ripple of laughter back in the control room in Scotland. All the conversations were live over their coms network.

Courtney, Jonathan's sister shook her head as she laughed. "He doesn't stand a chance, poor man."

"Zakariah, Dominique's father was standing next to Courtney, he smiled, "she doesn't get that from me, that's her mother all over."

The café doorbell rang again and Jonathan and Dominique turned around to see who it was.

The two Knights near the door had already recognised the two men as they were approaching the café, and the Knights outside had already announced their approach over their coms. They knew who they were. They were expected. Marie-Claude's crosshairs had tracked them the second they had turned into the street.

Cameron Jack smiled and acknowledged Jonathan and Dominique, then he sat at a table opposite them.

"Corpse, my old chap," the other person bellowed with a roar. "So very nice to see you again." The voice belonged to a man who had bounded through the café door with as much noise and gusto as the gale that followed him in. "I've not seen you since our exploits in Rome. My God Corpse, have you b ..." He stopped short as he noticed the person Jonathan was sitting next to. "Well, bugger me, Brigadier, and this is the missus, eh?" He turned to Dominique and planted a 'lip-pouting' kiss on both of her cheeks. She didn't have time to get up – she was pinned to the chair. "Damn, you smell good Missus. I'm Aldrich Manwin Tucker, witch hunter, professor and" then he whispered "not quite a Templar. At your service my dear," he was back to roaring again. He shot a glance in Sherry's direction. "Bet she's flattened some grass, eh?" Another roar of laughter erupted from his mouth.

Then the bell went yet again and two men walked in, an

older man and a younger man. The older man put out his hand to Aldrich and smiled broadly.

Aldrich grasped it and shook it vigorously. "Ah, Cardinal. How have you been old fruit?"

The Cardinal laughed. "I have been well, witch hunter."

"And who do you have with you?" Aldrich asked the cardinal.

The cardinal introduced Father Declan. "I have heard all about you Mr Tucker," the priest said.

"Ha. Good, good," Aldrich roared with glee. "And I will tell you more. But first, let me do the honours. Corpse you know," he said pointing to Jonathan. "And over here we have the Lionheart; no real names here mind you." More roaring laughter.

Cameron Jack was about to apologise to the cardinal for his and Dominique's masquerading over the last few days but he didn't get the chance.

The cardinal smiled. "Ah. I have been looking forward to speaking to the real you. Do I have this right, Aldrich? He turned to face the Lionheart. This man's name is Cameron Jack." The cardinal continued now turning to Cameron Jack. "If I'm not mistaken, sir, you finished your degree at the age of twenty-one, with a *first* in medieval history; you promptly joined the army, British Intelligence Corps, as an officer. You specialised in counterintelligence. At the age of twenty-five, you followed your grandfather's footsteps and joined the SAS. Once my friends had a name, they were able to do some more digging and we found something really interesting in old newspaper clippings. When you were sixteen, you won a competition, and the prize was a trip to Japan, more specifically to a dojo owned by Hinata Satō the 10th Dan grandmaster. We know he was the Templars' Master of the Blade. We also know you trained under Tanjkna Sugata San, Hinata Satō's understudy, whom we assumed eventually took over as Master of the Blade. And it seems logical that you would have taken over from him. We think you are the Templars' new Master of the Blade."

"You knew we were not the British Secret Service, didn't you?" Dominique asked the cardinal, interrupting him.

"Yes, I knew," he confirmed.

"Something's been bothering me," she said. "After the first lecture you gave, when you were coming back to the car, I had a sense you knew me, it was like you recognised me. It was just the look you gave. Was I wrong?"

"No, you were not wrong," he confirmed.

"And that put you on to the Lionheart as well?"

"Yes. I'm afraid I had my aide, Father Declan here, do some digging, he's very resourceful like that. Fingerprints are a marvellous thing. That's how we know about Mr Jack here."

Father Declan held up his briefcase, it still had some powder on the handle used to pull Cameron Jack's fingerprints. "Sorry," he offered. "We have friends in the city who helped us. From that, we found out about your army record, your fighting skills and even your grandfather, quite the warrior family. I'm sorry."

"But how can you know me?" Dominique asked. "There are no fingerprint records of me, and we have never met."

"You are wrong, my child," the cardinal said. "*Dominique. Sei bella adesso come lo eri quando avevi dieci anni* – Dominique. You're as beautiful now as you were when you were ten."

"*Mi conoscevi?* – You knew me." She had spent her childhood in Italy and unconsciously switched to Italian.

"Sì, e tua madre – Yes, and your mother."

"English please," Jonathan said.

"Seems the cardinal here knows me, Darling!" Dominique said. "And he knew my mother too, but I have no idea why."

*

Glennfinch Castle

Back in Scotland, Zakariah was listening intently. St Clair looked across at him but Zakariah gave him a look of *I don't know who he is or how he would know Dominique or Sophia.*

Zakariah's wife had been a Templar. A crucial planner and strategist in many of their most successful sanctions. She was attractive, had a great smile and could light up a room. Sophia was also a Seer. She lived in Tuscany, not far from where she was born. Dominique was ten years old when her mother died.

"Ask him how he knew your mum?" Zakariah spoke to his daughter over their coms. "Ask him how he knows you?" She didn't have to ask the cardinal as he was about to reveal all. The Templars in the control room could all hear what Del Luca told her.

"Your mother was seven years old when I first met her. I was just a young priest back then but I was already part of the Cabal, oh, don't worry, we'll come to that, and we'd heard of this young girl who lived in Tuscany who was a miracle child with numbers. A savant. I attended her Sacrament of Confirmation and supported the bishop that day. I followed her progress, as she grew, she did more and more astounding things with figures. At the age of fifteen, she completed her first degree and her second at seventeen. Her Doctorate by the time she was nineteen. She went to work as a professor at Milano University. She was a marvel, a beautiful, astounding marvel.

"Then we saw the marriage banns announced, as is the law, the announcement must be published publicly. She married a British man. He had no background, no history. We checked and double-checked. The man she married was a ghost. Your father didn't exist!

"Then that terrible, terrible New Year's Eve night." The cardinal seemed to falter slightly as he was remembering back. He took a second or two, and then, "that night the police contacted my bishop for help and he sent me. I was lucky, I was only fifteen minutes away in the next town. When I got there the police were still searching the grounds and trying to work out what had happened." The cardinal paused. "I'm afraid I am upsetting you, Dominique."

"Te ... tell him to finish the story," St Clair told her over the coms. "We need to know how much he knows. We must know."

She was silent. She didn't want to ask him. She didn't want to hear it: she didn't want to remember, to re-live it.

St Clair turned to his brother; Zakariah knew St Clair was right. "It's ok, Honey, please ask him. It'll be okay."

She asked him to finish the story. There was visible consternation on the cardinal's face. His intent was not to upset her.

He was a kindly man.

"Finish it." Her voice was clinical, with no emotion, that was buried deep inside her.

So, he did. "Abaddon assassins kidnapped your mother; they left you for dead. The Italian police found your mother's body four weeks later, after a nationwide police hunt. She had been tortured and raped. Her elbows smashed, her ankles broken and her ears, eyes and lips had been removed before they finally disembowelled her.

"You hit your head during your mother's struggle and fell from the bedroom balcony down onto the lawn. They left you for dead: you nearly were. The police found you sometime after they had arrived. At first they thought you had also been taken, so they were not looking for you. Then a policeman found you, I was there and they called me over—"

"And you picked me up in your arms ... covered me with a blanket ... and took me into the house." Now she remembered him. She'd been in shock. His face had been blurry, but the image of a man who had picked her up and wrapped her in a blanket, a kindly man with a soft voice, had filtered into all those bad dreams she had suffered from for years afterwards and the image was the only salvation she had during sleep.

"But then other men came and took you away," he continued. "They had the proper paperwork and you were released to them by the police. I assumed Templars because I recognised one of the men who took you away. The man was someone we had identified as a Templar a few years before.

"I, we, could only conclude your lovely mother was a Templar, and probably a Seer because of her exceptional gift. We also believed her husband, your father, was also a Templar and we assumed that you would eventually become a Templar too, like your mother and father."

"Give him your earpiece," St Clair told Dominique.

She did and the cardinal adjusted it in his ear.

"Can you hear me?"

The cardinal recognised his voice. "I can."

"Do you know who I am?"

"I believe the one who is the head of the Worthies, the one they call Grand Master."

"When we last spoke, cardinal, I asked you if you learned so much about us from one of our own. You said yes, from one who knew all our truths. You wouldn't tell me the name; you said I knew his name. Cardinal Del Luca, no more games, what is their name?"

"Jacques de Molay," the cardinal said. "The Templar Grand Master at the time of your near extinction, and his death in 1314. And because of him, we have kept a secret that has been a secret for seven hundred years, verbally passed down from one to another, decade after decade. It is the secret of the Ark key, given to us by the original one.

"Grand Master, I need to tell the Seer a story. A very important story about a farmer's boy called Thomas Dumas, a Spanish knight and the last Essene to have lived on this earth, a hermit called Caleb, who lived high in the mountains of the Cañon del Río Lobos, near Soria, in Spain, seven hundred years ago."

St Clair told him to take out the earpiece and give it back to Dominique.

When he had done so, she told them she was back on the coms.

"Leave the café now," St Clair told her. "All of you, bring the cardinal and his aide to Scotland, to the castle, to our castle, and bring our Seer with you."

Then, things went bad.

On the street

"Standby, stand by." Marie-Claude's voice came over their earpieces from her vantage point in the empty office, just across the street from the café. "Who else has eyes on him?" she called.

"We got him," one of the Templars who was sitting at the table by the café door confirmed. "He's on the opposite side of the street walking and looking at his phone. Wait one. He's stopped. Turning round ... he's turning back again slowly. It looks like he's trying to follow a map on his phone. Wait one, he's walking again.

Blue team, you should have him now."

"Roger that, he's just coming into our view. He's turning left. And ... now he's gone. All clear."

There was a pause in the communication between the Templars in Scotland, those inside the café and those positioned outside. The cardinal and Father Declan had no idea what was happening but they guessed from how the Templars inside the café were reacting, they were in touch with other Templars outside.

Luther Jones's voice came over the coms.

"What was he wearing?"

A member of the Blue team responded. "Wearing?"

"It's raining, right? You guys told us it was raining."

"He was ... he—"

"Was he wearing a raincoat or hat, or carrying an umbrella?" Luther asked.

"No ... but maybe he left when it wasn't raining," someone said over their coms.

"Luther is right," Dominique said. "It's been raining all day, from about four a.m."

Now the cardinal and Father Declan knew that they were in communication with others and there was a problem.

"Did you sweep him?" St Clair asked from the control room in Scotland. "Did you sweep the cardinal for bugs?"

"No, we haven't done it yet, they onl—"

"Do it," St Clair ordered.

One of the Templars sitting by the door got up and approached the cardinal; he made his apologies then he swept an electronic device detector over the cardinal's body. "He's clean," he said over the coms.

"Do it again," St Clair told him.

Again, the Knight apologised to the cardinal and again he swept the device over the cardinal's body.

"He's cl—"

"Frisk him," St Clair interrupted.

The Knight was just about to apologise for the third time when Luther spoke again.

"Wait. His aide, sweep his aide, if there's a tracker, they will

193

have planted it on him. He's never far from the cardinal's side. His security focus is the cardinal not his own. Check him, quickly."

The Knight walked towards Father Declan. The priest smiled and lifted up his arms in readiness.

"Standby, standby." Marie-Claude's voice was on the coms again. "Our man is back. Now walking back up the street. Inside the café, he will be in your line of sight in three, two and one."

"Got him."

Dominique began to open her coat. The cardinal heard nothing of their conversation but he knew there was trouble.

"Damn it!" the Knight sweeping Father Declan exclaimed over the coms. He'd just found a small tracking device on the underside of Father Declan's coat collar. "He's hot. I repeat he's travelling hot." He threw the bug on the floor and stood on it.

"Black transit van just stopped to pick up our mark," a Knight from the Red team towards the top of the street called. "Standby, standby. It's turned around. The van is heading back your way. Two hostiles in the front are wearing clown masks and black boiler suits; the one in the passenger seat is armed. Assume more hostiles in the back, armed. They are twenty seconds out. Make note, make note, the van has a side, sliding door, no back exit door. Inside the café, the sliding door will be on your side."

The van picked up speed very quickly and was travelling at high speed, in wet conditions with poor visibility. Its two windscreen wipers struggled to cope with the rain because the van was driving head-on into it. The force battering the windscreen.

Marie-Claude saw the transit van. "I have it. In three, two one." Her right index finger gently squeezed the trigger of the rifle. The sound of her shot rang out. The driver's head viciously snapped back as the bullet went straight through it.

The man in the passenger seat saw where the shot was fired from. He frantically grabbed the steering wheel but the van was still travelling at high speed, the foot of the dead man behind the wheel still pressed onto the accelerator. He shouted to the others in the back to get ready, they were going to crash.

He had no choice, he turned the wheel and aimed for some scaffolding rigged up on the outside of a three-storey building, two doors down from the café. He knew it was their only chance of stopping the transit from flipping over. There was a screech of tyres when he turned the steering wheel sharply and the transit swerved right to the other side of the street. It hit the scaffolding; poles, braces and planks flew everywhere, its collapse deafening. A second later the van hit the skip which was full of old roofing tiles. The van crunched to a metal-bending halt, smoke pouring out of its engine.

The passenger, their leader, checked the back, they were all still alive, seven armed men, he made it eight. He shouted to one of the hostiles by name and ordered him to make it to the other side of the street and fire from the doorway of the Chinese takeaway into the café. He knew that the shot that killed his driver was made from an upstairs window above the Chinese takeaway, if his man was in that doorway, the shooter upstairs would not be able to see him, or fire at him.

The side door of the transit van was jerked open. Seven masked hostiles all made quick exits. Their leader, also masked, kicked open the passenger door. A hostile ran across the street as the rest laid down covering fire into the window above the Chinese takeaway.

Marie-Claude rolled away from the window; bullets breached the room through the window – it was deafening. She caught a bullet to the leg. It was a surface wound but she knew she had to get out of there.

Next, the leader told two of his men to bookend – a covering-fire tactic. He'd seen the two Templars at the top of the street as they drove down and figured there would be others at the other end of the street to box them in. Both followed the order. They laid down, feet wide apart for a solid position, their rifle stocks pressed into their shoulders. They lay side by side, one man facing one way and the other facing the other - bookends. They were shielded from the sniper above the Chinese takeaway by the transit van.

"Don't fucking shoot us," the leader shouted in Albanian. They were just two doors from the café where their targets were. He made one last check: one man hiding in the doorway of the Chinese takeaway, safe from the rifle above, laying down fire into the café. Two in prone firing positions covering their front and rear. He sent two more men back several shops to a small alleyway that ran between the buildings and out towards the canal. He told them to work their way around to the back. Then he and the remaining two started to work their way through the scaffolding poles towards the café, hugging the façade of the building, trying to stay as close to them as possible to reduce their exposure.

Gunfire erupted.

Of the few people that were on the street at the time, some ran, they ran as fast as they could. A few ran into shops; all screamed. They did not come out again until the police arrived. Two red London buses, one at either end of the street, had stopped and all the passengers, including the drivers, fled the mayhem.

Inside the café

The two Knights who had been sitting at the table by the door, were already on the ground, they were dead seconds after the opening salvo. Their two blood pools merged into one in seconds. They had made two easy targets for the gunman tucked into the Chinese takeaway doorway. He had opened fire into the café, spraying bullets indiscriminately through its large window; shards of glass flying like darts. Bullet holes punctured the café's large, glass window, yet it stood.

The first to react was the Lionheart. He'd been in war zones and intense firefights. His instincts took over. He opened the door slightly and returned fire. As soon as he did, one of the hostiles lying down opened fire towards the café door, this gave the hostile in the takeaway door the chance to lean out slightly and start firing again.

"They have superior firepower," the Lionheart had to yell over his coms because the noise was deafening. "We're in trouble."

Next to respond was the cardinal, he too had been to war. He made for the Seer, to protect him; to shield him.

Events were now unfolding in double quick time.

Dominique opened her coat and pulled out a pump-action 12-gauge shotgun. She turned back and looked at Aldrich. He knew what to do. Aldrich joined the cardinal. They both grabbed Jonathan's arm and pulled him towards the back of the café near to the counter. Aldrich upended two tables and pulled Jonathan and Sherry, down behind them.

The Lionheart hurled a chair at the café window and it smashed – no more flying shards of glass hurtling into the café with every gunshot.

Dominique and Cameron Jack ran towards the wide, gapping aperture the window left behind and they both started returning fire.

On the street

The Red team was split into two, two Knights were three hundred yards further up the street than the transit van, but they were pinned down by one of the hostiles lying down. He was shielded by the transit van; they were now desperately trying to make it from shop doorway to shop doorway on the opposite side of the street. They could have tried to cross the street to get a clear shot at him but they knew a gunman lay in the Chinese takeaway doorway and he would have easily picked them off as they tried to cross. They knew if both sets of Knights started opening fire whilst making their way towards the café, the chances were one of them would kill the other. It was a dangerous tactic because they were firing whilst advancing towards each other's positions. The chances of any number of bullets firing into oncoming Knights was very high. The Knights at the top of the street knew they had to try and take out the man in the takeaway doorway first. This would stop his indiscriminate firing directly into the café and protect the other Knights coming up from the other end of the street.

The other two Knights in Red team were more than five hundred yards down the street from the café and running hard to get there. They stood a slightly better chance because the hostile lying down and firing in their direction, also had his leader and two other men in his firing arc. He fired more slowly, with his boss and two hostiles hugging the shop fronts heading for the café, his line of fire to the two Knights from the Red team, was radically reduced.

*

Two hostiles had found the small walkthrough alleyway between the buildings, it was just seven buildings further up. They ran through.

*

"They're closing in," Marie-Claude warned the people in the café. "Be good if you can get out of there."

Inside the café

"Sherry," Dominque called. "Other than the front door, is there another way out of here?" Sherry did not respond." "Hey, Sherry, focus. Is there a w—"

"There's a door in the back," Sherry shouted above the din. "I use it to sneak out and go and have a fag. We can get to the canal towpath."

Dominique looked at Father Declan.

"I'll take them," Father Declan said. He got up to go and she grabbed his arm. Her look was a look of desperation. She so wanted to protect her husband, to shield him, to keep him safe but she knew the Lionheart needed her. "He's my—"

"I know," Father Declan said.

"Yes, but he's also the S—"

"I know who he is and what he is. I got this."

"Has anyone got our six?" Dominique asked over their coms.

"Has anyone got our six?"

"Blue team has your six," the reply came.

"Five people coming out; don't kill them." Dominique pulled out her backup gun, a Heckler Koch .40 with a 13-round magazine, from a holster in her shoulder rig and gave it to Father Declan. She gave him an extra clip.

He gave her a reassuring smile. "They will have to take my life first before they can get to him." Then he got up and led Jonathan, Sherry, the cardinal and Aldrich into the back and out the back door. They cleared a small wall, then onto the grassy embankment that led down onto the towpath and to safety.

Glennfinch Castle

Back in Scotland, it was frantic. They knew what was happening. They had all the Templars' mobile phone tracking devices on a large screen. They knew where everyone was. St Clair was in direct coms with the Lionheart now and all coms conversations were on loudspeaker in the control room. "Lionheart," he said, "you have control."

"Roger that," Cameron Jack confirmed. "Blue team, confirm when you have them."

"Roger that."

Scotland estimated that there were nine hostiles. One, the driver, was dead thanks to Marie-Claude. Three were making their way to the café, two laid down covering fire from behind the van, one was hidden in the takeaway doorway, and two had been seen disappearing down an alleyway.

On the street

A delivery cyclist came speeding along the street. He saw the transit van and the pile of scaffolding poles scattered all over the road. He thought a crash. Then he heard the gunfire and he thought robbery. The cyclist made for the pavement opposite the transit van.

He was almost by the Chinese takeaway doorway when the hostile popped his head and gun barrel out to fire on the Knights at the top of the street, who were still desperately trying to make their way down to the café.

The cyclist saw him at the last minute and couldn't swerve in time; he ploughed into the hostile. Both fell sprawling to the ground. The cyclist raised his head with a moan, just in time to see a tall woman, all dressed in black and wearing a long black leather coat, blood oozing from her leg. A large rifle in one hand and a Samurai sword in the other. She knelt beside the hostile and, just as she was going to drive the sword into the hostile's heart, she looked directly at the cyclist – she was just three feet away.

"Where do you live?"

He said nothing, he was still in shock.

"Quickly, tell me."

He blurted out an address in Kilburn.

"When the police come, you didn't see me, so you can't describe me. Agreed?" He nodded in agreement "You may want to look away now."

Seven left.

*

Now the Knights at the top of the street crossed and immediately began firing at the two hostiles laying down in the prone firing position. The hostile facing them returned fire immediately but without the other shooter in the takeaway doorway to protect him, he was completely exposed. One of the Knights bullets finally found its mark and the hostile dropped his rifle and his head dropped onto the pavement. Now they were not being fired upon, they made good ground. One moving, and the other one covering, then that one moving and the other covering. In and out of shop doorways they weaved their way towards the people trapped inside the café.

Six left.

Down at the other end of the street, one of the two Knights was within one hundred yards of the café entrance. He was in a firefight with the leader and two hostiles. His partner was wounded, he lay tucked away in a shop doorway, a make-shift tourniquet on his leg to stop the bleeding. His hand had also been hit, he could not hold his gun. He could shoot with his left, but it was his weakest shooting hand and he could not risk it because his partner was directly in his line of fire.

The Knight making headway breathed heavily. He tried not to but he was exhausted and adrenaline started to sap his body strength. He tried to stay focused. *No slip-ups*, he kept telling himself in his head. He heaved, gasping for air. He fired, then fired some more; then fired again. The only way he stood any chance of hitting one of them was to stay out of the doorways and onto the pavement. He fired repeatedly. He heard the cry. He saw a hostile fall. He saw him dead on the ground. He dived back into a doorway.

Five left.

The last hostile lying behind the transit van was aware there were shooters closing in on him from behind. He raised himself to his knees. He needed to direct his fire behind him now. Those in front, he thought, were on their own; he needed to protect himself.

The two Knights saw what was going to happen; they saw who was crossing the street to engage the hostiles. They both knelt and started firing. They were now sitting targets – but not for long.

"Thank you, Knights," Marie-Claude said to them over the coms. "In three, two one, go." The two Knights got up, turned around and ran, intentionally drawing fire onto themselves. The hostile saw his chance, he got to his feet and ran a few feet forward, he was no longer protected by the transit van. From the back of the van a woman, all in black, stepped into his path. Her sword plunged into his chest and he instantly fell dead.

Four left.

Glennfinch Castle

The team in Scotland knew the Knights were running out of time. The London City police, along with an armed response unit, would soon be on the scene. They needed to get their Knights out of there and quickly.

"Blue team, confirm you have them." St Clair shouted over the coms to be heard above the noise of the firefight taking place. There was no answer. "Blue team, confirm you have them." Again, nothing.

Dominique looked at Cameron.

"Go," he shouted, "I'm good here."

The canal towpath

She ran to the storeroom and out of the back door. She cleared the wall. As she reached the top of the embankment, she could see their predicament. At the bottom of the embankment, and to her right, she saw two hostiles firing down the towpath. About one hundred yards away from them, and to her left was a four-foot diameter, concrete culvert pipe which carried rainwater into the canal. Shots came from within. She guessed the others had run into it to take cover because they came under fire from the hostiles.

"Jonathan," she called over the coms.

"I'm here," he replied straight away. "We are s—"

"I know. I know. "It'll be okay, I'm here now. Ask Father Declan how many rounds he has left."

A second or two went by. "Five."

"Okay, Jonathan, here's the plan. I have clear shots at the shooters. As soon as I start shooting, they will turn to me, you have to make a run for it then."

"But the Blue team, you need to wait for the Blue team."

"I don't think they are coming, honey, they haven't been answering. Jonathan, you have to listen to me now. Tell the others what we are going to do. As soon as I give you the command, make a run for it. just turn left and run as fast as you all can along the towpath."

Jonathan told the others and they made ready.

Inside the café

Cameron Jack heard her voice; it was almost a whisper. "Lionheart, two heading your way; they're coming in. Be ready." Marie-Claude watched the two hostiles. They were in the doorway of the shop next to the café. The shop owner had locked the door when the shooting started and was now in the back with two customers who happened to be in the shop when all hell broke loose.

"They're making their move," Marie-Claude announced. The team back in Scotland braced themselves. Billy Jack tensed up, The Lionheart was his grandson; he was a far more able soldier, more experienced, a better combatant, a better leader, a warrior but, he was his grandson and Billy Jack would never stop worrying about him.

The coffee machine inside the café hissed, then it exploded as a hail of bullets smashed into it. The two hostiles had left the shop doorway and were now standing in front of the opening, where the glass window used to be, and firing into the café. The Lionheart was standing against the wall behind the door, the door was open but the frosted glass of the door had remained intact. The Lionheart's back was firmly pressed against the wall. He heard the glass on the floor outside being crunched by the first set of footsteps. He let the first hostile through the door. The hostile ran through shouting and screaming at the top of his voice. It was the leader of the hostiles. He did not look back – why would he, the other hostile was right behind him.

The leader saw the place was empty. He called "clear" to the other hostile and then went into the storeroom. The back door was open. He pulled out his mobile phone and made a video call. "They're gone," he panned the phone around so the person on the other end of the phone could see for themselves.

"Seer?" he was asked.

"Gone."

"Cardinal?"

"Also gone. They must have gone out the back here but I have men out there, and I have sent four more."

There was a pause, and then. "he say don't kill. He say must be alive."

"I understand."

The leader took out another mobile phone, a burner, he sent the text message to the others. *'The Seer and the cardinal alive; kill all the others'.*

The second hostile had stayed in the café doorway, laying down fire back down the street at the Knight that had fired repeatedly at them and had hampered their progress all the way. The Knight kept breaking his cover to lean out of the doorway and fire in short bursts.

The hostile heard 'clear' from his boss. He was relieved to hear it and ran into the café and out of the way of the gunman just down the street. He was thankful to be unscathed. Seeing his arm completely severed sent him into shock. He'd run into the café, his arm outstretched, gun in hand, ready to fire just in case. Like his boss, he did not see the man behind the door holding a Katana sword. The Lionheart brought it down with fury onto the outstretched arm. The severed arm fell onto the floor, the hand still clutching the gun. The second movement by the Lionheart saw him step back and bring his sword down at a forty-five-degree angle, high to low. The hostile's throat lay open and his chin almost severed.

Three left.

The leader heard the commotion. He came back out of the storeroom and immediately saw the dead body on the floor, its clown mask bloody and sliced through; its throat gaping open. A man stood in front of him. The hostile lifted his weapon to fire. 'Click, click'. He threw the gun at the Lionheart. The Lionheart ducked. "Nice sword. Samurai. You better hope you are as good as you think you are." He pulled out a machete.

"Me see him." The voice from the phone called out. His pidgin English was distinctive. Cameron Jack already knew who he was.

The hostile still had the phone in his hand, still connected via video call. He raised his phone and pointed it at the Lionheart, who was now face-to-face with Bo Bo Hak.

"Before we meet each other, you not die then; now you die." Bo Bo Hak told him.

"You know this man?" There was another voice, a low scratchy, eerie whispering voice on the call. He spoke English but with a strong eastern European accent and in a low rasp that sounded like fine shards of glass being stepped on. His voice tapered off to a whisper at the end of every statement. "Let me see this man." Bo Bo Hak moved out of the way and a new face appeared. "Ah. Lionheart!"

Everyone back in the control room looked at each other. They all held their breath; they didn't dare believe it was who they thought it was but the voice, it was exactly as André Sabath had described it to them.

Cameron Jack saw an odd-looking man on the screen. A pallid-skinned man, with pure white hair, a pink eye, the other he presumed was missing because he wore an eye patch over it. It was semi-dark in the room, with just one small fluorescent light. His pink eye showed signs of photophobia, sensitive to sunlight but not fluorescent light. He was also instantly recognisable as an albino.

"You think your man can take him?" the man asked Bo Bo Hak.

"Yes," the answer was laced with disdain and contempt for the question.

"But you couldn't in Romania when you met him, he beat you. We killed the Lebanese Christian, the Templar Sabath and many others but not this man, this man beat you."

"He there can beat. I can beat." Bo Bo Hak rounded.

Over their coms, the team back in Scotland asked Cameron Jack to video link with them via his mobile phone; St Clair wanted to see what the Lionheart was seeing.

"Nystagmus," Tiff whispered as the image of the man appeared. "It makes his eye receptive to uncontrolled spasm movements, especially when he gets tired."

"Is this who I think it is?" St Clair asked the question out loud that everyone was thinking. "Is this the White Ghost? Is this Zivko Cesar Gowst?" They were all certain it was, the detailed description André Sabath had given them of his voice and appearance left them all in no doubt. They wondered why Gowst would reveal himself in such a way, there was no need for him to do it. To expose his image like that. But there was another momentous moment about to come.

"Let our man kill the Templar."

It was a new voice. There was another person in the room with Gowst and Bo Bo Hak. It was a man's voice. They could not see him. His voice was neither loud nor soft. Not distinctive.

"Yes, my Lord, as you wish," Zivko Gowst said.

Everyone in Scotland stopped what they were doing. St Clair looked over to Courtney and Bertram. They both nodded, yes, they had recorded the conversation; they had recorded that voice.

The hostile hit the red button on the phone and threw it to the floor.

"Got to go," the Lionheart said over the coms. Then he slowly put his mobile phone back into his pocket. He never took his eyes off the man in front of him; watching for any slight movement, any change in his eyes. The hostile wielded his machete for a second or two then he settled into his fighting position.

The Lionheart's eyes narrowed. "I recognise those moves. I know he trained you; Bo Bo Hak trained you. Though, as you have learnt, when we met last time I beat him. Let's hope you are better than him."

The hostile spat, and then he wielded his machete again, slowly turning, and then, he began his attack.

"Girl, tell me you have them." Cameron Jack used her nickname; rarely would they use their real names over coms.

"They're trapped. I'm trying to get them out. Could use some help. You done there yet?"

"Yup," he replied. He then held his sword in the middle of the blade like a spear and threw it. The hostile stopped dead, half of the Katana protruding out of his back, the handle part out of the front. He keeled over and fell.

The Lionheart retrieved his Katana sword from the body, wiped clean the blood and then drew a small red cross on each of the hostile's foreheads. He then ran out the back door.

Two left.

The canal towpath

As soon as they heard Dominique's plea for help, the two Knights from Red team, who had made their way down from the top of the street, doubled back and through the walkthrough alleyway between the buildings. They quickly made their way down the grassy embankment and onto the towpath. In front of them, they saw two hostiles firing towards a concrete culvert. They looked left and saw Dominique at the top of the embankment; she was soon joined by the Lionheart.

"Red team two in position," one of the Knights announced over their coms.

"Stand by Red team two. Jonathan, tell the others on my mark go, go left and go fast. We will lay covering fire down on the hostiles. They will be too occupied with us to worry about you."

"Got it," Jonathan said.

"On my mark, three, two, one." And with that Dominique, Cameron Jack and two Knights from the Red team, all opened fire and it rained down bullets on the hostiles. The two hostiles tried to fire back but they were outgunned. It was mayhem.

Cardinal Del Luca, Aldrich, Sherry, Jonathan and Father Declan all emerged from the culvert, they ran left and down the towpath. Father Declan brought up the rear and used up the last of his rounds helping to pin down the hostiles. He was now out of bullets and caught up with the others.

Cardinal Del Luca saw them first, two bodies floating in the canal, it was what was left of the Blue team. Then the others saw them. Sherry went to scream but nothing came out, she was in shock and in a bad way. Aldrich had held on to her ever since they had fled the café. He had not left her side and had placed his body in between the hostiles' bullets and her a number of times. She slowed him up; she stumbled several times, but Aldrich hung on to her. He stayed with her.

Four men stood across the towpath, armed: they were not Templars. They all wore clown masks and boiler suits: they were definitely not Templars! A black Range Rover was parked at the edge of the towpath behind them, all the doors were open. They knew they were looking at the people who had murdered the Knights whose bodies now floated in the canal.

The cardinal turned to Jonathan, "go back, go back," he shouted at the top of his voice. They were about two hundred yards from Dominique and the Lionheart but only one hundred yards from the four new hostiles. It was a hopeless situation.

"Red team, close in, we have the front, you close in on their six. Watch the crossfire, let's make sure every round is aimed at them, not each other." Cameron Jack told them. They advanced, keeping low, spread out, ten feet apart, firing on the move.

They had all stopped. They saw the four hostiles starting to run towards them. They were not firing. The cardinal called to Father Declan. "Take them. Protect them. Protect the Seer." The cardinal turned back towards the four hostiles and stated to run towards them, shouting at the top of his voice.

"Don't," Father Declan screamed after him. But he knew it was the right move, the only move. He knew that the Seer's life was the most important thing. He watched his boss, his mentor, his friend, and his Brother from their ancient Order, charge towards the hostiles. The one they called *Volpe Bambino* – baby fox during the war, but now called *l'esorcista del Papa* – the exorcist of the Pope, had no weapons, just heroism.

The Lionheart and Dominique closed in quickly on the two hostiles that were left from the original onslaught. Red team Knights made the same ground from the rear.

She heard his voice over the coms, Jonathan's voice, and she recognised the panic in his voice. "We have four new hostiles in pursuit; no way out, we are coming back to you. The cardinal ... the cardinal ..."

Just then the two hostiles decided to make a run for it. Both were shot the second they stood up. Dominique looked back for her husband. He was safe. The group ran to them and then they all collapsed onto the floor. Gasping for air. Afraid. They were exhausted. Sherry sobbed uncontrollably.

"The cardinal?" she asked her husband.

Jonathan looked back to see the cardinal, along with the hostiles, were gone. "They took him."

"They'll kill him," Father Declan shouted. "They will kill him."

St Clair heard Father Declan over Jonathan's coms. "Priest," he called to Jonathan, "tell him they won't kill the cardinal. If they wanted him dead, he would already be in the canal. I don't know if these are the same people that have tried to kill him in the past, and if they are, as I suspect they are, then something has changed and I think it is because he met with us. My guess is they will keep him alive as long as necessary because they will want to know what he was doing with us. Tell Father Declan and then get back here Priest, all of you. I don't know how much time we've got to find the cardinal and save him, but we won't have long. Don't lose Father Declan, I'm going to need to know everything Del Luca knew, I just hope he can tell us."

Dominique's voice came over the coms. "They all have it. They all have the three crescent moons tattooed on their wrists."

On the street

A slight crackle. Red team one. "I confirm, all dead hostiles on the street and in the café, all have the three crescent moons tattooed on their wrists."

Chapter 14

A green flashing cursor

Place: Llucmajor, Mallorca, Balearic Islands, the Mediterranean.
Time: The day before Del Luca's second lecture and the café meeting

The green cursor flashed away in the corner of the room. Day and night the old 1980s bulky computer monitor screen, attached to a matching bulky hard drive, both now yellowing with age, flashed. At first, she had found the fact that he kept the screen on, kind of cute. He never turned it off; would never turn it off. It was, he said, to remind him of the way it was before the helix. How they had struggled; how he had struggled to get his experiments accepted. Back then they had no money; he had no standing in the science community, within academia, no recognition. Then one day it happened and everything changed. He called it the pre-photon life and the post-photon life helix. It changed things. It changed everything. Before they would struggle to buy food, pay their rent. They rarely went to the movies and never ate out. After the helix, they ate well, went out, owned two properties, a two-bedroom apartment in Barcelona, just off the famous La Rambla and the Plaça de Catalunya, which they rented out and the other, their main residence, a three-bedroom house in the town of Llucmajor, Mallorca on the Balearic Islands. Now they had money; now he was celebrated within the science community: they had made it.

But now it was bugging her. She found it annoying but couldn't figure out why. Something had changed. Something was off. She'd stared at it for a week. It was driving her mad. She couldn't work it out. It was beginning to make her irritable. The cursor flashed away in the corner on the old monitor screen. Flash, flash, flash, as it had done for over forty years but now it was different. Was she going crazy? A thought that had crossed her mind several times a day. Was it different? Why did it bug her so? Was it because he was no longer there?

The letter he sent was brief, not his style, he was a scientist and everything he said or wrote demanded verbose explanation. It used words he wouldn't; it just didn't fit with him. However, regardless of the words used, their meaning was the same and devastatingly so:

My dearest Rosario

Please forgive me. The pressure has become too much this last year or so; my work is suffering, I am so, so unhappy. I need time, time to find myself again. To re-evaluate. To take stock.

Please do not search for me. I will contact you when I am clear how I feel about the purpose in my life.

I do love you but I need time.

Al x

Al, Allan Studerbaker, was an American who married Rosario over forty years ago. She was Spanish and a student and took some of the same classes as him at the Massachusetts Institute of Technology, MIT. It was clear even back then that he was special. He had one of those brains that saw physics and mathematics like a Da Vinci masterpiece, a panacea canvas: stunningly, impressively complex but with endless possibilities; potentially holding the answers to every single question about life that had ever been asked.

For forty years Allan Studerbaker had dedicated his life to his science, and she had dedicated her life to him. They had no children – she couldn't.

She always thought they were happy. There was nothing over the last forty years that would suggest to her that there was a problem in their marriage or a problem with his job or his work. It just didn't make sense to her. Of course, she was all too aware of how things could change. They had friends who had gotten divorced, surprising everyone when it happened. They had male friends who did crazy things at middle age and not just male friends, females too. But she knew that he was not a midlife crisis kind of guy. She called him her science nerd. He lived for his work; he lived for her. She lived for him.

In the second week after his disappearance, she found out he had also written a letter to the laboratory where he worked, telling them he was taking a sabbatical. His boss, Dr Drew Thomas, had not contacted Rosario because he assumed it had been a joint decision and he wanted to give them space. Feeling lost, confused and somewhat embarrassed, she had not reached out to Thomas when Allan disappeared. However, one week moved into a second week, she was getting desperate. She rang Allan's boss and Thomas told her about the letter he had received from Allan. She asked what the letter said. He read it to her. It was just four lines; it said he was exhausted and needed time. He would be in touch. She asked him the date of the letter, he told her, it was the same date as the letter she had received. She asked the post mark, it was Barcelona, the same post mark as on the envelope she received. Thomas said he was confused because there had been no indication of a problem, in fact quite the opposite, they were finalising some really interesting findings on the helix and Allan was excited. She then asked him if he believed Allan wrote the letter. It threw him for a second or two because he had just assumed that he had. He had not seen any mystery in it, no skulduggery or alternative meaning behind the letter. However, as he was looking at the letter, he started to notice the language, it too was a little off; not Allan-esque. Allan was more clinical – he was a theoretical physicist. Whilst Rosario waited on the phone, he called in one of Allan's close colleagues. She knew about Allan disappearing and the letter but had not seen it. Thomas showed it to her and she immediately said she did not think it was Allan who had written it. Both letters had been typed on a computer.

The fact that they were not handwritten was another big problem for Rosario because Allan loved writing to people by hand; he considered it good manners and always kept writing paper and a fountain pen with him. He would use emails, but sparingly and only to colleagues about specific work. Thomas told her he would ask around. He said she should go to the police if she felt Allan had not written the note. He offered to go with her if she wanted.

By week three, she had still not heard from Allan and had finally convinced herself that something had happened to him, something bad. By then, she had let his family know. Most, loving him but not understanding him, just thought it was another of his eccentricities and he would be back. They consoled Rosario with 'I'm sure it's nothing, you know what he's like', and 'that's Allan for you, he'll be back before you know it'. It was surprising to her that not one of his family thought it was suspicious.

It was embarrassing for her to reach out to their friends and ask them if they had seen or heard from Allan or knew anything about his intention to leave for a while. Nobody knew anything. Most had the same opinion as Allan's family, a few told her, if he wasn't back in a month, she should get on with her life and forget about the selfish bastard.

It was the start of week four and she finally decided to reach out to the one man she knew might just be able to help her find him. He was someone she and Allan knew well; he was someone who had once worked in the shadowy world of the CIA, a man called Ken Knox.

Kenneth (Ken) Knox was the son of an army officer. The family moved around a lot; it gave Ken a wide experience of life and other cultures and it fed his desire to learn and understand other people and see other places. An American from Florida, he joined the army, the Intelligence Corps. They taught him Russian and that became his speciality. When he left the army, he was recruited into the CIA. He became one of the country's most experienced operatives on the Russian desk.

In later life, he met and married the belle of the ball. She was a Canadian and eventually he settled there and changed his nationality to become a Canadian citizen. They lived a quiet life in a house on the rugged coastline of Nova Scotia with their dogs and cats. However, Ken wasn't a hundred per cent done with covert operations and sometimes took an occasional contract as a freelancer and because of this, he would regularly see low-level briefing papers from Langley, sent to their contractors.

Some years back, Ken had lived and worked in Cambridge, Massachusetts. There he met Allan Studerbaker and Rosario Cortez and they all became great friends. When they married and became Mr and Mrs Studerbaker, Ken was Allan's best man. Allan was Ken's best man when he married many years later.

Ken's work in Cambridge was to identify any Soviet operatives working the campus of MIT, looking for people who might be sympathetic to their country's cause. The CIA knew that MIT was, as with most universities, a hotbed recruiting ground for foreign governments. Young American minds driven and blinded by the righteousness of opposing Western movements, their own government. The injustice and oppression imposed by these governments and their government on the Soviets and others, was horrifying for them. It was Vietnam and Cuba all over again. Something must be done! Swayed by ideology based on such a thin veneer of understanding, some students signed up – and the flames of their rectitude ever fanned by the Soviet wolves in sheep's – student – clothing.

Allan and Rosario knew what Ken did for a living and at times they would help him – saving young, susceptible American minds from committing future treason! They all became great friends and had kept in touch, mainly via email and occasional skypes. They had not spoken for six months.

*

Rosario Studerbaker paced up and down the floor of the hall of their town house, staring at the house phone as she went. She was hesitant. No one knew how dreadful she felt, how worried, how utterly alone.

She opened the small, black phone book they always kept on the hall table and searched the Ks, for Ken Knox's number. She checked the time in Nova Scotia on Google, he was five hours behind, it was 7 p.m. his time. It rang five times and then Ken answered. He was delighted to hear from her but quickly grew concerned with what she had to say. She told him everything. She said she was scared. This was not Allan; Allan would never do this. He was happy at work; he was happy at home. She was crying, her frustration had built up, the burden of not knowing had made her a wreck. She'd agonised with multiple scenarios during all those sleepless nights – none of them good. She had not gone to the authorities, "perhaps I should?" she asked.

Ken smelt a rat! Something was wrong, she was right, this was not Allan. His intuition went into overdrive. His instincts, finely tuned over many years as a CIA operative, were telling him that Allan was in trouble. He told her he'd wished she'd contacted him sooner. This didn't help and she started crying all over again. He quickly added that he understood why she'd delayed, she had done it for Allan's benefit because it was, seemingly, what he wanted. They had a long conversation but he told her to hold off going to the police for a little while longer. He told her he would look into it. She felt better; it was a lifeline.

Ken put the receiver down and then paused. He pulled out his mobile phone and started looking at flights out of Nova Scotia. He was in no doubt that he needed to go there. It was clear to him that Rosario had no more information than what she had told him. She wouldn't know what to look for, he did. If he wanted leads, this was a boots-on-the-ground thing.

He moved out of the hallway – his wife was watching tv in the other room. There was something at the back of his mind, it was a bit hazy, foggy. He'd heard of this, surely, he asked himself. Had he missed Allan's name in something he'd read? *No, I'm not that bloody old*, he thought to himself. He quickly went into his den. His den was oak-studded, with an old 18th century desk and leather-bound chair. To one side a wall, full of books, on the bottom shelf, two years' worth of issues of the Monocle, a global affairs and lifestyle magazine, his magazine of choice; he had read it for years. On another wall, several guitars lay leaning against the wall.

He switched his desk top computer on. It loaded. He went to his floor safe and retrieved a small, black USB entitled 'Security Briefings CIA'. He put the USB into the computer's hard drive and sat down in his chair. He switched on his brass desk lamp, pen and notepad ready. The screen flickered and then the files index came up. It took him less than a minute to find what he was looking for; to find what the foggy thing was that had been at the back of his mind. It was there on the screen, two briefings, one from two months ago and one from six weeks ago, briefings about missing scientists. He checked for Allan's name; it was not there. The briefing paper asked a red flag question, had these scientists left to go to a foreign power? It went on to say that whilst these people were known as top scientists in their fields, none of their work was connected to either defence programmes or space programmes, the two areas that would create the most concern for the CIA and one for Homeland Security. Ken read on:

MISSING: Hans Augst
German
Electromagnetism engineering professor
Three children, one, Klaus also missing.
No note
No contact
Missing eight weeks

MISSING: Anna Petrof
Ukrainian
Microbiologist
No children
Note left for husband
No contact
Missing six weeks

He looked at the notes he made during the conversation with Rosario.

MISSING: Allan Studerbaker
American
Theoretical physicist
No children
Note left for wife
No contact
Missing four weeks

He read the note Anna Petrof had sent to her husband, it was remarkably like the one Allan sent to Rosario, same kind of language, same syntax. He couldn't prove it at that point but he was starting to suspect they were connected. After an hour or so he kept coming back to the same scenario, Allan did not leave of his own accord and neither had the others – Occam's razor, *the simplest solution is almost always the best; the most obvious answer is often the answer.*

He spent the rest of the night, all night, searching all the intel files. As a CIA contractor, he had access, so he could search for patterns and similarities. By 5 a.m. he had come up with one more, a British scientist called Theresa Tylor. She had also gone missing but the information was scant, other than she was an exceptionally talented cosmologist and had been missing for nearly six months. She had two children but one of them was also missing. She went missing at the same time. The police had drawn a blank. He saw the pattern but he needed more information about Theresa Tylor to verify it. He needed someone he could trust in the UK, someone who knew people. There was only one man, a friend, a man who had been at his wedding.

In 1992 Knox met a British Secret Service agent called Morgan Clay. This was one year before Clay left the Secret Service, after his superiors nearly got him killed by the IRA. That was one bureaucratic blunder too many for Clay and he left. Ken was one of very few people who Clay told he was leaving. He told him that he was going private and would take on contract work – which of course, was not true because he had joined the Order of the Knights Templar.

Ken always said that Clay was probably the best Secret Service agent he knew. He was average looking, average height, with average features and average ways. Nothing ever seemed to change about him – leastways, not outwardly. The kind of man you could see every day for a year and when asked not be able to describe him. He was a professional spook, a ghost man. Ken admired his work and his fieldcraft.

Ken Knox dialled the number he had for Morgan Clay. He knew what would happen, after the many years he'd spent as a CIA operative he recognised the small delays, the nuances each time he'd called Clay: the call was being checked.

Since Tiffany Clarke had been appointed to the Higher Council of the Knights Templar, she had spent less and less time in Islington. A deputy controller had been appointed. The call from Ken Knox came in, it had been routed through the secret satellite communication center in Islington, UK. The computer, in its electronically protected shell (EPS), checked the call's authenticity in the usual way and then connected the call. The caller was calling Morgan Clay's mobile number, the number was registered on Morgan's approved list. The deputy controller told Clay who it was and that it was clear. He put the call through to Clay. The two men exchanged pleasantries – neither man would embarrass the other by asking too many questions about what each had been doing. They knew they would not or could not answer.

Ken gave Clay the outline of the problem. He told him about the call he'd received from Rosario and the other scientists who had also disappeared. Clay agreed with Ken: if it looks and feels like a storm, invariably someone's getting wet: Occam's razor!

Clay agreed he would do some digging and they both agreed to try and find out via their sources, if there were any reasons why each of these people would want to walk away from their lives. Of course, they knew there were a myriad of possible reasons that might cause that action: perhaps they were in debt, big debt, maybe a gambling problem, maybe they borrowed from the wrong people. They knew that stress and depression causes people to do things outside of their norm, their character. One of the most common reasons for disappearing was due to affairs or any other type of marriage crisis. They may have become involved in illegal activity, like theft, fraud, selling copies of designs to competition, patent designs, formulas, know-how, work product ... perhaps they had been duped into it, perhaps they thought it was not as bad a thing to do as other things – but then it became as bad! The lure of big money might have been the reason. For some competitors, stealing knowledge through a competitor's employee was a short cut to allow them to avail themselves of research that otherwise would take them years and large investments to get to.

Clay and Ken Knox both agreed with the CIA's categorisation on the people missing: on the surface at least, it seemed that these people were not threats to national security: they were not working on defence programmes or any of the space programmes. But they needed to find out why they all left because then, they might stand a chance of finding where they were. They needed to interview the families of the missing people. Ken said they should start with Rosario in Mallorca because she was willing to talk and he knew the missing person, very well in fact. Clay agreed it was a good place to start and would give them valuable insight and validate, or not, any emerging thoughts. Ken invited Clay along to visit and meet with Rosario. He knew Clay being there would be invaluable. Clay told him he would check his schedule and let him know within the next few hours. Then, Ken emailed the three-missing persons' details to Clay, plus the name of the fourth, Theresa Tylor.

Clay knew he probably would not be able to go, the Templars were meeting with the cardinal the next day in London, after the cardinal's second lecture at the Thornburgh Society. He would be needed in London.

*

It was three hours later when Clay called Ken Knox back. Clay confirmed that he would not be able to go to Mallorca but he had asked a couple of friends, who were also in the 'game' as private contractors, if they would take his place, Ken agreed. He told Ken that they would meet him at Palma airport in one day's time, if that timeline worked for him. Ken agreed; the trail was already somewhat cold. Clay then told Ken he had found about one hundred and fifty-six scientists who had gone missing in the last sixteen months. However, five fitted the pattern: missing on their own, they had left a note. He said that all the notes were very similar. The second type: missing along with one of their children, no note. None had been in contact with their spouses since disappearing. The five were an astrophysicist, a Nobel prize winner for her work in quantum mechanics and quantum electrodynamics. Plus, a theoretical mathematician, a geobiologist and an evolutionary biologist. He also had the details on Theresa Tylor, the cosmologist. He sent it over via text and Ken read it whilst he was still on the call with Clay:

MISSING: Theresa Tylor
British
Cosmologist
One child, Annabel, also missing
No note
No contact
Missing six months – longest missing
*

Place: Palma Airport, Mallorca, Balearic Islands, the Mediterranean
Time: Afternoon

Their flight was on time, direct from Glasgow to Palma. They were entertained on the flight by two boisterous stag parties and one, even more boisterous, hen party. They refused several invitations to join them.

Morgan Clay had briefed them. He couldn't go because he was in London, on standby. Ever since Del Luca had had the conversation with Jonathan in the Church, at the slaying of the Hag, St Clair had got Morgan Clay to tail the cardinal. The Templars needed to know who the cardinal really was, what he knew and how he knew it! Clay was now in London waiting to pick up the tail again, but for now, the two Knights from Blue team were tailing the cardinal from the place of his second lecture to the meeting place with the Templars.

Clay's stand-ins waited just inside the arrivals meeting area, in a café called Paul's. Ken Knox's plane was just two hours behind theirs. They waited. The time went quickly.

They had a full description of him, given to them by Morgan Clay and when he walked out, they spotted him straight away. Broad man. Red hair combed back, a well-kept red beard and neatly dressed in khaki trousers, brown loafers and a blue, button-down collared shirt. He was carrying a small holdall.

Luther rose from his seat and introduced himself as Luther

Coats, an alias he used from time to time. Luther had served in the SAS for fifteen years. He was stocky and gave the impression he could handle himself. Along with Tiffany Clarke, he was one of the newest of the Nine Worthies, the Higher Council of the Knights Templar. He liked cowboy boots, his boots had metal toe and heel tips – people knew when Luther was coming. Morgan Clay had just given Luther's name to Ken Knox, no description. He told him to look for a cowboy – it was spot on. However, Clay felt the need to pre-warn Ken about Luther's travelling companion, the second stand in for Clay. He told Ken he was odd but a genius.

Bertram Hubert Klymachak De'Ath stood up, his black backpack, with an assortment of things in it, was strapped to his shoulders. His white, flash of teeth leapt out of his deep brown skin and they were the first thing to greet Ken Knox. His black square glasses, his unkempt, floppy hair and acne were the next. And if there was any mistake, Morgan Clay had told Ken that the other person with Luther Coats, would most likely be wearing a green tartan, tweed cloth suit, waistcoat, with a fob and scuffed brown shoes. He was.

Bertram shook Ken's hand enthusiastically. "I'm Cerebral," said the Oxford graduate who had a 'first' in Computer Science, specialising in Nanotechnology, Artificial Intelligence, Blockchain, Advanced Electronics and Gaming.

"I'm sure you are," Ken replied. "I'm Ken Knox.

"Ah, Mr Knox Ken."

"Actually it's ..." Luther was looking at Ken, with a look of I wouldn't bother trying! "Ah. Knox Ken I am then."

Ken had already rented a hire car via an internet booking, and after a few minutes he went off to the car rental kiosk in the arrivals area to sign for the car and collect the keys. He was only gone for ten minutes.

Two Knights from the mainland had arrived the day before as planned. They arrived by boat, and at night – they were carrying weapons, so no airports with customs. As they were giving Luther two 9mm handguns, with two spare magazines, they told him that they had watched the Studerbaker place for most of yesterday, ever since they arrived on the Island from Spain; they had watched from around 11 p.m. and had taken shifts to watch the house through the night. No one left and no one came but they did see more than one person pass the window a few times; they thought three people were inside. Luther didn't mention this to Ken Knox. As an organisation, the Templars were already on red alert, for now at least, they would play their cards close to their chest. The two Knights had disappeared by the time Ken Knox got back.

Ken drove them straight to Rosario's house; she was expecting him because Ken had spoken to her directly after he had spoken to Clay the first time. He told her he was coming to see her. He did not mention there would be others because at that stage, he didn't know himself.

Turning left out of Palma airport, which was on the outer edges of Palma city, at Can Pastilla, they eased out onto the MA-19A. The traffic was light, as the winter was slow to retreat and had not turned into spring yet; the white sandy beaches were empty, the sea was rough, the sky grey and most of the shops, restaurants and bars were still mainly closed.

The Templars' plan was to stay for a few days if they needed to. They had reservations at the Playa de Palma Court hotel for two nights, just in case. Ken planned to stay at Rosario's, this had already been agreed with her.

Luther sat up front with Ken, Bertram sat in the back ensconced in a textbook. The journey was light on conversation, up front, each knew that neither would give any personal details, and none were asked, so the conversation lingered around the weather and the lack of traffic. They were heading east to a town called Llucmajor. It was a twenty-minute drive. Their plan was to meet with Rosario and to find out as much detail as possible. The key was to determine if his disappearance was linked to something of his own making, like mounting debts, gambling, stress or the most sensitive, if she was aware of any affairs? There were several other possibilities but they would ask the most likely first. If there wasn't an obvious reason, they would need to think about something less obvious and perhaps more ominous.

The drive to the town of Llucmajor was an easy drive because the traffic was light, they made it in under twenty minutes. It wasn't a market day either, so there were plenty of parking spaces – the market was always held in the centre of town and caused major disruption. They parked near the bar Rosario had told Ken to park at and then followed the directions she had emailed to him. Luther insisted that he walked on the other side of the street. She was expecting Ken, and he wanted Bertram to stay with him, he said that three men standing at her door might cause her some consternation. They didn't know what the back story to Allan's disappearance was yet and the less they spooked her the better.

The Studerbakers lived in a three-bedroom town house on Carretera de Tor. It was old but they had refurbished it a few years back and now it had one of the better-looking facades in the street. Ken pressed the door intercom and waited. Luther was still on the opposite side of the street, directly opposite. He was looking into a shop window but through the reflection he could see all the Studerbaker's front windows. Down the street, three hundred yards away, the two Knights were sitting in the outside seating area of a café. They ordered coffee and waited. "In position," one of them said over the coms. "We have your six."

"Roger that," Luther confirmed. Bertram also heard it through his earpiece; he did not respond.

At first, there was no answer from Rosario. Ken pressed the buzzer of the door intercom three of four times more. Finally, she answered.

Rosario sounded flustered, worried; not herself. "Si?" it was curt; she wasn't curt, it wasn't her style.

"Hola Rosario, it's Ken," he said.

There was slight pause and then she said, "I am too busy today, Ken. Please go. I was mistaken. It's all fine now. I'm sorry to have troubled you."

Luther watched and knew there was a problem. The curtain at one of the windows had twitched, he saw a male figure. He was looking down onto Ken and Bertram.

"Get ready," Luther said over his coms. The two Knights down the street stood up, they left a five Euro note on the table and started to slowly walk towards Luther.

"But I have come a long w—" Ken didn't get chance to finish.

"GO AWAY. Please, Ken. Everything is alright now." He knew it wasn't. Then she added, "I'm sorry to have dragged you away from the kids. Go home." He didn't have kids, now he knew she was in trouble.

Ken looked over to Luther. Luther spoke to Bertram on their coms. "Tell him to leave." Bertram did. Ken was now aware that the two men were in communication with each other. Their earpieces almost hidden because they were built on nano technology. Ken then noticed the two men walking slowly towards Luther, he knew enough to know they were not just pedestrians. He turned to Bertram and said, "I think he's in trouble," he looked towards the two men. "My gut tells me they are not just out for a stroll".

"It's alright Mr Knox Ken, they are with us." Ken breathed a sigh of relief. Ken and Bertram moved away from the Studerbaker's door.

*

Inside the Studerbaker's main living room, the two criminals paced. They were anxious. Twitchy. Both were armed. One was a Moroccan, who had been in Mallorca for three years, after fleeing Madrid because of money laundering charges. He lived on the north of the Island, in a place called Alcudia. The other man was a Russian, who lived closer, in Palma Nova, next to the port, where he did most of his business! He was a hard, brutal man who had spent time in a number of European jails before he smuggled himself onto the Island of Mallorca. Between them they had committed numerous counts of murder, extorsion, torture and kidnapping, as well as a raft of other crimes. They were being paid – source unknown to them – to keep watch on a woman in Llucmajor. Her house phone and mobile phone were tapped – she was not aware of it. Once she'd made the call to Ken Knox, the unknown source contacted them and told them to go and sit on the woman, make sure she did not meet with the man and to make sure she didn't say anything else, to anybody. The two criminals conned their way into the Studerbaker's house and had imprisoned Allan Studerbaker's wife. She was surprised they knew about her call with Knox. They kept pressing her but she kept telling them he was a family friend and an insurance broker by profession. It was then that she knew Allan had not left her. They told her if she contacted anyone else, her husband would die; and if she did not get rid of the man at her door then her husband would die. She believed them. She needed to somehow warn Ken; she hoped he would know the slip-up about children was deliberate.

"If you go back, can you get in. Can you disarm the intercom and pick the lock?" Luther asked Bertram over their coms.

"Yes, Mr Luther. It's a standard single action, twin barrel—"

"How long will it take?"

"It will take twenty seconds to disconnect the intercom camera, because it is a C series—"

"Bertram!"

"Twenty seconds for the intercom and five seconds for the lock."

"Go back and do it, quietly. Then, leave and wait in the street."

"Okey dokey; the Pink Panther is back on the cas—"

"Bertram!

"On it, Mr Luther."

Luther met up with Ken just around the corner. The two Knights covered Bertram.

"How many of you are here?" Ken asked.

"Four of us."

"I know better than to ask but—"

"Then don't. Were you a field operative?"

"Yes"

"When I go in, are you rusty or good to go with me; I can use one of the others if you need me to, they're both good men."

"Carrying a little more weight, but not rusty."

"Then, you, one of the others and I go in." He gave Ken a gun. "I want her to see you, so she's less likely to panic and get herself killed. You make for her and keep her safe, we will handle the muscle."

Ken checked the gun, cocked it and put one in the chamber. Then he put the safety on. "Safety on and good to go," he told Luther.

A few seconds later one of the Knight's voices came over the coms, "he's got it open. You are clear to go, Luther."

"We'll need your Spanish, Ignacio."

"On my way." The Knight crossed the street, then he walked along towards the Studerbaker house, Luther and Ken approached from the other direction. Luther spoke to Bertram. "Walk down the street, cross over and join our Knight there." Bertram ambled across the street like a tourist and joined the Knight. They were a hundred yards away from the Studerbaker house.

Luther and Ken hugged close to the façades of the buildings, trying not to be spotted from the Studerbaker window; Ignacio did the same. Once there, Luther eased the door open. "Damn," he whispered. "Tiles!" He removed his boots. "Steel caps," he explained.

*

The criminals were thugs, not professionals. They were in the same room as Rosario. She was sitting in a chair petrified and hoping Ken had not gone away. One of the criminals was standing by the window. He was looking for the man with the American accent who had been on the intercom. He was sure though the man had gone now – he was lazy and not vigilant. The other thug, the Russian, sat drinking the Studerbaker's brandy in another chair opposite Rosario.

*

"We're going green," Luther said over the coms.

Bertram and the other Knight started to walk at pace down the street. They stopped opposite the Studerbaker house. "In position," the Knight with Bertram said.

"Okay, do it," Luther instructed. Both the Knight and Bertram looked directly into the window where the curtains were twitching earlier. Bertram threw a small stone at the window.

"Get here, they're back," the Moroccan spat out in broken English.

"Who's back?" The Russian rasped back at him.

"Two men, they're looking at us. I think one was here earlier. Look, there. Over there."

The Russian got up but kept his glass. "You're fucking *estúpido.*" As he was walking over to the window, he suddenly saw three men rush into the room – one was in his socks!

Ken dived towards Rosario, grabbed her arm and threw her off the chair and on to the floor. Ignacio ran at the Moroccan man at the window. He was taken by surprise and he faltered. He went to pull the gun from the back of his trousers but couldn't get to it in time. Ignacio fell to his knees, skidding along the marble tiled floor, his right hand reached behind the back of his neck. His hand found what it was searching for. He gripped the *tuska* – handle of his Katana sword. The whole thing took less than five seconds. Still skidding along the tiled floor on his knees, Ignacio leaned back, withdrew his sword, held it at right angles to his head and, at the last minute, thrust it forward. The Moroccan went to scream, he wanted to but his voice had gone, what came out was a fountain of blood.

Ken Knox rolled onto his front. He held his gun at the Russian. "No, we'll need him," Luther yelled.

The Russian didn't have his gun with him. He'd left it in the kitchen when he took the bottle of brandy from a cupboard – not a professional, just a brutal thug. Shaven head, neck and arm tattoos, he looked dangerous. Luther ran at him. The Russian turned, looked towards the kitchen and then at the woman. The woman was being protected. "Fuck you, bastard," he rasped. He slung his glass at Luther and it caught Luther on the side of the head.

As soon as Luther, Ken and Ignacio had entered the house, Bertram and the other Knight ran across the street and entered the house too. The Knight with Bertram then ran upstairs, his gun drawn, he cleared all the upstairs rooms. Bertram locked the front door; he left the intercom disconnected. Seconds later they all heard the word 'CLEAR' shouted out from upstairs. They knew then that the criminals were all contained in one room, there were no other hostiles in the house.

Luther shook his head to clear the fuzziness from the blow of the glass. Blood poured from his head. He stepped forward towards the Russian but his footing was not secure and his foot slid slightly on the marble tiled floor. The Russian was on him in seconds.

Ken Knox pulled Rosario to her feet and led her out of the room as quickly as her trembling legs would carry her. They headed for upstairs; Bertram went with them. The Knight who had cleared the rooms ushered them into the master bedroom. The four of them stood silent in the room, door shut. The Knight and Ken Knox had their guns drawn and trained at the door. They waited.

The Russian lunged at Luther. He was just a thug but he was a hard thug. His fist caught Luther on the side of his head, on his ear and it hurt! The Russian brought his knee up fast, aiming for Luther's groin but Luther had already read the move. He crossed his arms and formed them into an aikido x and forced them down hard against the oncoming knee, absorbing the knee and its thrust. Then he grabbed the Russian's knee, crouched quickly, brought his right leg out and swept it towards the Russian's leg in an arc. The Russian, still on one leg, fell with a mighty crash. He fell on his back; he bounced as he hit the hard, tiled floor. The wind was completely knocked out of him. He rolled onto his side and gasped for air.

"CLEAR." Luther called to the others. "Bertram, I need you." They all ran downstairs.

"Got it." Bertram replied. He ran over to the Russian, took out plastic ties from his backpack and restrained the Russian, who wasn't going anywhere for a while anyway because he was still gasping for breath.

One thug, the Moroccan, was dead, the blood had spread quickly on the non-absorbent floor. The sign of the cross had been made on his forehead and in his own blood. Ken Knox saw it but did not say anything,

The other, the Russian, had been dragged into the kitchen, all knives and any other utensils removed, and he was left in there with the door shut, on the floor, restrained and still heaving; he was guarded by one of the Knights.

*

It had been over an hour since the Templars and Ken Knox had entered the Studerbaker house and rescued Allan Studerbaker's wife from her forced imprisonment. The Russian, as they had expected, knew very little. He confirmed he and the Moroccan had been hired to watch her, initially from outside only. Check who visited her and who she visited and report back when they were called. They were never given a number to call. The Russian said her house phone was tapped and so was her mobile phone. He said someone was pissed off, he didn't know who, because she had been talking and asking for help from someone; she'd called Ken. They knew he was coming. So, he and the Moroccan had been told to sit on her and get rid of the visitor when he arrived. Ken asked him roughly what time of day the calls would come through to them, when they had to report back in. The Russian was unsure and said that they would come through at any time. Ken pressed him further, "Generally sometime between 10 a.m. and 6 p.m." he told them reluctantly. Ken told the others that whilst it's not an exact science, the general assumption would be, given those times, that the other party was in the same time zone or close to it. He wondered out loud how many countries were on the same time zone as Spain. Luther shrugged his shoulders; the others did the same.

"Forty-eight," Bertram called out from the corner, "or is it forty-nine?" Bertram had been quiet for some time.

They all looked at him astonished. "Who carries that kind of information in their head?" Ignacio asked. Luther just smiled.

They hadn't noticed before but for the last hour Bertram had been sitting in front of the old computer screen in the corner, with a writing pad and pen in his hand. In fact, he had not moved. In fact, he was quite still except for his left foot tapping ever so slightly.

"It's Allan's," Rosario said, when she noticed him staring at it. "He has kept it going for the last forty years. It just flashes away in the corner, the green cursor flashes away. He never turns it off, would never turn it off. He said it reminds him of the way it was before for us. So, he leaves it on. I used to think it was cute but not of late. I can't work out why but it's started to irritate me."

Bertram sat on.

*

Ken Knox told Rosario he would now stay there until Allan was found. She was relieved. The two Knights were also staying. They would get rid of the Moroccan's body, and then stay to guard the

229

Russian. They needed the Russian because they knew he would get a phone call to see what had happened with Knox. The Templars managed to do a deal with the Russian, his life for a day or two, or as long as it took of lying to his bosses, when the call came through. He could also keep the money he'd been paid. They wouldn't go to the authorities and they would not cut his head off. The Russian needed no further persuasion to agree to the terms of their deal – he knew at least one of them had a very sharp sword!

Luther went into the hall to put his boots back on and to make a call. He took out his mobile phone and called Morgan Clay. The call, as always, was routed via Islington.

"It's a kidnaping. Don't call the families of anyone else, not yet. We have to find out what's going on. We're wrapping up this end. How did the meeting with the cardinal go in London, it should be over about now."

Clay didn't respond straight away.

"Morgan?" They rarely used their real names on calls but he knew the Templars' mobile calls were cloaked. "Morgan?" Luther asked again.

"Not good."

"How bad is not good?"

"Bad," Clay told him.

"How many, Morgan?"

There were a few seconds pause and then, "four Knights dead. Marie-Claude shot in the leg and a Knight from the Red team, shot in the leg and hand. They are both with the Doc but I'm told they will be okay."

"My God! The Seer?"

"Safe."

"The Girl, Lionheart?"

"Also, safe."

"The cardi—"

"Taken."

"What ... How?"

"Somehow they managed to plant an electronic tracker on his aide; led them straight to us."

"Didn't we sweep him for bugs?"

"They did but it didn't matter, they were already inside the café, our position was blown the second the cardinal and his aide walked through the door."

"Damn it. We're on our way back." He hung up.

Luther took a few minutes to digest what Clay had said, then he rang St Clair. Again, the call was routed via Islington.

"I just spoke to Morgan."

"There's nothing you can do from there, tidy up and catch the first flight back, we will need you and Bertram here in the days to come."

"Roger that," Luther confirmed.

"Give me a quick overview; do we know what happened to Allan Studerbaker?" St Clair asked Luther.

"Without thinking Luther was about to scratch his head but stopped midway up when he remembered he had a lump on his head the size of a golf ball and dried blood all down his face. "No idea yet."

"What's your best guess?"

He told St Clair about the thugs who were sitting on her and what they had learnt from the Russian, which was not much. "My best guess is it's a big tech play. Whatever he's working on, Studerbaker, one of the competitors wants it, wants what he knows; maybe the others too."

"Are all the missing scientists linked?" St Clair asked him.

"His wife doesn't know, we asked her if she thought he would have known any of them. Ken will reach out to Studerbaker's employer tomorrow and start to draw up a list."

"Okay, let Courtney have that list and she can start running back checks from here; I will ask her to brief Bill Meeks, he can check with the FBI, and Proctor can do some digging within the British Secret Service this end."

"I really don't see this as a Russian play, and neither does Ken, and he's a bit of an expert," Luther said. "Perhaps the Chinese, it's something they wouldn't hesitate to do, but I don't know about this one, St Clair, it's odd. We checked the mobile phones of the two hostiles but when they get the calls from whoever is doing this, the caller always withholds the number. Bertram said it's not going to be possible to backtrack and trace, so, we have to wait until they call again and be ready and try then, whilst the call is happening."

"Sounds like a plan, Luther."

"Well, let's see, Bertram said that if they use a satellite phone then we have no chance and—"

"And if they've gone to all this trouble to kidnap a bunch of scientists, they are not likely to use a standard, call tracing mobile phone for our convenience."

"Yup."

"Tell our Knights to sort out security cameras for the lady and install trip pads on all windows and doors so she feels safe. They should stay with her and Knox, for as long as it takes to get her husband back or—"

"Agreed."

Just then there was a call from the other room. "Got to go, St Clair, Bertram is calling me. I'll tidy up this end and then he and I will get the first available flight out tomorrow."

"Okay. I'll let the control room know your plan and I'll tell the deputy in Islington."

They hung up and Luther went back into the main living room where everyone was crowded round the 1980s computer screen and Bertram.

"It's a series of sequences," Bertram said.

"What is Bertram?" Luther asked him.

"The cursor. It's a series of sequences. It does not follow a regular cursor beat." He was staring intently at the flashing green cursor. "This computer cannot do this, it's an old Commadore computer, a Commadore 64, it came out in 1982."

"Well, it used to flash regularly," Rosario told them. "Maybe that's what has been bugging me, it's changed from the last forty years."

"Look, the pause between the flashing is very, very slightly different each time, but then it repeats the sequencing. You would not see it Mrs Allan because the change is only slight each time."

They couldn't help noticing that all the time he was talking, and watching the screen, and scribbling notes, he was also tapping his foot to keep time.

"He's using his foot like a metronome to determine the beat sequences," Ken Knox whispered to Luther.

"I know," Luther answered. Then turned back to Bertram. "Deliberate?" he asked him. "Or is it the machine has gone out of sync because of its age or something?"

"Very," Bertram said. "Very deliberate. The pulse sequencing is very man made. Someone programmed this."

"Morse code?"

"More sophisticated, Mr Luther." He looked down at his notes. "The sequence is twenty-five flashes, then seventy-three, then thirty-two, a total of one-hundred-and-thirty flashes per sequence. Then it repeats it all over again, and again and again. I think there are five spaces though in the twenty-five section, sixteen in the seventy-three and five in the thirty-two. Which means, if I am right, there are twenty-one spaces, which leads me to conclude we have five words in the first line, seventeen on the second line and six on the last line. I think you have been sent a message, Mrs Allan."

Luther asked him how smart you would have to be to programme it like that. Bertram told him the average person couldn't do it, a good programmer could but on a computer this old, very few. "This person not only created the programme to do this, he or she ... Look," he opened the Properties Folder, then hit the advance key, then several other keystrokes.

"What are we looking at Bertram?"

"This wasn't done at the computer here. It was done remotely."

"Can you decipher this thing?" Ken Knox asked him.

"No, Mr Knox Ken, there is a piece of code missing. Without that I don't think I can decode it. Whoever did this—"

"Allan could do this; he is more than capable of programming his computer like this and from anywhere," Rosario said.

"Anywhere?" Luther asked."

"Absolutely," Rosario answered.

It had them perplexed for a long time. Bertram knew that without the code their only hope was to insert a series of possible passwords, on a code search tool, and run a multi-sequencing programme that would apply a different password every three seconds. He knew it was a long shot and could take days. His mobile phone rang. "It's Miss Courtney," he told the others. "I sent her access to view the screen a few minutes ago, so she has been looking at what we are looking at."

Bertram put the call on speaker. "Miss Courtney, you are on speaker phone and the room is not secure." This was his way of telling her that there were other people in the room besides Templars – she would keep it brief.

"The programme has a binary trap door and a back door. Don't use a code search tool for passwords, if you get it wrong it will block you out, there's the trap door. The backdoor is there to allow someone to go into the programme, which means they will be able to read whatever this thing is trying to say to you. And I agree with you, it is trying to say something. My only guess is, having read Dr Studerbaker's bio, he built the programme; and given he's missing; and this programme was built and installed remotely; and installed into the computer sitting in their home, well, it's got to be a message for his wife. And so, she has the key, the password."

"Do you and Allan have a shared password or a secret set of numbers you share or a date that is important to you, a name, anything?" Ken Knox asked her.

She thought about it but told them that they didn't share passwords. She gave Bertram some obvious numbers, like their birthdays and wedding anniversary but, when Bertram tried to apply these the rhythm of the cursor changed. Each time they tried something and the cursor changed its beat, it took longer and longer for it to resume its previous rhythm and sequencing. Courtney told him she didn't know how many chances they had left. She was certain that very soon it would scramble and not return to the sequence, then the message would be lost forever.

"I think it's numbers," Bertram said.

"Are you sure it's a numbers thing," Ken Knox asked.

"Yes, Mr Knox Ken, it's binary. So yes, numbers and it has to be something only the two of them would know. Something so important that they would never forget it. Like, only their secret."

That's when the penny dropped. She gave Bertram eight new numbers to try.

Ken looked at her. "Are you sure?"

"We lost our child; a miscarriage." Rosario said. "That is the date."

"I'm sorry Rosario, I didn't know."

"No one did, Ken. After that the doctor's told me we only had a ten per cent chance of being successful if we tried again, we stopped trying. At the post examination, the doctors detected that the issue was with me. The number is the date we lost our son, Luis Allan Studerbaker."

Bertram inserted the numbers on the keyboard into the sequences. The screen cleared, it went blank and everyone held their breath. Seconds ticked by. Then, after what seemed like an age, a smiley face appeared with a kiss after it.

"That's him," Rosario said. "He always puts that in his letters or emails to me, or his damned 'post it' notes to remind me of things. That's Allan." She ran over to the computer screen. "Is he there now?" her voice beginning to crack with emotion. "Is Allan there at the other end?"

"No, Mr Allan's wife." Bertram said. "It looks like he set this up a week or so ago."

"Bertram, the screen," Courtney's voice came over the mobile phone speaker and everyone stopped. "Look at the screen."

He looked; they all looked. The smiley face had gone and it was replaced with:

From the end of the world
You would see it before 110 sea captains would see it but if right they would not get wet on Job 267
Then look for the Alabama window

They all looked at it. Then they looked some more.

"Has anyone got any ideas what this means?" Luther asked.

No one spoke; they were all deep in thought trying to work out what Allan was trying to say.

Then, the screen cleared again. It was now blank. The cursor was still there but now it flashed at its normal pace, no change, no sequencing. This went on for two minutes.

Finally, she could not contain her frustration any longer. "What's happening?" Rosario said in a panic. "Have we lost him?"

Then the cursor moved, it moved into the centre of the screen, all eyes were on it. It flashed several times more, then it typed out a new sentence: WHAT IS THE PARADOX?

Chapter 15

The control room

Place: The M1 motorway heading out of London
Time: 3 p.m.

They were all exhausted.

Getting out of London took all their patience: there were accidents on the roads everywhere. No matter which way they tried, it was the same everywhere. The satnav was full of redlines. The rain had not stopped all day; the roads were slippery; the traffic was backed up everywhere because of the weather; there were major delays; drivers were already irate, and now it was the early build up to the rush hour! It would take them seven hours on a good day to reach their destination: this was not a good day; seven hours seemed like a pipedream to the exhausted Templars. When they did finally make it out of London and onto the MI motorway, the traffic was almost at a standstill in many parts. Delays went on for miles – five accidents and a broken-down delivery truck in the middle lane took over an hour to clear. The Templars' two black Jaguar cars slowly made their way back to Scotland.

*

The control room in Glennfinch castle

In the control room the mood was frantic, they knew time was not on their side as they searched for clues where the cardinal's abductors might have taken him. They had started monitoring airports, train stations and ferry ports as soon as it was reported he had been taken. All their satellite centres were put on alert, with the edict: FIND DEL LUCA AT ALL COST! They knew who had taken him, the Abaddon's three crescent moon tattoos were the give-away, they just didn't know why they had taken him, not for sure anyway. St Clair's theory was that they had taken him because they wanted to find out what he was doing meeting with the Templars. They would want to find out all he knew about them.

*

The motorway back to Scotland

Cameron Jack drove the lead Jaguar, Dominique sat in the front, Jonathan sat with Father Declan in the back of the car.

Not much had been said since leaving the café near London Bridge. It had all happened so fast; people had responded on instinct; they hadn't had time to think. There were wounded; people died and the cardinal was taken. It was a mess, 'a bloody mess', someone had said over the coms – nobody disagreed.

Father Declan sat in the back staring out of the window. He was worried for the cardinal's safety, for his life! He replayed the shoot-out in his head. He went over and over it in his mind to see if he could have done something different. Something that would have protected the cardinal but it was the cardinal who had protected him and protected the others too. It was the cardinal who had sacrificed himself so that they could get away.

He'd asked the Templars in the car, a number of times, what was being done to find the cardinal. 'Everything', Dominique had told him each time. She was in constant communication with the control room in Scotland but she knew it was the proverbial needle in a haystack scenario. They might get lucky or the cardinal might get lucky and find a way to escape. She knew every positive scenario required a massive amount of luck. She also knew that the first forty-eight hours were vital, seventy-two hours at a stretch, after that, she knew the trail would go cold and their chances of finding the cardinal would become virtually zero. She didn't share those thoughts with the young priest sitting in the back of the Jaguar. She knew he was in turmoil. She knew what it was like to be responsible for protecting someone and what it was like when that went wrong. She tried to reassure him. "Right now, the best way you can help the cardinal, is to let us do our thing", she told him. "We have people working on it, lots of experienced people, in lots of different places. Remember, the cardinal, you, came to us, asked us for a meeting, so you have got to trust us now". After that, the young priest fell into silence again but they all knew what he was thinking: the worst and, blaming himself.

Hours passed by with only the hypnotic sound of the car wheels revolving on the endless black tarred motorway to break the silence. Mile after mile with nothing but the dark night-time outside their side windows and bright, dazzling headlights speeding towards them on the opposite side of the road through the windscreen. All the features they would have seen in the daytime as they sped by, showing their progress, were now hidden in the darkness. Like a dark, endless, featureless tunnel they journeyed on.

The further north they went, the easier the traffic started to become and the more consistently they were able to achieve and maintain their optimum speed. Cameron Jack put the car in cruise control. They were now making good time.

It was Cameron Jack who finally broke the long silence in the car. "Dominique."

She looked at what he was looking at, it was a sign: Cumbria. It was the last county in England before they would cross the border and enter Scotland.

"All coms off, only issued mobiles to be used and only sparingly, we are going dark," Dominique announced over their coms. The Knights in the car behind confirmed they were going dark. She turned around and spoke to Father Declan. "Sorry, I'm going to need your mobile."

"Can't I just turn it off?"

"It might be bugged."

"Can't be, it has been with me all the t—"

"They planted a tracker on you."

He thought about it for a second or two. She was right and he was no fool. "I need to make three calls, then."

Dominique didn't answer.

"Look, I know what's at stake. I wouldn't ask if they were not important, vital even, to me and to you."

She looked at his face, she saw the sincerity but she also saw the desperation in his eyes. "Make them," she said, "but do it before we cross the border."

At this point with still many miles to go to reach their destination, even if he used his mobile phone and it was being tracked, it wouldn't help the trackers, the Templars were still far enough away that they could have been heading anywhere.

The Lionheart made him put the phone on speaker. "No disrespect, Father but we don't know you. All our dealings have been with Cardinal Del Luca, for now at least, let's play it safe."

Father Declan agreed – and understood. He punched in the first number. A man answered after five rings.

"Si?"

"His Eminence has been taken."

"*Capisco* – I understand. *È vivo?* – is he alive?"

"I pray to God he is. Tell your guardian to burn everything; leave no trace. Get your guardian out. I don't know how much time we have if ..." he didn't want to say it but he knew he must, "if the cardinal is tortured and reveals what he knows. Find a new safehouse. Post in the usual way when you are safe. I will keep checking."

"*Dio velocità fratello* – God speed Brother." The person at the other end of the phone hung up.

Father Declan made two other identical calls, then gave his mobile phone to Jonathan. Jonathan took it. Cameron Jack was watching in his rear-view mirror. Jonathan saw him. Cameron Jack nodded to Jonathan.

"Sorry," Jonathan said to Father Declan. He then took out the sim card from Father Declan's mobile phone and snapped it in two, he then threw it out of the window. Twenty miles or so later, Cameron Jack slowed down, moved over to the nearside lane and

Jonathan threw Father Declan's mobile phone out of the window and onto the grass verge.

*

Back in London

Morgan Clay had remained behind in London. Once things had started to go wrong, he'd called in other Knights who were based in London, they were on the scene before the police arrived – they had been on standby. They removed the bodies of the four dead Knights. They then checked the bodies of the nine dead hostiles for any identification, credit cards, phones anything that would give them clues as to where they had taken the cardinal. Then they made the sign of the cross on the foreheads of the dead men, in their own blood. They left the bodies for the police.

The wounded Knight from Red team and Marie-Claude were taken to a Templar doctor, near to Tower Hill. The doctor, like all Templars, was hidden in plain sight. He had a private practice, and a very private practice!

Aldrich volunteered to take Sherry home and make sure she was safe. He said he would ensure she understood the importance of not saying anything to anyone about what had happened. He would help concoct a story that because of the rain, she had shut early and had spent the afternoon with Aldrich. He said he might tell them that he and Sherry were an item – he'd roared with laughter at his emerging ruse. The Templars knew that if anyone could sell it to the police, when they came calling, it was an eccentric, University of Cambridge, medieval studies professor from the department of Supernatural, Occultism and history of Satanic Medieval Renaissance. They knew the police would be so confused by him; they would only conclude that his story had to be true.

*

Place: Glennfinch castle, Scotland
Time: Nearly midnight

It was dark when the two black Jaguar cars pulled up on the

forecourt of the castle – it was pitch black, no outside lights came on. The lights would have been seen for miles around and so they had been turned off in preparation for their arrival – re connected when the doors were locked. Father Declan didn't know where he was or at what, other than the building they pulled up in front of looked oddly like a castle. They approached the large, arched, oak, double door. Either side, a myriad of lattice windows remained lightless. There was no sign of life within. As they approached the door, it opened and an armed man stood and welcomed them. They moved Father Declan quickly through the castle, he barely had time to look and take it all in. They went into the reception room and then through one of the closed doors off of the reception room. Behind the door lay another door, a four-inch steel door that required a retina scan to open it. Dominique placed her face up to the scanner. The door opened. A lone tungsten bulb lit the way to an iron spiral staircase, Father Declan followed her down, and the rest of them followed on behind. As far as anyone could remember, he was only the third non-Templar to be allowed through that door, Jonathan was the first, his sister Courtney the second.

There were a number of people in the room, all busy; all using the technology. Father Declan was amazed. The technology hummed and buzzed, accompanied by an array of lights, some static, some flashing.

"Wow," was all he could muster – he was genuinely impressed as he looked on.

"You know technology?" Courtney moved to his side.

"No, I don't but that doesn't stop me from being impressed. Is this all you?"

Courtney laughed, "no," she turned around, "all of us and some who are not here right now. This is our CR, our control room." She then hit him with it. "We've upgraded a lot but we have 256-way symmetric multi-processing mainframe running Unix, Linux operating systems, Quad TFT Plasma display terminals. Hard drives with petabytes of storage, satellite uplinks, combined CPU speeds cloaking into terahertz stealth technology. Whilst we love to hack others, people trying to hack into us is one of my primary concerns. Hackers surfing the internet occasionally stumble on us, on one of our digital trails. So, we have reduced the digital 'attack surface' and bolstered our legacy encryption systems. All that simply means we have just 'future proofed' our infrastructure." As she was speaking, he noticed that the people that had entered the room with him, all but Dominique, had quickly sloped away as soon as the tech-speak began. She saw him looking. "I gave up trying to tell them a long time ago."

He chuckled. "The cardinal does exactly the same if ever I start speaking about anything technical, and that is just with his mobile phone, or the tv remote control. Do you have a name?" he asked her.

"Me?"

"Yes," then he checked himself, he didn't want to overstep the mark. "An alias is fine. I've met the Girl, the Lionheart and the Priest, which might get confusing, but what do they call you?"

"Me? I'm just Courtney, no alias, don't need one, I don't get out much."

He smiled. "Well Courtney, who doesn't get out much, I am really grateful for all of the information you have given me. However, in all of the films I have ever watched, when they start to tell the newcomer everything about themselves and all their secrets, it normally means they're going to bump him off!"

Courtney laughed. "I wouldn't kill you, Father, it's not my thing. He, on the other hand ..." She said, looking to her left at the man walking directly towards them.

Father Declan turned around, then the second 'wow' came out of his mouth. "Wow. He looks just like Sean Con—"

"My advice, Father," Courtney whispered, "don't mention to him who you think he looks like, he gets very irate and probably will kill you."

"Father Declan." Payne St Clair held out his hand. White hair, beard and moustache, he stood over six feet tall and towered above the cardinal's aide. "You've had a busy day. You must have a lot of questions, please feel free to ask. No more secrets between us, ay?"

Father Declan could see that the man in front of him was blessed with grace and reverence; and by the way the others reacted to him, he guessed who he was. "Grand Master," Father Declan bowed.

"We stopped bowing to Grand Masters a few Grand Master's back," St Clair said.

"We have been searching for you and the Seer for a very long time."

"Well, here I am now and the Seer you have already met. It could have been better circumstances I agree, but here we are. Now, questions."

"He thinks he's going to get bumped off once we've shown him everything," Courtney said.

St Clair laughed. "You can relax, nobody is going to bump anybody off. I wanted you to see all of this. I want you to ask any and all the questions you might have and I promise you we will answer them all, if we can. And tomorrow, I will show you more, much more, because I want you to understand what you risked your life for, back there. Plus, I am going to have to tell you everything, for you to tell me everything, right?" He then asked Courtney to finish the tour; to introduce him to the others and to show him what she and her team had been doing to try and trace the cardinal. The next hour was a whirlwind for the young priest but he felt a slight easing in the pit of his stomach because of the sheer amount of work they were doing to try and find the cardinal.

An hour later and Father Declan had seen almost every part of the control room and interacted with over twenty different people. Everyone had answered every one of his questions, without hesitation or ambiguity. He had no idea how many of them there were in the organisation, but he knew it had to be in the hundreds and they had global reach. He felt if the cardinal was going to be found, the Templars he now moved amongst, would be the ones that could do it.

Finally, his tour was done and Courtney took the young priest out of the control room and back upstairs and into the reception room.

Father Declan now had more time to look at his surroundings. He could see that the building he was in, was spacious but sparsely furnished. Other than the people in the control room, it looked like it was all but empty – still, he had the sense that there were more people there than he had seen.

The reception room, as always, had a welcoming log fire burning in the stone hearth. Two armchairs were placed in front of the fire. Off to one side of the room, on a large wooden table, stood an assortment of honey pots brimming with golden honey, on another, an assortment of whiskies. The walls of the room were almost bare, but for a few old pictures, which were too small to make out. The wattle and daub ceiling was yellow in patches from the smoke of countless log fires. The floor was laid with light-coloured flagstones, about four inches thick and partly covered by a large blue ornate rug that took away the coldness of the stones. Three doors leading off to other parts of the castle remained shut.

St Clair was standing in front of the fire. He thanked Courtney and she left, then he greeted the priest and handed him a large, crystal glass with rich, amber coloured whisky inside it. He indicated to the priest to sit down and they both settled themselves in front of the fire.

Father Declan's body ached. The adrenaline had now gone, it was the only thing that had kept him going. Now it left a deep void and his whole body was trying to shut down. He was physically and mentally spent. The whisky helped a little; it helped numb the pain. Despite his exhaustion though, he so desperately wanted to help the Templars. They were out there searching for the cardinal and he was inside drinking whisky. He needed to help them and he knew that the best way he could do that, was to tell them everything. He took a mouthful of his drink and it ran down his throat and seeped into his body and started to heal it. "I think it's my turn to tell you some things," Father Declan started. "I want you to know that his Eminence had fully intended to tell you everything anyway because you, the Seer, all of this, is what we have been waiting for, searching for. It is the reason our Cabal exists. The secret we have kept for so long Grand Master, is not our secret, we have merely been guardians of it. Guardians of an Ark key, which we have kept hidden from the world. And that Ark key belongs to the last Seer." He stopped and thought about it for a second or two. "Perhaps first though, is there something specific you would like to know?"

St Clair asked the question, the one he had been waiting to ask since that first phone call with Del Luca. "Who are you?"

"I believe by that you mean the cardinal and myself and others that work with us?"

St Clair nodded.

"We are a *senza volto cabal,* a faceless cabal. Nobody other than our members know we exist. And now we can add the Templars to that list."

"Does that list also include the Vatican?" St Clair asked. He knew that as far as secrets were concerned, the Vatican was like a sieve!

"If you are asking me if they are aware of the Cabal, no, they are not, so they are not involved. In fact, only myself and the cardinal are priests, the other members of the Cabal are not of the church."

The priest sipped his whisky, this time he savoured its taste more, and then took a deep breath. "Today from the café, using Dominique's coms, the cardinal told you that he needed to tell the Seer a story. A very important story about a farmer's boy called Thomas Dumas, a Spanish knight and the last Essene to have lived on this earth, a hermit called Caleb. If he was here, he would have told you that the hermit lived high in the mountains of the Cañón del Río Lobos, near Soria, in Spain, seven hundred years ago. So, Grand Master, that is where I shall start because that is where, our *senza volto cabal* started, high in the mountains of the Cañón del Río Lobos, near Soria, in Spain, seven hundred years ago."

The fire hissed. Still there was no outward sign of any others in the building, yet still Father Declan had a sense that there were many more, everywhere.

"It was one of your own past Grand Masters, Grand Master Jacques de Molay, who was ultimately responsible for enlisting our Cabal before it was even formed. He had a secret, and that secret was that the Ark of the Covenant had a key, the Ark key. The key was discovered lying beside the Ark over nine hundred years ago in the Holyland by the first of your kind, Grand Master Hugues de Payens. As you know, the original nine Knights found the Ark of the Covenant buried deep in subterranean passageways and catacombs of the Temple Mount, the Holy of Holies. But what you don't know, because all the nine Knights, the original Worthies all swore an oath to never tell another soul, was that there was something else they found lying by the side of the Ark of the Covenant that day. They pledged not to tell any other person, not even another Templar.

"Whoever placed the Ark there, also placed three scrolls alongside it: the Ark key. The scrolls, Hugues de Payens finally figured out, were the key to unlocking the Ark's true purpose." He leaned in a little. "The Ark is far more powerful than most people think, although I suspect you, Grand Master and your Seer, may have already worked out its true purpose." He waited but St Clair said nothing. He neither confirmed nor denied, so Father Declan continued. "Hugues de Payens knew the danger of having the Ark and the key together and so he sought out a small, ultra-religious community of Essenes who lived a semi-nomadic life on the edges of the desert. Whilst the Grand Master knew most of what was written because he was, as you know, a scholarly man, there were sections written in a language he did not understand. The Essene however, did understand it because it was written in an ancient Aramaic dialect, which the Essene still used. They confirmed that he was right about the Ark's true purpose according to what was written. They then told him that the scrolls were meant for a person described as a Seer. They said there would be many Seers who would be able to see symbols rise from the Ark. Some would be able to decipher a number of these but they warned that only the last Seer would understand the Ark key and how to use it. They called this the Paradox."

St Clair had never heard of the Ark key but it would explain, he thought, a number of things, especially his and Jonathan's frustration with their lack of progress in understanding and reading all the symbols. St Clair had seen the symbols so many times. Jonathan had first seen them, those floating symbols, back at the battle with Salah El-Din in Cumbria. He'd said he'd felt the hand of God. He'd lifted one of the tablets, it was weightless – as the Ark is when it is inside the alloy box. Then, to Jonathan's astonishment, in between the written words of the Ten Commandments, he saw additional lines of faded symbols that seemed to lift from the stone. St Clair had asked him what he could see, and Jonathan had replied, 'I see thousands of symbols and images, I see … it's like I am looking at them through running water. They are there, but distant. It's like they are alive, like the symbols are alive'. He saw them moving and rotating, lifting themselves from the stone and slowly forming a three-dimensional orb. He said the symbols dismantled as they touched each other and then spun off at great speed to form another. He didn't recognise the symbols and yet he could make some of them out. 'Look', he had said to St Clair, 'the resurrection'. Then he saw the Law and the Lore of numbers, geometry, science, astronomy, the universe, chaos, sincerity and healing. They are the esoteric knowledge, he said. It was the blueprint for the most perfect celestial plan – *Spiritus Mundi* – the Breath of the Universe. It was the sacred science. For centuries the Templars had tried to understand them. Templars in France first discovered their presence but all these centuries later, St Clair and the others knew only a small part of their meaning. Jonathan had been amazed that St Clair and the others could not read them and it was then that St Clair told Jonathan he was a Seer.

St Clair got up and refilled their glasses again. He handed one to Father Declan.

Again, the whisky helped the priest. "Hugues de Payens entrusted the Essene with the key. And so that was the way it was up until the time of de Molay's death. The Essene protected the key and kept its existence a secret. The Templars protected the Ark, your 'Charge' and kept its existence a secret. They could not come together until the last of the Seer's came."

"So, I presume de Molay spoke about the Cathar prophecies we have?"

"Yes, but we have never seen them, nor do we know what they say, except for the one prophecy that talks about the last Seer. I cannot remember it fully but—"

"The sixth prophecy says: *The flower of the martyrs and the plaited crown shall join to battle 'El S'hhan te Abyann' for the way back*. We thought the red rose was something to do with martyrs because it was sometimes used as a sign of the martyrs, red signifying the blood they have shed. But it wasn't until the cardinal gave Jonathan the small wooden cross that we were able to figure it out. From the Bible, *And when they plaited a crown of thorns, they put it upon his head ... And they bowed the knee and mocked him, saying Hail, King of the Jews.* The wooden cross has both the plaited crown of thorns upon it and the red rose. I think the prophecy speaks of your Cabal joining with the Templars to battle 'El S'hhan te Abyann' for the way back.' We don't know what 'El S'hhan te Abyann' means because it has never been translated."

Father Declan told St Clair he knew what it meant. "It is an ancient Aramaic dialect. It is another name for the man who appears in 2 Thessalonians 2:3 where it tells of the coming of the Man of Lawlessness, also called the Man of Sin, Man of Perdition and the Son of Destruction. The Essene hermit Caleb, used this name to Don Pablo, the Spanish knight, and when he asked what it meant, Caleb told him who it was talking about." St Clair looked confused so Father Declan proceeded to tell the story of the poor farmer's boy, Thomas Dumas, *Petite Pomme* – Little Apple. His visions; joining the friary and his great uncle, Benoit. He told him about Thomas's meeting with de Molay when de Molay was on his way to his own execution.

"It was the eighteenth of March 1314, when de Molay and Thomas finally met face-to-face but they had seen each other in their visions. In Thomas's visions, the Archangel Michael came to him. The leader of the Seraphim, the fiery ones, and one of the seven archangels that serve as the throne guardians of God. The Angel told Thomas to find the bearded warrior. When Thomas and de Molay met on that dreadful night, de Molay knew Thomas was the one he had to pass on the secret to about there being an Ark key. He asked him to warn the Essene because he knew, if he was tortured and his resolve failed, it would be a secret no more.

"De Molay told Thomas that they, the Templars had the Ark of the Covenant but he said it was gone, removed in 1307. De Molay told Thomas he must go and find the one who had the key, the Ark key; he had to find the guardian of the Ark key.

"Get the key and hide it, de Molay told Thomas. He said that the Ark was always separated from its key, right back to when the Templars first found the Ark under the Temple Mount, in 1118. De Molay told him that the key did not open the Ark, it was not that kind of key, but it opened what the Ark was, what was really inside it. He called the Ark, the *weapon*, and the *way*.

"De Molay told Thomas that only the last Seer would know how the key works. The last Seer knows the answer to the Paradox and Thomas must protect the key until the last Seer comes. He warned Thomas that others were also seeking the key, they hunt it because it will tell them what the Paradox is. When Thomas asked who else hunted it, de Molay told him, the followers of the Man of Lawlessness."

Father Declan then told St Clair that de Molay had instructed Thomas to find an Essene hermit, Caleb, who lived at the Cañón del Río Lobos, near Soria, in Spain, near to the San Bartolomé hermitage, and that he had hidden the secret for decades.

"Essene from the Essenes from the time of Jesus, that sect?" St Clair asked.

"Yes," Father Declan told St Clair. "When Thomas asked de Molay how he would know such a man, de Molay had said, 'you will know him when you see him. He is one hundred and three years old and around his neck hangs a small wooden cross with a crown of thorns carved upon it and a rose carved within the crown."

"So, that's where the cross came from?"

"It is the same cross. Does Jonathan still have it?

"He still has it."

"Ah, good. Grand Master de Molay knew the fate that awaited him that night, he was going to be burnt alive. He didn't know if his resolve would hold. He didn't know if he would give up the hermit and the other Templar secrets.

"Thomas left the friary that night. He took with him two travelling companions, his great uncle, another friar by the name of Benoit Duvall and a knight called Don Pablo Santiago de Aragon. Benoit Duvall gave his life for the quest to find the guardian of the Ark key. I'm afraid to say Thomas Dumas also lost his life, in the Pyrenees Mountains. Don Pablo, the only survivor of their journey through France and into Spain, barely made it through the mountain pass himself."

St Clair listened intently as Father Declan went on "The

Spanish knight finally found the Essene hermit, Caleb. And so, Don Pablo became the guardian of the Ark key and the hermit was finally able to pass away in peace, he'd done his job. But on his way out of the canyon, Don Pablo stumbled across a reconnaissance party and was wounded in the fight. He was in a bad way. He manged to escape and headed for the farm he'd stayed at on his journey in.

"Don Pablo was in a bad way. His wounds needed tending. He convinced himself he needed one night, just one night to rest and he would be gone in the morning. It was the farmer's son, Ignacio, who found him, weak and exhausted slumped under one of the groves' olive trees. The boy shouted for his father who came, quickly running to see what the alarm was. Together they helped Don Pablo back to the farm. There, his wife tended to his wounds. She cleaned them and dressed them. She told her husband he could not travel; his wounds could easily reopen again and if he did, infection would set in, followed by fever and then death. The farmer knew that the soldiers would be looking for the Spanish knight. He needed to hide him. Many years before, the farmer's father had installed a food store in the ground of the barn, it was meant for storing food away from the rats and other vermin. It was a cellar, but it was also big enough for a man to remain hidden. The wooden door to the cellar lay flat on the ground, covered with straw, it was tucked away in the corner of the barn so anyone walking in there, would be less likely to walk over the door and hear the hollow sound.

"Two weeks passed and Don Pablo's wounds had finally healed and he was feeling strong again. He felt like he owed the farmer an explanation and so told him his story, from the time Thomas met de Molay, all the way through the Pyrenees pass, the abbey and, finally, Caleb, the Essene and the Ark key.

"The farmer said he wanted to help and help he did. Between them they compiled a list of true and trusted men. Then, one by one they approached them and slowly the Cabal was formed. Two of the farmer's uncles, the ones who had fought for Don Pablo during the wars, became members of the Cabal, along with one of Don Pablo's brothers. The eldest of the Cabal was the village doctor, the youngest was Ignacio St. Barrello, the farmer's son, who was just fifteen but he had stood guard over Don Pablo as he lay healing in the underground cellar. And so, the Cabal to protect the Ark key was formed and so it has been for the last seven hundred years."

St Clair rose from the armchair and poured two more drinks. He didn't put anymore wood on the fire, he was letting it burn out. He was exhausted. He had not had more than a few hours' sleep in the last three days and he needed rest. He needed his mind sharp. Besides, he still had one more place to go before he could retire but before that he had one more question to ask the young priest.

Father Declan again sipped at his whisky and again he felt its rejuvenating qualities and his nerves settling a little bit more. He was in a strange place, with the people they had been searching for, for a long, long time. The man he was supposed to protect was gone, captured and he had no idea where. Now he was in front of a Grand Master of the Knights Templar, telling him every secret he knew.

"Tell me," St Clair asked him, "how did you and the cardinal come to be involved in the Cabal? I'm interested to hear your story."

"The reason I got involved is easy. I went to work for the cardinal and after some time he revealed the work of the Cabal to me and invited me to join, and so I did. I have been honoured to serve the cardinal, God and the Cabal."

St Clair finished his whisky and placed the glass on the small side table by his armchair. "And the cardinal?" he asked.

Father Declan smiled. "Ah, I can seldom tell this, but love telling it when I can. When the cardinal was about nine years old, both his parents sadly died in a horrific car accident. He was orphaned and lived on the streets. A year later he, along with many street children at that time, started working for the resistance. After the war he was brought up by foster parents. However, what the cardinal didn't know was that the man in the car crash was not his real father, it was his mother's second husband. His real father had died not long after the cardinal had been born; his mother remarried. What he also didn't know was that both his mother and his biological father were Spanish.

"His mother's new husband was a kind man and a successful businessman; he was also an Italian. He legally adopted the young cardinal, and he changed the boy's last name to his, but he also changed the boy's first name to Gino, so he became Gino Del Luca.

He did this because he lived in Rome and he and his new wife were worried that the child might be harassed and picked on when he went to school because he was not Italian. His stepfather taught him Italian and by the time he went to school, he was fluent. He joined a local school in Rome and was saved from certain torment. He lived a perfect life until the car crash." Then Father Declan stopped talking.

"You're going to want me to ask, aren't you?" St Clair said, seeing the pause for what it was a mile away.

A big grin spread across the young priest's face. "Please, it's the best bit."

"Okay, you have me. What was Del Luca's real name?"

"Ah. His real name was Gael Pablo Santiago de Aragon." He is a direct descendant of Don Pablo Santiago de Aragon, the first of the Cabal, the Spanish knight. There has been a de Aragon in the Cabal ever since that very first day.

"You see, when the cardinal was old enough, the Cabal members came looking for him, they found him. They told him about the Cabal. They also told him that his father, his biological father, had been the head of the Cabal before he died and, now let me get this right, his great, great, great, great, great, great, great, great, great, great, great grandfather was the founder and the first non-Essene guardian of the Ark key."

The fire was almost out, but its warmth lingered as they left the room. St Clair walked Father Declan to his room; both men had walked in quiet contemplation along the corridors. It was quiet. No sound but Father Declan still had the sense the place was full of people – he hoped he would find out tomorrow.

Both men had learnt so much in the last hour or so, but Father Declan was anxious. He was there but the cardinal should also have been there. He should be giving the answers to the Templars, the answers he had waited so long to tell; entire generations of his family had been waiting to tell. It should be the cardinal, not him.

"Do you think they will kill him?" he finally asked St Clair as they walked along. "Will they kill the cardinal?"

"I don't know. As I said, I think they have spared him

because they want to know what he was doing with Templars, or they would have killed him on the tow path. But what puzzles me is, why did they want to kill him in the first place? Do they want to kill the cardinal because he holds the Ark key?"

"No, because like you, up until some hours ago, they don't even know that there is an Ark key."

"If they don't know he holds the Ark key, then ... then it makes no sense to me. There is no reason to kill him."

"There is every reason to kill him," Father Declan assured him.

St Clair stopped walking. "I'm listening."

"The young priest in the book, in the *Morto Vivente* - Living Dead book, that was the cardinal."

St Clair shook his head. "And that's how he knows about the books, the only three copies?"

"Yes. After your conversation with him, he then knew you have one. He had one and he already knew who had the third one, and that's the reason they wanted him dead."

St Clair asked him to explain.

"He had asked the journalist, who was there in the village when it all happened not to write the story, but he did. So, it was the Cabal that purchased the small print company that was about to publish the book. It was all printed and ready to go out but they stopped it and then set about destroying all the books, but three survived. One the Cabal kept and one we now know you have."

"And the other?"

"It is owned by a man whose name is Samir Fancy."

"What am I missing here?"

Father Declan then told St Clair about how the Cabal did not want the story to be known, the story of a dead man coming back to life. That they were greatly concerned it would start a panic, especially in the small, rural Italian villages; worried it could spark another Inquisition and they would see the re-emergence of the witch hunts of the dark ages.

He continued "The Cabal had been searching for the books for years. The cardinal knew that three copies survived. He had one, but the whereabouts of the other two books had eluded him, despite his and the Cabal's best efforts. However, as the new digital age dawned, computers and the internet, searching got easier, but it was still an almost impossible task. Finally, after years of searching, they got lucky. The Cabal made it known over the internet that they were searching for an old book and would pay a high price for it; they named the book and included a contact email address in their postings. Somehow, the right person in Canada saw it. It turned out he was a contractor; he had worked for a security firm that installed high specification laser and infrared security systems. They had a branch office in Qatar for their Middle East business. The Qatari office had been retained to install a new, top of the range security system in offices in Cairo, Egypt. The man and two others were seconded to the Qatari operation for this large install. A few years later, the man got fired for some reason and then greed got the better of him. He sold the blueprints of a security system they had installed in a mansion on a private estate, in the leafy suburbs, he'd sold it to a well-known thief. The thief and his three accomplices raided the house but got caught by the private security firm that patrolled the estate. The thief then gave up the name of his source and the man in Canada was arrested and served two years in prison. When the man got out, he was an ex-con and so found it hard to get a job.

"After seeing one of the posts, the man in Canada wrote back to say that he knew where the book was but he did not know the name of the owner. He said it was housed inside a glass case in one of the offices in an office block in Egypt. To convince them, he explained how he knew. The Cabal arranged a bank transfer to the man for fifty-thousand Canadian dollars, to be released to him upon receiving the information. The Cabal got the information they wanted and the man got his fifty-thousand dollars.

"Then the Cabal engaged a firm of private investigators from Syria and sent them to Cairo, to the office building where the man in Canada said the installation was done. They checked the records and eventually, after much digging, found out that the owner was a man called Samir Fancy. Nothing else was known about him, no other records to show that the man existed, just a name on one set of property deeds. They watched the building, took photographs and kept a log of the comings and goings.

"The third report they submitted to the Cabal talked of a wall of silence about the owner of the property, Samir Fancy. Apparently, in Cairo his name was associated with rumours of bad things that went on there. Everybody they tried to speak to about him were too scared to talk but they said that they felt there was something malevolent, evil and criminal going on in that building. That report also contained four photographs. The cardinal had read the report and looked at the photographs. The third photograph was of a man that had entered the building several times a day. The cardinal recognised the man, it was Vincente from the book *Morto Vivente*. The same Vincente whose body was discovered hanging from an olive tree on the south road that led out of the village where the cardinal, at that time, barely a priest, had tried, with two other priests, to exorcise a demon from his body. The man who had been hung and had died of strangulation; had been stabbed over forty times after his death. His body was eventually taken down and buried in a secret place outside of the village by his family. The last time the cardinal saw him, was seven miles outside of the village. He and the journalist had come upon a man walking along the road as they drove out of the village. Taking him for a hitchhiker, the cardinal slowed down, then stopped to see if they could offer him a lift. He honked his horn, wound down his window and called out to the man. The man on the side of the road turned around. Clearly visible on the man's neck were the rope burns from the hanging, it was Vincente. His stare was fixed. The cardinal put the car in gear and sped away as fast as his car would allow."

"And that's why someone has been trying to kill the cardinal," St Clair said.

"The Cabal believes that only the darkest of evil resides in that place and only the Man of Lawlessness has the power to do what the rumours spoke about. So, in the end the cardinal sent an assassin to Cairo to kill Vincente, the man that had already been dead. He also told the assassin to kill the man known as Samir Fancy, who he believed was a lieutenant for the Man of Lawlessness. The assassin was successful and killed Vincente but he died in his other attempt. The operatives from the private investigators in Syria went missing the same day. Twelve hours later their offices were ransacked and a client's file stolen. A week later, the first attempt on the cardinal's life took place.

The last attempt on his life was just a few weeks back and the assassin, Michael, was the second dead man walking that the cardinal had seen. He believes there are others and it is the way the Man of Lawlessness intends to win *the* battle. When we raided Michael's room, we found a black leather-bound book, small with a sliver metal clasp. It was embossed on the front with three crescent moons, the same design we found on the underside of Michael's wrist, which was always covered by his watch. Inside the book, it was inscribed: *the end will be the beginning. Samir Fancy.*"

"I am beginning to think he might be the one Zivko called Lord on the mobile phone today. Have you encountered Zivko Cesar Gowst, also known as the White Ghost?"

"No."

"Bo Bo Hak?"

"No."

"Well, they are names you need to become familiar with. I will get Zakariah to brief you fully tomorrow."

St Clair paused and thought about the question he was about to ask, then he asked it, "Do you think Del Luca will hold out if tortured?"

"Could you?" Father Declan asked him back.

"I don't know," St Clair answered honestly. "If he dies, will the secret he holds die with him and render the Ark key useless?"

"No. The cardinal does not have the Ark key. In fact, he's never seen it, neither have I!"

They had reached Father Declan's bedroom door. St Clair opened the door for him. He wanted to ask Father Declan so many more questions. The revelation that the cardinal had not seen the Ark key was indeed a revelation and one he was not expecting. However, he was tired and Father Declan was tired, a lot had happened in one day. "You'll find fresh clothes," he said pointing to the bed. "I hope they fit. There are toiletries and fresh towels in the bedside cabinet." St Clair wished him good night and started to walk away.

"You have not asked me who the others are, the other Cabal members or where the Ark key is. Nor why the cardinal and I have never seen the Ark key, or what it is. Or the Paradox?"

"You will tell me tomorrow," St Clair called back from down the corridor.

"How can you be so sure?"

St Clair smiled, he turned around, "because tomorrow two things will happen. The Templars and the Cabal will come together for the first time in seven hundred years."

"And the other, Grand Master?"

"You will stand before the Ark of the Covenant."

St Clair made his way back to the control room to check on their progress in trying to find the cardinal. They had drawn a blank. A small group in the control room had also started to look at the riddle Bertram had decoded from the old computer screen in Mallorca.

St Clair left a skeleton crew but told all the others to go to bed. He had a sense that there was not going to be much sleep for any of them in the coming days.

Chapter 16

The Ark

Place: Glennfinch castle, Scotland
Time: The following morning

Father Declan awoke. The smell of lavender was all about him. He had not slept well. The sun pierced his bloodshot eyes as he drew back the curtains. It had been pitch-black when they had arrived the previous night; he still had no idea where he was. All he knew from last night was that he appeared to be in a castle. He looked out of the window. Now he knew he was in a castle. The structure, with six-foot-thick walls, looked and felt solid; it was inspiring and he knew it was a safe sanctuary for its owners, the Templars. It looked to him to be semi-isolated from civilization, standing in miles of Scottish wilderness. Everywhere he looked he saw bracken-covered hills, a dense meandering spruce forest. He breathed in deep, the lingering smell of lavender again filled his nostrils. He opened a window, showered and dressed.

Jonathan Rose knocked on his door.

"Come in," Father Declan called as he was brushing his hair. Jonathan entered. "It's just me, Father," he said as he walked in.

"It's okay, Father, come in, come in."

"This is going to get confusing," Jonathan commented. "Perhaps you should call me Priest, it's what most of them around here call me. Although, I would be obliged, and prefer it if you would just call me Jonathan."

Father Declan walked over to him. "Jonathan, I am very

pleased to meet you," he held out his hand. "Please call me Declan." They both smiled and instantly liked each other.

"We didn't get time to introduce ourselves in the café yesterday." Jonathan said. "But I want to thank you for protecting me and the others."

Father Declan smiled. "Can I ask you two things?" he asked.

"Please do."

"Through the window I can see some other houses quite close by, small houses?"

"Cottages. There's thirty of them. They were all upgraded and refurbished some years ago now."

"They look like holiday homes, like summer-lets."

"That's the idea," Jonathan told him, "but in fact they are our first line of physical defence of the castle. They are run, operated and manned as fully equipped garrison posts. Electronically protected – linked to the control room here. Heavily armed, fitted with perimeter sensors, sound sensors, night scopes, infrared cameras and a range of small arms. They are our 'eyes on the ground'. Every three months new Templars come and take their turn at the outposts. The rotation ensures that all Knights get a chance to come to the castle for training and briefings. In fact, Dominique and I live in one of them, you must come to dinner. So, that was one thing, what's the other?"

"Is it me or is there a strong smell of lavender in here?"

Jonathan burst out laughing and proceeded to tell Father Declan his story. About Salah El-Din, John Dukes, his search in Scotland, meeting St Clair and, after his first night in the castle, waking up with the strong smell of fresh lavender about him. They talked for a while like old friends catching up and they both forgot about the time, until Jonathan finally looked at his watch.

"Oops," he said. "I came to take you to the control room so, we'd better get moving. The team are back from Mallorca and St Clair wants you to meet them. Plus, they have a riddle we all need to decipher, any help would be greatly appreciated."

"Riddle?"

"Bertram will explain everything. And, whilst I'm talking about Bertram ..." He explained about Bertram, which took a while longer!

The control room was as busy as it was the night before but there were a few more new faces there for Father Declan to meet. Most of the people were gathered around a large, wall mounted screen, he and Jonathan joined them. He read what they were all looking at:

From the end of the world
You would see it before 110 sea captains would see it but if
right they would not get wet on Job 267
Then look for the Alabama window

On a swivel chair directly in front of the screen a man was sitting staring at the words on the screen. He wore black square glasses and looked about twelve years old. His white teeth flashed out from his deep brown skin and his curly, unkempt hair flopped about and acne. He was dressed in a green tartan, tweed cloth suit. Waistcoat, with a fob. Brown shoes, scuffed.

"Bertram," Jonathan whispered to Father Declan.

The sound seemed to break Bertram's concentration. He swivelled around on his chair. "*Ha. maidin an-mhaith duit, sagart Deagh*-án – a very good morning to you, Priest Good-full."

"*Tá áthas orm bualadh leat, Bertram* – I am pleased to meet you, Bertram," Father Declan replied. "How did you know I was Irish?"

"I heard it in your voice just now when you said hello to people; slight but it's there, Cork I believe? And because your name is Declan. Well, it is really from the Gaelic name Deaglán. Deagh means good, and lán means full. Priest Good-full, I hope we shall be friends."

Father Declan looked at Jonathan. Jonathan had one of those 'I told you so' looks on his face. "Good-full you are then," he whispered. Jonathan couldn't help but smile.

Luther walked over to them and introduced himself to Father Declan. He asked if he would care to help them decipher the riddle on the screen. He explained where it had come from and the fact they thought it had come from the kidnapped scientist who was trying to tell them where he was. "We've been brainstorming for a while now. We've got lots of ideas, pages full of ideas but nothing we have feels right, too random. We're struggling a bit."

Father Declan looked at the screen again. "Well," he began,

"if it's a place you are looking for, then it's less than one thousand, three hundred and twenty miles away, but I don't know one thousand, three hundred and twenty miles away from where?"

It took a few seconds, and then, "ha." Bertram exclaimed. "Jolly well done, Priest Good-full."

Then Courtney got it. She smiled. "Clever," she said.

"What, what?" Jonathan and Luther, both asked her almost at the same time. Everyone drew in closer and looked at Father Declan and Courtney.

Courtney turned to Father Declan, "you cracked it, you tell them."

"If you stand on the shore and look out to sea," he began, "the average distance you can see towards the horizon is about three miles. However, look from the bridge of a ship and the distance is twelve miles. One hundred and ten sea captains would equal one thousand, three hundred and twenty miles. My brother is in the Merchant Navy," he added. "You just need to know either from where, or to where, because once you have one of them, you will get the other one."

Now they all had renewed energy because they knew that if you get one piece of a puzzle, just one, then often the other pieces will fall into place fairly quickly. They were hopeful.

They decided to tackle the Alabama window part of the riddle first. It was a place name and perhaps it was linked to the one thousand three hundred and twenty miles. First, they looked at distances from the south part of Alabama, then north, east and finally western edges of the state. Nothing. Blank. So, then they looked at locations from its capital, Montgomery. It was a scatter gun approach that yielded nothing but an ever-growing list of places and a deepening sense of frustration. They even called John Wolf, the Indian – it was around 3 a.m. for him. Next, they looked at prefixes and suffixes to the word Alabama. After ten minutes they had over three hundred written down on their list but none of them made any sense in the context of a place. They looked at window styles, shapes, sizes, titles, nicknames, designs, no Alabama window. Thirty minutes later they were no further forward. They called Ken Knox in Mallorca – who was still with Rosario – he put his mobile phone on speaker so she could hear.

"Has Allan ever been to Alabama?" Courtney asked Rosario.

"No, not that I know."

"Does he have relatives there?"

"No."

"Friends, colleagues or ex-colleagues?"

"No. I don't think so ... No, he's never mentioned anyone in Alabama."

The questions went on for fifteen minutes. Everyone was making suggestions, trying to find the Alabama link but nothing. They were all getting tired and frustrated.

It was John Wolf who thought it may not be a place name and they might be barking up the wrong tree. He decided to change tack. He spoke to Courtney. "Ask her, if we said Alabama to her husband, what would be the first thing that would come into his head. What would he instantly say?"

Courtney asked her.

"Music," Rosario said without any hesitation.

"Why do you say music?" Courtney asked.

"Because his favourite group is Alabama."

"And how would the word window fit with that?"

"Because he plays that song every Christmas, 'A candle in the window', by Alabama."

Then it dawned on them all but it was Rosario who verbalised it. "He's telling us he will leave a light at a window for us to follow" Rosario's words were full of excitement.

"He is indeed," Courtney said. "Well done, Rosario. If it's okay with you and Mr Knox, we'll have you both stay on the line to help with the rest of this because you're doing great so far."

They were all still staring at the message on the large screen trying to figure out their next lead, Billy Jack took charge of that. He suggested, whilst he was in a room full of people of strong religious convictions, they did have two priests in their midst and they might like to take a stab at ... *but if right they would not get wet on Job 267.* Jonathan and Father Declan found an empty desk. Its computer was already on. They gathered up two large pads, pens and coloured marker pens and set about their detective work. Everyone else worked their desk top computers, laptops, phones and tablets to try to determine what *From the end of the world,* meant. About half the people in the control room were focused on solving the riddle; all electronic devices were working overtime. The other half had remained at their desks and all seemed focused on a number of individual tasks.

The priest and the ex-priest took no time on *Job 267*, because there was no *Job 267*! Job numbering did not go to 267. So, Father Declan asked how the message was coded. Jonathan explained how Bertram had discovered the message from a beating, green cursor on an old Commadore computer. Bertram had figured the corresponding letter to each beat type. The two then pretty much figured it out at the same time but it was Jonathan that said it.

"There was no punctuation. He used no punctuation in the message. There is no *Job 267*, but if we put a colon in there—"

"We get *Job 26:7*," Father Declan said.

They then went back to the others and both recited it. *"He stretches out the north, over the empty space and hangeth the earth upon nothing."*

"So, who is *right* and not getting *wet?*" Ken Knox asked. "It makes no sense, ... *but if right they would not get wet on ... He stretches out the north, over the empty space and hangeth the earth upon nothing. They* are the sea captains. *If right they would not get wet*. So, that's either right as in correct or right as in opposite to left."

"Verdens Ende," someone said. "We've had that listed down about thirty times now, but we thought that it is just too easy, too obvious. He is a scientist, we figured he would have found a better clue. It seems far too easy because it literally means from the end of the world. We think it's more to do with a book, or film or something."

Rosario's voice came over the speakers. "Yes, but he was sending me the message. I guess he was hoping I would be able to get help, he would know I would have reached out to Ken, but the message is primarily for me, right? So, he would not want to make it too difficult, which means, that's exactly where he could be."

"Or," Bertram interrupted, "he is where he is, so, that's the name he had to play with. And if that's the case, he is less than one thousand, three hundred and twenty miles away from it!"

St Clair asked Courtney to show a map on another large screen. It flickered, then the map was there. They all looked at it. St Clair asked her to zoom into each of the suggested places but to leave Verdens Ende till last. "Let's eliminate as many as we can before we get to the most obvious." Twenty minutes later, they had eliminated them all but one, Verdens Ende. Courtney zoomed in to that part of the world: Norway.

"It's in south Norway," Billy Jack said as it appeared on the large screen. "Can you draw a line as the crow flies directly north for one thousand three hundred and twenty miles, Courtney?"

The pointer landed in the Greenland Sea.

"*But if right they would not get wet ...* move the pointer to the right until you hit the first land mass. There!" They landed on a place called Longyearbyen, Svalbard, a Norwegian archipelago surrounded by the Greenland Sea, Barents Sea and the Arctic Ocean.

"*... He stretches out the north, over the empty space and hangeth the earth upon nothing.* Well, we have our north, our empty space and our nothing, look at it, its desolate. He is somewhere south of Longyearbyen, Svalbard."

And there it was, just as they knew, get one part of a puzzle and very quickly you will normally get the rest. They'd found him. There was elation in the control room, but not as much as there was coming out of the speaker from Mallorca!

Someone quickly looked it up. "It belongs to Norway. Its sparsely populated, Russians mostly."

"Seems the perfect place to hide a bunch of top scientists. Now, to find where they are hiding them," St Clair said. "Assume it's a building because we know it has a window. It's south of Longyearbyen, going to be extra isolated. See what buildings are out there, what type, who's using it, who owns it. Check with oil and gas suppliers, either there or on the mainland, they need to burn fuel to keep warm. Plus, I would imagine there's not much day light there, if at all, it's still winter there.

"Billy Jack, Lionheart, did either of you do arctic training?" They both confirmed they had. "Good. Billy Jack, you're the

Sergeant at Arms, prep for a rescue and extraction operation with a high chance of enemy contact; we'll send a twelve-Knight team, this will include one medic and one doctor. Lionheart, you will be team leader, choose your Knights and prepare them. Be ready to go in an hour or so."

The control room became quite frantic but St Clair noticed that Father Declan was not joining in the celebration. He walked over to him.

"You are not happy?"

"Yes, yes, I am but ..."

"But what?"

"I am pleased about the scientist, of course I am, but—"

"But you are wondering why no one is talking about the cardinal. Let me show you why. Bertram, put up the rest of Allan Studerbaker's message please."

A second or two later, there on the screen was the answer for Father Declan. There in large bold letters: *WHAT IS THE PARADOX?* "So," St Clair continued, "we know the Abaddons have the missing scientists and, I'm betting they have the cardinal there too."

For Father Declan, this changed everything. "Can I go with them, with your Knights?"

"I've already told the Lionheart to give you one of the twelve places, should you want it."

"I want it."

St Clair looked over to Cameron Jack who had been watching them and nodded affirmatively. He turned back to Father Declan. "We have an hour, it's time for you to see the Ark, are you ready, Father?"

The hectic control room became even more hectic as St Clair, Jonathan and Father Declan left.

As they walked along the tunnels, St Clair told Father Declan that he and Jonathan tried to make the journey once a week. They were in the bowels of the castle. It was a maze of underground tunnels that had been dug out of the rock foundations of the castle centuries before. They had been expertly excavated and formed. Supporting the ceiling, at ten-yard intervals, were the most stunning vaulted stone arches, barrel, domed, ribbed and pitched vaults. In perfect symmetry, the stonemasonry looked like subterranean art: the proportions and balance, stout and strong, yet integral and beautiful.

They carried burning torches with them that lit the way. There was also light from the wall-mounted burning torches. The air was fresh, a vertical ventilation shaft had been constructed so that there was always clean, fresh, cool air flowing through, slightly fanning the flames of the torches and causing them to flicker and dance.

"De Molay did not yield his secrets, did he?" St Clair asked out of the blue as they walked along.

"No," Father Declan confirmed, "and in fact as he burnt, he called for revenge. He called for the death of both the king and the Pope. Pope Clement died just thirty-three days after Molay's execution. Seven months later, King Philip himself became gravely ill and unexpectedly passed away on the 29th of November. Over the next decade, the Capetian dynasty, which King Philip was so proud of, fell and each of Philip's childless sons briefly became King and died. Was Jacques de Molay's curse divine or not? Who knows for sure but it certainly created a domino effect because all of that led to the Hundred Years' War with England."

They paused as they always did. It was a stretch of about five hundred yards. Along the walls were small niches and in every niche an urn, ten inches high, black in colour, a rounded body but with a narrowed neck. Each had a lid on it. And on each black urn, the Templar red cross.

St Clair told Father Declan that they held the ashes of nearly every Knight that had fallen. Centuries of proud and valiant men and women who had served their God and their Order. St Clair lingered by the urn of André Sabath. He whispered, "I miss you, my friend." Then he walked on.

Above them, as they walked and at intervals of every three hundred yards, were a number of alloy steel doors hidden in the tunnel ceiling. They were big, six inches thick and they were solid and strong. St Clair said that they were built to seal off the tunnels at given points. They were the Templars' escape route, should the need ever arise.

They were about two miles in when one of the tunnels suddenly turned sharp left at a 45 degree angle. It looked to Father Declan like they had come to the end of the tunnel, it was just rockface – many had made that wrong assumption. However, as they approached and their flame light hit the rock, Father Declan could see that there was a door nestled back in an alcove. St Clair pressed in a seven-digit code and it opened the reinforced, tungsten door to reveal a small, perfectly rounded room with the same exquisite stonework in the form of a cupola domed stone ceiling.

"I wanted you to see this," St Clair said. I wanted you to see what you and Cardinal Del Luca had risked your lives for. It will not stay long though; it never does, so we must hurry."

There was a dull, silver alloy box in the middle of the room. St Clair approached it with reverence. He then pressed the tips of his fingers against the side of the box so that his fingerprints were held flat. He whispered something, an incantation, a prayer in Latin. The sides of the alloy box slowly folded down into small, one-centimetre concertina sections, taking the lid with it. The blue smoke, small at first, but it would grow. A strange rumbling noise, like far away thunder, seeped out of the empty space before them and echoed. Then a shimmer appeared, slowly forming a shape, hazy and glimmering, transparent. A square shape. Gold, then silver, then a myriad of colours appeared, all fusing into one another like a rainbow exploding in front of their eyes. The thunder intensified. St Clair, his voice raised above the noise, recited ancient words. The shape grew more pronounced. And then, the Ark appeared and Father Declan fell to his knees. It was made of acacia wood and overlaid in pure gold. Four gold rings attached to it and on the lid, two gold cherubim faced each other. The cherubim wings spread upwards, overshadowing the cover. St Clair and Jonathan removed the gold lid.

"The Ark gave me my life back," Jonathan told Father Declan.

"Life?"

"I was dead."

"Dead as in really dead and back to life like the assassin Michael and the villager, Vincente?" he asked.

Jonathan nodded. "The miracle of life had been given back to me through the Ark. Not only did it give me my life back, it also gave me my belief back, my faith. When I look inside the Ark, I see the tablets of stone, the Ten Commandments, the words of God. When I touch them I feel history at my fingertips: centuries of time, the ancient ones: the people of the Promised Land. Then, in between the written words of the Ten Commandments, I see additional lines of faded symbols, lifting from the stones. Floating."

"What is it like?"

Jonathan smiled; he'd been asked the question a thousand times. "Try to imagine a map of the London underground system, now overlay the Paris Metro, now overlay the New York subway. Now do it one thousand times more, layer upon layer. Now do it again in three dimensions and that's still clearer than what I see above the Ark. It's like every breath every living creature has ever taken is crammed into a space no bigger than a small table, and it's all in motion. I see thousands of symbols and images. It was like looking at them through running water. There but distant. Alive. Moving. Rotating. Lifting themselves from the stones and slowly forming a three-dimensional orb. The symbols dismantle as they touch each other and then spin off at great speed to form another."

St Clair told him that for centuries they have been trying to understand the Ark. Templars in France first discovered their presence but they still knew but a small part of their meaning. He lamented that their progress had been slow, disappointingly so. Often the symbols did not appear for weeks. Sometimes when they appeared, they would only stay for a short while, sometimes for less than a few seconds, at other times for a few minutes, five at the most, but never more. He told him that one of the discoveries that he and Jonathan made was that if they took the two stone tablets out of the Ark and moved them away from the Ark by more than a few feet, the symbols would fall from their levitated, rotating orb shape and then disintegrate into nothing. They would just fall mid

269

shape and disappear, as though they were linked in some way for their energy.

"They have a symbiotic relationship, the tablets and the Ark, you can't have one without the other," Jonathan said. "Now you are here, we have learned so much more. You have confirmed what the Ark is for. You, the sixth prophecy, the cardinal, your Cabal, the Ark key, all point in that one direction." He recited it. "The Apocalypse of John, the Book of Revelation. Revelation 9:2-11. ... *And he opened the bottomless pit; and there arose a smoke out of the pit, as the smoke of a great furnace; and the sun and the air were darkened by reason of the smoke of the pit.*

"And there came out of the smoke locusts upon the earth: and unto them was given power, as the scorpions of the earth have power ... And they had hair as the hair of women, and their teeth were as the teeth of lions.

"And they had tails like unto scorpions, and there were stings in their tails: and their power was to hurt men ... And they had a king over them, which is the angel of the bottomless pit, whose name in the Hebrew tongue is Abaddon ..."

Just then a Knight came running in. He stopped breathlessly and knelt before the Ark. He made the sign of the cross across his chest. Then he stood and spoke to St Clair. "The chopper is ready and Father Declan's kit is on board. The Lionheart said it's time to go, Grand Master."

"Do we have a location, a building?" St Clair asked.

"Bertram has narrowed it down to three possible locations but there is one that stands out. An old government research complex that had a laboratory, kitchens, sleeping quarters ... it ticks all the boxes. Plus, it's had fuel delivered there a number of times in the past six months. Zakariah told me to tell you that it is being leased from the Norwegian government by an organisation called the Thornburg Society. He said you would like that one."

St Clair looked pleased. "Tell the Lionheart he is coming now."

"Yes, Grand Master." The Knight left.

The Ark went and St Clair closed the alloy box. They left the Ark room and for the next ten minutes Father Declan answered all the questions that the night before St Clair had told him he would answer once he had seen the Ark: who the others were, the other Cabal members, where the Ark key is, and why the cardinal and he had never seen the Ark key, or what it is. Or the Paradox?

"Don Pablo was the first to spilt up the three scrolls. He thought it safer. Our first Cabal was made up of three key guardians and a number of people who protected the guardians. This worked well for a long time but it was not without its problems. The more people you tell, the higher the risk you have and the more likely that one of those people will say something to somebody. There are many reasons why someone might give the key away, and not always for malice, gain or a different ideology. Sometimes people just let things slip, or they drop their guard or they think they can trust someone and they can't. We know of two cases when a person got drunk and ... well, you can guess. And, of course, if one of the Cabal should fall into the wrong hands, torture is a persuasive tool to get what you want. The Cabal tried a number of different ways to protect the scrolls over the years but it was the cardinal that really defined the modern security protocols that we now use."

He continued telling St Clair "There were three key guardians. Each holds one scroll. Each are not aware of the other two, who they are, or where they are. The cardinal chose each one of the guardians and it is a lifetime position. And, to ensure total secrecy, each of the guardians keeps their scroll in a safety deposit box, and each in a different bank, in a different country. So, each guardian lives in a different country to the other two. They never, ever communicate with each other.

"Each has the same system in place with their bank. The safety protocol is the same for each. Once a month they visit the safety deposit box. They register each visit with the bank. If they miss a visit, if they don't turn up, the bank has an envelope with instructions inside. It tells them to remove the contents of the safety deposit box and put it into a different one. Then, they have a name and a number to call. They call the number." St Clair was about to say something about the loophole he had just spotted in the cardinal's safety protocols when Father Declan added the next layer of security.

"Each key guardian has a watcher. The watcher also does not know who the other key guardians are or even the other watchers. They don't even know in which safety deposit box the scroll is kept. They know the bank of course because they accompany the key guardian but that's it. The watcher's job is to keep their key guardian safe. Another lifetime job. They dedicate their lives to protecting their key guardian. So, if ever a bank has to call the number in the envelope, it is to the watcher. The watcher calls the cardinal. The cardinal then makes arrangements for the scroll to be retrieved from the bank by a new guardian that he appoints.

"We always have two reserve guardians in waiting should the need ever arise. And also two watchers. The new guardian will make the same arrangement with a bank of their choosing. Remember, no one other than the guardians know where their scrolls are kept. And one scroll is no good without the other two because the key is what is in the total of the three scrolls."

St Clair asked him, "when was the last time someone saw all three scrolls at the same time?" He was not expecting the answer.

"Probably two hundred years ago, give or take a decade or two."

"How do you get in touch with the guardians if you need to?"

"Through their watchers, we have an emergency number."
"Those were the calls you made yesterday, to their watchers?" Jonathan asked him.

"Yes."

They moved quickly now through the final tunnel; the sound of the helicopter's rotor blades whirling becoming louder as they approached the exit. Father Declan's stomach churned: he was about to go into the unknown.

Chapter 17

Lone little girl

Place: An ex-government research centre, somewhere in the frozen wasteland of the Svalbard

They tried the door; it was unlocked and slightly ajar. The Knights prepared for entry, A handgun in one hand – safety off, one in the chamber. In their other hand, a Katana sword, normally these were black *saya* – scabbard, and black *tsuka* – handle, but they were carrying arctic weapons: white. They were trained to fight with weapons in both hands if needed, gun in one, sword in the other, a deadly combination: it gave them options. Dressed in their white, arctic, all-in one combat gear, with white ski masks, they blended in. Their night vision goggles allowed them to see. The lead Knight pushed against the door. The large ten-inch-thick metal, grey door moved easily, it was an obvious sign it had been used a lot.

The decision to go in by stealth and not by shock and awe, using thunder flashes and charging in en masse, was taken because they believed there were prisoners inside, the missing scientists and the cardinal.

Two Knights entered the building, the others waited in a semi-circle outside the entrance door. Their firing arc was now one hundred and eighty degrees behind them – no one could surprise them from the rear.

It was way below freezing, their breath clearly visible. No one spoke. They all had coms; they were all connected. They waited for the advance team to report. Seconds ticked by like minutes, they seemed to have been waiting an age, but in reality, the advance team were only gone for about four minutes. All the Knights had high hopes that the rescue and the extraction mission would be a success.

*

Glennfinch castle, Scotland

There was absolute silence in the control room. Each of the extraction teams coms were linked to the sound system in the control room – they could hear them breathing. Via the teams' headset cameras, they saw the bleak, white, frozen landscape they had just crossed via six two-man snowmobiles.

There had been a light in a window, just like Allan had promised, a candlelight and because of the darkness they were able to see it from two miles away. They left their machines there and had walked the rest of the way so as to approach in silence. It had been slow going though, despite using snowshoes, it had been a long and difficult slog – something Knights who were ex-forces referred to as a yomp.

On a large wall mounted screen, the people in the control room watched multiple mini scenes with live footage being relayed back via each Knight's camera headset.

Two Knights had been left behind to guard the snowmobiles. The Knights had placed the snowmobiles in a circle, the two Knights remaining were crouched in the middle, using them as cover. They waited in the cold.

They had left the castle by helicopter, landed at a private airfield just west of Glasgow and then took a private carrier plane to Hammerfest Airport in northern Norway, it was a six-hour flight. Two Knights, part of the satellite station based in Norway, met them at the airport. The satellite team had already hired a small, airside hangar. They had also arranged all the necessary provisions for the rescue and extraction team and extra provisions for the prisoners. They had acquired six snowmobiles; these were loaded on to the plane. They oversaw the refuelling of the plane, which eventually flew to Svalbard Airport, the flight took a little under six hours. From there it was a ten-minute drive by snowmobile down to Longyearbyen. It was nearly midnight when they finally fired up their snowmobiles, it had taken them nearly thirteen hours to get there, they had another two hours' drive south across barren, white wasteland. The two Norwegian Knights from the satellite station waited at the hangar to support the team upon their return, and offer any medical assistance needed to freed prisoners,

*

Ex-government research centre

There were no lights coming from inside the complex. The only light that they had seen on their approach was the light of the candle. There was also no sound coming from inside the complex. Off to the right was, what looked like a generator building, but it was silent. Nothing seemed to be feeding the complex with power. Cameron Jack checked his temperature gauge, it read ten below. He knew that without power, if anyone was in there, and not in arctic gear, they would have less than an hour to survive.

Then a voice came over their coms. "Clear."

Cameron Jack turned to one of the Knights and indicated towards the building, a hundred yards away to the right – the generator room. The Knight nodded and then left the group, keeping low as he moved stealthily. They covered him until he reached the generator room, then he went inside. Then Cameron Jack indicated to another Knight to stay outside by the entrance door. His job was to cover the Knight who had gone to the generator room. When he returned, both would stay outside and guard the teams six. This was the prearranged plan. They all knew what they had to do.

Cameron Jack raised his hand and indicated towards the door, he, Father Declan and the four remaining Knights entered the building – the medic and doctor were part of the four. Inside the air was stale. It was clear that the walls had been covered with condensation, a tell-tale sign that there had been activity in there, with the air temperature slightly higher inside than outside, but the condensation had frozen.

They were in a long corridor. It was empty but for cables running along the top of the corridor wall. They looked like power cables. It was spooky inside. Each footstep they took caused an eerie sound and it echoed, reverberating several times, its sound diminishing each time as it spiralled away. It was pitch black and if they had not had their night vision goggles, they would be moving totally blind, in a hostile place, with live ammunition pre-loaded into handguns – *God bless Billy Jack* they all thought.

Another voice came over the coms. "Lionheart, we can go live on the power whenever you want." It was the Knight in the generator room.

Cameron Jack looked around at the Knights with him. "Switch your head set cameras night vison off and remove your night vision goggles. V formation for possible contact. No blue-on-blue, we are in a tight space." All the Knights kneeled down and raised their weapons in readiness.

For a few seconds they were in pitch black. Back in Scotland, their screen went black.

"On my mark," Cameron told the Knight in the generator room. "Three, two, one." The Knights inside closed their eyes as the lights in the complex came on. The sound of the ancient hot water pipes rattled and growled as the generator powered the oil burners that produced heat and hot water. The Knights squinted trying to get used to the white light from the green, low luminous light of their night vision goggles.

All the Knights carried photographs of the missing scientists and any family members that had also gone missing with them. But they had also memorised their faces, so if there was a firefight, they would be able to identify the prisoners from their captors.

They removed their masks and then it hit them. Cameron Jack knew what it was straight away, that stench had never left him, he would never forget it. When the White Ghost was in Romania, he had spent up to five hours a day in a germ free, clinical atmospheric dome that was maintained at a certain heat temperature, which acted as an antiseptic environment. The Templars determined from what they found that he had had his skin treated three times per day with a lotion of Aloe Vera, Llama milk, honey and antiseptic components, like chlorhexidine gluconate, hexachlorophene, boric acid, Lugol's iodine and formaldehyde. The smell was distinctive, overpowering, ghastly and resembled the smell of a mortuary. For Cameron Jack and the others that rescued André Sabath from Zivko's lair that day in Romanian, he would never forget the smell.

"He's here," Cameron Jack announced over the coms. "Control room, Gowst, his stench is here." They edged forward; there was still no sound of anyone else in the complex. "Stay alert," he told the others.

There were a number of doors leading off the corridor, both on the left and on the right. All were open; all were empty of people. There were papers scattered all over the floors. In some of the rooms someone had tried to burn papers but had made a bad job of it. "I think they've left," Cameron Jack said over the coms. "Control room are you seeing what we are seeing. It looks like they tried to burn evidence on whatever has been going on here but they left in a hurry and didn't finish the job." He told one of his Knights to start to collect any papers that had not been burnt, they would take them back to Scotland.

Then things changed. They started to find bodies. Some of them had been shot, others had had their throats cut. The Templars knew exactly who they were. It didn't take them long to find all of the kidnapped scientists and their family members. Everyone was dead, including Allan Studerbaker, he lay face up with his throat cut.

"We're too late," Cameron Jack said.

St Clair asked him to take the count. Cameron Jack did. Every missing scientist and any of their family members also missing, were lying dead on the cold, concrete floor of the complex.

"Keep looking," Cameron Jack told his Knights. "Keep looking."

Father Declan continued to search the rooms off the corridor, there were only a few left, the others moved off into the main area of the complex. What greeted them as they walked in there stopped them all in their tracks. There were over a hundred computers, all linked into a mega mainframe stack system of colossal size and that was wired into what was standing in the centre of the room.

"You seeing this?" Cameron Jack asked the control room in disbelief.

"We're seeing it," St Clair replied, struggling to get his words out. He didn't want to think it but he did; he didn't want to say it, but he did. "They look as if they are real."

There were five, skilfully and articulately designed, expertly built exact copies of the Ark of the Covenant, all in different stages of development. Each one looked like a prototype. The fifth one looked almost complete. Five Arks standing in the centre of the room, each one on a magnetised, metal plinth, hovering just above the ground. But then they saw that there was a sixth plinth, and that was empty. One Ark was missing. Everyone was thinking the very same thought: they have built their own. The original was constructed by the Israelites in the Sinai desert after they left Egypt, more than three thousand years ago. It held the foundation of God's covenant with man, the Ten Commandments. In the Hebrew Bible it says that it stopped the Jordan river from flowing. The Israelites took it into battle. It was captured by the Philistines and they suffered for it. They broke out in tumours, disease. Death came to anyone who touched it or looked inside it. It was carried around the walls of Jericho, on the seventh day, the walls fell down.

*

Glennfinch castle, Scotland.

The Ark was far more than a container to house two tablets of stone and now St Clair knew the Abaddons knew that too. The sixth prophecy replayed in his mind: *The flower of the martyrs and the plaited crown shall join to battle 'El S'hhan te Abyann' for the way back.* He was in shock. If they couldn't take it from the Templars, they would build their own.

"Is that even possible," Dominique turned to St Clair. "To actually build another Ark?"

He just shook his head, "I ... I don't know."

She turned to Bertram. "Can they replicate its power?"

278

"Theoretically, I guess ... yes, if you have the right and exact construction, and you are able to measure, code and replicate a number of other dimensions and matter driven anomalies. If you can manipulate using the golden ratio, plus use accelerated, multivariable and differential calculus. It would be like taking the Riemann Hypothesis, which is one of the hardest problems to solve in all of mathematics, and times that problem by a thousand. There would be so much science involved, so, so much, most of it theoretical, it's mind blowing. To do that you would need a dedicated, specially programmed bank of computers and, you would need—"

"An astrophysicist, you would need to cover quantum mechanics and quantum electrodynamics and a theoretical mathematician. Geobiologist an evolutionary biologist and I guess a cosmologist." St Clair said. "Exactly the specialist fields of the kidnapped scientists,"

"But what about His part in the Ark, God's part," Luther asked. "How would they ... how could they replicate that?"

"There are two forces that could enrich an Ark built by man with such power. One was carried out over three thousand years ago on Mount Sinai."

"And the other?" Luther asked him.

St Clair looked at him, his face grave. "The other is El S'hhan te Abyann!"

"So, they are building their own Ark because they have never been able to find the original one," Luther said.

"And even if they did get the Ark, they know they don't have the answer to the Paradox, the Ark's fail safe."

"So, they are building one without a failsafe, without a Paradox." Luther just said what they had all just been thinking.

*

Ex-government research centre

They all heard the cry – it belonged to Father Declan. They ran towards where it was coming from, it was coming from inside the last room along the corridor. They rushed in. Father Declan was on his knees; he was crying. In front of him was the sad, limp body of

279

the cardinal, hanging, strung up by his arms, spread out like a crucifixion. On the floor a large pool of blood below his body. On a chair lay a small tape recorder. A note by its side read *'Templars'*. The presence of the note told them that the prisoner's captors knew they were coming.

Cameron Jack was first to react. "Control room, the Knights at the hangar, you need to get them out. They knew we were coming, that means someone's tipped them off. They must have had informants at various airports ... We have to warn our Knights at Hammerfest Airport, if they knew we were there, they will know they are still there."

"We've been trying ever since you started finding the bodies," Luther told him. "There's no response. "We're talking to the satellite station now; they have Knights en route."

"Play the tape recorder," St Clair instructed.

"But—"

"Play it, we need every morsal of information we can get. Play it, Bertram will record it here and then try and work his magic and see if there are any background noises or voices he can pick up that might tell us where they've gone. Something. Anything."

Cameron Jack turned to Father Declan and asked him if he wanted to leave. The priest shook his head. Cameron Jack pressed play. Everybody went quiet. They heard the voice.

'Shhh, we have practised, we have. Zivko has. We will do a good job on you.'

Every Knight felt the same chill down their spine; they knew it was just one man speaking; they knew he was speaking to himself; he was deranged. Zivko Gowst was deranged.

'It will be neat but it will hurt.'

They could almost see Zivko cut along the length of Del Luca's spine – from top to bottom. Then cut along his back waistline so he could open him up.

'It is called the 'blood-eagle'. 'I cut some more. Deep. I want you to know what we are doing for you. We will pull your skin back.'

The cardinal screamed as he did it. He roared and screamed as the flesh on his back was peeled back.

The Templars heard another voice, it was clear.

'*Tell me what the Paradox is, man of God?*'

Then Zivko's voice again. '*Tell my Lord*'. St Clair knew Zivko would have smiled at that point, smiled but with a vacant look in his eye: the look of a psychopath, empty.

The screaming went on for another fifteen minutes. Several people back in Scotland left the control room, it had gotten too much for them. The questioning went on, they were asking about the Paradox and interrogating the cardinal about the Templars, where were they, what he knew. After they had strung him up and cut his back open, peeled back his skin and then finally, pulled his lungs out from his back, they heard Zivko say he knew that the Templars had the Ark, Salah El-Din had told him he had seen it in Cumbria.

The cardinal did not utter any words to them. He said nothing – but he screamed and it filled the control room and the research complex.

'*Now, are we ready?*' his voice was back again. '*Yes, Zivko, we are ready. Now we must detach his ribs from his spine and open them out. Then, we will pull his lungs out*'.

The cardinal must have passed out because the Templars no longer heard his screams. Then the silence was replaced with the sawing of bone.

'*We must saw the ribcage, where it is attached to the spine and then open his ribs outwards; then we will push our hands inside and pull out the priest's lungs.*'

There was a long silence. Three maybe four minutes went by. They could hear noises but not voices; people were still there. Then, his voice again, Zivko's. This time he was closer to the microphone. His voice filled the control room, his low, scratchy, eerily whispered voice.

'*Templars, we will leave him here for you. We know you are coming. We will see you soon. Yes, we will Zivko.*' Then the voice recording ended.

They all walked around in a semi daze. Disheartened by the failed rescue. They were checking every room looking for anything that might help them determine where they had gone.

More bad news came. Luther confirmed that the Knights at

the hangar in Norway were dead. There'd been a fire in the hangar, no survivors. The Templars began to realise that the Abaddons reach was as extensive as their own, if not more.

*

Her papa had told her to stay still. Stay hidden inside the box, inside one of the Arks he had put her in.

There had been someone screaming, screaming for a long time. Her papa had gone to comfort her. He had sat with her in their cell. He told her not to listen but she couldn't help it, it was loud. He knew it was a man of God, a cardinal, one of the others said he had overheard.

When he heard the first shot, he knew things were about to change. He crept back into the main area with Priya. All of the others had been at their workstations when they had been gathered up and taken into various rooms. He saw his chance; the area was empty but they had trashed all of the computers, all the other electronics, all the many machines, and burning documents where laying everywhere: he knew they were leaving. He hid his daughter in one of the Arks, the last place he thought they would think of looking. He then went in the direction of the shooting. He had already guessed what was happening but he went anyway, sacrificing his own life to try to protect his daughter. He had been a master carpenter. He was skilled in silver and gold inlay work and ornate carvings and features. He'd produced some of the finest furniture for royalty all over the world. When the Templars found him, he lay dead on the freezing concrete floor. His throat was cut.

It had been quiet for so long. Priya didn't know how long.

She heard their voices. They spoke differently to the others and she could understand them. She wanted to see if her papa was ok; to see if Mr Hare was ok. She was cold and she couldn't stop her teeth from chattering. She moved the lid slightly but it was too heavy. She peered out of the gap. There were some people there. They were dressed differently. There was a man standing right next to her Ark, right next to her. He looked like he had a kind face.

He saw the movement out of the corner of his eye. Then he

saw two small, peering eyes. They were human eyes. Dark and sunken. Sad. They were a child's eyes.

"Have you seen my papa," she asked the man with the kind face, through chattering teeth. "I would like to see Papa."

Father Declan was filled with emotion. He lifted the lid. A miracle lay before him and he wept.

Chapter 18

Charlie B and War

Two weeks later

The service for Cardinal Gino Del Luca took place two weeks after his death. It was led by the pope himself. The pope spoke fondly of the cardinal, his colleague, friend.

Lots of people had turned up for the service. The cardinal had been a popular man; many spoke about him as a possible successor to the pope. A large number of cardinals had gone to show their respects too.

Dámaso Nef was there, the chief of police sat with his family, his wife and young daughter. Three rows behind him, sat Jonathan, Luther and Aldrich Manwin Tucker; the three who had been with the cardinal when they slew the witch – the service was in the same church. Right at the back, on his own, a man sat quietly. He'd come to pay his respects to the man he had never met in person, but in the last few days had come to know him well. He was tall, with silver hair and beard. He caught some glances, a few people thought they recognised him. Was it Sean Connery? No, surly not, they thought. The man had arrived after the service had begun and he would leave before it ended. Seemingly he had travelled to Rome alone and when he left, it would look like he left alone, but two men from in the shadows watched over him.

It had been a service befitting a man much loved.

Nef had been asked to stand near to the door where the pope would leave from. His Holiness, they said, wanted to speak to him briefly. Nef waited his turn as a line of other people stood waiting, including Father Declan. His Holiness spoke with each one. He lingered longer with Father Declan. Then finally his Holiness was in front of Nef.

"I just wanted to thank you my son." The pope's voice was serene. "Thank you for finding our Holy Thief and for arresting him. He languishes in a jail and will do so for a very long time. The church thanks you."

"I had help," Nef told him. "If it wasn't for an anonymous note from someone calling him or herself Charlie B, I would never have caught him."

"Rome is blessed to have you as its chief of police." The pope said, he smiled and then he left – with a small entourage in pursuit.

Father Declan stopped by Nef and they greeted each other.

"I shall miss the Cardinal," Nef said.

"We all will," Father Declan replied.

"You know, his Holiness thanked me for arresting Cardinal Cristoforo John Paradiso but I explained to him, I would never have been able to without that note. I think Cardinal Del Luca sent it."

Father Declan chuckled a little. "Oh no, Dámaso, it wasn't him. As a young boy, the person who sent it looked so much like the cartoon character Charlie Brown, that everyone called him by that name Charlie Brown. Whenever he wants to send a sensitive message to anyone, he would always use Charlie B."

"Not the cardinal?"

"No, no, no. The cardinal received a few of those messages himself."

"Then who?"

"His Holiness. His Holiness is Charlie B. He wrote you the note. He writes them with his left hand so people will not suspect, they would tell his handwriting otherwise. However, he is in fact left-handed. It was the nuns who made him write with his right when he was four years old, as they did with all left-handed children. His Holiness could not get directly involved in a police matter, so he gave you a helping hand."

*

Ciampino Airport, Rome

He was wating for his flight. He sat in a row of seats near a large window overlooking the runways. He had no luggage, no carry-on, all he had was his passport and a bottle of water.

A row of seats attached to his row faced the opposite direction. Directly behind him Luther sat reading a magazine – but not really. Cameron Jack, the Lionheart, was about twenty feet away on another row of seats. It was busy; it was noisy, it was Rome airport!

Luther leaned back slightly; he lifted the magazine up towards his face and then spoke to St Clair. "What next, then?"

St Clair looked up, checked no one was near them. "He was a good man, the cardinal."

"He was," Luther agreed.

"They've killed too many good people, Luther. We're going to change our game."

"Are we going to war, then?"

"We are, a biblical war. We've been fighting them for centuries but now it changes, Luther, too many good people are dying. This time we're taking the battle to them."

Cameron Jack was stretching his legs, he walked by. He slowed when he approached them. "What have I missed?" he whispered.

"We are going to war," Luther whispered back.

"About bloody time." The Lionheart smiled.

Just then their flight was called and people started to head for the departure gate. St Clair and Luther stood up. Now the three of them looked at each other.

"We are with you with Grand Master," Luther said.

"*Ubi positus est, ut omnis* – where one stands, so stand us all", St Clair said, "as it's always been. Let's go then Templars, we have a plane to catch and a war to win."

THE END

Book I ~ ARK
Reviews

5.0 out of 5 stars
Ark: A Templar thriller series. Book 1
Thoroughly enjoyable book. A fast paced read, fabulous character introduction and build up. Can't wait to read the other books. *Reviewed in the UK*

5.0 out of 5 stars
Fab read
Excellent read from page to page with a great twist at the end. He's Looking forward to the next one! Absolutely loved it! *Reviewed in the UK*

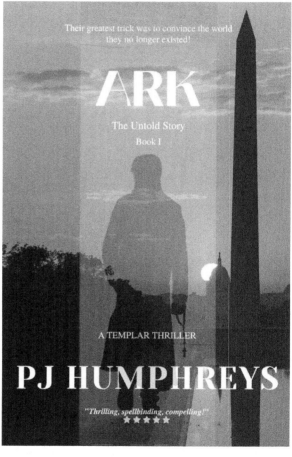

5.0 out of 5 stars
Fantastic read
A great storyline and frantic pace, in a world of chaos and instability it's what we would all wish for. I would highly recommend this book. *Reviewed in the UK*

5.0 out of 5 stars
Excellent yarn!
Really well paced and involving story, good mix of fact and fiction which keeps the interest level high throughout a very engaging tale. *Reviewed in the Italy*

5.0 out of 5 stars
Gripping read front to back from a truly visionary author
Reviewed in the United States
I loved this book. Like other reviewers I finished it in a matter of days and am excited to pick up the next instalment in the series- which is already out! So exciting. Amazing first book to what I imagine will be an amazing series of novels. *Reviewed in the United States*

Book II ~ PROPHECY
Reviews

5.0 out of 5 stars

Excellent read. Couldn't put it down.

So fast paced that my heart was racing. The story is so interactive that you feel like you are in the story with the characters. Can't wait to read the next book. *Reviewed in the UK*

5.0 out of 5 stars

Excellent Read!!!!

Great follow on from Ark Return of the Templars. Keeps you on your toes and edge of seat. A lot of thought and research went in to this I believe, to create realistic feel. Hard to put down. *Reviewed in the UK*

The Rise of the Ghost...

PROPHECY

It's in their DNA

Book II

TEMPLAR THRILLER

PJ HUMPHREYS

"Thrilling, spellbinding, compelling!"
★★★★★

5.0 out of 5 stars

Leaves You Wanting More

Really enjoyed reading this, it is a great follow up to book one - Ark.
Loved the characters and the plot. Can't wait for the next one. *Reviewed in Australia*

5.0 out of 5 stars

Tremendous

Once again gripping and not able to put the book down. These characters are fascinating and the information on the templars is leaving me wanting more x *Reviewed in the UK*

5.0 out of 5 stars

Excellent read. Totally engrossing.

The second book about the Knights Templars of today. As like the first book I just couldn't put it down. Totally lost myself in it. The characters came to life with each word. Brilliant read but be warned once you start reading it everything around you disappears and time stands still. Roll on book three. *Reviewed in the UK*

Book III ~ PERDITION
Reviews

5.0 out of 5 stars
Gripped by chapter II
I devoured the 3 books in the series so far and found myself wanting more, much more. The last time I had been gripped so by a series of books was way back in the 80's with James Herbert Rats trilogy.
Exciting, action packed, thrilling, affectionate but deadly these books are unbelievably good and caution, extremely addictive. Please write more, much more. *Reviewed in the UK*

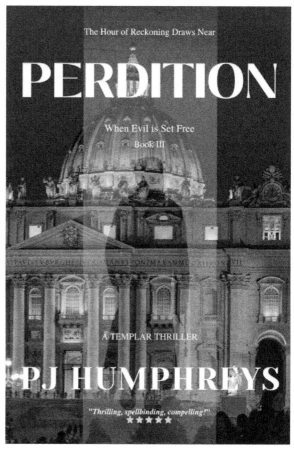

5.0 out of 5 stars
Outstanding.
Another Gem , Can't Wait for the next One. Totally Addicted To These Books. *Reviewed in the UK*

5.0 out of 5 stars
Brilliant read
Gripping to the end. *Reviewed in the UK*

5.0 out of 5 stars
Super Templar series
Brilliant fantastic read as were the first two books. Awaiting the next one with bated breath. *Reviewed in the UK*

5.0 out of 5 stars
Excellent read.
Just finished Perdition. Like the other two Ark and Prophecy absolutely brilliant read. The story takes you with it. Well written, intoxicating and makes you wonder if some of it might just be true. Here's hoping the Templars are guarding us. *Reviewed in the UK*

Printed in Great Britain
by Amazon

27822010R00172